# THE
# DEADLY
# SHALLOWS

COASTAL GUARDIANS // BOOK 3

# THE DEADLY SHALLOWS

## DANI PETTREY

BETHANY HOUSE
a division of Baker Publishing Group
Minneapolis, Minnesota

© 2022 by Grace & Johnny, Inc.

Published by Bethany House Publishers
11400 Hampshire Avenue South
Minneapolis, Minnesota 55438
www.bethanyhouse.com

Bethany House Publishers is a division of
Baker Publishing Group, Grand Rapids, Michigan

Printed in the United States of America

Library of Congress Cataloging-in-Publication Data
Names: Pettrey, Dani, author.
Title: The deadly shallows / Dani Pettrey.
Description: Minneapolis, Minnesota : Bethany House, a division of Baker
    Publishing Group, [2022] | Series: Coastal guardians ; book 3
Identifiers: LCCN 2022001431 | ISBN 9780764230868 (paperback) | ISBN
    9780764233456 (cloth) | ISBN 9781493431595 (ebook)
Subjects: LCGFT: Novels.
Classification: LCC PS3616.E89 D44 2022 | DDC 813/.6—dc23
LC record available at https://lccn.loc.gov/2022001431

Cover design by LOOK Design Studio

Author is represented by Books & Such Literary Management.

Baker Publishing Group publications use paper produced from sustainable forestry practices and post-consumer waste whenever possible.

22  23  24  25  26  27  28        7  6  5  4  3  2  1

To Steve Oates, David Horton, and Jim Parrish

You three took an unknown author under your wings. You supported me, championed my work, and made me feel like part of the BHP family from the moment I met you. I was so nervous the first day I visited Bethany House, and you three welcomed me so kindly. You have a lasting legacy with BHP, with all the authors you shepherded over the years and the vast number of books that are out in the world because of you. I'm forever grateful for the privilege and honor of working with you. May God bless you all.

Death was a breath away.

# ONE

Crisp night air slapped his cheeks, but he'd long since learned to endure the elements. Tonight's op was nothing compared to some of the filth he'd crawled through. Their objective simple, his targets unaware.

The four-person catering crew loaded trays into the back of their van, along with their tools of the trade.

Standing at the edge of the woods, the ground tight beneath his boots, he shifted his gaze to the house. *Quiet. Still.* His team held position, awaiting his signal.

Lights clicked off, shrouding the house and van in darkness.

The last member of the catering crew climbed into the rear of the vehicle.

Shifting his grizzled jaw, Dwayne signaled his team forward with a flick of two fingers.

They swept from the woods, moving across the driveway at a fast, silent clip before the van's ignition turned.

They hit the back of the van, doors still open and silent shots finding their mark.

Climbing into the van, Max pushed the slumped body out of the driver's seat and took position behind the wheel.

The rear doors shut, and Dwayne, now situated in the passenger seat, tapped the dash.

Max turned the key, and the taillights spilled red across the circular drive behind them.

In the blink of an eye, they were rolling for the road and on to Fairpark Cemetery.

# TWO

The mission's execution was flawless. The van taken. The cemetery gate lock picked. The bodies discarded in the mausoleum, where no one would find them—at least not in time to stop their primary objective.

Back at headquarters, Dwayne stood, inspecting his team as they loaded the arsenal into the van.

*Nearly time.* A commencement unlike any other was about to begin.

"The van is outfitted, sir," Adam said.

Copenhagen nestled deep within his lower lip, Dwayne spit into his cup. "Well done," he said, the chewing tobacco tingling behind his lip.

His gaze swept over his team, zeroing in on Dylan's eyes. Few men could douse the shadow of fear from their gaze, and Dylan certainly wasn't one of them.

He lifted his chin in Dylan's direction. "Something wrong?"

"No." Dylan's voice hiccupped.

His jaw shifted on instinct. The kid was lying. "You got a problem with the mission?"

Dylan swallowed, his Adam's apple bobbing down his thin, pasty neck. He shook his head too vehemently. "No, sir."

Dwayne eyed the sweat sizzling down Dylan's pulsing temple.

"I demand honesty. Honesty is essential. This is all in or all out. Understood?" He stepped forward, the wooden boards creaking beneath his boots. "Which is it?" He set his cup on the wooden railing beside him, fingering his gun grip.

Dylan hesitated, and Dwayne fired.

The kid's body crumpled to the floor, blood pooling at the base of his skull.

"Anybody else unsure?" The words slithered through his coffee-stained teeth.

His question was met with stony silence.

# THREE

Brooke zipped her walking jacket, the temp hovering at fifty-one. Her family would crack up if they saw her wearing a jacket on what they'd view as a warm day back home in northern Colorado. But she'd adapted to Wilmington's weather and swore her blood had thinned.

She spotted Gabby across the street and waved. The red light shifted to green, the walk symbol flashed, and Gabby crossed over. "Good morning."

"Good's two coffee cups away." Brooke worked a kink out of her neck. It'd been a long night, but they'd made three saves— well worth the aches and pains.

Gabby jogged in place, her knees nearly hitting a ninety-degree angle. "Down to the Riverwalk?" she said.

Brooke rubbed her mittened hands together. "You're entirely too peppy. The sun isn't even up."

"You're the one who suggested the earlier run," Gabby said as they jogged down the sloping sidewalk leading to Wilmington's gorgeous walkway along the Cape Fear River. Birds chirped among a cascade of insect hums in the marsh grass lining the path.

"I'm meeting someone for breakfast before the graduation ceremony."

"You aren't surfing with us?"

By *us* Gabby meant herself; her fiancé, Finn; and her brother, Noah.

Brooke took a steadying inhale. *Noah Rowley.* He was even more addictive than riding the winter swells.

But any hope she'd had for that relationship flatlined weeks ago. She'd fallen hard for the kind, handsome man, but he clearly hadn't fallen for her. And she couldn't keep going with the status quo. As much as it would break her heart, it was time to move on. She sniffed back the pinch of tears pricking her eyes.

Thankfully, Gabby was too busy ruminating to notice—her brows deeply furrowed.

"No." Brooke finally answered her friend's question. She cleared her throat, knowing Gabby would be beyond bummed, but it was time.

"Can I ask who you're having breakfast with?"

"Always the investigative journalist." Brooke chuckled. The lady couldn't help it. It was woven into her being.

"Sorry." Gabby offered an impish grin. "You don't have to tell me."

"I know." Brooke smiled back. "But that would be cruel. I can see the curiosity is killing you." She took a steadying inhale and released it slowly. "I'm having breakfast with Dave Keller."

"Hmm . . . Dave Keller?" Gabby eased her pace. "The name is familiar . . . but I can't place it."

"He's a friend of Brad and Jason." Her Coast Guard "brothers." She'd been paired with the two rescue swimmers since her first flight-medic duty. They wouldn't steer her wrong.

Gabby pursed her lips as she did when mulling something over.

Brooke shook her head, unable to smother a smile. Gabby

was a mess, but she'd figure out where she'd heard Dave's name soon enough.

Casting her gaze across the Golden River—as folks in Wilmington called it—Brooke scanned its dark-hued surface, searching for eyes. Nearly every morning she saw at least one alligator, often more. It was something she still hadn't gotten used to, and she'd been stationed in Wilmington for years.

"Church." Gabby snapped, making Brooke jump as they rounded to run the Riverwalk's nearly two miles again.

Gabby tightened her ponytail. "Was he the guy Jason was introducing you to after service on Sunday?"

"Yes." Maybe if she left it there Gabby would too, but she knew better.

Gabby's breathing increased along with their stride. "What about Noah?"

Brooke knew how much Gabby wanted them to be together. How much *she* wanted them to be together. But that dream was hopeless. "What *about* Noah?"

"I know you like him," Gabby said, never one to mince words.

"Of course I like him." And *like* was putting it mildly.

"So?" Gabby nudged.

"*So* we've been spending tons of time together for the last *two* months and . . ."

"And?" Gabby nudged.

"And nada." Nothing that said he wanted to move beyond friendship, and it stung.

"He spends an awful lot of time with you to call it nada," Gabby said, adjusting her fleece headband to better cover her ears.

"Yes," Brooke admitted, "he's over most Saturdays to help restore the bus." But helping her fix her grandparents' VW bus was far from a romantic overture.

"He spends time with you at Finn's for surfing and breakfast most mornings and at Nana Jo's weekly dinners."

"Yes, he spends time with me but not like that. You guys treat me like family, and I love it, but it's not like Noah's asking me out on a date or to go with him to those events." She searched for the right words. "I'm just one of the gang." It took Brooke a minute to realize she'd left Gabby standing at the top of the hill.

"What do you mean 'just one of the gang'?" Gabby said, catching back up to her. "You know that's not true."

Brooke sighed rather than arguing. Gabby meant well and wanted them to be together nearly as bad as she did, but it was beyond frustrating. There'd been moments—a lingering gaze in her direction, a charming smile on his lips, a level of deep comfort in his presence—when she'd thought . . . *maybe* he cared the same way about her, but clearly, she'd been misreading the situation.

Even after so much quality time together, he'd never made a move beyond friendship. It sucked, but she could only linger in the muck for so long. Today she was hauling herself out. Dave seemed like a nice guy. If her Coast Guard brothers said he was solid, he was solid. And it was time for some solid in her life.

Dwayne tapped the Copenhagen tin against his palm, then opened it and pulled a fresh pinch out. He rolled his lip forward and had barely settled it in place when his cell rang.

Fishing the phone from his shirt pocket, he answered the call but remained silent.

"Are we a go?" she asked.

He rolled his tongue against the inside of his cheek. Well, if it wasn't Miss-High-and-Mighty herself. "Affirmative. And you?"

She snorted. "What do you think?"

He curled his fists, a silent curse wagging in his mind.

"Don't be late, and don't mess this up," she snapped.

The line went dead.

Adrenaline surged through his limbs.

He glanced at his watch. *Not long now.*

He smothered any hint of pleasure from his face. It'd been years since he'd attended a graduation.

Gabby's face softened as they hit the final stretch of the Riverwalk. Pausing, Gabby laid her hand on Brooke's arm, took an inhale, and blew it out as if she was about to share something big.

Brooke stepped closer, almost expecting Gabby to whisper in her ear.

Gabby gazed across the river—pondering? Brooke fought the sudden urge to shake it out of her. Whatever *it* was.

"Gab?" Brooke asked

Her friend turned to face her, the rising sun's rays silhouetting her.

Brooke shielded her eyes with her hand. "You clearly want to say something."

Gabby slid her jacket zipper partly up and then down, then exhaled. "Just remember Noah has a past too."

"Which he never shares," Brooke said, then glanced at her Apple watch. She needed to hurry to make breakfast with Dave and get to the graduation in time. They trudged up the steep incline of Main Street, her calves burning with the good warmth of exercise, her mind spinning on Gabby's cryptic comment. What past? Was she indicating something bad had happened? "That's just part of the frustration," she said. "I know nothing of Noah's background other than professionally." He never confided in her.

"But you know *him*, and that's what matters." Gabby stuck her hands in her pockets, stretching her arms out and the jacket along with them.

"I know *about* him. I know he loves his family. I know he loves Jesus. I know he excels as a CGIS special agent in charge. He's disciplined and always in control."

"See, you know the important things about him—his love of family, the Lord, his country, and his team."

"Which is *about* him. Not *him*." Brooke shook her head. "You know what I'm saying. I'm sorry if I'm being short. I'm just . . ." *Heartbroken.*

Gabby's shoulders slackened. "I understand and I'm going to share something with you. Something I think will help you understand Noah better, and maybe you won't give up on him just yet. But it has to stay between us." She dipped her chin, her brows hiking.

"I promise." It felt wrong learning something about Noah from his sister rather than from him, but if it gave her insight into the man she'd fallen for—a peek beyond the wall he'd erected so firmly in place—she'd listen.

"Noah has a *complicated* relationship history."

*Seriously?* Brooke tried to smother her sarcastic chuckle. But, seriously, didn't Gabby know who she was talking to? Her collective dating experience looked like a who's who of losers. "Who doesn't?" she said.

Gabby shrugged a shoulder. "Fair enough."

"I thank you for sharing, but whatever this complicated history is, it's either affecting him enough that he *won't* move forward with me, or he simply doesn't want to." The moments when she thought there might be more between them than friendship were amazing, but he always pulled back, keeping her at arm's length.

"Give him time," Gabby said, a hint of hope holding tight in her voice.

Brooke exhaled. "It's been two months. If he cared enough to trust me and share even a little bit of life or his past with me, it would be different. But at some point, I have to let go of the dream and live in reality."

She glanced at her watch. *0640.* "Shoot. I've got to go."

"What time are you meeting Dave?"

"0715 at Belle's."

"Oh, yum," Gabby said. "She makes the best French toast. Well, you best scoot."

"Thanks." She waved, then headed right, toward home. It was the first house she'd actually owned, and she loved the feeling of being settled.

Gabby headed left. "Have a nice time," she called.

"Thanks," she said before rounding the corner. With the silence of early morning enveloping her, she released an exhale and turned to her Father in prayer.

*Help me to be open to giving Dave a real chance, Lord. I've fallen for Noah, but he clearly doesn't feel the same way. It's time I accept that our relationship will only be that of friendship. Please help me move on, even though it's the last thing I want to do.*

# FOUR

He would not ask.

Noah took long, determined strokes toward the breaking ridge of waves.

He couldn't ask.

His 1mm wet suit kept December's biting water from penetrating his body, but his toes were numb. He pumped them in and out to regain feeling. Gabby wore boots, but he liked the feel of the board beneath his feet.

The bracing temps would never deter him from riding the winter swells. They were addictive, just like Brooke Kesler's presence.

The last two months had been exquisite torture. He yearned to spend every chance he got with her—laughing with her, admiring her . . . falling for her, and that's where the torture came in.

The deeper he fell, the more he knew he had to walk away.

On a deep inhale, he dove beneath the roaring wave, cresting up in time to hear it gurgle and crash behind him.

He looked over his right shoulder at Gabby, then past her to his CGIS teammate Finn. The fact that Finn would be his brother-in-law come April was still surreal. But he and Gabby . . . well, they just *fit*.

Seeing them together made him miss Brooke all the more, but he absolutely refused to utter the question burning inside.

Cold water slipped over him and his board. He stroked farther out toward the horizon, but the question wouldn't shake loose from his mind. Where was Brooke?

She joined nearly every morning for a quick surf followed by breakfast at Finn's, but not today. Maybe if he asked whether she was feeling all right, that would show concern but not give Gabby fodder to think—to *know*—he'd fallen for the woman. But he cared too much to let Brooke settle for him, no matter how deeply he ached to be with her.

Spotting the perfect wave about to form, he paddled hard for it. Cutting through the water with rhythmic strokes, he reached position and waited. The wave lifted him, and he angled into the curl, letting the frothing wave carry him in until it dissipated about ten yards from shore.

"Nice one," Gabby said. Looking back at the horizon, she smiled as Finn also rode a stellar wave in. "About time for breakfast."

The half hour had flown by. Noah had best hurry. He had a stop to make on the way to work.

Grabbing their boards, they headed up Finn's sloping beach to the house, the damp sand shifting beneath their feet.

Reaching the surf shack, Noah rested his board against the wall and pulled off his neoprene gloves, shaking out his fingers. He headed for the shower stalls Finn had installed last month.

Stepping inside, he lost his suit and let the hot water roll along his skin, trying not to focus on how much Brooke's absence was bothering him.

He'd grown too dependent on having her in his life, and that would burn them both. Giving the water another minute to cascade warmth over him, he hung his head. He had to do the right thing, had to distance himself, painful as it would be.

Dressing in dry clothes and slipping his feet into a pair of flops, he emerged from the stall. He'd grab his work shoes from the car after breakfast.

"Speaking of breakfast," he said, entering the house to the scent of cinnamon, sweet icing, and yeasty dough. And, as was always the case with Finn, bacon. "Let me guess," Noah said, snatching a piece. "Finn was in charge?" Not that he was complaining. His future brother-in-law was a great cook.

The bacon left a heated sting on his fingers and his mouth. The sizzle of it on the plate should have been a warning. Just like his deepening feelings for Brooke. "Can I help with anything?" he asked, trying to shift the direction of his thoughts onto anything but Brooke.

"Thanks, but I got it," Finn said, loading a fresh heap of steaming bacon onto the platter while Gabby artfully arranged cinnamon rolls and pineapple slices along the rectangular serving plate.

He noticed the table was set for three. So they knew Brooke wasn't coming.

"She went out for breakfast," Gabby said, of course catching his glance at Brooke's usual seat.

"I didn't ask." He popped a slice of still-sizzling bacon into his mouth. Better to burn his tongue than spill the truth—at least in this case.

She smiled that mischievous smile he swore she'd come out of the womb bearing. "Of course, you didn't."

"Stop razzing your brother," Finn said, wrapping his arms around her from behind and placing a kiss on her neck.

Noah raised his hands. "Oy. Big brother here. No need to see that."

Finn stepped back. "Sorry, man."

After a prayer of blessing for the food, Noah shoved a cinnamon bun oozing with icing into his mouth, hoping it'd dissuade his investigative-reporter sister from probing him about Brooke.

Gabby sat back and crossed her arms—her telltale sign of

an interrogation to come. "You didn't ask, but I saw your face slacken when you looked at her empty chair."

Yes. He missed Brooke. A longing resonated in the pit of his stomach at her absence, but he'd never admit it. And most definitely not to his sister, though she wanted them to be a couple nearly as desperately as he did.

She poked at the pineapple with her fork, moving the chunks about her plate. "She joined Dave for a breakfast date."

*Dave?* Noah struggled to keep his expression even. *Who the heck is Dave?*

# FIVE

Brooke pulled up to the active-duty line at the base gate. The visitor line wrapped around the bend—everyone, no doubt, excited to attend their loved ones' graduation.

She swiped her ID, trying to push all thoughts of Noah Rowley from her mind. Dave was sweet and had a great sense of humor. She'd truly enjoyed her breakfast with him, but her foolish heart still belonged to a man who didn't want it.

Passing the CGIS station, she forced her gaze straight ahead. It didn't matter if his Jeep was in the lot or not. She wouldn't look.

She banked left, taking the shortcut to the Ida Stiller Hall's rear lot. As she rounded the corner of the large white building with the American, Coast Guard, and North Carolina flags rippling in the wind, she saw others had discovered the rear lot. Finally locating a space, she parked and strode for the entrance. The brisk December gusts ruffled her skirt about the top of her knee-high boots.

She could hardly believe Molly, the sweet young lady who'd shadowed her for several weeks before entering Flight Medic A-School, was graduating today. Entering the building's outer glass doors, Brooke rubbed her chilled hands together.

"Brooke."

She followed the direction of the familiar voice. "Hey, Austin. What are you doing here?"

"My neighbor's grandson is graduating, and she just had a hip replacement. She didn't want Grant graduating without anyone here to support him."

"That's sweet of you to come."

"They don't have much family. I'm happy to be here for them. Shall we?" Austin asked, holding the inner wooden door open.

"Thanks," she said, slipping through.

"Who are you here for?" Austin asked.

"Petty Officer First Class Molly Allen. Such a great kid." Though she was only a half dozen years older, somehow Brooke felt a strong mentor role with Molly. "Speaking of . . ." she said, turning to greet Molly as she approached. "Hi, honey," Brooke said, wrapping an arm around the petite redhead. "Molly, this is my friend Austin Kelly."

Molly smiled. "Pleased to meet you."

"Same here," Austin said. "Congratulations. This is such a big day for you."

"Thank you." Molly smiled as she scanned the room.

Brooke spied Molly's friend Peter beckoning her up front as the instructors huddled on the stage chatting.

"I better go."

"I'll be cheering for you, and afterward we're hitting the hard stuff at Maggie Moo's."

"That place has the best rocky road, hands down," Austin said.

"Next to their cookie dough, it's my fave," Brooke said as Molly hurried toward the front row for what would be one of the most memorable days of her life.

A sardonic smile flickered across Dwayne's lips as they pulled up to the building. It'd worked. The planning had paid off.

Now the execution needed to be flawless. He slid his gun into his side holster.

---

"Shall we find a seat?" Austin asked.

"The trick is going to be finding two together," Brooke said, scanning the full rows.

"There's two," Austin said, pointing toward the far left of the hall. She booked it to them, and Brooke quickened her step to keep up.

Settling into the cold metal chairs, Brooke tugged her sweater wrap tightly about her. "How's work going?" she asked.

Austin sighed.

"That good, huh?" Brooke smiled.

"No. I mean, it's a good case, and it's about wrapped up." She exhaled, her hair whipping about her forehead. "It's the second case since September where Caleb and I are both involved. It's his case jurisdictionally, but the family hired me to make sure everything is being done that can be done, and he's so . . . so . . ." Her shoulders tensed. "Stubborn."

Brooke bit back a smile. Caleb said the same about her.

Instructor Fleming stepped to the podium and cleared his throat. A hush fell over the room. "We'd like to thank you all for your presence today as we acknowledge the hard work and dedication of these graduates of Flight Medic A-School. With me today are Instructors Baker and Denson, who I have the honor of teaching with." He nodded his head in each instructor's direction, then turned his attention to the graduates filling the front row. "Graduates, as I call your name, please step forward." He looked up at the audience. "Each graduate will receive their certificate of completion along with their duty orders."

Brooke prayed Molly stayed in Wilmington, but she knew her friend would do a phenomenal job wherever she was based.

Instructor Fleming lifted the first certificate encased in a blue leather folio with the Coast Guard motto, *Semper Paratus*, embossed across the front. "Petty Officer First Class Molly Allen." Molly stepped onto the stage.

A mixture of pride and joy bubbled in Brooke's chest.

Molly aimed a quick smile her way as Instructor Fleming handed her the graduation certificate and shook her hand, both posing for a quick picture. The flash went off.

"Guns!" a man yelled a breath of a second before shots retorted, and Brooke watched in horror as Molly's stomach caved in. She staggered back, red seeping through her dress whites.

Brooke stood to race forward.

"Duck!" Austin hollered as an explosion of gunfire riddled the room.

# SIX

Noah pulled into his spot in front of his CGIS station, noting everyone else's cars present. He had the luxury of a late arrival today, due to several after-hours interviews that were nothing more than a screening process. But rather than volunteering one of his team, he'd offered this go-around. Anything and everything to keep his mind off Brooke. Though, as special agent in charge, it went against his constitution to arrive after any of his team, regardless of the reason.

He stepped from his Jeep, Brooke living in his mind. He wanted her desperately. Wanted to hold her hand, to sit silently beside her in the movies, to snuggle up on the couch at night. He wanted her—period. But what he wanted didn't matter. *She* did. She deserved the world, and he wasn't it.

*Crack, crack, crack.* The sound of gunfire, popping like Black Cat firecrackers, reverberated in his chest.

He swung in the direction of the noise.

*Crack, crack, crack.*

Caleb rushed out of the station. "Shooting at the graduation." He tossed Noah a bulletproof vest.

Noah slid it on, fastening it in place.

Caleb handed him his M4, a set of magazines, and an earpiece.

Noah slipped the earpiece in place and shoved the auxiliary

mags into his vest pockets as he raced for Ira Stiller Hall. Caleb kept pace, the rest of the team—save Emmy, who ran logistics from the station in a crisis situation like this—were tight on their heels.

"SRT is gearing up. ETA five minutes," Emmy said over the comms. "I notified them you'd be on-site."

"Details?" Adrenaline burned Noah's thighs as he rounded cars and jumped over the concrete dividers.

"Cameras are offline, but Austin called. She didn't speak. She must have rung the station and left her phone on the floor, giving us ears in the room. Multiple shooters. By voice inflections, I'd say at least four, possibly more."

"Did you say *Austin*?" Caleb asked, his voice heated.

"I'm afraid so," Emmy said.

"What is she doing there?"

"She's not the only one." Noah's throat tightened, squeezing the words out through a near-chokehold. "Brooke's there too."

"Brooke?" Rissi and Emmy said in unison, one behind him and the other in his ear.

He only managed a nod.

"We'll get them," Mason said, his tone resolute.

Noah prayed his teammate's confidence proved true.

Ira Stiller Hall was perched at the top of the hill they'd just raced up. Noah signaled his team to lay low as he scanned the area, determining how to position his crew. The special-response team wasn't on-site yet, but with gunfire continuing in bursts, they couldn't wait.

He lifted his fist, immediately halting his team.

*Please, Lord, let Brooke and Austin be okay. I know that's a selfish prayer. I do pray for everyone there, but please, let them be okay.*

Another burst of gunfire.

They were well armed. But were they trained?

He signaled for Rissi and Logan to head around the south

side of the building, Finn and Mason around the north, and Caleb to enter the front with him.

"Noah." Deacon Stiles, head of SRT, spoke over Noah's earpiece. "ETA three minutes."

"Roger that. Six CGIS agents in labeled vests entering now."

"Roger that," Deacon said.

Noah pressed his back against the outer brick wall, flanking the glass front doors. Caleb held position on the other side.

He pumped deep breaths in and out. M4 in hand, he dipped his chin at Caleb, who nodded his readiness.

Following a quick heartfelt prayer for his team's safety, Noah gave them the go-ahead.

He opened the front door, Caleb covering him. No one was between the exterior and interior doors. With two fingers, Noah signaled for Caleb to take the right side of the double doors. Both eased their gaze up to the porthole windows. Noah's body grew taut at the scene of chaos before them. People wailed and scrambled for cover as bullets riddled out in bursts. *Why bursts?*

Two shooters, in gray-and-white fatigues and ski masks, stood twenty-feet ahead—their backs to them.

Noah signaled *One, two, three.* Opening the doors just enough to slide his muzzle in, he fixed his aim at the base of the shooter's head. On a slow release of air, he squeezed the trigger. The shooter on the left dropped. In near synchronicity, Caleb fired, and the shooter on the right landed limp on the floor.

Noah signaled forward, and they entered the hall.

Both men were dead.

Two more shooters dropped at the back of the auditorium.

"Two shooters down," Rissi said over comms.

"Good job. Any more shooters?" he asked, as he and Caleb kept their backs to the wall, their eyes scanning the room, at the ready if any more appeared.

He signaled for Caleb to keep watch on the doors and room

as a whole, while he started to scan the ground in case the cowards were trying to hide within the crowd of wounded and dead.

"Not within sight," Rissi's voice echoed the question in his mind. Were there more out of their line of sight?

Noah's gaze moved toward the podium and locked on Brooke behind it, her hand and blouse covered with blood. His heart raced. *Was she hit?*

His gaze shifted down to her friend Molly bleeding out, Austin applying pressure as Brooke cried. She spoke to Molly, no doubt trying to keep her conscious until shock trauma arrived.

His heart broke for Molly, but at the same time, gratitude filled him that Brooke was okay. He yearned to run to her, to take her in his arms, but he had to help clear the rest of the building.

"I'll clear the lobby and front stairwells," Noah said over the comms. "Caleb, take the hallway to the right. Rissi, hallway to the left. Mason, check the back stairwell. Finn and Logan, hold the rear of the hall."

Everyone acknowledged in turn.

Noah moved back into the lobby. The echo of footfalls resounded behind him.

Turning, he caught sight of a shooter moving up the west stairwell. "Freeze!"

To his shock, the shooter stilled. One more step, and he would have rounded the corner.

"Lower your weapon," he ordered.

The shooter hesitated.

"Lower your gun," Noah barked out, his muzzle aimed at the man's chest.

To his surprise again, the shooter laid down his gun, his hands up, palms out.

Before Noah could take a step forward, the crack of gunfire echoed from behind the shooter, and he flailed down the steps, hitting the ground, gasping for air.

"Entering in sixty," Deacon said over the comm.

"Roger that. We've got five shooters dow—"

*Crack, crack.*

Searing pain burned through Noah's thigh. *A sixth shooter.*

He pivoted swiftly and shot, hitting the sixth shooter's center mass twice. The man sank to the ground, his eyes frozen wide in death.

Warm blood seeped down Noah's leg.

# SEVEN

"Noah!" Brooke yelled, rushing for him.

"Stay put," he hollered, waving her back.

She only raced faster as SRT swarmed around them, guns drawn. *Please, Lord, let him be okay.*

Her gaze shifted to the blood saturating his pants on his right thigh. *Please, Lord, not his femoral artery again.*

Deacon Stiles took a knee by Noah. "Special agent down. We need a paramedic—"

"I'm fine." Noah waved him off. "We've got many critical. This guy"—he gestured to the shooter slumped at the base of the steps, gurgling for air—"and Molly . . . among them." He winced, his brow hardening.

"Medevacs landing now," Deacon said. "I got this guy. Who and where is Molly?"

"In here," Caleb called, kneeling by Austin's side as she continued to keep pressure on Molly's chest.

Gratitude for Austin's help filled Brooke, but the only way her sweet friend would survive was if God performed a miracle.

Two of her fellow flight medics, Cal and Leo, pushed through the doors with stretchers, followed by their supervisor, Oscar, who caught sight of Brooke. "You okay?" he asked.

She swiped tears from her cheeks and nodded.

"We need you on Medevac Three if you aren't injured."

"I'm not injured." At least not physically.

Oscar bent to assess Noah's thigh.

"I'm not critical," Noah said, and Oscar moved on to the shooter, who was still gasping.

"If it hit your femoral artery, you are critical," Brooke argued. "It's only been a few months since your artery was severed. If the bullet hit it . . ." She swallowed, the words lodging in her throat.

"I'm fine waiting for an ambulance. There are many more critical than me."

Oscar looked over at her. "Grab a set of scrubs in the copter and sanitize up," he said. "I'll get the shooter prepped for you to escort him." He turned to Cal. "Take the woman bleeding out on the stage."

"Yes, sir." Cal nodded and moved for Molly.

Brooke yearned to stay by Noah's side or to be with her friend. She'd taken an oath to heal all those in need . . . but to go with one of the shooters, a man who'd taken lives . . .

She exhaled. It was her job.

"Medevac Three, Kesler," Oscar repeated.

"Yes, sir." Brooke nodded. Tears burned as she stared into Noah's eyes. *Please let him be okay, Father*. "I'll see you at the hospital."

"I'll be fine," he said, but concern still warred inside.

Relief loosened Noah's tight chest. Brooke was safe and uninjured.

*Thank you, Father. I pray healing for all the injured and comfort for all those who lost loved ones today.*

EMTs flooded in with stretchers, defibrillators, and crisis-response gear as Cal rushed Molly's stretcher out the double-glass doors.

Noah glanced around at the sorrow, the echoes of sobs, the blood . . . and righteous anger filled him. *Senseless. Senseless death and heartache.*

Flight medics and EMTs worked fast and yet methodically to assess, treat what they could on-site, and transport all the critical and wounded to Wilmington General.

"Let's get you on the stretcher." Leo knelt beside him and flagged another EMT over to aid in lifting Noah onto it.

"I can help," Caleb said as he and Austin moved to Noah's side.

"Thanks," Noah said, "but I've got this." He pushed up on his arms, readying himself to climb onto the stretcher.

"Whoa!" Leo halted him with a hand on his arm. "Don't move your leg. We don't know what level of damage has occurred."

Not liking it one bit, he reluctantly agreed.

"On three," Leo said. "Try to keep his leg as stationary as possible." Leo lifted Noah from behind, underneath his shoulders, while Caleb lifted him by his calves.

Noah situated himself on the stretcher, his leg shaking. He looked up at Austin. "Thank you for helping Molly."

"Of course," Austin said. She started to cross her arms, then winced hard, her lips thinning into a tight grimace.

"Are you injured?" he asked.

"It's nothing." She shrugged, then winced again, favoring her left arm.

"I'm pretty sure she dislocated her shoulder," Caleb said.

"Get her in line for an ambulance," Leo said. "It'll be quite a while, given . . ." He gazed at the hall and shook his head before fixing his eyes back on Austin. "X-rays will be needed to see the full extent of damage before treatment."

Good thing Austin was a tough lady, because treatment for a dislocated shoulder consisted of popping it back in place. Most definitely not a pleasant experience. Neither was pain pulsing through his thigh.

Leo opened his supply bag and pulled out a few items, laying them carefully on the stretcher beside him.

"Your car's at the station, right?" Noah asked Caleb.

"Yes." Caleb nodded.

"Take Austin to the ER, then."

"Good idea," Leo said. "You'll get there a lot faster." He gestured over his shoulder, and they all looked in that direction.

Lines of wounded and medics waited for an available ambulance or helicopter.

"Take her to the ER and then stay," Noah said. "I need you to be point at the hospital." Needed him to track everything happening there and to speak with the victims as they were able. It sounded cold to bother them at the hospital, but talking with them as soon after an incident as possible often provided the most accurate details.

"I'm going to apply a tourniquet to try to slow the bleeding," Leo said, pulling Noah's attention back to the paramedic. "I'll get a better look and get it cleaned up in-flight," Leo said, setting to work.

Rissi approached. "How you doing, boss?"

"Hanging in," he said. *Keep your focus on the case, not the injury. It's a bullet wound. Not your first.* "How many shooters did there end up being?"

"Six," Rissi said, "including the two you shot out here."

"I didn't shoot the one who laid down his weapon," Noah said.

Rissi's eyes narrowed. "One surrendered?"

"Yeah. The one who's on the Medevac with Brooke." Copter blades whirred outside, along with the wailing of more arriving ambulances.

"If you didn't shoot him, who did?" Caleb said. "I was with Austin and Molly once we cleared the hall."

"Mason and I were in the rear stairwell and hallway. Finn and Logan were holding the rear," Rissi said.

Noah frowned. "I have no idea. Did we miss a shooter?"

"No." Mason shook his head. "The building was swept by us and then confirmed clear by Deacon and his team."

"Time to go," Leo said. And before Noah could blink, they were moving toward the doors.

"Rissi," he called back.

"Yes?" She jogged to his side.

"You're point here." She and the rest of his team would do a fantastic job regardless of his presence, but frustration anchored deep inside at being sidelined.

"Yes, sir," Rissi said, as Leo loaded him into the ambulance.

"I want regular updates," he called before the rear doors shut.

"You got it!" she hollered a nanosecond before the sirens blared, and they pulled away from the chaos, though he anticipated just as much at the hospital about to be flooded with victims.

# EIGHT

Zeke took a quick glance from the pilot seat back at Brooke working hard at the shooter's side. "Five minutes out," he said.

"Roger that." Brooke relayed their ETA to Wilmington General, along with the kid's critical status. Shock had surged through her when she'd removed his ski mask for treatment and saw how young he was.

She'd managed to slow the bleeding from the gunshot wound to his back, but listening to his lungs, she knew his right had collapsed, resulting in tension pneumothorax. She had no choice but to perform needle decompression to release the trapped air in the pleural space, or he'd likely die before reaching the hospital's helipad. No wonder he'd been gurgling on-site.

The shooter lulled in and out of a hazy consciousness. So much death and destruction caused by one so young.

Had *he* been the one who shot Noah? There'd been two shooters in the lobby. Either could have been the one to pull the trigger on the man she loved. Her thoughts shifted back to Noah.

*Please, Father*, she started in prayer as wind rattled the bird. *Please let Noah be okay. Please don't let it be his femoral artery again*. It had recently been sliced in the line of duty. If it was compromised again . . .

She cut off the thought and continued her fractured prayer.

*Please be with Molly.* Tears burned her eyes. *Please be with everyone harmed by today's tragedy, whether physically injured or not.*

Questions rumbled through her mind. Why the graduation? Why them?

She looked back at the shooter. He was staring at her, eyes filled with defiant fear.

Hovering above Wilmington General's helipad, she spotted Dr. Kent and his jump team awaiting them.

Her thoughts tracked to Molly. The comms said she was arriving soon.

Zeke set the copter down. "Clear."

The shooter moaned as she slid the bay door open. Kent's jump team rushed forward.

"Vitals?" he asked as she raced with them for the hospital doors.

"Blood pressure is eighty over sixty, blood oxygen is stable, and heart rate sixty-seven," she said, continuing to relay the treatment she'd performed as they rolled toward the glass sliding doors, where another rolling gurney waited. They had to make the transfer as quickly as possible to allow the other Medevacs to land.

A hand clutched her shirt before they rolled inside. She looked down at the shooter, straining to raise his head. He struggled to form words. His terror-filled eyes latched on hers, silently pleading for her to lower her head.

She leaned down.

"Gator," he uttered barely above a choked whisper.

"What?"

"Gator," he wheezed, then flopped back onto the stretcher.

She frowned. What on earth did *gator* mean?

"We need to get him into the OR stat," Kent said, rolling him inside and making the transfer to the hospital gurney in rapid fashion.

Before she could ask the shooter what he was trying to say, what the word meant to him, Kent's team was vanishing through the inner set of doors.

Turning, she headed back for the copter.

Zeke signaled for her to hurry. "Medevac Two's ETA is one minute," he said as she climbed into the copter, closing the bay door.

Medevac Two. *Molly.*

Dwayne's cell rang. He looked down at the number. *Saul.* Everything had gone according to plan, with the notable exception of Connor's survival. "Yeah," he answered, hoping for the good news Connor was dead.

"He talked," Saul said in a quiet muffle.

"I thought he was nearly dead?" he asked between gritted teeth.

"So did I, but they're wheeling him into surgery."

He gripped the phone tight. "Who did he talk to and what did he say?"

"To the female medic who brought him in."

"What did he say?" he asked again, his muscles coiled tight.

"I don't know." Saul cleared his throat. "They were on the helipad, and I was staying out of sight as instructed, watching from the tinted window of an empty room. What do you want me to do?"

"Take the medic," he ordered. "We need to know what Connor told her. The entire operation could be compromised. Grab her when you can."

"Yes, sir."

"Once you have her, bring her to the black site. We'll dispose of her after we get what we need."

In what seemed like mere minutes to Noah, the ambulance arrived at Wilmington General. He wondered how long ago Brooke had lifted back off.

*Please, Father, carry Brooke through her duty today. Her heart must be breaking for her friend's critical state. I pray for Molly, that you will be with her, and if she doesn't pull through, welcome her home in your loving arms.*

He'd barely finished his prayer when the rear ambulance doors opened. Blotny and her head surgical nurse, Mandy, stood waiting. Clearly, he spent far too much time at the hospital, being on a first-name basis with the majority of the staff.

They whisked him inside and transferred him to the hospital gurney. The pressure throbbing in his leg began to burn as the adrenaline that had been coursing through him since the first shot sounded dissipated.

The EMT briefed Blotny as they moved down the hall. "His vitals are stable, but the bleeding was quite heavy. He has a tourniquet above the wound along with layers of gauze to keep infection out. I started an IV line with penicillin."

"Thank you," Blotny said. "We can take him from here."

"Take care, man," the EMT said before heading back to the ambulance.

Noah looked up at Blotny. "Any news on the shooter who was brought in?"

"He's in surgery with Dr. Kent," she said as they rolled down the hall, the harsh smell of antiseptic burning his nose.

"Any idea of his chances?" Being the only assailant to survive—at least Noah prayed he survived surgery—he was the only one who could provide answers. What had prompted him and his crew to open fire at a Coast Guard graduation, of all places?

"It's touch and go, but I'll try to keep you posted," Blotny responded as they passed through the imaging center's double-glass doors. "Now, let's focus on you." Blotny frowned. "What is it with you and this leg?"

"Bad luck." He shrugged and winced at the lancing pain.

"We need an MRA stat," Blotny said to the imaging tech.

---

Brooke returned on-site to help the next victim. It would be so easy and natural to fall into the pit of emotions warring through her, but she had a job to do. She was trained to focus on what needed to be done, rather than on the trauma surrounding her.

Rissi hurried to her side as Brooke headed for the main hall, where she'd been directed to find her next patient. Paramedics relayed they had the elderly woman on an IV and oxygen while she waited for the Medevac to return.

"How is Molly doing?" Rissi asked, hurrying her stride to keep up.

Tears welled in Brooke's eyes, but she quickly swiped them away. She was on duty. She'd have to deal with her sorrow later. "Molly was arriving moments after we took off. I imagine she's in surgery by now."

"We'll keep praying." Rissi clutched her hand. "Em is keeping tabs on Noah. They are prepping him for surgery now."

"Did the bullet hit his femoral artery?" Brooke's chest squeezed tight.

Rissi's face softened, compassion strong in her gaze. "We don't know."

"Ris," Finn approached from across the room. "Hadley is ready to transfer the first body to the morgue."

Brooke looked at the sheets draped over the bodies surrounding them—her heart aching as she counted. *Twelve.* Twelve lives senselessly lost. And the number would rise. Not all the patients in critical condition at the hospital would live. She prayed Molly would pull through, but deep inside she knew better.

"We thought taking them out the rear exit would be less traumatic for those still here," Finn said, offering Brooke an expression of sympathy.

She appreciated how Noah and his team all loved on her.

"Definitely use the rear," Rissi said. "Give Hadley the go-ahead, and let Caleb know the ME is starting to transport the deceased. He'll want to speak with Hadley for sure. Though I can't image Hadley will have time to start with autopsies today."

"I'll let Caleb know." Finn turned to Brooke. "We're praying."

"Thanks." She nodded and moved for the EMT triaging the elderly lady not twenty feet from her.

She bent down beside the woman. "Medic Brooke Kesler."

"This is Mrs. Kilpatrick," the EMT said. "I'm Kyle Michaels."

"Glad to have you aboard, Kyle." She turned her attention to the woman. "I'm going to get you to the hospital and take care of you on the way. Don't worry. I've got you."

"Than . . . Thank . . . you," Mrs. Kilpatrick whispered, her eyes glazed with fear.

EMTs and ambulances continued arriving in waves as they moved for the Medevac. Nearby bases and statewide agencies were sending help in what was surely one of the worst domestic tragedies on a military base.

# NINE

Hours after arriving at the hospital and seeing Austin into an ER room, Caleb got the go-ahead to interview the first victim who was stable and settled into a room.

He rapped on the door for room 203. "Grant Miller?"

"Yes?"

"I'm CGIS Special Agent Caleb Eason. Could I talk to you for a few minutes?"

"Sure," Grant said.

Caleb slid the door open and stepped inside.

The young man scooted up in the bed, a cast on his left leg and a bandage wrapped around his forehead and right ear.

"Sorry about your injuries," Caleb said.

"Thanks. They just need to watch the knock I took to the head for a couple of days, and then I'm free to go. I got off lucky." Moisture pooled in his brown eyes.

"I appreciate you talking with me," Caleb said, standing several feet from the bed. Interviewing the victims was vital, but he always hated intruding in the midst of suffering or loss.

"If it can help figure out why the . . ." Grant paused. "If it can help figure out why they did what they did . . ." The moisture brimmed over his lashes, tears slipping down his freckled cheeks. He swiped them away with the back of his hand. "Please take a seat." He pointed to the empty chair on the far side of his bed.

"Thanks." Caleb slid the cushioned chair closer to the bed. "The sooner we talk with the—" *Don't say victims.* Most people hated the term. "The sooner we speak with those present," he continued, "the more helpful it often turns out to be."

"On determining their motive?" Grant asked.

"That's one thing," Caleb said.

"And the other?" Grant frowned, then reached for his head, wincing at the facial motion.

"Are you okay to continue?" Caleb asked.

"Yes," Grant choked out, then reached for the mauve pitcher on his rolling cart but came up short.

"Can I help you?" Caleb asked, standing.

"Some water would be great."

"No problem." Caleb poured him a cup of ice water, then moved the cart closer so Grant could reach it if he wanted more.

"You were saying the other reason was . . . ?" Grant asked, reclining back against his pillows.

"We always need to determine if anybody not present at the site played a role in the tragedy."

"That happens?"

Caleb retook his seat. "More often than you'd think."

"Wow. I hadn't thought of that. Ask me anything you like."

"Hey, Grant," Austin said, rounding the corner with an oversized gift bag.

Caleb frowned. "I thought you were discharged and went home?" He couldn't leave to take her until he'd finished interviewing all the injured once they were able to talk, but she'd said she had a friend who could give her a ride home.

"Yes, I was discharged. But, no, I didn't go home," she said, shifting her attention to Grant. "I brought you some goodies." She handed him the gift bag. "I figured you'd prefer magazines and candy to flowers."

Grant riffled through the bag's contents, pulling out a sudoku book and Peanut Chews with a big smile. "Thanks, Austin."

"No problem." She smiled, though it wasn't lit with her usual brightness. Caleb hated that she'd been in the tragedy. That kind of trauma stuck with people, leaving an indelible mark.

"I didn't realize you'd be interviewing Grant," she said.

"And I didn't realize you weren't heading home," he replied.

"There are plenty of people here who could use someone to bring even a nanosecond of peace to them, whether it be through flowers or someone to pray with."

He loved her giving heart, but her arm was in a sling, and her relocated shoulder had to be painful. "That's very kind of you, but you are injured. You should be resting."

"I can rest later." She took a seat on the bottom edge of Grant's bed. Clearly, they knew each other well. "Besides, now that I'm here, I can chat with you and Grant."

Caleb cocked his head. When she'd offered to help him with questioning victims, he'd insisted she go home and rest, but that advice clearly hadn't been taken. Though, he wasn't the least surprised. Austin Kelly was the most stubborn woman he'd ever met.

He exhaled. "I think it would be best if I talked to Grant privately."

"I'm fine with Austin staying," Grant said. "She's a friend of the family."

Austin smirked.

If it weren't the most annoyingly cute thing he'd ever seen, he'd have throttled her. "All right." She may have inserted herself into this interview because she knew Grant, but that wouldn't be the case with the rest.

He cleared his throat and began. "Grant, could you tell me how your day started, up through arriving at the graduation ceremony?"

"Sure. That part is easy." He shifted his right leg over his casted left and rubbed it back and forth. Caleb knew from experience how much casts itched.

"I woke up at 0600," Grant began. "I went for my morning run, ate breakfast with my grandmother." He looked over at Austin. "Austin's our next-door neighbor."

So that was the connection.

"We were told to be early for the graduation ceremony, but I didn't get there until 0850. My grandma had a little fall, and I wanted to make sure she was all right."

"Did you drive yourself?" Caleb asked.

"Yeah."

"Where'd you park?"

"At the Sadgewick building so we didn't take up visitor spots, then I walked over," Grant said.

"Did you notice anyone or anything out of place?" Caleb asked.

"No." Grant's lips shifted as if in thought. "But I did almost get taken out by the catering van."

Caleb and Austin shared a glance. On-base events were self-catered. But it wasn't hard to imagine someone driving to the graduation in their catering van.

"Where did that happen?" Austin asked, then looked over at Caleb. Clearly, she wanted to take part in the investigation, and she was a top-notch private investigator. It was a good question, and Grant obviously felt comfortable with her, so Caleb gave her a nod to proceed.

"About halfway between Stiller Hall and that white building across the street."

"Can you describe the van?" Austin asked.

"At first, I just saw a flash of white. It all happened so fast. The van swerved mere feet from me, and I jumped for the sidewalk. When I looked back up, it was at the end of the road and rounding the corner."

He'd provided the van color—that was a good start. It might

lead to nothing but was probably something they should check in to.

"But," Grant continued, "when I passed it parked right next to Stiller Hall, I got a much better look."

Caleb furrowed his brow, and Austin leaned forward.

"Can you describe it?" Austin asked. "Any chance you noticed the make or model?"

"It was one of those . . . what do you call them? Sprinter vans."

"That's very helpful," Caleb said, then dipped his chin for Austin to continue.

"Was there anything painted on it? A name, a logo?" she asked.

"A logo," Grant said. "It was black and gold, and the writing was fancy."

"Do you remember the name on the logo?" Caleb asked.

"It started with a *J* . . . maybe Jacob something . . . or Jason. . . ." He shook his head, then winced. "Sorry. It's this darn headache. It's hard to think, and I wasn't paying a ton of attention."

"It's okay," Austin said.

"You're doing great," Caleb added. It was a wonderful start to go on, now knowing the van had been parked outside the hall. A visitor would have parked in one of the lots—or, at least, most visitors would. The van might be inconsequential, but as an investigator he couldn't ignore the possibility. Often it was the small details that became the biggest clues. "Did you happen to see the driver?" he asked, thinking it would almost be too good to be true if Grant had.

"Yes, but there wasn't a whole lot to see. He was wearing sunglasses and a baseball hat."

"Can you describe the hat?" Caleb asked, refusing to admit how well he and Austin Kelly worked together.

"It was a Red Sox cap, so at least he has good taste," Grant said.

"Anything else?" Austin leaned a smidge forward. "His hair, build?"

"I'm not sure. . . ." Grant's lips twisted again in contemplation.

"Close your eyes and replay the scene in your mind," Caleb said, having found the exercise Rissi recommended to be helpful in situations like this.

Grant closed his eyes. "He had a dark shirt on—maybe black or navy," he said after a moment. "He was tapping the wheel and staring toward the building, like he was impatiently waiting for someone and they were taking too long. I couldn't see his hair color with the hat on."

"So it's most likely short," Austin said. "Anything else?"

Grant left his eyes closed another moment, and then his jaw clenched—no doubt his mind had moved to the shooting.

"That's plenty," Caleb said, and Austin nodded in agreement.

Grant opened his eyes, tears slipping out. He swiped them with the back of his hand, then cleared his throat. "Hope that was helpful."

"Extremely," Caleb and Austin said within a second of each other. "Thanks again for your time."

"Thanks, Grant." Austin clutched his hand. "I'm praying for a swift recovery."

Caleb closed Grant's door as he and Austin stepped into the ward's main corridor. "That's a great lead to follow," he said.

"Definitely." She shuffled her feet.

"Yes, you can help me interview," he said, noting her questioning tell. When had he become so in tune with her gestures, expressions . . . with *her*? He took a stiff inhale, shifting his full focus back on the case. Why did his thoughts always track to her?

"Thanks," she said with a soft smile. "I want to help find out why this happened, who the shooters were, and if anybody else might have been involved. In the Oklahoma bombing, Terry

Nichols wasn't present but helped build the bomb, and Michael Fortier was aware of the plot."

"It's more the norm that others are involved in some aspect, even if it's just the knowledge of the coming tragedy. Those are the people we have to find, especially if the only surviving shooter doesn't make it." They needed answers. He looked back at Austin.

Having been in the shooting, of course she wanted to work the case, and Noah had had her collaborate on several CGIS cases in the past, so he was sure that wasn't an issue. And it probably would help distract her from the trauma she'd been through.

He reached over and squeezed her good shoulder. "I'm so sorry you had to endure the shooting."

She slipped her lip into her mouth as tears beaded in her eyes. "Thank you."

He hated seeing her in pain. He just wanted to pull her into his arms and comfort her, but they didn't have that depth of relationship. *Not yet.*

He started. *Not yet?*

# TEN

Well after nightfall, and once recovered from anesthesia and settled in his own room, Noah was more than ready to dive fully into the case—albeit from a hospital bed.

Rissi had erased the nurses' information from the whiteboard on the wall after noting it down so Noah still had it, then used it instead as a makeshift case board.

Rissi and Caleb were handling the witness interviews—each working a different avenue of questioning—Rissi at the crime scene and Caleb at the hospital. He'd also approved Austin joining the investigation since she'd already been assisting Caleb with his interviews. She was a brilliant private investigator. He looked forward to hearing her insights.

Considering the strict limit they were placing on visitors due to the high influx of patients, the hospital had made a big exception allowing Caleb, Rissi, and Austin to be present so soon after his surgery. But the one visitor he was aching to see was Brooke. Last he saw her, she was heading for the Medevac with the only surviving shooter.

He clenched his jaw at the realization he could have lost her today without telling her he loved her. But that love was precisely why he couldn't tell her, so he shifted his thoughts onto something he could do.

"What do we have so far?" he asked.

"We have the identity of the shooter in the ICU," Rissi said. "Despite his fingerprints coming back unknown like the other shooters, he was wearing a medical-alert necklace. Each one has an individualized ID number."

That was a solid start.

"His name is Connor Andrews," she said, the marker squeaking as she wrote it in purple ink on the whiteboard.

"What do we know about Connor Andrews?" Noah asked.

"He's nineteen, from Georgia, and his work history is limited to a two-year gig at an Apple Genius Bar," Rissi said.

"All right, let's find out when he showed up in Wilmington and how he got involved in the mass shooting," Noah said, wincing as he shifted his weight, his thigh throbbing. "I'll put Logan on him. He may very well be our only link to discovering the other shooters' identities."

"Agreed," Rissi said.

"Did anything come from your interviews?" Noah asked.

"Mostly very general details. It seems that most people were still too stunned to have clear memories," Rissi said. "But I had an interesting conversation with a Mrs. Talbot. She was there for the second graduation of the day—IT C-School. Her husband was one of the IT C-School instructors. She'd agreed to join him early to help set up the refreshment tables. She survived. Her husband and the two other instructors scheduled to present at their graduation ceremony did not. What's of particular interest is that the three instructors were in a meeting room off the back hall. Not accessed directly from the main hall."

"Hmm," Noah said. "Maybe that's where Connor Andrews and the other shooter on the steps were coming from."

Rissi nodded. "Could be."

Noah shifted his attention to Caleb. "Anything interesting come from your interviews here?"

"We found out some interesting details about a vehicle seen

on-site," Caleb said. He relayed his and Austin's conversation with Grant Miller.

"Good work," Noah said. "I'll put Em on the logo. That's a lot to go on. Be sure to follow up with those you both questioned in a day or two, even if by cell," he said. Following up a few days later often proved helpful. Time allowed memories to surface as the traumatized mind began to settle—though it never truly did.

He took a steep inhale, bracing himself for the information he needed to have. "Can you give me the current casualty stats?" he asked.

"There were twelve dead on-site," Rissi said.

"And another three have died at General," Caleb added.

Noah grimaced. They were looking at a death count of at least fifteen. Anger seared through him.

"At last count, the injured treated here is twenty-three," Caleb added. "A few have been cleared to go home. Only one of those still in the hospital is critical."

*Molly.* Caleb didn't have to say it. As of the latest update from Blotny, Molly's chances of surviving were less than one percent. He glanced back at his phone. *2110.* If Molly was going to pass, he prayed he could be with Brooke to comfort her.

"Emmy is compiling the list of people Mason and I interviewed on-site," Rissi said as they shifted to wrap up.

"As well as those we interviewed here," Caleb said.

"Good. Ask her to also compare it to the list of attendees that were slated to be at the hall," he said. It'd be interesting to see what, if any, discrepancies arose.

# ELEVEN

Brooke entered Wilmington General for what she prayed would be the last time that day. She rubbed her arms, trying to wrest December's chill from her bones. It'd been over twelve hours since the shooting, and most of those hours were a hazy blur sifting through her rattled brain.

She made her way through the throngs of agitated family members pacing the lobby or lined up to speak with—or rather, holler at, as a man nearly lunging across the visitor's desk was doing—the volunteer who was trying to keep order in the midst of tragic loss.

Two security guards stood watch, making sure no one got out of line. But she understood. There could be no peace for the throngs of relatives clamoring to learn more about their loved ones.

With the ER filled to overflowing and the tension pulsing through the air, visitors were limited, if not fully restricted, to the lobby.

Brooke swallowed, her throat parched. There hadn't been time to eat or even drink more than bottled water during the intensity of the day. Once they'd wrapped up medic duties and everyone on-site had been seen to, Oscar had called a post-emergency briefing. It was important, but thankfully he hadn't taken too long, because they were all weary, and her heart was cracked. Last she'd heard, Molly was still clinging to life—barely.

"Brooke," Gabby called.

Brooke spun around, searching for her friend. She spotted Gabby waving from the center of the crowd as she maneuvered her petite frame through the tight-knit mass of people.

"Hey," Gabby said, wrapping her arms around Brooke.

It was the first hug she'd gotten today, and heaven knew she needed it.

"How's Noah?" Gabby asked. "You probably have or can get more details than me. All I could get was that he's out of surgery and in a room."

"The femoral artery wall wasn't hit, thankfully," Brooke said, the news one strong bright spot in her day. "They removed the bullet with no severe damage. He should be released within forty-eight hours."

"Ha! My brother stay put for forty-eight hours? Yeah, right." Gabby shook her head.

"I know. We might have to chain him to the bed." But even that wouldn't do it, knowing Noah. She was half-surprised he hadn't already checked himself out of the hospital.

Gabby lifted a Trader Joe's bag. "Rissi said you've been running all day. I thought you could use some fresh clothes, since I imagine you'll be here awhile. And your purse is in there too. Finn cleared it from the scene. I also drove your car over. It's in the rear parking lot—second row."

Brooke took the bag from Gabby's outstretched hand.

"Thank you. That's so thoughtful."

"Have you been cleared to go up?" Gabby asked.

Brooke smiled shyly, feeling a little reluctant when so many other people weren't being allowed to see their loved ones. "Yes. Professional courtesy, I guess."

Gabby squeezed her hand. "I better let you get up there, then."

Brooke nodded.

"I'm praying for Molly. We all are."

"Thanks," Brooke said, trying not to cry. If she started, she feared she'd never stop. She gave Gabby one last hug and headed for the elevators.

The doors slid open, and Caleb and Austin stepped out.

"Hey there," she said. "You two heading out?"

"Yeah. I'm taking Austin home," Caleb said.

Brooke knew Austin had injured her shoulder but didn't know the extent. "Anything broken or torn?"

"Nope," Austin said. "Just a dislocated shoulder. They popped it back in place. Right as rain."

While popping it back in place was a quick procedure, it certainly wasn't a painless one. "Did the doc give you pain medicine?"

"He said NSAIDs are best, so I grabbed her a handful of over-the-counter options from the hospital pharmacy." Caleb held up a bag.

By the bulging bottom, she saw Caleb wasn't joking about a handful. It looked as if he'd bought every painkiller on the shelves.

"I hope you're able to sleep well," Brooke said.

"Thanks." Austin offered a soft smile.

Unfortunately, *she* wouldn't be able to. Even if she could manage to fall asleep, she'd no doubt be stuck in night terrors.

Just thinking about it made the sound of casings dinging off the pile around the shooter's feet twang in her ears.

Caleb's eyes narrowed. "You okay?"

"Yeah." Brooke shook off her thoughts. "I'm good. Just tired."

"I can imagine," Caleb said. "We just left Noah's room. Hopefully, he'll get some rest."

"That'll be the day," Brooke said.

"We should let her head up," Austin said to Caleb.

"Of course." He nodded. "If you need anything, just call."

"Ditto," Austin said, pulling her into a one-arm hug.

Brooke clutched Austin's hand as she stepped back, giving it a gentle squeeze. "You be easy on that shoulder. I know it's back in place, but your arm is probably going to bruise, if it hasn't already."

Caleb rocked back on his heels. "There's a better chance of pigs sprouting wings than Austin taking it easy."

Austin perked her brows.

Brooke shook her head. They really were a stubborn lot.

Caleb pressed the Up button, as Brooke had let the elevator go rather than holding it while they talked.

The circle above the elevator doors dinged brightly, and the doors slid open.

Caleb held the door as she stepped in. "Room 304."

"We're praying," Austin said as the doors slid shut.

The elevator bounced to a stop on level three. Stepping into the corridor, she headed for unit 34 and found Noah's room, the second door on the left. "Knock, knock," she said.

"Come in," he called.

She took a settling inhale. It was good to hear his voice. She wanted nothing more than to curl up beside him, rest her head on his shoulder, and bawl, but she wouldn't. Noah had kept things friendly but at arm's length, especially over the last few weeks.

She rounded the corner, vowing to be strong.

"Brooke," Dr. Blotny said. "You finally done for the night?"

Brooke nodded, her eyes weary, her body riddled with tension.

She looked at Noah, and her heart thumped in her chest, as it always did in his presence. She couldn't help imagining what it would be like if he actually loved her back. Meeting his gaze, she paused at the deep intensity there, far deeper and different than she'd ever seen before.

She shifted her attention to Blotny, though Noah's gaze held on her as she peeked out of the corner of her eye. Warm and, dare she say it, loving concern radiated there.

"How's our patient?" she asked as Blotny scanned the chart in her hands.

Blotny shook her head. "Stubborn as always."

Noah opened his mouth to no doubt argue, but Blotny shushed him.

Brooke bit back a smile. She'd only seen two women effectively do that—Noah's mom, affectionately known as Nana Jo, and Dr. Blotny.

"His femoral artery?" Brooke asked, wanting to confirm Noah was out of the woods.

"His angiogram showed no leak, but the bullet missed the artery by only a hair, and the artery wall is only seventy-five percent healed since his last injury." She dipped her chin and arched her brows at him. "You should be grateful and not tempt the blessing you received. I do not want to see you back in here for another leg injury. Understood?"

"Yes, ma'am." A humble expression fixed on Noah's face.

"Good. Now, I'll leave you two alone." Blotny turned for the door, then paused at the sight of the bag Brooke had set on the table when she entered. "For you?"

"Yes. Gabby thought I could use a change of clothes."

"Great idea. Why don't you use the nurses' locker room. Take a nice hot shower. That is, if you're staying."

"I . . ." Brooke began.

"I already know the answer to that," Blotny said. "The locker room is at the end of the unit on the far-right side."

"Thanks." Brooke nodded her head and turned her attention back to Noah.

He held out his hand. "Come sit by me a moment before you go shower." He patted the mattress beside him as he scooched with a slight grimace of pain toward the left rail.

Taking a steadying breath, she sat beside him on the bed.

He gripped her hand firmly, caressing the back of her knuckles with the pad of his thumb. "When the shooting happened . . . knowing you were there . . ." His thumb stilled, his grip tightening. "Seeing your blouse covered with blood . . ." He cleared his throat, still holding her gaze. Love radiated there. "I thought I lost you."

"Lost me?" she asked, her head dizzying from his intent, loving gaze.

"I thought you'd been shot. I thought . . . I feared I'd . . ."

"You'd . . . ?" she nudged.

"Hello?" Dr. Blotny said, knocking on the door.

*Nooo.* Brooke frowned. *Not now!* What had he been about to say?

As Blotny stepped through the doorway, the air left Brooke's lungs. Blotny's expression said it all. Molly was dead.

# TWELVE

Brooke's bottom lip quivered, and Noah grasped her hand tightly.

He pulled her toward him, letting her nestle against his weight.

"I'm so sorry, Brooke," Blotny said. "Molly was quite the fighter."

"Yes." Brooke nodded, her words thick, as if trying to smother burgeoning sobs. "She was." Her limbs trembled.

He rested his other hand over their joined ones.

"Would you mind giving us . . ." he began, but Blotny was already heading for the door.

He heard it click shut behind her and engulfed Brooke in his arms.

Within seconds, sobs wracked her body, and he cradled her against his chest, wishing he could will it all away—that he could carry the pain and sorrow for her.

She pulled back, swiping her tearstained cheeks. "I'm sorry," she said between jarring hiccups.

His brows dipped. "Sorry for what?"

She sniffed on a hiccup. "For not holding it together."

"Your friend just died. No one could hold it together with that kind of loss."

She shook her head. "But I'm a soldier and a medic."

"And a person. We have our jobs, our service, but that's what we do—not who we are."

"True, but I see tragedy all the time."

"See, but not endure personally."

She nodded, sobs breaking forth once more.

Austin's neighborhood wasn't what Caleb anticipated. Though he wasn't quite sure what he'd anticipated.

Dimly lit by the glow of his headlights, single-story ranchers made up the neighborhood lining the sound. Mature trees lined both sides of the street between the asphalt and the sidewalk. Their overhanging branches and remnant of leaves provided a canopy over the narrow street.

"Fourth one down on the left after you cross Beacon," Austin said, shifting slightly. She hadn't complained about her arm. Acted like it was a bump or scrape. He worried she wouldn't take Brooke's advice to take care of herself, so he'd make sure he was around to help if she needed any.

He stopped at the four-way stop, happy to see speed bumps stretching out in front. No doubt there were kids running about during the day. It was one of those neighborhoods. The kind with perfect families of four—Mom, Dad, and two kids. He'd always longed for that kind of home, though it needn't be perfect. He would have taken *happy*, or even one filled with basic love. Looking around, he bet Austin had grown up in a loving home, and the thought of that made him happy.

"Thanks for bringing me home," she said.

"My pleasure." It truly had been. Horrific circumstances aside, he'd enjoyed her company immensely today. He couldn't put his finger on it, but seeing her try to help save Molly . . . the tender, vulnerable side of Austin had burrowed into his heart, and he didn't want to leave her side. Not now. Not yet.

He cut the ignition and walked around the car to get the door for her.

She took his hand and stepped out. "I have no clue what's in my fridge, but as neither of us has eaten since breakfast, would you like to stay for a very late dinner?"

Her invitation warmed him in a way he hadn't felt in . . . he didn't know when. But he played it cool. "Sure." He chuckled. "Who can turn down an invitation like that?"

"Come on in," she said, kicking her shoes off and dropping them into the white woven basket under the coat hooks.

He stepped inside, admiring the photographs on the wall. At first, they appeared abstract, but as he studied them one by one, he realized they were all shots of the ocean and the land surrounding it. The ripple of a conch shell close up. The sway of marsh reeds in the wind with a blur of motion captured in a sped-up time lapse.

"These pictures are amazing," he said.

"Oh, thank you. Most people think they are messed up—like I don't know what I'm doing."

*She took these photos?* Another facet of an amazing woman. Caleb shook his head. "Then they aren't looking close enough."

She smiled. "I'm going to check out what's in the fridge." Nervousness flashed across her face as she turned toward the kitchen just beyond the front room.

"I'm starting to wonder if I'm risking my life dining here," he said, hanging his jacket on one of the empty hooks on the wall. He slid his boots off, adding them to the basket.

"It's not that bad," she called, her voice echoing, her head inside the fridge. She popped out, biting her bottom lip. "On second thought, how about takeout? There's a great deep-dish pizza place that delivers fast." She looked at her watch. "They take orders until eleven, so we should be good."

"Sounds great." His stomach was growling, and who didn't love pizza?

Austin called it in, and they were given a twenty-to-thirty-minute delivery window.

"Would you like a glass of wine?" she asked. "We can sit out on the patio. I have heaters, and the stars are pretty spectacular this time of year."

Caleb nodded. "That'd be nice." He couldn't remember the last time he had a sit-down, one-on-one meal with a lovely—albeit frustrating as all get-out—lady.

"Red or white?" she asked, facing her small wine rack with exactly two bottles in it.

"Red with pizza, please."

"You read my mind." She pulled the bottle from the top rung.

"Can I help you with that?" he offered as she struggled with one arm in a sling to screw the corkscrew in the cork.

"I've got it, but thanks."

He chuckled under his breath. Of course she did. She had to be the most stubborn woman he'd ever met, and he knew Gabby and Rissi, for goodness' sake.

Her brow set in a hard line, she gave it her best, then finally exhaled and looked up at him. "I suppose a little help wouldn't hurt."

He smiled and opened the bottle. She set two long-stem cobalt glasses on the counter beside him.

He poured into both glasses, and she handed him one.

"Thank you," he said, warming even more to the idea of more time spent with Austin Kelly. This had to be the first time they were alone while not actively investigating, and there was something so . . . entrancing about her.

She lifted her chin toward the patio door. "Shall we?"

He nodded and held the door open for her. The screened-in patio was the definition of relaxing. A small iron table and chairs with oversized cushions sat on the far right, the perfect spot for a view of the sound during the day, and the ripples of moonlight across it at night. Wind chimes—or were those spoons dangling down?—jangled in the wind. He glanced at the love seat bolstered with pillows and two heavy throws draped over it.

Austin flipped on the heaters, and before long, the small area warmed up nicely.

She stood at the edge of the patio, staring at the sound. He moved to stand beside her.

"Beautiful view," he said, lifting his glass toward the marsh. The grass swayed in the breeze, the sound of waves lapping along the shore, and the stars . . . She hadn't exaggerated. With the majority of the surrounding houses dark for the night, the sky shone with sparks of illumination. It reminded him just how small he was in the majesty of God's creation.

"Dirk," she called back toward the cracked screen door.

Caleb turned to the door, assuming Dirk was a pet, but they hadn't been greeted by any when they entered the house.

A chubby bulldog nosed the door farther open, waddled out, and quickly collapsed with an oomph onto the oversized cushion on the patio floor by the love seat. His breathing was lethargic, his movements stiff.

"Is he okay?" Caleb asked.

"No." She walked over to Dirk and knelt to rub his big round belly. "I don't know what it is. I'm taking him to the vet tomorrow. Hopefully, Lucy will be able to help."

He prayed whatever was wrong was an easy fix. He saw the love in her eyes as she continued rubbing Dirk's belly. He knew the deep love of a pet, and the horrific stabbing pain of losing one.

"I don't know what's going on around here," she said, looking up at him.

Caleb took a sip of wine. "What do you mean?"

"Dirk's the third dog on our street to get sick."

"That's odd."

"Agreed," she said, standing up and taking a seat on the love seat.

Caleb joined her. "I hope your vet is able to quickly treat whatever it is."

Fifteen minutes of chatting later, the doorbell rang, and Austin moved to stand, but Caleb beat her to it.

"I've got it," he said. "You just relax. It's been a trying day, and that's putting it mildly."

"Thanks." She sat back.

Caleb strode to the front door and grabbed the pie from the kid in a red T-shirt and baseball hat with a slice of pepperoni imprinted on it. "What's the damage?" he asked, setting the pizza box onto the edge of the entry table as he pulled out his wallet.

"Oh, it's already covered. She orders so often, we keep her card on file." He chuckled.

"Must be good pizza."

"It's pretty rocking, dude."

Caleb pulled a twenty out of his wallet. "Here you go, kid."

"Geez. Thanks, mister."

"Have a good night." Caleb shut the door with his socked foot and, grabbing the box, headed back to the patio. "This," he said, settling the pizza in the center of the round mosaic tabletop, "smells out of this world."

She smiled. "Wait until you taste it."

"Should I go grab plates?"

"Nah, I got it." She stood. "I'll get a pizza cutter too. Their pizzas are so cheesy I find it helpful to run back over the slices."

Regardless of how she played it down, her shoulder had to smart, but he didn't argue this go-around. Quick as a firefly's light blinked, she returned with two plates, a stack of napkins, and a pizza cutter. He examined the latter and smiled. The cutter had a red monkey for the handle, and the blade made it look like he was riding a unicycle.

He laughed under his breath. Austin Kelly was full of surprises.

# THIRTEEN

Brooke's mind flooded with the vivid image of Molly's face in shock and pain as blood soaked through her white uniform. She swallowed and looked down at the scrubs she'd changed into in-flight. They were clean, and she'd used antiseptic wipes to clean off what blood she could see clinging to her skin, but no doubt some of Molly's blood remained, even if only a trace.

She should go home and shower and get some sleep, but she was terrified the terror would return when she'd close her eyes. Instead, she'd take Blotny up on her offer to use the nurses' locker room.

She sat up, and Noah, who had dozed off, roused. "Where are you going?" he asked, wiping sleep from his eyes.

"To shower."

"You're going home?" He gripped her hand firmly, as if he didn't want to let go.

"No." She wanted to remain with Noah. One, she wasn't ready to be alone yet, and two, she still worried about his femoral artery. Fear had had a stranglehold on her chest that was just loosening up. She didn't want to leave him. "I'm going to use the nurses' locker room."

"Okay." His bleary eyes studied her. "Can I pray for us first?"

She nodded. She and everyone involved needed to be bathed in prayer.

Noah cleared his throat, and she bowed her head.

"Father, we cry out to you today. Our hearts are broken. So much innocent bloodshed. Please be with all who sustained physical injuries. Continue to give the doctors and nurses deft hands as they treat them. Also be with everyone emotionally wounded through this tragic event. Help us discover the motivation behind the attack and, especially, if anyone else had a hand in this. If so, please help us bring them to justice. And lead everyone touched by this to you, our refuge, and our rock. In our Savior's name, we pray."

"Amen," Brooke whispered.

When she opened her eyes, his locked on hers with a gaze she'd swear was full of love. But she must be reading too much into it. He was a compassionate man. That was all. If anything, it was a love of friendship. She was kidding herself to think it any more.

She stood, grabbing the Trader Joe's bag Gabby had brought her, along with the catchall bag she always kept in her purse. "I'll be back."

"I'll be right here," he promised.

But for how long? Until the trauma passed, and then was it back to him pulling away?

Dwayne rocked forward in his chair, rage searing through him. "*What*," he gritted out, "is taking so long?"

"She's been surrounded by emergency personnel all day, and now she's with the agent who got shot," Saul said.

"She should have been in hand hours ago. The longer we wait, the more we risk her sharing what Andrews told her. Get her now!" Or he'd suffer the consequences.

"Hang on," Saul said, putting him on hold.

His limbs burned in the silence, and then the call reconnected. "Did you just put *me* on hold?"

"Sorry. She just walked past me. She's in the women's locker room. I'll grab her now."

"Good. And, Saul . . ."

"Yeah."

"Don't. Screw. It. Up."

The call dropped, and he chucked his phone across the room. It bounced off the far wall. This was Saul's last chance. Either he came through, or he was the next fatality.

Brooke stepped into the locker room, the scent of Pert shampoo hanging in the air. A nurse was fixing her braid in the mirror.

"Hey there," the woman said.

"Hi." Brooke nodded. "Just heading for the showers."

"They're in the back. Be careful. The water comes out surprisingly hot in here."

"Thanks for the tip." She grabbed a towel from the bin—thin and rather scratchy but clean—and acquainted herself with her surroundings, like she always did. Two doors in and out. Two entrances to keep an eye on.

The towel tucked under her arm, she stepped into one of the curtained shower stalls. There was a bench with two hooks above it, far enough away from the spray radius to remain dry. She set the Trader Joe's bag on the bench, hung the towel on the hook, and pulled the plastic curtain closed behind her.

Leaning forward, she turned the faucet. A high pitch sounded, then the water spurted out. Steam filled the space with a warm cloud before she even stepped back to disrobe. The nurse wasn't kidding about hot.

Fishing the hotel-sized shampoo, conditioner, and soap from the bag, she set them on the soap dish jutting out a few inches from the ceramic wall.

She pulled off her scrubs and looked down, her breath hitching at the sight of Molly's dried blood along the band of her white sports bra. Grabbing hold of the straps, she tugged. The dried blood had crusted the band to her skin. Fighting back sobs, she tugged harder, peeling it away from her body.

Tears streamed down her face as she punched it along with the rest of her dirty clothes into an empty Target bag Gabby had included. Her friend had thought of everything. She hung the bag on one of the hooks, then stepped under the spray.

Hot water rolled over her, and she leaned deeper into it, praying it would somehow wash the sorrow of the day away.

The door to her right opened and slowly creaked shut.

Something inside her hitched.

She peeked out of the curtain but saw no one. She ran the shower curtain hooks back across the bar the few inches she'd opened it and moved into the water's spray.

A moment later, footfalls echoed across the tile.

"Hello?" she called, expecting a nurse to respond. Nothing but footfalls drawing near.

# FOURTEEN

Brooke shut off the water, yanked a towel off the hook, and wrapped it about her. "Hello?"

The heavy steps grew closer still.

She quickly glanced about for a weapon and, finding her keys in her catchall bag, fashioned several to stick out between her fingers and made a fist.

A shadow crept across the curtain.

Her chest seized.

A door opened, and two chattering nurses entered.

The shadow disappeared.

"Hello?" she called.

"Yes?" one of the women asked.

Adrenaline let loose, flooding her limbs with shaky warmth. She poked her head out of the curtain. "I thought I heard someone in here just before you came in."

The two nurses—one blond and one brunette—looked about.

The blonde paused on the far door. "That door just shut, so someone must have been in here, but it's just us now."

"You didn't see who went out?" The nape of her neck wouldn't stop tingling.

The blonde frowned. "No. Are you all right?"

"Yep." She was being ridiculous—her body still on high alert from the shooting. "Just got startled—that's all."

"Showering in here at night spooks me sometimes too," the blonde said.

"Yeah," the brunette chimed in. "It can be isolating in here."

"And creepy," the blonde added. "Especially when the overhead lights flicker, which they always seem to do when I'm in here alone, running late after shift."

Okay. So she wasn't the only one creeped out, but they were talking about short-circuiting lights—not someone heading for her without a word.

She swallowed, then released a tight exhale. "Thanks, guys," she said, appreciating their kindness.

"No problem, honey," the blonde said.

Taking a moment, she changed into the clothes Gabby had brought—a soft pair of jeans, comfy T-shirt, and long-sleeve burgundy knit hoodie with hunter green stripes on the arms. Dressed, she sat on the bench, thankful the ladies were still in the locker room, and pulled on the wild-patterned wool socks and fleece-filled UGG boots from the bottom of the bag. She lifted out a cosmetic case and unzipped it to find a hairbrush along with an unopened blush, mascara, and lip gloss.

No sense using the mascara because she'd be crying for days, but maybe a little blush. As she'd glanced in the mirror running over the sinks and noted how pale she was, how red her eyes were . . .

She grabbed the plastic bag she'd shoved the bra she'd been wearing in and tossed it in the trash. Even if the blood came out, she'd never wear the sports bra again because every time she'd see it, Molly's contorted face would flash before her eyes.

"I better go," Caleb said. Though going was the last thing he wanted to do, but Austin needed her rest.

"Okay," she said. Was that a twinge of disappointment in

her voice? Was she becoming as addicted to his presence as he was to hers?

He rubbed his hands along his thighs, then forced himself to stand.

She followed suit. The blanket she'd draped across them slipped to the love seat.

"Come on, Dirk," she said. "Time to go in."

Dirk grumbled—actually grumbled. Then even more reluctantly than them, he roused himself to a standing position and lumbered lazily into the house.

"Sure you have to go?" she asked, flooring him.

He wanted to stay with everything in him, but . . . he looked at his watch. Almost 2400. "You need to get some sleep. I'll be back at 0600 to pick you up."

She'd ride to the base with him, and he'd drop her at her car still parked outside the site of the shooting. No longer would folks think of it as Ira Stiller Hall. It would now be known as the site of a horrific tragedy.

He stepped into the brisk night. *Idiot.* She'd pretty much asked him to stay, and he was leaving. *Why?*

Because she needed rest.

He looked back at her locking her door. She waved, then shut off the interior light.

He raked a hand through his hair. He shouldn't have stayed so late. That was selfish, but he hated leaving her. He could breathe around her—be himself around her.

Taking a deep inhale, he climbed into his car and fought the urge to head back to her door.

# FIFTEEN

Noah looked over at the strongest woman he'd ever known—and he was surrounded by strong women. What Brooke had gone through today, how she'd performed her duty in the midst of chaos, how she'd let loose when her heart was cracking, how she shouldered the trauma—she was amazing, and he was an idiot. He loved her. Wanted nothing more than to be with her. Ached to be with her. But he loved her too much to do so.

Leaning over and ignoring the searing pain in his thigh, he gently tossed a blanket over her as she lay curled up in the recliner. They'd ordered food from the hospital kitchen, and she'd planned to leave after eating, but she hadn't even stirred when they brought in the food.

In the silence, he prayed for everyone hurt today. The ramifications of the shooting would run the gamut from massive to minute. It would remain imprinted on them at best, consuming them at worst.

*Crack. Crack. Crack.* Rapid fire drilled through her mind. Shells dropping to the ground, clanged off the growing pile at the shooter's feet.

Gunsmoke enveloped the room crowded with chaos.

A bullet whizzed by her head as she raced for Molly's fallen body, blood seeping out—wide, frightened eyes staring back at her.

Brooke lurched up, gasping for breath, cold sweat clinging to her skin.

"It's okay," Noah said. "I've got you." He reached over and clutched her hand.

A thin blanket pooled in her lap.

The hospital. Noah's room. What was she still doing here?

"You were having a nightmare," he said, shifting closer to her.

Oh, it was a nightmare all right, but the nightmare had been real—though distorted in fragments in her mind. She rubbed her forehead.

"You okay?" Noah asked, his just-woken voice husky.

She nodded and glanced at her watch. 0600. "Oh, shoot. I'm going to be late for duty. I'll have to use the gear I store on base."

"Duty?" Noah sat forward, then winced. "You're not going to work, are you?"

"Yeah." She ran her fingers through her hair. "Why not?"

His eyes softened, light creases in the corners. "Honey, don't you think you should take some time off?"

She stood. "Oscar tried to get me to take the shift off, but keeping busy, helping others—it's what's best for me."

He nodded and reached out his hand.

She clasped hold, and he tugged her down, then leaned forward and pressed a kiss to her forehead. "Be safe."

Her forehead still tingling, the rest of her shaky, she headed out into the rear hospital lot, where Gabby said she'd left her car. The chill morning air hit the dampness of her skin, causing her to shiver, but the cold gust that ruffled her hair and swirled about her face helped bring her fully back to the present.

She clicked her key fob and spotted the yellow reflection of its blinking lights on a white van parked in the slot in front of it.

Noah had kissed her. Granted, not where she'd dreamed of, but a kiss was a kiss. She just hoped it wasn't a pity kiss, but a true, genuine one.

She took a sip of the coffee she'd grabbed from the nurses' lounge, needing to shake herself awake. She reached her car door. An arm slid around her neck, placing her in a choke hold. She struggled for breath, trying to pull the arm down, trying to kick, but a hand smothered her nose and mouth. Her coffee tumbled to the ground as a sickly sweet scent engulfed her.

# SIXTEEN

Caleb walked up the winding stone path that led to Austin's kitchen door, her outside light clicking on as the sun still hadn't crested the horizon.

Brushing her hair behind her ear, she opened it before he reached for the handle. "Hey," she said, his handsome face leaving her a bit breathless. Then, again, it always had—even when he annoyed the heck out of her.

"Hey." He smiled, then frowned. "Where's your sling?"

"I couldn't sleep with it. Took it off, and I'm good."

He cocked his head.

"It's all good. Just a little sore."

He inspected her shoulder.

"Stop," she said, shooing his glance away with her hand.

"Fine," he said, chuckling. "I'm just glad to hear you were able to rest."

She bit her bottom lip. *Rest* certainly wasn't the term she'd use.

Concern erased his smile. "That bad, huh?"

She shrugged her good shoulder. "Yeah . . ."

"Nightmares?"

She nodded, hoping he didn't delve deeper than that. She'd relived the terror last night—woke drenched with sweat and trembling.

He slipped his long fingers through hers, startling her in a good way, as he took hold of her hand. "I'll pray harder."

She bit her bottom lip. "Thanks."

He looked past her at Dirk, and she turned to see her buddy lumbering along, his belly sliding across the kitchen floor.

"How's the pup today?" he asked.

Sadness and worry swelled inside. "Not any better, I'm afraid."

"What time's your appointment?"

"Four. I'll swing back and pick him up." She grabbed her keys. Finn had cleared her purse after she'd left it at the shooting, and Gabby had kindly dropped it by the hospital for her. "Should we head out?"

"After you," he said, gesturing toward the door. Always such a gentleman. An impossible man when they first collided, but a gentleman all the same. But something had changed. He hadn't, but she saw past the stubbornness to his heart, and what she saw was captivating.

She stepped outside, and he followed. After she locked her door, he gestured for ladies first.

Angling her neck to slip her crossbody purse strap over her head, she winced.

"Let me help you," he said.

"Thanks."

"Here." He took the strap from her hand, lifted her hair in one hand, his fingers brushing her neck.

Gooseflesh rippled her skin.

He paused. "You cold?"

She swallowed. "Uh-huh . . ." If she thought about it, she was . . . a little. And it sounded a whole lot better than, *No, your touch just rippled my senses.*

"I have an extra coat in the car. It's a lot thicker than yours."

"Thanks." Sweating was a lot less embarrassing than explaining that one.

He slid the strap across her good shoulder ever so gently, settling the purse on her hip—his fingers brushed across it in the most innocent of touches, but gooseflesh rippled across her skin all the same.

Her hair still cupped in his other hand, he released his hold, his fingers dancing across her neck.

She took a shaky inhale, and he didn't move.

Why wasn't he moving? Was she that obvious? Mortification set in. "Ready?" she asked, her voice coming out in a high-pitched twang. She cleared her throat. "I mean, ready?" she said, forcing her voice lower. Probably too low.

"Mmm-hmm." He exhaled.

The riff from "Sweet Home Alabama" sounded, and Noah lifted his phone from the tray table. No one called this early unless something was wrong. He frowned as the number registered as coming from on base.

"Rowley," he answered, shutting off the early morning news.

"Hi, Noah. It's Derek Greer."

Noah straightened. "How are you, Chief Greer?"

"You can call me Derek. We've known each other long enough," he said in his raspy voice.

Nicest guy, but he'd seen his share of combat and carried himself like a soldier who had.

"How can I help you, Derek?"

"First things first. How's the leg? I heard you were shot."

"Sore but good. Though I'm being held hostage at the hospital for another twenty-four hours."

"I'm glad you're good, but always listen to the doc."

"Yes, sir."

"Derek," he reiterated.

"Derek. How can I help you?"

"I need one of your personnel, the top one you'd recommend in your stead, to come down to the lab."

That certainly didn't indicate anything good. Not at this hour. Not at Chief Greer's request.

Who should he send? His entire team was stellar—each with their own areas of expertise.

"Sir . . . Derek, is it possible for you to give me the scope of the situation? My team members excel in different areas."

"Fair enough, but I'm afraid I can't discuss this matter in any detail over an unsecured line."

The muscles in Noah's shoulders constricted, tension hitting his frame. That *really* didn't sound good. "Understood," he said, frustrated to be restricted to the hospital walls. "I'll send Agent Eason."

"How soon can he be at the Kellen building?" Greer asked, an unsettling urgency in his voice.

"I'll call him now and send him right over."

"Great. And send your CSI guy too. I'll meet them out front."

His mind racing through the possibilities of Greer's inquiry, Noah dialed Caleb.

"Eason. How are you doing, boss?"

"Eager to get out of here."

"I bet."

"How quickly can you meet Chief Greer outside the Kellen building?"

"Austin and I are on the way to base now. ETA ten minutes."

"Great. And call Finn. He needs you both."

"Any idea what's going on?"

"He couldn't give details over the phone, which means you won't be able to either."

"Understood. I'll head over to the hospital as soon as I can to catch you up to speed."

After hanging up, Noah pulled out a piece of paper to scribble some notes. The tentacles of this case seemed to be ever expanding.

"Knock, knock," Gabby said as the door cracked open. "Brooke's morning coffee delivery."

"Come on in."

Gabby rounded the corner with two coffee tumblers with the Raul's Roast Coffee logo. She took a quick sweep of the room and frowned. "Where's Brooke?"

"You just missed her. She left for duty maybe twenty-five minutes ago," Noah said, still wishing she'd stayed. She was pushing herself to keep going. He'd done the same numerous times.

Gabby took a seat. "Who picked her up?"

He furrowed his brow. "She drove herself. She said you brought her car by."

"I did," Gabby said, kicking her feet up on the recliner portion of the chair. "But she didn't take it."

Noah tensed. "Her car is still in the parking lot?"

Gabby's smile disappeared, and she sat up, planting her feet on the floor.

Noah picked up his cell and called Brooke. It went straight to voicemail.

He called Jason, Brooke's rescue-swimmer coworker.

"Hey, man," Jason said. "How you doing?"

"Has Brooke arrived yet?" Panic sifted through him.

"Nah, man. I'm sure Oscar told her to take leave after . . ." He cleared his throat. "After yesterday."

Noah released a heavy exhale.

"Everything all right?" Jason asked.

"She said she refused Oscar's order to take the shift off. She left the hospital for the base a half hour ago."

"She's not here. Have you called her?"

"It's just going to voicemail, and her car is still in the parking lot."

"Do you think she's okay?"

Every warning signal in his body said otherwise. "Call me if she gets there."

"Will do, and let me know if we can help search if . . ."

Noah swallowed, not wanting to even consider the *if* he was referring to. "I will." Hanging up, he swung his legs over the side of the bed, hot pain searing his thigh.

"How can I help?" Gabby said, standing.

"I'm going to the security office to watch the video footage from when she left. You go outside and check around her car, see if you can find anything that might indicate a struggle." He had zero clue why she'd be taken, but his expertise was saying that's exactly what'd happened.

"Please, Lord," Gabby uttered to God as Noah said a prayer in his heart.

*Please don't let this be what I think it is.* Noah hobbled as fast as he could for the door.

"Here," Gabby said, shoving the crutch the nurse had set in the room for when he had to use the restroom.

He shoved it under his arm. "Thanks."

"Do you think it's because of what the shooter told her before surgery?"

Noah stopped dead in his tracks. "What?"

"Yesterday, Dr. Blotny mentioned the shooter whispered something to Brooke before they rolled him into surgery."

"Why didn't anyone tell me?"

"I guess . . . with everything going on . . . it didn't seem important." Regret hung heavy in her voice.

He took a stiff inhale. "Unfortunately, the circumstances indicate otherwise. I'll call in the rest of the team. We need Finn out here ASAP." Finn and Caleb would have to give up their cells to enter the high-security labs. He had to reach them another way. He'd start with Emmy. She coordinated like none other.

Brooke blinked. Darkness engulfed her. Fabric scratched her eyelids and the bridge of her nose. A solid surface was beneath and behind her. A chair?

She tried to move her arms, but they were bound. She yanked them, only to have abrasive material cut into her flesh.

The odor of fish swirled in the air. The lap of water mixed with muted conversation trailed around her.

"Well, look who's awake?" a man said, his deep baritone voice reverberating in her chest.

His breath smelled like raw tobacco, and she turned her face away. He clutched her jaw, his fingers biting into her flesh, and turned her back. "You are going to tell me what he said." His hot breath was mere inches from her face. He didn't release her jaw. Instead, his grip bit into her bone.

"What *who* said?"

"Can you believe this?" He exhaled a cold chuckle. "She thinks she's dealing with fools."

He released her jaw, but what felt like his knee bore into her thigh. He leaned in, his breath stroking her lips when he spoke. "Because I'm a generous guy, I'm going to give you one last chance to tell me before we slowly and painfully pry it from you. What did that betraying fool tell you?"

The shooter who'd whispered to her. How did this man know?

Regardless, whoever this man was, he was not bluffing, but the minute she gave them what they wanted, she was dead.

"Okay," he said, stepping away. "The painful way it is." A sharp blade grazed her neck.

Terror shook her limbs.

"I'm going to enjoy this," he said hot against her ear.

# SEVENTEEN

"Chief Greer," Caleb said, extending his hand. "I'm Agent Eason, and this is Agent Walker."

"Eason." He shook Caleb's hand and then Finn's. "Thank you for leaving your cell phones and service weapons with security," he said, opening the first set of doors after security.

Caleb had reluctantly handed over his phone and gun. Both were essential for his job, but he understood the importance of where they were.

Noah was right. Something had to be very wrong.

Following Greer, he wondered which lab they were headed for. There was one that had everyone intrigued. Rumors of something highly classified swirled around base. But those who worked in it wouldn't confirm its location—even when they came and went from the Kellen building daily. Caleb bet they were headed for the chemicals lab or the materials and equipment lab, though he was curious why Chief Greer had called in CGIS.

Chief Greer exhaled a whoosh of air as they walked through yet another set of doors that required his badge and fingerprint scan.

They reached a set of elevators Caleb had no idea existed, since the Kellen building was one story—at least from the exterior.

The thick silver doors opened, and they stepped onto the elevator.

Chief Greer pressed 3.

Greer looked over at him and Finn. "What I'm about to tell you is highly classified. Understood?"

"Yes, sir." Caleb and Finn both nodded as the elevator went down three flights.

"We've been collaborating with a specialized Army unit on a new kind of weapon adaptation. They started project Strike First at their RAD location in Duck, North Carolina, and invited us to collaborate."

Caleb's mind raced through the possibilities for their presence.

"They believed they had a mole in their ranks, so they moved the project and assets here, and only sent their top trusted men and women."

"And the project is . . . ?" Caleb asked.

Greer performed the same verification outside another silver door, and it slid open.

They stepped inside the lab, and to Caleb's surprise, it was devoid of personnel. "It's a high-tech laser weapon," Greer said. "Applications include shooting enemy aircraft midflight and destroying a vehicle from over a mile away. You can imagine the possibilities available to strengthen our military." Greer slipped his hands behind his back, rocking forward on his black boots. "Someone broke into the lab and stole a printout of the design plans for the last component being worked on."

*Odd.* "Just the last part?" Caleb asked.

"Yes." Greer gave a single nod.

"That's strange," Finn said. "Maybe they didn't realize what they were stealing."

"That was our initial thought as well," Greer said, "but given the circumstances and the weapon itself, we have to think worst-case scenario."

"Of course," Finn said.

"Do you believe it was someone on base?" Caleb asked, getting to the nitty-gritty.

"That's exactly what you're here to determine. We have video surveillance that picked up two men entering the room. The time stamp places it during the mass shooting."

A phone rang, and Caleb followed the sound to a black land-line on the far wall.

"Excuse me a moment," Greer said, stepping to the phone. "Chief Greer. . . . Yes. . . . Will do." He hung up, and when he looked back at them, his face had hardened, his gaze intense. "You two are needed ASAP. We'll have to continue this later."

Caleb frowned. What on earth would pull them away from this?

"Petty Officer Brooke Kesler has been abducted."

Caleb's jaw set as questions raced through his mind. Questions he didn't have time to ponder. Action was needed.

"Agent Rowley needs you both now," Greer said, leading them through the door and out to the elevators. He used his thumbprint to open them and then held the door with his hand as they climbed in. "You can grab your phones and weapons from security on the way out. Tell Noah we'll assist in every way possible."

"Thank you, sir," Caleb said as the doors slid closed.

Noah's heart seized as he watched Brooke walk out of sight of the security camera and not return. The only vehicle to pull out of the lot was a white Dodge Sprinter van. Like the one a witness had described as sitting outside the graduation. Noah didn't believe it was a coincidence.

Gabby wrapped her hand around the doorframe to the open security booth where Noah sat. "Her car is definitely still there.

I didn't touch them, but her keys and a coffee cup are tossed about under her car."

Turning to Felix Cruz, the security guard, he said, "Call 911. Explain we have a missing person and that CGIS is on-site. We need a full manhunt. Police Commissioner Brick can call Special Agent Noah Rowley's cell if there are any questions."

Felix nodded and did so.

Noah speed-dialed Em, each ring feeling like a lifetime.

# EIGHTEEN

In rapid fashion, Noah's team—minus Caleb and Finn—arrived at the hospital, where security had aided in setting up a command center in the west conference wing. He needed to be able to coordinate the search, and he wasn't wasting time discharging himself or heading to the station. With no hospital events occurring, they had the wing to themselves.

"Em got ahold of Finn and Caleb," Gabby said. "And I just spoke to Finn. They're on the way."

"Thank you," Noah said, trying to stall the fear biting at him. He'd never experienced fear on a rescue before. But it'd never been the woman he loved missing. "I've set up a grid. We have DOT scanning all the traffic cams in the area, and Wilmington PD and the local FBI field office have put out a BOLO on the white van."

"What about the plate number?" she asked as Rissi and Mason raced around the corner.

"Bogus."

"We'll get her back," Rissi said with the same tone of confidence he'd used, but fear had its claws in deep. *What if . . . ?*

He couldn't go there. They'd get her back. They had to.

"Take her out to the boat," the man with the gravelly baritone voice said, the man who'd been hurting her for what seemed like an eternity, until, unable to endure the pain any longer, she'd finally given up the word—"Gator!"

The one named Saul—the only name they'd used thus far— had cussed, and a hush fell over the room, and the pain inflicted finally eased. Clearly *gator* meant something to them. They'd pressed to see if she knew what it meant—did they know the meaning or didn't they?—but she couldn't give them something she didn't know.

Wherever they were smelled old, like her grandma's cellar. And the odor of brackish water and fish swept in on the cold wind that whistled through whatever walls or windows surrounded her.

She took a shaky inhale, her cuts stinging.

A man with calloused fingers unfastened the bonds around her wrists, and the instant her raw flesh met the air, she fought back a cry. She wouldn't give them the satisfaction. They may kill her, but she knew where she was going and did not fear death. But Noah . . .

She closed her eyes despite the blindfold and pictured his ruggedly handsome face, the sound of his voice with the slightest hint of a Southern drawl, the strength in his touch, the tenderness in his actions.

"Let's go," the man she recognized as Saul said, as he reached under her armpits from behind and hauled her to her feet.

Her legs weak, she prayed, *Lord, I know you are with me. Flood me with your presence.*

"Go with him," the man with the gravelly voice said to someone else in the room.

"All right."

"I've got this, Dw . . ." Saul froze, his grip tightening on her flesh.

So the gravelly-voiced man's name started with *Dw.* She'd hang on to that information if she survived this, which she'd fight for with all her might. She'd learned on rescues that the people who survived were the people who never gave up, no matter how surmounting the odds.

"I said"—the gravelly voice deepened to a frightening register that sent cold fingers clawing down her chest—"he's going with you."

Saul dragged her toward the draft, her feet tripping over some debris on the floor. After cussing her out, Saul hauled her tightly against him. He smelled of harsh liquor and . . . grape?

A door creaked open, and Saul pulled her through it. Cold assaulted her.

"I'll grab the boat. You get her in," the second man said.

Stepping forward, she tumbled, her jaw colliding with the harsh edge of something hard smarting her swollen cheek. The surface beneath her bobbed, and the sound of oars against rippling water pushed them off from shore.

"Why did he have to send you?" Saul said to the man.

"I don't question him. That's the difference between us."

"Whatever," Saul scoffed. "Then I'm not rowing." The oars clanged off the surface inches from her head.

"I'm sure as heck not rowing."

"Make her do it," Saul said.

The second man chuckled. "Fair enough."

He dragged her up onto the bench and placed two oars in her hands.

"Row!"

"I can't see."

He bent in front of her, his stale breath hot on her face. "You don't have to see to row."

Noah hobbled at a quick clip to Gabby's car, the crutch propped under his arm.

"Noah," his sister said, "are you sure you should be—"

"Don't bother. You know if it was Finn out there, no one could hold you back. At least I'm letting you drive." He popped the extra cherry Caleb kept in his car onto Gabby's dash.

"True," Gabby said, then turned the ignition. Within seconds they were pulling out of the hospital lot and onto the main road—each car in the caravan of search teams splitting off in different directions.

He'd put Caleb with Mason, Rissi with Finn, Logan with Emmy, and himself with Gabby. As an investigative reporter, his sister knew how to search and drive.

He looked at the speedometer for the third time as search helicopters buzzed overhead.

"Could you speed it up?" he asked, his skin nearly crawling with adrenaline.

Gabby depressed the accelerator, the red light swirling across the dash, reflecting on the windshield.

His heart was in his throat. No. His heart was with Brooke, wherever she was.

His cell rang, and Noah pulled it out so fast he fumbled to answer. "Yeah, Em?" he said, putting it on speaker.

"We got a hit on the van."

*Thank you, Jesus!*

"They found it on the traffic-cam footage. It was last seen passing through a traffic light fifteen miles from here heading due east."

Gabby frowned, her brows bowing. "Due east of here is the warehouse district down by the old port. Most of those properties have long since been abandoned."

"The perfect place to take someone . . ." He stopped the thought of anyone hurting the woman he loved in its tracks. He needed to remain focused on finding her—not letting his mind wander.

"How long ago did it pass through?" he asked, fully redirecting his attention on the details.

Em cleared her throat. "It was time stamped at 0615."

"That was well over an hour ago," he said, the blood draining from his face.

# NINETEEN

Oars lapped in and out of the brackish-smelling water. Her cuts stung deeper with every aching rotation of her arms.

The scent of sugary grape filled the air, stronger than the thick, marshy odor. Saul had to be within inches.

"Dude, how can you chew that stuff?" the second man asked.

Grape bubble gum. That was the smacking she heard off and on.

"It's better than that dip you and Dw—"

"Shut up!" the second man roared.

"What? She's going to be dead and buried in the marsh soon enough."

So she was right. She was in a marsh, and not a deep one. Her oars kept meeting resistance every few feet—seagrass. She submerged the oar as far as she could, praying they didn't notice. Was it deep enough for her to swim? It would be her only way out, but how?

She gripped the oar handle tighter in her bleeding hand, the lacerations burning. *Please, Father, give me a way.*

"That's your problem," the second man bit out.

"My problem?" Saul said with another smack of his gum.

"Yeah, you talk too much."

"What the—"

A shot fired, the blast reverberating in her ears.

She stiffened as the boat rocked.

"He sent you to kill me!" Saul hollered, the boat rocking harder. One of the men fell back on her, and the boat wobbled as he righted himself.

She pushed her blindfold up enough to see the two of them wrestling. A gun in one man's hand. Another beneath the front bench.

They stood, the gunman trying to get a shot off, their arms entangled.

She looked to the water. She might be able to make it to shore if she swam long enough and kept to the bottom. She might be able to lose them. Lifting the oar, she swung with all her might, whacking both of them.

They fell into the boat, and she lurched out of it into the water.

The men's hollering grew more muffled the deeper into the dark water she swam, her arms and legs crushed with agonizing pain as she maneuvered around the clumps of seagrass tangling around her arms.

She pushed free and kicked forward. She had to keep going.

Bullets whizzed by her. She fought to hold her breath. No way she could surface.

Cold water rose from below. Deeper water. She dove, bullets straying farther from her. *Please, Lord. Carry me.* Her breath nearly bursting in her lungs, she swam as fast as she could toward shore.

"What's the latest, Em?" Noah asked, his throat tight, his nerves taut. But this is what he did. He saved people. The fact that he loved the victim was a first, but he had to keep his head on straight, had to focus on the search.

"Copters are sweeping the warehouse district and abandoned

buildings, but it covers a ten-square-mile area. So far, no sign of a white van or any cars down there, but Mason and Caleb are forming search teams with local police and starting to go through them one by one."

Noah raked a hand through his hair. That could take time they didn't have. But it was the right move. "Keep me posted."

"Will do."

"And no further sightings of the van on the traffic cams?" he asked, hoping to close in on a more defined area.

"No," Em said, the ache he felt in his heart echoing in her voice.

Noah laid the map across the dash. "There are a few state parks in the area. Very few visitors this time of year, especially the ones out by the warehouse district. Let's start searching those."

"On it," Gabby said.

He looked at the clock on the dash. They were losing precious time. The more that went by, the less likely . . .

He took a steadying breath.

*Please, Jesus, let her be alive. You know exactly where she is. Please guide us there.*

Brooke scrambled onto shore. Hair clinging to her face, cold seeping into her bones, she army crawled her way for the tree line.

"There!" Saul shouted.

*No. Please.*

She took a rapid glance back. The two men remained in the boat, rowing furiously toward her.

Pulling the clump of seagrass from her ankle, she mustered herself upright and raced for the trees.

*Pop. Pop. Pop.* Gunfire ricocheted around her, a chunk of

the tree an inch to her right blasted off, sending splitters into her hair.

Ducking and hovering low, she raced deeper into the brush, ignoring the pain riddling through her. Cold air seared her lungs as adrenaline burned her limbs.

A splash sounded behind her and footfalls followed.

They were coming.

Nearly stumbling over her own feet, her limbs trembling with pain, she pushed forward.

She likely couldn't outrun the men, so she scanned the woods for a place to hide.

*Please, Jesus. It's all you.*

Copter blades whooshed overhead. She looked up through the leaves that remained, still heavy for this time of year.

Coast Guard Search and Rescue. *Thank you, Jesus.* She waved her arms as it circled overhead.

The men's thrashing through the underbrush grew closer.

"Please," she whispered, waving her arms as she ran, stumbling over tree roots and rocks.

The copter circled once more and banked west.

*No!* Tears rolled down her cheek, burning her swollen left eye.

Footfalls pounded heavily on the hard ground. They were closing in.

She raced forward. There was no turning back.

An engine zoomed by less than sixty feet ahead. A road. She just had to make it to the road and pray another car showed. Someone. Anyone she could flag down.

"Get her now!" the second man yelled.

She looked back and saw who she guessed was Saul. His grisly gaze hardened as he aimed and fired. She ducked, running as low and fast as possible up an embankment.

Another car zoomed by. *So close. You can do this.*

She scrambled, tumbling forward, catching herself on her outstretched hands, righting herself and continuing.

Saul had not yet crested the embankment as her feet hit pavement.

She looked to the left. No cars.

To the right. No cars.

Her heart sank.

Then an engine roared. She looked back to the right as a semi rumbled around the bend. With a deep breath, she steeled herself and raced in front of it, waving her arms.

"Please," she breathed.

His horn blared as he waved for her to get out of the way.

She remained fixed in place. This was it. *Please, please, stop.*

The engine barked as the trucker hit the Jake brake and slammed on the brake pedal, straining back as they shrieked. The rig fishtailed, and the cab shuddered to a stop inches from her.

The driver's door opened as Saul crested the embankment.

"Are you crazy?" the trucker exclaimed.

"He's going to shoot us," she yelled as Saul lifted his gun. She raced around the rig for cover as the trucker slammed his cab door shut.

A line of construction vehicles rounded the bend, yellow swirling lights bouncing off the pavement.

A police car followed the construction vehicles, and Saul slinked back into the woods, where, no doubt, the second man was already hiding from view.

Collapsing in the passenger seat of the trucker's cab, she rolled her head toward him. "Thank you."

The man's eyes widened as his gaze slipped over her. "What happened to you, lady?"

# TWENTY

"They found her," Emmy said over the cell. "Or rather, she found them."

A level of relief he'd never felt before swept through Noah, loosening his taut chest muscles. *Thank you, Jesus!* "Wait . . ." His brows arched. "Did you say she found *them*? As in one of our teams?"

"No," Em said. "She flagged down help on Highway 67, across the inlet a mile or so from the warehouse district. Ambulance is en route. I'll text you the GPS coordinates."

"Thanks, Em." He didn't think he'd ever heard better news, yet fear of what she might have been put through hung fast in his mind.

Gabby headed for 67 as they waited for the exact location to come through.

Within a matter of minutes, Em sent the GPS coordinates, and Noah punched them in. "We're six minutes out." He released a shaky exhale. It would be the longest six minutes of his life.

"Caleb and Mason are two minutes out," Em said.

"Let them know we're en route, Brooke too if you can patch through to one of the officers on-site."

"Will do, boss."

With Gabby's driving, they made it in under four minutes. Commotion awaited them. A semitruck, followed by a string of construction vehicles, held up the right lane. A police car wedged across the left, blocking traffic. Patrol car lights twirled along with those of an ambulance that sat with its bay doors open behind the police vehicle.

Gabby hadn't even put the car in park when Noah jumped out and rushed as fast as his stupid leg would carry him. He could make out Brooke's form on the stretcher, the EMT injecting something into the IV bag.

Several K-9 units rushed past him toward the woods.

*Please let them find who took her. Don't let them escape.*

Increasing his stride caused his wounded leg to wobble, but he ignored the throbbing pain, pressing for the ambulance.

Caleb stepped in front of him, and Noah shifted to maneuver around him. Whatever Caleb had to tell him could wait. He needed to be by Brooke's side.

"Hang on, boss." Caleb clutched his arm.

"It can wait."

"Noah, you need to know this before . . ."

Noah stilled. Caleb only responded that way when it was dire. Steeling himself for what was coming, or doing his best to do so, he turned his full attention on Caleb.

Caleb looked down, then back up with a pained expression. "They"—his voice cracked—"tortured her."

Noah squeezed his eyes shut. *Dear God. Please be with her. Be her shield.* Because he'd failed her. They'd taken her right from under his nose. If only he'd walked her to the car.

He pinched the bridge of his nose, knowing he needed to ask but terrified of the answer. "How bad?" he asked. He didn't want to walk in uninformed, to let shock steal his composure. Brooke needed him to remain strong for her.

Caleb looked down and shuffled his feet.

Noah swallowed. *That bad?*

"We won't know the full extent until she's examined at the hospital."

"Make sure Finn's there too." She needed to be processed as a crime victim.

His chest closed in on him, the air horse-kicked from his lungs. *No.* Brooke was *not* a victim. She was a fighter, a survivor, and she'd gotten free on her own.

"Sir, did you want to ride with her to the hospital?" an EMT asked Noah. "They asked us to hold the ambulance until you arrived, said you'd want to be with her."

"Definitely." He strode for the ambulance, then looked back at Caleb. "Thanks, man."

Caleb nodded. "Mason is spearheading the manhunt."

Noah prayed the perpetrators were found and brought to justice. Better Mason catch them than him. Right now, he'd be tempted to apply his own brand of justice.

Approaching the ambulance, he said a quick prayer. *Please let me be what she needs right now.* Noah prepared himself to keep his expression full of love and not react in shock or outrage when he saw her wounds. Brooke would need his outrage for the criminals responsible, but not right now. Now she needed his love and steadiness.

The EMT attending to Brooke stood and moved toward the open doors, concern etched on his brow. "Sir, you should let me look at your leg."

Noah glanced down at the blood seeping through his pants, feeling the warm moisture for the first time now that the adrenaline was dissipating. How long had it been bleeding?

"I'll be okay until we get to the hospital. Just tore open my stitches."

"If you're sure?" the EMT said, climbing out of the ambulance. "She's stable, so I'll give you two some privacy."

"Thank you."

"She's going to need to be examined by a CSI," the EMT said quietly.

"My guy, Finn Walker, will be waiting."

The EMT nodded, his dark eyes full of compassion.

Noah returned the nod and climbed up into the ambulance, wincing as pain shot through his thigh with the motion. The EMT shut the rear doors behind him.

She rolled her head to face him, then reached out her hand and grimaced.

A blanket covered most of her, but as it slipped from her outstretched arm, he saw the marks those animals had made, imagined the scars they'd leave, and a rage he'd never known lit inside.

But she was alive.

He fought to keep the tears from his eyes.

"Hey," she whispered.

"Hey." He clasped her hand, vowing never to let it go. He couldn't. He wasn't strong enough to walk away. *She* very well might when he told her what happened, how it changed him . . . but not today. Today he was here, and she was safely back with him.

He brushed the hair from her eyes, trying not to focus on her wounds. "I've got you," he whispered, pressing a kiss to her forehead.

"Promise not to let go," she said, tears spilling from her eyes.

"I promise." He blinked back the tears beading in his eyes.

# TWENTY-ONE

"Noah, this would go much faster if you'd stop bouncing your leg," Dr. Blotny said.

It was a habit he'd had since he was a kid—his way of getting out restless energy. He hadn't realized he'd been doing it, but it certainly explained the pain throbbing through his thigh.

"Sorry," he said.

"I know you're anxious to be with her, but these examinations take a while."

He hated Brooke having to go through the exams, the questioning, but it was necessary if they hoped to catch the men responsible.

Blotny finally finished and sat back with a shake of her head. "You've really got to be more careful. That poor leg is going through the ringer."

He shrugged. "Comes with the job."

She exhaled. "Speaking of your job, I thought you'd like to know Connor Andrews is stabilizing. He's still unconscious but seems to be reviving. If he wakes, he'll be moved to unit 3 sometime tomorrow."

"Thanks for letting me know." He and Connor were going to have a long chat.

"Okay." Blotny placed her hands on her thighs and stood. "You're taken care of. Let's try to keep these stitches in place, shall we?"

"I'll do my best."

"That's what I'm afraid of. Your best pushes your limits, and this needs to heal."

He nodded. She was right, but if it came to Brooke's safety or the opportunity to catch the men responsible for not only her injuries but also the deaths and injuries of so many others, he'd act without even taking his leg into consideration.

Blotny grabbed the crutch and handed it to him. "And *please* actually use this."

"Yes, ma'am."

She shook her head, clearly knowing better than to expect him to listen. "I suspect this isn't our last round of stitches."

His cell rang. "Mason, what's the latest?" he asked, anxious energy still pulsing through him.

He mouthed *Thank you* as Blotny silently exited the room.

"We found the boat," Mason said. "I'm having it transferred to the station's garage for Finn to examine."

"And the men?"

"We're still searching. We now have two US Marshals helping us."

"Extend our thanks for their assistance."

"Already done."

"Good. Keep me posted."

"Will do. How's Brooke?"

"She's been examined and treated. Now Finn's in there with the medical team."

"I'm sorry she's having to go through all this," Mason said.

"Me too."

"I better get back to it."

Noah prayed he didn't stop—that none of them did until the people who had unleashed this terror were caught.

After what seemed an eternity, Finn entered the hall. He closed Brooke's door and sat on the bench next to Noah.

"How did it go? Was there anything that might identify the kidnappers?"

"Do you want me to go into detail?"

No, he didn't. He cringed at the thought of hearing the extent of what they'd done to her, but it was his job. He cleared his throat. "I think you'd better."

"It's likely I can figure out the type of blade used for the wounds. That could lead us somewhere. The rope used to bind her hands . . ."

Rage burned through him at what they'd done to her. The pain they'd inflicted both physically and mentally. Torture was never completely forgotten.

"You want me to continue?" Finn asked.

He nodded.

"The rope left a pattern on her wrists. I should be able to figure out the type of rope used, and what she was burned with. If anything unique was used, that could be a strong lead. Though, what most often provides the strongest evidence is the vic—" Finn cut himself off.

Noah's stomach lurched. One of his teammates better find the men before he did, because he didn't know if he would be able to restrain himself from inflicting pain or death on them.

But Brooke would hate being labeled a victim, and he didn't blame her. She was a fighter—one he admired beyond measure.

"Sorry," Finn said, understanding without Noah having to say a word. "What's most telling in this situation," Finn continued, "is the evidence her clothes might provide." He lifted an evidence bag in his hand with her clothes sealed and labeled in it. "She was in the water for several minutes, so it's hard to say if I'll find any trace evidence, but it's worth a try."

Finn stood, and Noah joined him.

"Okay to go in?" Noah asked.

Finn nodded. "I'm done, and the medical staff was just getting her settled in a pair of hospital scrubs rather than a gown at her request as I ducked out. I'm sure she's set for you to come in. She was asking for you."

"Thanks."

"Of course," Finn said before clearing his throat. "Are you going to have Caleb interview her since Mason is spearheading the manhunt, and Rissi is helping search?"

Those were his top three interviewers.

"Yep. I'm texting Caleb for the interview, and Logan to do a sketch of the men Brooke saw chasing her. She said it all went very fast. But she got a decent look at the man she identified as Saul. The other man held back farther, but anything she recalls about him could help."

"Sounds like a plan," Finn said. "I'm going to head back to the lab and get started on this evidence, then I'll turn my attention to the boat." He turned to go, then paused and turned back around. "Noah . . ."

"Yeah?"

"You should know that what she endured was painful and horrific, but there's nothing that should have prolonged physical effects, other than scarring."

Noah nodded and asked the question he least wanted to. "Did they . . . ?"

"No," Finn said. "That was the first question the nurse asked."

Noah breathed a sigh of relief. The physical and emotional wounds she was bearing were bad enough, but he thanked God the trauma of rape wasn't added to the list. "Thanks," he said. "Keep me posted."

"Will do." Finn headed down the corridor.

After shooting quick texts to Caleb and Logan, he knocked on Brooke's door. Caleb was on his way, Logan—in the midst of attempting to track down the van used—would be by for case board and do the sketches with Brooke after.

"Come in," she answered, her voice shaky.

"Hi." His throat constricted at her black eye. Rage reared its head again, burning through his veins. He pumped his fingers in and out of a fist, trying to head off the surge of adrenaline. Brooke didn't need him amped up.

"Hi," she said, smoothing back her hair.

"Okay if I stay?" he asked, wanting to make sure she didn't need some time alone.

"Of course. I want you here." She tilted her head in the direction of the recliner positioned beside her bed.

He stepped around her bed, but before sitting, he leaned over and pressed a kiss to her forehead. "I'm so sorry," he said, clasping her hand. "I should have protected you better. Walked you to your car."

"This wasn't your fault, Noah. The men who took me are at fault—fully at fault. And . . ." She took a long inhale and blew it out slowly before continuing. "It's my fault for not being strong enough."

He frowned. "What could possibly be your fault? You are amazingly strong to survive something so horrific, not to mention escape."

"Connor Andrews whispered something to me as we were entering the hospital. I didn't think it meant anything so didn't even think of telling anyone, especially with all the chaos going on. But somehow they knew about it, and I couldn't keep holding out." A red flush blanketed her cheeks, and she looked down, fiddling with the edge of her blanket. "I told them he said something that sounded like *gator*. It seemed so important to them. I should have been stronger, held out longer."

He gently tipped her chin up, their gazes holding. "You have been through hell, and you feel you should have done more?" He shook his head. "You are tough. Extremely tough."

She shrugged off the compliment. "I knew they'd kill me as soon as I told them. But I just couldn't hold out anymore."

He leaned in closer. "Sweetheart, you held out far longer"—based on the wounds she carried—"than ninety-nine percent of people would. And there is no way you could have known a random word Connor Andrews whispered to you might mean so much to them."

She nodded, tears welling in her eyes.

"And you fought for your freedom. You got away." He moved his hand from her chin, wanting to cup her face, but he worried the pressure might hurt her bruises, so he rested it over their joined hands. "I want you to listen to me. To really hear and believe this. You are the strongest woman I know. Don't ever doubt that."

Her gaze darted down.

He dipped his head, once again drawing her to look at him. When she did, he spoke words he prayed soaked into her soul. "You are a fighter. A warrior. Promise me you'll take me at my word."

She exhaled.

"Promise?"

A soft smile crept on her lips. "I promise."

"Good." He straightened the pillow behind her. "Now you need some rest."

"But you have to question me."

She was exhausted. He could read it in her glazed-over eyes. "It can wait until morning."

"No." She shook her head. "As soon as possible after the crime is the most vital time to question. You taught me that."

"You're right, but . . ."

"No buts." She shifted to sit higher up and winced as she pressed up on her arms.

"Hang on," he said. He grabbed the bed remote and raised it up. "Better?"

"Better." She sighed.

He so didn't want to do this now, but she was right. "I've asked Caleb to do the questioning."

She frowned. "You're not staying?"

"I'll stay right here, but I think Caleb can be more impartial as someone . . ." he hesitated. "Someone without deep feelings involved."

"Deep feelings?"

He nodded. "I—"

"Knock, knock," Caleb said at the door.

Noah inhaled. That conversation would have to wait. "Come in."

Caleb entered the room.

"That was fast," Noah said, having only texted him minutes ago.

"Finn texted me a few minutes before you. How can I help?"

"I'd like you to question Brooke," he said, hoping Caleb would understand why without him having to go into detail.

"Of course," Caleb said. He gestured to the empty chair at the edge of the room. "May I?" he asked Brooke.

She nodded.

Caleb scooted the chair closer and sat. His six-four frame was less intimidating when seated. Not hovering over the victim while questioning showed respect and empathy. Noah thanked God for blessing him with such a stellar team.

Caleb lifted his chin at Brooke. "Would you like to begin?"

"Yes. I'm ready."

Caleb pulled out his notepad and pen.

"Start from the beginning."

She ran them through being abducted and knocked out in the parking lot, waking up blindfolded, being threatened with harm if she didn't share what Connor told her, and then came the part that squeezed Noah's chest to the point of breathlessness.

"The man who . . ." Brooke took a deep breath. Her swollen cheeks were raw and bruised, but the skin around them grew pale. "His name started with *Dw*."

Caleb straightened. "You heard his name?"

"The man named Saul almost said his name but stopped himself after the *Dw*."

"That's a great start to go on. All these pieces just need to be put in the right order until the full picture develops." He leaned forward, a kind expression on his face. "We're going to get these men."

She nodded, a tear slipping down her cheek.

Noah still held Brooke's hand as he sat in the chair on the opposite side of the bed from Caleb. Holding her hand wasn't exactly professional, but they'd already crossed that line. Hence Caleb's questioning.

A thorough forty-five minutes later, Caleb wrapped up the interview and gave them privacy once more.

Noah prayed they'd catch the men responsible. Every case was important, but this one hit on a profoundly personal and painful level.

# TWENTY-TWO

Brooke's phone had rung practically nonstop for hours—her family in Colorado calling to make sure she was okay for the second time in forty-eight hours, her Coast Guard coworkers, the pastor at her church. . . . While she clearly appreciated the calls, Noah could see she was ready for a break. Thankfully, the rush had ceased a while ago. The one phone call he waited for hadn't come. Yet.

Finn had been working at the lab on the evidence taken from Brooke's exam as well as the boat she'd been held in, but so far there was no update.

Noah was itching for news—for something, *anything*, that would lead them to Brooke's abductors, and most likely to the people responsible for the shooting. Maybe even to the lab break-in. He was now convinced they were tied together. Otherwise, why were the men who abducted Brooke so concerned with what the one surviving shooter uttered to her?

He remained in the recliner beside her bed and had no plans to leave her alone. Gabby had agreed, most happily, to spend time with Brooke while he led his team's case-board meetings in what was technically his room next door. It'd taken pulling some serious strings, but given the dire circumstances of the last two days, Blotny and the hospital chair had agreed to let him run the investigation from his room. But the longer he remained at Brooke's side, the more content he was.

She sat up in her bed, pillows propped behind her, reading the Bible they'd borrowed from the hospital chaplain. He watched her, amazed. She was so strong . . . so brave.

Austin smoothed her dress, lifted the blue sea-glass vase brimming with sunflowers in her left arm, wedged the tin of cookies under her right, and knocked on Brooke's door.

"Come in," Brooke called.

"Hey," Austin said, peeking around the corner. "Is it an okay time to visit?"

"Of course." Brooke smiled. "Come in."

"How are you?" Noah asked, standing up from the recliner next to Brooke's bed. "Shoulder not too bad?"

"Just a little twinge in tendons surrounding it."

Noah's cell rang. "Excuse me a moment," he said, giving Brooke's hand a squeeze before exiting the room.

"I hope I didn't interrupt anything," Austin said.

"Of course not," Brooke said. "Thank you for coming."

"I just wanted to bring you these."

Brooke's face lit. "Sunflowers are my favorite."

"I thought so," Austin said, trying not to react visibly to Brooke's swollen eye or the various bandages covering her arms.

"They're beautiful," Brooke smelled them and smiled. "How did you get these this time of year?"

"A friend runs a greenhouse and grows them, and a plethora of other plants, year-round."

"How fun," Brooke said.

"You'll have to come with me sometime."

"I'd like that." Brooke's gaze remained on the flowers. "Thank you again. They'll brighten up the room."

"I also brought you some cookies." Austin scanned the room, finding a spot for both the flowers and the tin.

Noah stepped back in. "That was Hadley. He'd like me and Caleb to see something." He looked at Austin. "Will you be here for a bit?"

"Yeah." She looked at her watch. "I don't have to leave for the vet for another hour."

Noah tapped the doorframe. "I won't be that long." He looked at Brooke. "Be right back."

She nodded and offered a soft smile, but Austin didn't miss her wince at the movement. Her cheek was so swollen, it broke Austin's heart.

"You've definitely got me intrigued," Noah said as he greeted Hadley. "You said you found something interesting?"

Hadley whistled. "That's one way to put it. With no identification, I've labeled each of the shooters as John Doe and differentiated with a number," he said. "This is John Doe One." He gripped the sheet and lowered it from the shooter's shoulders to his waist.

Curiosity raked through Noah. Hadley hadn't started the internal autopsy yet, so it had to be on the shooter's person.

It was insanely frustrating that they still hadn't been able to identify any of the shooters but Andrews. Noah prayed Hadley's autopsy or the shooters' dentals, at the very least, would remedy that.

Hadley adjusted the swing light over the man's right shoulder. "Grab a pair of gloves." He tilted his head at the box of latex gloves on the edge of the counter to his left.

Noah and Caleb stepped around the head of the autopsy table, each grabbing and slipping on a pair of gloves.

"Good, now come around by me," Hadley said. "I'm going to roll John Doe One over."

"Let us help," Noah offered.

"That's all right," Hadley said, sliding one hand under the man's neck, the other clasped on the man's arm as he rolled him over.

Noah's gaze narrowed in on the image. "Is that . . . ?"

"A branding mark," Hadley said. "On his upper left arm."

"I've never seen anything like it," Caleb said.

Neither had Noah. "What is the image of?" He leaned in closer, studying the interlaced lines, the image interpreted in a variety of ways depending on the part he focused on. Three interlocking triangles.

"I don't know," Hadley said after Noah and Caleb had examined it thoroughly.

"Is it Celtic?" Caleb asked, his gaze pensive.

"Possibly," Noah said. "I'll send images—" He looked up at Hadley. "If it's okay with you, I'll photograph it and send the images to Em and Logan."

"Please do," Hadley said. "I'm convinced that pair can find anything."

"Agreed," Noah said, snapping pictures on his phone.

Once done, Hadley rested the man's back flat on the exam table. "Another point of interest," he said. "After finding this, I had a hunch and checked. All of the shooters have the same brand."

# TWENTY-THREE

Caleb caught sight of Austin walking past the door of Noah's hospital-room-turned-satellite-office.

"Austin," he called, hoping she'd stop, hoping he'd get to be with her for a few minutes before their case-board meeting started. He shook his head. What was happening to him?

"Hey," she said, entering.

He wouldn't bring himself to note how the dipping rays of the sun highlighted her blond hair, or how the dress she wore fit her curves perfectly. He was a man, for goodness' sake. Men didn't comment on shimmering hair—at least not men like him.

"Wow!" she said. "How did you get the hospital to let you bring in a giant whiteboard?"

"I bribed the front-desk volunteers with an appetizer platter from Dockside and, of course, sweet tea for the sweet ladies."

She arched a brow. "A charmer? Interesting . . ."

He chuckled. "You don't have to sound so shocked. I can be charming when I want to be."

She smirked. "I just might have to hold you to that."

Man, he loved bantering with this woman. "Noah said you came by to see Brooke. Did you have a nice visit?"

"Yeah. I wanted to let her know I'm keeping her in prayer, and I brought her some flowers and my grandma's red velvet cookies."

"Those sound good."

"I'll have to make you some—" She cleared her throat. "I mean, if you'd like . . . one day . . ."

"I'd like that. Maybe we could make them together sometime." The thought of more time with Austin, no matter how they spent it, made him happy. She warmed his soul in a way he'd never experienced before. The woman still drove him mad at times, but there was so much more there.

Red flushed Austin's cheeks.

Had he just made Austin Kelly blush?

"I'd like that." She shrugged.

Recognizing a small grimace of pain, he asked, "How's the shoulder?"

"Pretty good."

"Uh-huh." Of course, she'd never admit pain.

She took a deep breath. "All right, it's a little sore but manageable."

"How'd it go at the vet?" he asked, switching gears. He prayed Dirk was doing better. The strong bond between Austin and her pup was evident.

"I'm actually on my way to pick up Dirk and head there now. Lucy was running late, so she moved me to the end of the day." She glanced at the time on her phone. "Yikes! I better scoot."

"Let me know how it goes."

"Will do." She smiled and headed toward the open door.

Caleb watched her go, wishing he'd said something more, but having no clue what. He just hadn't wanted her to leave.

Austin paused in the open doorway and waggled a few fingers good-bye.

He waved back, and she strode away, her dress swirling about her knee-high boots.

The woman was breaking down his walls. Oh, who was he kidding? She was obliterating his fastidiously placed guard.

And the scary thing was he didn't mind at all.

"Hey, Caleb," Rissi said, rounding the corner with Mason behind her.

"Hey, man," Mason said, lifting his chin in greeting as the two entered Noah's room, though Noah hadn't spent any time in it, remaining with Brooke practically every moment since she'd been found, as far as Caleb could tell.

"Can I help set things up?" Mason offered.

"That'd be great." Caleb lifted the manila envelope that tied in the back with a red string—just like the ones they'd used in elementary school to send papers home. Unfortunately, this envelope was full of crime-scene photos Emmy had sent over. "You and Ris know far more about these images than I do," he said, handing the folder off to Mason. "You want to take care of placing and noting them?"

"No problem," Mason said.

Caleb's gaze inadvertently shifted back to the door, the image of Austin waving good-bye tracking through his mind.

Rissi smirked as she caught his gaze, then she and Mason exchanged a knowing glance.

"What?" he asked a little too defensively and, of course, being an amazing profiler and body language expert, it wasn't lost on her.

"Nothing," Rissi said, holding up her hands.

He glanced at Mason.

"Like the lady said, nothing."

"Uh-huh." He wasn't buying that either.

*Great.* Soon everyone would know he was falling for Austin.

Mason used a magnet to place the next photo on the board. "How'd you manage to get this board in here?"

Caleb explained again, and Mason laughed. "Brilliant."

"Noah next door with Brooke?" Rissi asked.

"Yep. Apparently, Gabby's riding over with Finn, and she is going to hang with her."

"I think I'll pop in and say hi before we start the meeting," Rissi said.

"Sounds good," Mason said.

Rissi smiled back at him, a woman deep in love.

Mason was a good guy. Caleb was truly happy for them. And, looking back, he could see that what he'd felt for Rissi had been basic affection. Nothing more, and certainly not love. Not like the love she and Mason shared.

His feelings for Rissi had completely ceased a few months back. Right around the time Austin—no matter how infuriating the woman was at first—entered his life like a whirlwind.

"Hey, guys," Finn said as he and Gabby entered.

Everyone murmured their greetings, and after a minute, Gabby gestured in the direction of Brooke's room and said, "I'm going to head on over."

Finn pressed a kiss on her lips. "Love you, babe."

Noah looked up to see his sister entering the room with a coffee-carrying tray and two duffels—their straps slung across her body.

"I brought coffee," Gabby said as she set the drink carrier on the side shelf and the duffels in the cubby beneath it.

He gave his sister a look, knowing she'd understand what he was silently asking, and she nodded. *Good*. He would surprise Brooke tonight. It was nothing fancy, but he prayed it would be enough to distract her from the pain she'd been enduring—both mentally and physically.

"Those are beautiful," Gabby said, gesturing to the sunflowers.

"Austin brought them." Brooke smiled.

*Really* smiled, and it warmed Noah's heart.

Speaking of his heart, he hated leaving her, but he needed

to be at the case-board meeting, and she was in loving hands. Besides, she might feel more comfortable confiding in a female friend about certain aspects of what she went through than with a man.

"I'll leave you ladies alone," he said, his gaze fixed on Brooke. "I'll be right next door if you need anything."

"Okay, shoo," Gabby said, signaling with hand motions for him to scoot. "We're good."

He headed next door, a hollow ache in his gut at leaving Brooke.

# TWENTY-FOUR

Noah entered his hospital room—his for at least another day. Everyone was present except Emmy, who was supposed to have the entire day off but had, of course, refused to take it until Brooke was found and safe. He'd insisted she take the rest of the day off, and she very begrudgingly listened, but only once she was assured that Logan would fill her in on what they discussed during the meeting.

"I can't believe Emmy actually agreed to take the afternoon off," Caleb said.

"I didn't give her a choice." Noah looked directly at Caleb. "Just like I won't give you one tomorrow."

"With so much going on . . ." Caleb said, tapping his pen against his notepad.

"No *ifs*, *and*s, or *but*s. You're off," Noah said. "This case has so many facets, it's going to take a while to solve—and plenty of other agencies are working with us. We can afford one person off a day in rotation."

Caleb nodded in agreement, but his tight jaw said he still wasn't happy about it.

"Okay." Noah rubbed his hands together. "Let's get started. We have a lot to cover. Finn, how about you start us out?"

Finn started by explaining he'd processed most of the evidence collected from Brooke and the rowboat and had some interesting leads, but because they had not yet found the site of her interrogation and any evidence on her clothing had been compromised by her swim, most leads were dead ends.

"It's difficult to determine the influence of the river's current," Finn continued, "but considering the approximate time Brooke was in the rowboat and swimming in the water, I'm guessing we are on the right track with this area of the warehouse district." He pointed to an enlarged section of the map.

Noah shifted his attention to Caleb. "Let the team know what you learned from your interview with Brooke."

Caleb nodded, then cleared his throat.

Noah braced to hear the information once again.

"She remembers going out to her car," Caleb said. "Went to unlock the door, but before she could even lower the key to the lock, someone grabbed her in a choke hold from behind and smothered her with something that smelled sickly sweet—most likely chloroform. She woke up blindfolded and bound. She said wherever she was smelled old and musty."

"Any idea what kind of building she was in?" Rissi asked.

"She guessed an old barn or warehouse. The ground was hard beneath her feet and the cold wind was whistling in, indicating either poor insulation or possibly a cracked window. She said the walk from the structure to the boat was less than forty paces."

"I can continue spearheading the search, focusing on buildings situated directly by the water," Mason said.

"Brooke also provided some helpful details about her captors," Caleb said. "She heard one man being called Saul, and she saw his face in the boat and during the chase, so she thinks she can recall a fairly accurate description. She only briefly saw the second man but will attempt a description of him as well. Though, she said the second man tried to kill Saul, and their fight enabled her to escape."

Noah closed his eyes for a brief second, whispering a prayer of thanks.

"Also," Caleb continued, "Saul referred to the man who appeared to be in charge at the warehouse as *Dw* before he was cut off. That's probably the reason the second man in the boat tried to take him out."

"So we have one first name and a partial, as well as a chance at helpful sketches," Noah said. "One more note on Brooke before we move on, Connor Andrews whispered the word *gator* to her before he went into surgery, which I believe is the reason she was abducted. Andrews is still unconscious, so he hasn't spoken to anyone else. His age and the fact he still had on his medical notification necklace indicate he was a green recruit. His surrender only confirms this in my mind."

"Agreed," Mason said.

"Brooke has no idea what *gator* means." Noah pinched the bridge of his nose as anger and pain sifted through him. "She held out as long as she could but eventually told her captors the word. Despite their cruel attempts to get more out of her, she insisted she knew nothing else, and they finally gave up."

Noah raked a shaky hand through his hair as fury quivered his limbs. If the men hadn't taken her out in the boat, if she hadn't escaped . . . she would be dead. She'd nearly died, and he'd nearly lost her twice, in less than twenty-four hours.

Turning his attention back to the board, Noah forced himself to concentrate fully on the case. He had to put all he had into finding and punishing the men responsible for it all. He would not rest until they were behind bars where they belonged.

"How you holding up, hon?" Gabby said.

Brooke smiled at the term of affection Gabby, Noah, and the rest of their family had brought from Maryland.

She clutched the hazelnut latte Gabby had brought, allowing

it to warm her hands. Raul must have made it extra hot for it to still hold its heat despite the chill outside.

"You cold?" Gabby asked.

"Yeah. I have no idea why they have to keep it so frigid in here." Brooke shivered under the sheet masquerading as a blanket the hospital had provided.

"Then good thing I brought this for you," Gabby said, pulling a beautiful quilt done in blues and seafoam green with starbursts of yellow throughout from one of the duffels she'd carried in.

"It's beautiful. Is it one of Kenzie's?" Gabby's sister made the loveliest quilts. No matter how many she made, they always sold out at the craft fairs. "It's so sweet of Kenzie to let me borrow this." She snuggled into the comfy warmth as Gabby spread it over her.

"It's yours. A gift from Kenzie," Gabby said.

Brooke considered arguing but knew better. Gabby lived to win arguments. Watching her and Noah go at it was hilarious. Brooke and their whole family placed bets on who'd win any given argument. Noah's family really had taken her into their fold, and considering her family was in Colorado and wasn't tight-knit, she adored being an adopted part of the Rowley clan. If only she and Noah . . . if only she could become a real part of it.

"And . . ." Gabby said, fishing something else out of the duffel bag, "Nana Jo's peanut brittle."

"Oh, you guys are too sweet," Brooke said. "Between these and Austin's red velvet cookies, y'all are going to put some pounds on me." She chuckled for the first time since— She cut off the thought before it consumed her. "What's in the blue duffel?" she asked, curious what else Gabby might have brought.

"Stuff for Noah." Gabby shrugged.

Of course. "That's nice of you to bring him stuff too. I can't get him to go rest in his room. The recliner in here can't be as comfortable as a bed." She wished he'd never leave her side, but her concern for his well-being overrode that.

"He's stubborn," Gabby said, taking a seat in the recliner.

Brooke chuckled. "Pot, kettle." And that went for his entire family.

Gabby smirked. "Fair enough." Her face softened, and Brooke feared Gabby would ask her for details about what happened.

It wasn't that Brooke didn't want to confide in her friend. She just wasn't even close to ready to talk about it more. She'd already gone over it twice—in general terms with Finn and in more detail when Caleb questioned her. Both had been kind and let her take her time, but it was too painful to breathe even a word of what happened again.

Gabby must have read her face because she didn't ask a thing, just sprang up from the chair. "I almost forgot." She strode back to the open duffel. "I also brought you some flannel jammies so you aren't stuck in those scrubs, and I've got some fuzzy socks, slippers, and a robe. Oh, and a book of fill-in-the-blank famous lines from literature."

"Thank you," she said as Gabby handed her the book along with a set of colored pencils. "This is wonderful. It'll help keep my . . ." *Mind off of what happened.* "Keep me occupied," she said.

"Speaking of staying occupied, do you want to take a walk?" Gabby asked. "Maybe to the chapel, but only if you're—"

Brooke didn't even wait for Gabby to finish. She was out of bed and heading to the bathroom to change into the pjs, robe, and slippers.

A few moments later, she emerged feeling fresher and far more comfortable. She'd run a brush through her hair, rubbed lotion on her face, and smeared Chapstick on her lips.

Gabby smiled. "That definitely looks cozier."

"It is," Brooke said, thankful for her friend's smile. She understood why, but everyone else's faces had been fixed with concern. It was nice to see a happy face, even if she still felt broken inside.

She popped a Bit-O-Honey chew Gabby had brought in her mouth as they headed for the chapel. She hadn't had one since she was a kid, didn't even know they made them anymore, but apparently the hospital gift shop sold them, and she was delighted.

They rounded the hall. Recessed lighting illuminated the beautiful stained-glass windows in the upper half of the chapel's mahogany doors. Scenes of Jesus with a lamb on one side and calming the storm at sea on the other. Peace and turmoil.

She was in turmoil, but she trusted Jesus could calm the tempest raging inside her as He'd calmed the storm at sea. She didn't anticipate it being instant, but that's what she needed—for Him to comfort her, to shelter her under His wings, to be her safety after the horrific experiences she'd endured—to be her peace in the midst of it all.

Gabby studied her. She always saw too much. Brooke blamed it on her reporter's eye. She was singularly gifted for the job, but it meant there was no hiding anything from her. "You okay?" she asked. "We can head back, if you'd prefer."

"Thanks, but I could really use some quiet time with God." There always seemed to be personnel popping in her room checking her wounds, checking her vitals. She just needed silence and to sit at her Savior's feet.

Gabby opened the arched doors leading into the chapel, and Brooke stepped in. It was empty, save them.

Small and old-world in style, the chapel boasted dark wood walls and three rows of pews. Plush carpet cushioned her steps as she made her way to the middle pew, studying the stained-glass windows donning the side walls. One of the Garden of Eden, one of the fall of man, one of Christ on the cross, and one of His transfiguration. It was the gospel summarized in four images.

Gabby slid in the pew beside her. "Would you like me to say a prayer," Gabby asked, "or would you prefer silence?"

"I'd love a prayer. Where two or more are gathered," she said.

Gabby clasped her hand, and as Brooke closed her eyes, suffocating sorrow draped back over her.

"Dear Lord," Gabby began, "you know everything that has happened. We don't understand, but your Word says, 'Now I know in part; then I shall know fully.' We long for that day, Lord. Please bring healing and comfort to all concerned." Gabby paused, releasing a long exhale, her hand clasping Brooke's loosely, and then continued, "I pray for everyone whose life was taken in the horrific tragedy today and all who loved them. I pray for peace for their families, and especially peace for Brooke. In Jesus' name, I pray."

"Amen," Brooke whispered, leaving her eyes shut and head bowed. She sat in the silence, feeling the Lord with her and soaking up His presence.

# TWENTY-FIVE

"Caleb, let's shift gears back to the shooting and to your conversation this morning with Greer," Noah said, glancing at the analog clock ticking on the wall. It was going to be a long case board, but there was much to cover.

"With Brooke's abduction, our initial conversation with Greer wasn't long, but I met with him this afternoon to gather the details." Caleb moved for the whiteboard. "He emphasized how highly confidential this information is." He looked to the door, and Noah followed his gaze. It was shut. "And that what he told us must stay within the confines of our team and our investigation."

"Of course," Noah said, looking across the space at his team as they all nodded. He trusted each of them, knew he never need worry about leaked information.

"The Coast Guard's RAD unit has been working with a specialized branch of the Army's RAD on a laser weapon."

Noah's jaw clenched. *Laser weapon?*

"The program, named Strike First, began at the Army's RAD facility in Duck, North Carolina," Caleb continued. "They invited the Coast Guard's top scientists and ordnance specialists to collaborate with them at their facility but recently moved the project to our base."

"Why was it moved?" Mason asked.

"They believed they had a mole in their midst. Certain information went missing—plans for the early part of the weapon's development. When they moved the project here, they pared down to only the top-tier personnel they were confident were loyal."

"Do they believe that took care of the problem?" Logan asked.

"They did until yesterday," Caleb said. "At 0915, the lab was evacuated due to the mass shooting, and the personnel were sequestered in one of the guarded holding rooms."

"0915 is less than ten minutes after the shooting began," Noah said.

Caleb nodded. "Greer believes the two events were part of a coordinated attack."

"Or," Noah said, "the shooting was a distraction for the theft."

"That's a heck of a distraction," Rissi said.

"Agreed," Caleb said. "A paper copy of the plans for the final component of the laser weapon was stolen."

"So the initial plans were stolen at the Army's RAD facility in Duck, and plans for the final component were stolen here," Mason said, his expression one of disturbed contemplation.

Rissi sat back in her chair. "Are we leaning toward the belief that someone on the inside was part of this attack, and whoever stole the plans is building their own laser weapon?"

"That's the fear," Caleb said.

Noah turned to Finn. "I assume you didn't have time to work the lab?"

"No," Finn said.

With everything going on, they'd have to rank by priority, and this just took top spot. "Take the time needed to process it first thing tomorrow."

"You got it, boss," Finn said.

"All right." Noah rubbed his hands together. "What about

visitors coming through the building's main entrance before the theft?"

"None." Caleb shook his head. "But the rear emergency exit alarm went off two minutes before the men entered the lab."

"And no one checked on it?" he asked.

"The alarm was drowned out by the base alarm going off in response to the shooting. The primary objective for all the soldiers in security roles was to get the rest of the building's soldiers and civilian contractors safely into the holding room," Caleb said.

"I'm curious," Logan said, shifting forward. "What makes lasers important or unique enough to spend so much time developing them?"

"They are smaller and, therefore, easier to transport than conventional weapons and heavy ammunition." Caleb started squeaking his marker across the board in bullet points beneath the photograph. "They use electricity or batteries for their ammunition, so they have an endless magazine."

Noah sat back and listened as Caleb continued with a list that made the weapon in question—or at least the plans for one—beyond frightening if in the wrong hands. The laser light was invisible, so the enemy or target wouldn't know where it was coming from, and they couldn't return fire. Due to their stealthy operation, lasers were ideal for surprise engagements . . . and the list went on. He prayed whoever stole it was never able to make it or, heaven forbid, use it.

# TWENTY-SIX

All the leads his team had collected raced through Noah's mind as they wrapped up. He was even more convinced that everything was interconnected, and that those who planned it possessed a high level of intelligence and a long reach.

"I'll just slide this over here," Caleb said, rolling the whiteboard with Logan's help to the open wall in Noah's room. Noah would be here at least until tomorrow evening—especially after ripping out his stitches—so it only made sense to gather in his room again in the morning.

"I'll pull the photos off the board and keep them with me," Finn said.

Noah nodded. "Perfect." They didn't want the crime-scene photos scaring a nurse, but more importantly, they couldn't risk someone removing any of them.

"I can either take a picture of our notes and erase it all," Caleb said, "or drape a sheet over it."

"I think the picture and erasing is best."

"You got it," Caleb said, getting to work. "I'm good here if you guys want to head out."

Finn just needed to get Gabby from Brooke's room, but Logan still had a significant job to do.

"Okay." Noah lifted his chin at Logan. "You ready?"

"Sure. Let me grab my bag," Logan said, lifting the worn brown leather satchel that housed his sketch pad and pencils.

Noah exhaled. He hated to put Brooke back in the headspace of recalling the men trying to kill her. But with Logan's artistic skills, they'd hopefully have an accurate face to ID—at least for the man named Saul.

"Thanks, Caleb," he said as he, Finn, and Logan headed into the hall and took the handful of steps to Brooke's room.

"Knock, knock," Noah said, rapping on the door.

No answer. No sound of his sister's or Brooke's voices. And Gabby definitely took after their mom with a volume setting stuck on ten.

His muscles grew taut.

Finn cracked the door and stuck his head in. "Hey, Gabs?"

Nothing.

Noah's chest compressed, wresting the air from his lungs. He strode fully into the room, only to find it empty.

Dwayne finally had time to deal with Ted, though keeping him waiting all day had its perks. The kid had been nervous the entire time. Sulking about when he thought Dwayne wasn't watching. But didn't his men understand he was always watching? He took a sharp inhale. *His men.*

They were his, but under provision by the boss. And if they didn't get this debacle taken care of ASAP, it'd be all their heads.

He looked at the clock in the space he'd claimed for his office, as poor of an excuse for one as it was. But it had four walls and served its purpose.

Ted had two minutes to be on time. The second hand clicked and clicked again. *Tick. Tock. Tick. Tock.* One minute.

A rap rattled the old door on its hinges.

"Enter."

Ted stepped in and closed the door uneasily behind him.

So he was uneasy? *Good.* He'd screwed up. So much so, it could threaten their primary objective. Years of preparation nearly undone at the two fools' hands.

Dwayne signaled the scrawny man in. Six feet and a featherweight, he'd always come through until now, and that was the only reason he was still breathing.

"You want to tell me what happened?"

Ted swallowed, his protruding Adam's apple bobbing in his thin, pale neck.

A neck Dwayne would snap in a second if he screwed up again.

"We were headed out in the boat. I told Saul to row, but he had the girl do it. I waited for the right moment and pulled my gun on Saul. He lunged at me, and it fired in the air. He knocked me back on the girl. I got up, we struggled, then she nailed us with the oar. While we were scrambling to get up, she jumped in the water."

"Continue," Dwayne said, stuffing a wad of dip into his lip.

Ted rubbed his flannel-covered arm. "We looked for her, shooting into the water, but she stayed under for a long time. I started rowing, and we finally saw her scrambling up the riverbank. Saul jumped out and ran after her. By the time I pulled the boat ashore, he had already disappeared into the trees."

Dwayne arched his brows, indicating for Ted to lay it all out on the table.

"Saul was shooting at her. I was a ways behind. When we got to the top of a hill, she'd flagged down a semi, followed by a long line of construction vehicles. Too many witnesses to do anything. Saul and I returned to the boat, and when we were far enough out of sight, I killed him with a punch to the windpipe and dumped him in the shallows. I ditched the boat and worked my way back along the far shore."

"Did she see your face?"

"I don't think so. I was pretty far back."

Dwayne sat forward, the old metal desk chair creaking as he swiveled to face Ted head on. "You don't *think* so? Son, this is a yes or no answer."

Ted fidgeted with the cuffs of his shirtsleeves. "Her blindfold was on until just before she hit us and jumped in the water, and then I was too far back for her to see me in the woods. Saul, she saw."

Dwayne sniffed, then pushed up on the metal arms of the chair. "Okay, that's all I needed to know. She might be able to give a description to a sketch artist." That's usually how these things went. "But Saul's identity is wiped, so we have nothing to worry about. Besides, the police or *special agents*," he said with a mocking tone, "will be searching the shallows, working the boat. That'll be a nice distraction from what's really going on." He took a sharp inhale, then released it. "So"—he clamped Ted's bony shoulder—"you just redeemed yourself."

The tension left Ted's shoulders.

"But you only get one redemption. If you jeopardize the mission again, you know the consequences."

Noah and Finn were about to split up to search the hospital for Brooke and Gabby when the two rounded the corner.

Noah's chest loosened. *Thank you, Lord.* He kept telling himself that she was fine, that they'd just gone for a stroll, but after just getting her back . . .

"Hey." Brooke offered a small smile. "We went to the chapel," she said, clearly aware by his expression that he'd been worried.

"That's nice," he said. He could only imagine the tumultuous emotions roiling through her, but she quieted herself in the Lord. He'd seen it as she read the Bible in her room. She trusted God, and what happened at the hands of those men hadn't dented her faith. Rather, it appeared she leaned even more heavily into the Lord.

"You guys all wrapped up?" Gabby asked.

"Yep," Finn said, slipping his fingers between hers and clasping her hand. "You ready to head out?"

"Sure." She took the few steps to Brooke's side. "I'm just a phone call away. Anytime."

"I know." Brooke smiled as Gabby gently hugged her.

Noah wanted nothing more than to envelop Brooke in his arms and never let her go. He flat-out loved her, but love was supposed to be selfless, to put the others' needs before your own. He had to keep that fixed in his mind. She deserved the best, and he wasn't it.

Gabby grabbed her purse and slid the strap over her shoulder. "Love you guys."

"'Night," Finn said, nodding his head at Brooke.

Gabby looked back and waved before they slipped out the door.

Brooke's gaze landed on Logan's bag.

Noah smiled, hoping to affirm this decision was up to her. "Do you feel up to describing the men who took you out on the boat? I'd like Logan to do some sketches."

Her jaw clamped, but she nodded.

"Are you sure? We can wait. . . ." Though they all knew the sooner, the better.

"I'll be fine," she said.

Wanting to be close to her but knowing they had work to do, he leaned against the wall, giving them space. "Logan," he said, gesturing to the chair, "why don't you take the recliner."

"Thanks," Logan said as he lowered into it. He pulled his sketch pad and pencil bag out of the bag. Resting one foot on the opposite knee, he propped up the blank pad. "I always recommend taking a deep breath, shutting your eyes if you feel comfortable, and just walking me through what you remember of their faces."

Taking a steeling breath, Brooke tried to get comfortable in the bed, but it was useless. She couldn't shake the terror of their faces flashing before her eyes, of reliving the heat of that moment of tremendous, consuming fear.

She looked up at Noah, standing against the wall on her left.

She swallowed the voice in her head whispering all the reasons not to—the fear he'd say no, that she'd be embarrassed, but none of that mattered. She looked up at Noah and asked for what she needed. "Would you sit with me?"

His face softened, his eyes smiling, the creases along their edges deepening. "Of course," he said, pushing off the wall and moving to the foot of her bed. "Down here?" he asked.

"Maybe a little farther up?" She patted the space by her hip.

He moved closer, and she melded into his strong presence beside her.

He reached up and took hold of her hand.

Her gaze locked on his, and something unspoken passed between them. Maybe Gabby was right. Maybe he had feelings, deep feelings, for her. Or maybe he was just being kind.

Shaking off that dilemma, she did as Logan suggested and took a deep breath yet again, and despite the fear clawing at her, shut her eyes.

# TWENTY-SEVEN

"That was brave," Noah said to Brooke as Logan left for the night.

"I don't know about that. . . ."

Still on the bed beside her, he wove her fingers with his. "I do."

Their gazes held, and she nearly forgot to breathe.

After a moment, he released her hand and moved away from the bed. "Wait just a minute."

Her entire body tensed. *Don't leave.* Not with those men's faces stuck in her head.

He set the blue duffel at the foot of the bed and unzipped it. "I've got a surprise for you."

She arched a brow. Not at all what she'd expected him to say.

He pulled out a round white tub with black lettering: *Fisher's Popcorn.*

He tapped the lid of the tub. "This is from back in Maryland. It's the best caramel popcorn ever."

"Yum." She wiggled her fuzzy-socked feet, wondering what other goodies he had.

He pulled out an old-style green thermos, with the cup inverted on the top. "Hot chocolate," he said, setting the thermos on her tray table. "And"—he reached back in the bag—"mini marshmallows!"

"Delicious."

He rested his hand on top of the thermos. "This baby keeps things hot for a crazy twelve hours, so be careful when taking a sip."

He pulled out two red tin mugs speckled with white, adding them to the collection of goodies.

"And," he said with a smile, "the best part."

She stretched up, trying to snag a peek.

"*Miss Congeniality*," he said, pulling out a Blu-ray.

She cocked her head. "How'd you . . . ?"

"Gabby told me it's your favorite."

"It is, but we don't have a Blu-ray player."

He reached into the bag again.

"No way." She chuckled as he pulled out a square Blu-ray player in one hand and an adapter cord in the other. "You thought of everything."

The joy on his face, echoing her own, shifted into one of deep care. "I hope so."

Caleb smiled when he saw the lights on in Austin's kitchen and living room. He hadn't called. He'd wanted it to be a surprise, but doing so ran the risk she wouldn't be home. He warmed at finding her there.

Climbing from his car, he opened the rear door and pulled out the Outback bags filled with their dinner. Being careful not to spill the French onion soup, he made his way to her door and knocked with his elbow. His technique wasn't pretty, but it got the job done.

A moment later, she pulled back the sheer curtain donning the door's paned window and smiled.

"Hey," she said, opening the door. "I didn't expect to see you."

"Hope it's okay I just dropped by," he said, trying to gauge her reaction. She seemed happy, which made him happy. When had making her smile begun to fill him with such joy?

"Of course," she said. "It's even more okay when you bring dinner." She raised up on her tiptoes to peek into the brown bag resting in the crook of his left arm. "French onion soup?" she asked.

"Very good."

"Let me help you," she said, taking the bag before he could answer.

He chuckled. "I'm guessing you haven't eaten yet?"

"Nope. I was about to call DeNucci's Pizza Parlor."

"Mind if I wash up?" he asked.

"Of course not." She angled her head toward the hall. "Bathroom is the first door on your left."

When he returned, they settled at her patio table to eat, a tall outdoor heater situated on either side. Both put out some serious heat, but all faded away as they slipped into easy conversation.

An hour of eating and chatting later, or maybe it had been longer—somehow time seemed to slip by when he was around her—her cell rang.

His gaze shifted to the phone vibrating toward him across the wrought-iron table. He picked it up and handed it to Austin.

"Vet," she said before answering. "Hi, Lucy."

Caleb glanced out at the black sky overhead. It rarely snowed in Wilmington, but the density of the air and the scent of snow lingering in it suggested tonight might be an exception.

"Uh-huh," Austin said after a moment of listening. "Any idea where it came from? A plant, perhaps?" She tilted her head. "What about something in the water?"

He surveyed the dark water, his eyes narrowing. That didn't sound good.

"Okay," Austin said, her voice wobbling.

He cleared his throat, and she looked over.

"Apologies for interrupting," he said. "But what did she say about the water?"

"She said Dirk has something in his blood that she's never seen before. She is going to run more tests, but it doesn't seem to be plant borne."

"Ask her if you can borrow the blood sample and let our CSI team look at it tomorrow. I'll come by in the morning and take a sample of the water, and we can compare the two."

Austin nodded and relayed the question. "Okay. Thanks, Lucy. 'Night." She ended the call and looked up at Caleb. "She said no problem. I can pick it up first thing in the morning."

"Great, but I don't mind picking up the sample."

She slipped her long blond hair behind her ear. "Are you sure?"

"Positive."

"Okay, thanks." She moved to the edge of the patio, staring out over water nearly as black as the night. "I never considered the water, but Dirk loves to swim."

Caleb glanced at the large lump snoring in the corner where the patio met a plant bed. He chuckled under his breath. Dirk had that ugly-cute quality Emmy was always talking about in certain breeds of dogs, which she and Logan argued about until both were nearly winded.

His eyes flashed back to Austin standing beside him, her perfume tickling his nose in a very good way. Somehow, she smelled like the ocean. He didn't even know they made perfumes like that, but it was captivating.

Dirk launched a cacophony of snores, each louder than the one before it.

They both laughed.

"Yeah," she said, "he's a mess."

"Well, hopefully the samples will help us nail down what's

going on. I'm guessing a good number of the neighborhood dogs spend time in the water," he said.

"Yep."

"I'll get Finn or Emmy to take a look at the samples. We should have an answer by midmorning."

"That would be great. Dirk sees Dr. Lucy Chang at Happy Paws on Birch Street. I'll text you the address. She opens at seven."

"It's a plan," he said, helping her clear the table. She'd transferred all the food from takeout containers to regular plates. He didn't want to leave—not yet, but they both needed rest. It'd been a long day. "I'll put these in the dishwasher and get out of your hair."

She nodded, her lips pressed tight.

He raised a brow. "You okay?"

She blinked, moisture misting her eyes. "I know it's silly, but . . ." She shrugged as he slid the plates into the dishwasher before leaning against the counter and giving her his undivided attention.

"But . . . ?"

She shifted her weight onto her left foot. "I hope I don't see them in my dreams again."

"The shooters?" he asked.

She shook her head, looking down. "The victims. Especially Molly."

This was not an area he excelled in—comforting. He'd tried, but always felt awkward. He stepped closer. "I'm sorry," he whispered. "That can be difficult."

He'd had plenty of nights where he'd woken up in a cold sweat, though most of those memories had nothing to do with the job.

Shuffling her foot around the edge of the sink floor mat, Austin looked up at him, her eyes soft as her voice. "Has that ever happened to you?"

He inhaled. Details of the horrors he'd seen, of the dreams that haunted him wouldn't help. But he could still be truthful. "Yes. It has."

She pressed her lips together and tilted her head as tears welled in her eyes. "Do they ever go away?"

He rubbed her arm, and she leaned into him. He stood stock-still, scared if he moved wrong, she'd leave his hold. He slowly wrapped his arms around her, and to his surprise, she nestled deeper in. Her tears soaked through his shirt.

He rested his chin atop her head. "It'll be okay. You're strong."

"Clearly," she said, hiccupping in his hold.

He leaned back just enough to look her in the eye, not willing to release the sweet feel of her in his arms. "I'm serious. You are one of the strongest women I've ever had the privilege of meeting."

She swiped at her red cheeks. "You're just saying that because I'm a mess."

He cupped her chin. "You are not a mess, and I never say anything I don't mean."

She chuckled at that. "You are pretty straight to the point."

He shrugged. "I suppose in an effort to always be truthful, I lost the ability to cushion it somewhere along the way."

She sniffed, composing herself—though, despite the tears, she'd really never lost composure.

She shifted her jaw as she leaned back against the kitchen counter, and his arms felt achingly empty.

"How do you make it go away?" she asked.

He slipped his hands into his pockets. "Time. I know it's the cliché answer, but God brings healing. Unfortunately, it often takes far longer than we'd like." And that's when healing was actually possible, but he wasn't going there with her. She needed encouragement, not the stark truth. And for once in his life he was going to listen to the Holy Spirit's nudge to keep his mouth shut.

She pushed off the counter. "I'll see you around seven-thirty tomorrow morning?"

"Yeah." He shook himself out of what felt like a dream. Not in the rainbows and unicorns way, but as if he'd been lost in the moment, and the jerk back to reality was startling. One moment she was in his arms, the next he was stepping onto her front porch.

"Thanks for stopping by the vet," she said.

"Happy to help. Noah insisted I take tomorrow off"— suddenly following Noah's command didn't seem so bad— "so my day is yours." He turned, but when the door squeaked behind him, he spun around before she'd fully shut it. "If . . ."

"Yes?" Her brow furrowed.

"If you need anything between now and then, my phone's always on."

"The life of a special agent," she said.

"'Night," he said, turning toward his car. Yes, it was the life of a special agent, but that wasn't why he'd said it.

# TWENTY-EIGHT

Caleb's tires crunched across the gravel lot as the sun crested the horizon. He pulled parallel to the only other vehicle present—a sky-blue Nissan Pathfinder. Early '90s model, he was betting. He glanced over his shoulder at the one-story brick building. A series of lights shone inside.

His hands balled into fists. He hadn't been in a vet's office since . . .

He swallowed. Since his mom made the decision she no longer wanted to be saddled with the responsibility of a dog after the divorce. The fact that Skipper was *his* dog and that he took care of him made no nevermind to her.

When they'd left the house that morning, he'd had no idea where they were headed. His mom saying he could bring Skipper for the ride should have sent red flags waving, but he was six. What did he know?

He took a stiff inhale, his jaw clenching. Standing there, watching the vet give Skipper a shot, then realizing what she'd done, had changed him. He'd tried to rouse his dog, his best friend, but it was useless. He couldn't rouse Skipper no matter how hard he shook him, screamed his name . . . cried.

He had hated his mom that day. Hated her for years until he'd accepted Christ as his Savior. But to this day, he kept her and her string of divorces and loser boyfriends as far away as possible.

He clenched his jaw as he stepped from his new Forester SUV and moved for the front door. A giant white paw print sat in the center of a large blue circle. *Happy Paws Veterinarian Clinic* curved along the top, and *Lucy Chang DVM* curved along the bottom. He was definitely in the right place.

Climbing the handful of concrete steps, he did as the *Come On In* sign said.

"I'll be right with you," a woman yelled from the back, nearly drowning out the sound of the bell twanging over the still-open door. Turning, he grabbed the door handle. A strong swoop of wind fought against his hold, trying to yank the door with it, but he won out. The door finally shut, he raked a hand through his windblown hair and moved for one of the lobby chairs.

A tan mop of a dog scampered toward him, his fluffy tail wagging furiously. He stopped in front of Caleb and sat, his breath warming Caleb's shin through his jeans. The dog's thick tail swished back and forth across the linoleum floor. His big eyes looked up with hope until Caleb caved, bending to pet the pup's back.

A petite lady, no taller than four-eleven, with dark hair and wearing lavender scrubs with colorful paw prints scattered about them, stepped around the corner. "I see you've met Jaxon," she said.

"Yeah," he said, still petting the mop, surprised at how good it felt to love on an animal again.

"Better be careful." She smiled. "He will steal your heart." Her white vet coat hit halfway down her thighs. *Lucy* was scrolled in bright purple above the right-side pocket. "You must be Caleb."

"Yes, ma'am," he said, standing.

"I appreciate the formality, but not having hit thirty yet, I prefer Lucy. Or if you're wired to be formal, which I'm betting you are"—she gestured for him to follow her toward the exam room hall—"*Doctor* will work just fine."

"*Doctor* it is." He smiled.

Paw steps pattered behind them, and he turned to find the mop following, his tail still wagging.

Lucy smiled over her shoulder. "He likes you."

"He seems like a friendly dog. I'm sure he likes everyone who comes in."

"Actually, no. He's usually extremely shy with anyone other than me."

Caleb frowned, unsure what to do with that.

"Someone just abandoned him on the doorstep. Tied his leash around the door handle and left him," Lucy said, turning to fluff the fur on Jaxon's head. "I'd adopt him in a heartbeat, but my cats would have a fit, so he's staying here until I'm able to find him a good home."

"That's awful someone just abandoned him." Poor guy. How some people treated their animals . . .

"Are you looking for a dog?" she asked. "He's really taken to you."

"I'm a CGIS agent. I don't have time for a pet."

Lucy's lips shifted slightly into an expression of *I ain't buying it*. "Working in the area, I know a lot of law enforcement and soldiers who have pets."

It was an excuse on his part, but it seemed the easiest way out, and he did, in all fairness, work long hours.

"He's a sweet guy, very easy and trained. Do me a favor," she said before he could respond again. "Don't say no. Just take a few days and think about it."

Caleb shoved his hands in his coat pockets, looking back at Jaxon sitting beside him, wagging his tail. He was a cute mutt, but after Skipper, he'd sworn off having a pet. Having anything his mom could snatch away whenever she capriciously felt like it. After leaving home, the pattern had just stuck.

He shook off the thought. Shook off the blip of memory—of

his mom and her wildly shifting moods. Instead, he focused on what was before him.

As Lucy led him down the back hall, they passed four pristine exam rooms, each with a different theme. The first had dog pictures all over the walls and a box of Milk-Bones on the counter. The second room had cat pictures and a glass jar of knitted balls with strings. The third was the bird room. He guessed the final room was for reptiles and exotic pets, since pictures of lizards, turtles, and sugar gliders hung on the dark green walls.

Lucy opened the door at the end of the hall, leading him into a lab and surgical suite. She grabbed a white case with vials inside. "Here you go." She handed them to Caleb.

"Thanks. Any idea what was making Austin's dog sick?"

"Not just Dirk. I've seen three other dogs from her neighborhood over the past few weeks."

"Yeah, Austin mentioned there'd been other dogs." He linked his arms across his chest. "I don't imagine you'd know if each of their owners' homes backs to the sound?"

"Sorry." She shrugged. "I do know they are all on Austin's street, if that helps."

"It does." He looked down at the vials. "So what are you thinking it might be, Doc?"

Lucy shook her head with a sigh. "It's a chemical, but not one I've seen before. Actually, I haven't seen *anything* like it before. With any luck, your CSI can zero in on it. Once the chemical is identified, and we can track down where in Austin's neighborhood it's coming from, then hopefully we can prevent it from continuing to spread."

His gut said it was coming from the water, and stopping anything from spreading when a current was involved was nearly impossible. But he'd hold his tongue until they were sure. "Finn is a great crime-scene investigator. We'll get this figured out."

"I hope so because I have another dog coming in at eight with suspiciously similar symptoms."

"Is it from the Wild Pines neighborhood as well?"

Lucy exhaled. "Yes."

Caleb's jaw tightened. "I was afraid you were going to say that."

# TWENTY-NINE

"Join me for breakfast?" Austin asked after Caleb arrived from the vet.

"Sure. If it's not too much trouble," he said, stepping inside the open doorway. Sharing meals together was quickly becoming a habit he very much enjoyed.

She moved to the blender. "I'm making smoothies."

"Sounds good."

Minutes later, with smoothie tumblers in hand, they took a seat on the patio love seat. They settled under the blue fuzzy blanket she'd added to the couch. The heaters ablaze, he looked over with a smile. He'd never met someone who enjoyed spending so much time outdoors in winter.

He took a sip of the fruit-and-protein-loaded smoothie. "This is delicious," he said, half-surprised, as she'd yet to make anything homemade around him.

"Thanks." She nuzzled deeper under the blanket. "It's one of my go-to breakfasts. I can just whip it up and take it with me."

He chuckled.

She tilted her head. "What?"

"Nothing." He shook his head, his smiling growing.

Her face scrunched. "You're clearly thinking something . . ."

"You're just always on the go." He liked to move but was quite content to enjoy a good book, watch a movie, or simply sit on his back deck to watch the sunset.

"I'm not always on the go," she insisted. "For instance, I am *sitting* here enjoying breakfast with you." Of course she'd argue the point.

When didn't the woman argue? But he found it an oddly enjoyable method of flirting, strange as it might seem to onlookers. Between them, it was all in fun . . . with maybe a smidge of competition.

"And I sat out here during our last two dinners together," she added.

He smirked.

Her beautiful green eyes narrowed. "What?"

"Do you ever just sit when a meal is not involved?"

"Yes," she said a little too quickly.

He dipped his head, trying to fight how entranced he was in her presence. "So you enjoy just being still?"

Her lips pursed. "What do you mean by *still*?"

"You know. No agenda. Just chilling. Enjoying a cup of coffee on the dock to start off your day?"

"Yes." Her voice hit a higher-than-usual octave. She cleared her throat. "Yes, I do," she said again, clearly forcing her voice to settle.

He arched his brows. "*Really*?"

She pursed her lips. "We really ought to get that water sample, don't you think?"

She stood, and he let her off the hook . . . for the moment.

Caleb headed to his car and retrieved the water-sample kit from his trunk but had barely rounded the house when a high-pitched scream pierced his ears.

Austin raced past him. "I think that's Megan."

"Who?" He set down the kit and caught up with Austin's frantic pace as they raced for the water.

"Neighbor kid," she said. "Next to the canoe, about a hundred feet out."

"Who's in the canoe?" he asked, yanking off his boots.

"Her brother Billy."

Billy was pulling his sister's arm, struggling to get her up into the canoe—not an easy task.

"I'm coming," Caleb hollered. Once the cold water hit his waist, he swam for Megan and Billy.

A moment later a splash sounded behind him, ripples moving along the water.

*Austin.* Stubborn as the day is long. With her sore shoulder. But given the situation, he'd have done the same.

"My leg is stuck," Megan cried as he got closer, the water level dipping.

"There's a sandbar out there," Austin said between strokes, "but the water's too deep for her to stand."

Megan struggled, screaming with each movement. Billy still gripped her hand but wobbled in the unsteady canoe.

"There's—" Billy lost his balance and fell back into the canoe, letting go of Megan. She dropped below the water surface, then back up, gulping for air, screaming.

"There's blood in the water," Billy cried.

They couldn't be dealing with a tiger shark, could they? Caleb finally reached a very panic-stricken Megan. "It's okay," he said, keeping his voice even. "I'm a policeman. I'm going to help you."

"I'm stuck, and it hurts," she wailed.

"Megan, I'm going to go under and take a look," he said as Austin settled Billy in the canoe.

Megan nodded, and he dove. The water was murky, but thankfully, the light was bright this morning. He saw something tall and round with a jagged hole in it. Somehow Megan's leg had gotten caught inside. Every time she and Billy tugged to pull her free, the jagged edges had cut deeper into her little leg.

He rose back above the surface. "Your foot is caught in a broken barrel. Don't worry. I'll get you out, but the less you move, the less it'll hurt. Okay?"

She nodded, eyes wide, but she appeared to be calming.

He turned to Austin. "Head back to shore with Billy, call for an ambulance, and I need something to cut the metal around Megan's leg. Gardening shears, maybe?"

"Okay, I'll be right back."

She paddled for shore and returned minutes later with what looked to be a large pair of shears. She handed them off, saying, "The ambulance should be here soon. Billy's in the house. I'm going to call their dad. He works just a couple minutes away. And I'll grab some blankets."

"Good idea." He ducked back under and cut the barrel until he had a wide enough opening. Then he looped his arm around Megan's stomach and gently pulled her up.

As Caleb settled Megan on the shore, he saw deep lacerations covered her left calf, and blood streaked down, dripping off her foot.

"Megan! What are you doing out here?" A crass brunette stomped up. "Who are you? What are you doing with Megan?"

"Celia!" Austin said, striding up with blankets in hand. She dropped them next to Megan and turned to the woman. "We found them in the water, and Megan's leg is all cut up. If you turned off the TV and stayed off your phone long enough to actually watch the kids you're paid to watch, everything would have been fine."

Sirens wailed in the distance, growing closer until the red swirling lights rounded the corner.

Celia looked between the arriving ambulance and them. "I had nothing to do with this." She shook her head. "This—" she waggled her finger—"this was not my fault."

"Clearly it was," Austin said, as she sat next to Megan on the grass, wrapping her in a blanket, holding her cold, trembling hand.

Billy ran out of the house just as their dad, who Austin whispered was Thomas, pulled up, jumped out of his car, and rushed down the driveway. "What happened?"

Billy fastened to his dad's leg as Austin explained.

"I can't thank you enough," Thomas said. He lifted Billy into his arms and hurried to Megan's side, holding her hand as the paramedic, who identified himself as Trent, triaged her.

"Would you like to ride in the back with your daughter?" Trent asked Thomas when she was settled in for the ride.

"Of course."

"We can watch Billy if that would help," Austin offered.

"Carol is meeting me at the hospital. We'll watch him, but thank you. Thank you so much."

"The big guy is welcome to ride up front with me," Trent said.

Billy smiled. "Cool."

Thomas climbed in the back of the ambulance with Megan, his stiff gaze on Celia. "Don't think we're done yet."

"I didn't do anything. I . . ."

His hardened gaze said he wasn't buying any of her excuses.

Trent shut the rear bay doors, got Billy settled up front, and pulled down the drive.

Caleb strode to his car.

"What are you doing?" Austin asked.

He popped his trunk. "Diving down to assess the situation." He turned back toward her, holding his dive gear. "Do you mind if I use your bathroom to change?"

"Of course not." She opened the back screen door. "You know where the hall one is."

"Thanks." He slipped into the room and changed, pulling on his wet suit more for protection from the cut-up barrel than for warmth. Though, given how quickly hypothermia set in, he ought to pay more attention to the cold.

He opened the bathroom door and headed outside. Reaching his car, the back hatch still open, he slipped on his tank and took hold of his mask.

As he headed for the sound, the screen door squeaked behind

him, and he turned to find Austin in a black wet suit that fit her to perfection.

He quickly turned his attention back to the water. "What are you doing?" It was obvious what she thought she was doing, but he could handle this on his own.

She grabbed her tank and gear. "I'm going to see for myself." She pulled her hair back, wincing as she lifted her arm.

"You should rest your shoulder."

"It's fine." She planted her hand on her shapely hip. "If roles were reversed, would you sit on the sidelines?"

He exhaled. "No."

"Then why do you expect me to?"

He sighed. "Point taken." He caught a glimpse at the base of her neck and noticed a tattoo of two intertwined hearts. "Who's the tattoo for?" he asked, unable to stem his curiosity.

"What?" She slipped her tank in place.

"Two hearts. Did you get it for a boyfriend?"

"Nope." She slid her mask in place.

"Not wanting to share . . . *interesting*." He slipped his mask on, and they headed for the water together. "Be careful," he said before lowering himself in.

"You too."

He quickly found the barrel Megan's leg had been stuck in. They were going to need to haul it out. He pulled the flashlight from his side zipper pocket. Austin was right. A sandbar wove in an erratic line away from his line of sight, but the barrel Megan had been stuck in sat smack in the middle of it—just high enough to grab the girl's leg.

As he approached the barrel, he felt several quick tugs at his elbow. Austin.

She swam a few yards away and pointed toward a submerged outcropping.

He swam to her side, and his eyes grew wide.

# THIRTY

Caleb's flashlight shifted to rest on another barrel, then another and another.

Austin's chest squeezed. There had to be at least a half dozen around the outcropping. Only the one had landed on the sandbar.

She followed the flashlight's circle as it landed on dead fish—tarpons, black drum, and butterfish—all dotting the sandy bottom of the sound's floor.

Pulling his underwater camera from his dive pouch, Caleb snapped pictures of the barrels and dead fish. Lifting a lifeless rigid tarpon, he tucked it into his pouch and pointed to the surface.

With hesitation at leaving the barrels without a full examination, she followed him to the surface. He was just trying to keep them safe. Whatever killed the fish could endanger them. They needed to pull the barrels from the water and test the contents, in addition to collecting and testing a surface-water sample. Hopefully, the blood sample Lucy sent from Happy Paws would provide answers as well.

Caleb hopped onto her dock with a quick swoop and extended his hand. "Come on," he said before she could argue.

She reached out her hand, and he effortlessly pulled her up as if she were a weightless rag doll. She'd never felt particularly petite, but compared to his tall stature, wide handspan, long legs, and broad shoulders, she was certainly feeling so now.

She handed him one of the towels she'd set atop the pylon.

"Thanks." He swiped it over his face and strode toward shore.

"Are your brothers as tall as you?" she asked, her bare feet freezing in the cold December air.

"I don't have any brothers."

"Tall sisters, then?"

"One sister." He lowered his hand to his side, his grasp tightening on the yellow terry towel. "She's about your size."

She narrowed her eyes. "*My* size?" She couldn't help herself. She loved arguing with the man, so she took just about every opportunity to provoke him and didn't feel a bit bad about it. As much as he provoked her, it was certainly mutual.

He raised his brows, looking down at her. "You know what I mean."

She did, but the furrowing of his brow when he was frustrated with her was oddly appealing.

What was it about this man that had gotten under her skin in the most delightful way?

When he reached Austin's patio, Caleb immediately started making phone calls.

"Hey, Caleb. Enjoying your day off?" Noah asked.

"I tried, I really did. It's a long story, but Austin and I found a half dozen barrels of what I'm assuming is chemical waste dumped into the sound behind Austin's house. I'd bet money there are more littered about the sound."

"I'm sorry to hear that."

Caleb sighed. "Yeah, unfortunately, the barrels are corroded, and their contents are leaking into the water. I'd say we've found the source of the neighborhood pets' illness. I've called in the *Diligence* and its support vessels that can fit back into the shallower depths. I know you ordered me to take the day off, but I'd like to stay and see this through."

"Of course you'd find work to do on your day off."

Caleb chuckled. "You know me."

"Don't worry about leaving to run the samples in. I'll ask Em to swing by when she has time."

"Is that your way of keeping me from heading into the station?"

"It is your day off, though I think that concept is lost on you."

He couldn't argue.

"Since you did land in the middle of a case though, you should brief us at tonight's case board."

"Yes, sir."

"It's in my room again, for the last time, thank goodness. I'm ready to blow this popsicle stand."

Caleb smiled. He hadn't heard that saying since he was a kid. "I'll be there."

"1700, and bring Austin. She's part of the barrel investigation too."

He tried to keep his smile from widening. He wasn't at all happy about the chemical waste sitting in the sound off Austin's backyard—it was horrible—but the thought of working another case with her, of being with her day in and out, warmed him. "Will do," he said.

"Make sure you take the proper precautions. You don't know what's leaking out of those barrels."

Austin paced while they waited for the crane retrieval ship Caleb had called for. Her limbs were warm despite the damp chill in the air. The wet suit protected her body, but not her cheeks or soaked hair.

How could someone do this? She gritted her teeth. She knew how. Because unconscionable men and women existed, and they didn't care who they hurt.

Caleb approached, his eyes narrowing. "You okay?"

"Just mad." She swiped the wet hair off her face. In these temps, it wasn't going to dry anytime soon. "What's the crane ship's ETA?"

"They said they'd be underway in twenty." Caleb looked at his watch. "So . . . forty minutes is a safe bet."

Austin exhaled. Time would crawl.

# THIRTY-ONE

Noah's cell rang again. He answered quickly so it'd stop playing music and moved as fast as he could on his tender leg for the door. Brooke had finally drifted off to sleep, the literary-lines book still clutched in her hand.

He was just happy she'd found some rest.

"Rowley," he whispered, shutting her door behind him.

"Noah?" Mason said.

"Yeah. Sorry. Brooke just fell asleep."

"Hope I didn't wake her."

"I don't think so." He lifted his chin at the head day-shift RN as she passed by, then leaned against the wall beside Brooke's door. "How's the manhunt going?"

"I'd say it just ended," Mason said. "At least for one of the men."

Noah pushed off the wall, regretting the swift movement on his injured leg. "Which one?"

"Saul. Brooke and Logan did a remarkable job on the sketch. Looks just like him, minus being in the water for a while."

"Where'd you find him?"

"He was caught up in the reeds along the shallows—a couple miles downstream from where Brooke waved down the truck," Mason said.

"Any idea on time of death?" Noah asked.

"No. I'm waiting on Finn and Hadley—that man's been working nonstop."

"I know." Noah ran a hand through his hair. Between the shooting victims, the shooters, and several questionable deaths that came through the ER, the morgue was at near capacity. It was no wonder Hadley was backed up on autopsies.

"But," Mason continued, "I'm guessing Saul's body went in the water not long after Brooke was found."

Noah rubbed his chin. "So did the nameless man with Saul kill him, or did someone else take care of them both for failing to kill Brooke?" Praise God they'd failed.

"All the joint jurisdictions, from local police to forest rangers, are still searching the shallows," Mason said. "I'll let you know if the other man is found."

"Thanks. Be careful out there. You don't know who else might be around. Everyone on this case is a potential target."

The 210-foot Coast Guard endurance cutter *Diligence* arrived on scene with the orange retrieval crane on its bow and a series of environmentally friendly containers large enough to fit the barrels inside at its stern. Mooring about a hundred yards beyond the sandbar and hidden shallows, they sent a red skiff for Caleb.

"Hey, Caleb," Petty Officer Greg Nains said, sidling the rubber skiff alongside Austin's weatherworn dock. "Figured you'd want a ride out to the *Diligence*."

Caleb lifted his chin in thanks. "Much appreciated."

"And who's this?" Nains asked with a smile.

"Austin Kelly," she said, holding on to the pylon and extending her hand.

"Pleasure."

Caleb frowned. Was he going to take him out to the *Diligence* or continue flirting with Austin? He couldn't tell if Austin was simply being friendly, or if she was flirting back. After climbing into the skiff, he looked back at her, studying her smile. It was different from how she smiled at him, but he wasn't sure if that was good or bad.

"Ma'am." Nains tipped his hat to her.

She waved as they pushed off, her gaze shifting to Caleb. "You be safe out there."

Was she worried about him?

Watching Nains's reaction to her and seeing her smile back in return still clenched his gut.

The spray of the inlet's brackish water spurting over the skiff's low sides showered him and Nains with heavy drops of water.

He glanced back at Austin. She remained on the dock. Frustration anchored inside him. She was going to freeze if she didn't take a hot shower, dry her wet hair, and get some warm clothes on. The temp was dropping by the minute, the sky shifting to a deep winter gray.

A damp heaviness clung to the air, seeping into his bones despite the wet suit. He prayed she wouldn't be her stubborn self and remain outside for the duration of the retrieval, but he knew better. Now he was the worried one.

A thick blanket of depressing gray covered the sky as the cold earth penetrated the soles of Austin's neoprene boots.

Time ticked achingly slow as the orange retrieval crane lifted one barrel at a time—each one encased in a containment vessel by Caleb and the other hazmat diver. Soon the rusted barrels would be out of their water, but the damage had already been done. Clear bubbles of hazardous liquid had pooled in puddles on the water's surface above the men.

*Hurry up, Caleb.* She wanted him out of the water, safely decontaminated on the *Diligence*, and back at her side in warm clothes. Though he'd be equally frustrated she'd remained outside rather than taking a hot shower and slipping on warm clothes. But she'd grabbed a blanket and a hot cup of coffee—at least that was something. But she wasn't going inside until he was topside. Concern for his safety gnawed at her gut as she tapped her foot. *How much longer?*

"Come on," she whispered under her breath.

"Come on?" Emmy asked, making her jump. Her heart thudded, a splash of coffee rolling off her hand.

"Sorry," Emmy said. "I didn't mean to startle you."

Had she seriously been that focused on Caleb that she hadn't noticed someone—even if it was someone with the lightest step she'd ever heard—approaching?

Emmy's brows furrowed. "Please tell me you've taken a warm shower since you called me?"

"I'll shower when this is all wrapped up."

"Honey, you're freezing, and with the chemicals . . ."

"I'll be okay. They've got to be nearly done."

"Okay, but shower well. I hate to think of your and Caleb's exposure to whatever is in those barrels."

"He's still down there."

Emmy's already big eyes opened wider still. "What?"

"He's in hazmat gear, but he's directing the barrel retrieval."

"Of course he is." Emmy exhaled. "Frustrating man."

Austin laughed. "Aren't they all?" Though she swore Caleb was far more so than any other man she'd crossed paths with. He had a way of burrowing under her skin. At first it had felt like a chigger, but now . . . it was in a yummy goosebumps sort of way. How that happened, she had zero clue.

"Austin?" Em asked.

"Yeah. Sorry. Dazed out there a minute."

Em pursed her lips, no doubt in an attempt to smother her

smile, but she failed miserably. Leave it to Em to recognize her feelings for Caleb, probably well before she had herself.

"Let's get you those samples," Austin said, trying to redirect her focus. "They're on my back porch. Follow me."

The sooner Emmy identified what they were dealing with, the sooner they could hunt down those responsible.

# THIRTY-TWO

Caleb pulled off the hazmat suit, inhaling a deep breath of fresh air. How long had it been? He glanced at his watch—1330.

As expected, Austin remained in her yard—still in her wet suit, her hair still damp. He'd never met a more perpetually frustrating woman in his life.

Nains sidled up beside him. "Beautiful woman you've got there."

"*I've* got?" Caleb said before realizing the words had left his mouth. Adrenaline shot heat through Caleb's veins, flooding him with hope he hadn't realized how desperately he desired.

"Yeah. No one stays out in the cold that long without a reason." Nains looked at him and sighed. "She's clearly into you."

Within fifteen minutes, Caleb was thanking Nains for the ride back to Austin's dock. She met him at the end of it.

"What are you doing?" he asked. "Why didn't you go in and shower," he continued before she could respond, "get into warm clothes?"

She braced her hands on her hips, her right foot tapping. "The suit is made for cold temps."

"You still should have showered and gotten warm. It's been hours and you had nothing to do."

Her chin lifted, her brows arching.

"With the retrieval, I mean."

"This is my backyard. My dog. My neighbors' kids." Pink flushed her pale cheeks.

Good. At least some color was returning to her face. He fought the inexplicable urge to pull her in his arms and warm her.

"This is personal," she said.

That he got. "Fine. Now that the retrieval is completed, can we get warm?"

Red deepened her cheeks. "We?"

He cleared his throat. "I meant . . ." He swallowed. "Would it be okay if I used one of your showers?"

"Sure."

"Thanks."

Austin strode up the slope toward her house, Dirk jumping up and wagging his tail at her approach.

"He's looking better," Caleb said.

Her stiff shoulders softened as she bent to pet Dirk in her screened patio. "Thankfully."

He smiled as she sat back on her heels, Dirk climbing in her lap. "Did Emmy come by for the samples?" Surely before now.

Austin nodded. "Yeah, about a half hour ago."

"Great." He raked a hand through his hair, water sprinkling off his fingers. Maybe if he went first, she'd follow suit and take a hot shower. "Is it okay if I . . ." He pointed to her back door.

"Right." She sat Dirk on the clay patio tile beside her and got to her feet. "Follow me."

Heat wafted over Caleb as he trailed her inside with Dirk lumbering behind him.

"Could you grab the door?" she asked over her shoulder.

"Yep."

Opening the powder room door, she stepped to the teal armoire.

"That looks like Rissi's work," he said. She refinished and distressed older furniture.

"It is." Austin smiled. "I love her house and asked if I could hire her to refinish a few pieces for me. Of course, she refused to let me pay her." Austin opened the door and pulled out a fluffy white bath towel and washcloth, handing them to him.

"Sounds like Ris."

Austin looked down, tracing her finger over the now-closed armoire door. "Not that it's any of my business, but . . ."

He furrowed his brows. "But . . . ?"

She cleared her throat, her gaze finally meeting his. "Are you over Rissi? I know she's with Mason, but Emmy said you'd had pretty strong feelings for her?"

Blindsided by the question, he bumbled out the truth. "Yes. I had feelings for her, but in retrospect they were more feelings of closeness, a friendly affection at most."

"And now?"

"I respect her as a colleague. I'm very happy for her and Mason. Any feelings I had beyond friendship for her are definitely gone." Warmth spread through his chest. "Why do you ask?"

Looking down again, Austin shifted her foot across the thick rug. "Just curious." She gazed back up at him, her green eyes the color of the sea glass he had on the wind chimes Emmy had made for him and each of the team members, but all unique and different. Just like Austin—unique and different from anyone he'd ever met.

"Curiosity goes with the job," she added. "I'll let you . . ." She pointed at the shower curtain as she headed for the door.

He fought the undeniable urge to pull her into his arms, but he reluctantly restrained himself.

She paused with her hand on the open door's handle. "I'll see you in a bit."

He nodded and switched the shower on to cold.

# THIRTY-THREE

Austin unlocked her downtown office door, flipping on the wall switch, illuminating her desk lamp. She was old school, preferring antique lamps to bright overhead lighting.

Cherrywood bookcases lined with burgundy, forest green, and navy book spines exuded the feel of a library, where she felt at home.

A chill bit through the office building, and Austin cranked up the space heater. "It shouldn't take long to warm up," she said as Caleb followed her in. He smiled—a different way than she had seen before—like anticipation hovered in it.

"Could you close the door?" she asked. "It'll help it warm up faster."

"No problem."

The door creaked shut, and his footsteps moved toward her, halting mere inches behind her. The scents of honey and vanilla swirled about him. Why'd she buy such good-smelling soap for her hall bath? Because she never would have pictured Caleb in her shower. Not that she pictured . . .

Heat rushed up her throat, spreading through her cheeks. She sped to the mini fridge and bent, pulling out two bottled waters. Their food order from the restaurant in the building's lobby wouldn't be ready for a little bit, and her parched throat couldn't wait until the two-liter of Coke she'd ordered with it arrived.

She straightened, her back still to him. "Want anyth—?" She squeaked as she turned and found him barely a breath from her.

"You're flushed. Are you all right?" His already-deep voice had dropped a register.

She blinked and nodded. "I . . ." Words failed her. She cleared her throat, finding her voice—at least a whisper of it. "Did you want anything?" She held out the water bottle, but instead of taking it, he rested his hand over hers.

She tilted her head. "What are you doing?"

"Something I've longed to do since the day we met." Reaching up, he cupped her face, his fingers warm and caressing.

She swallowed, unable to move.

He lowered his warm lips to hers.

Her dizzying head struggled to determine where one kiss began and another ended.

Her office door creaked open, jarring both of them.

Caleb pulled back. His hand fixed his gun's grip. "Can I help you?"

Austin's gaze met that of Ian—the sixteen-year-old son of DeNucci's Pizza Parlor's owner.

"L-lunch?" Ian's voice cracked at Caleb's approach. He held up the plastic bag in one hand, the two-liter of Coke resting in the crook of his other arm. "Sorry. Miss Kelly says never to worry about knocking. I didn't mean to . . ."

"All good," Caleb said, pulling out his wallet and handing Ian what looked like a ten from her vantage point. "Thanks."

Her hand free, she untwisted the cap on her water bottle and took a swig, trying to settle her rapidly beating heart.

He turned. "You hungry?"

She didn't want the kissing to end, but she really needed to clear her head. "Yeah." She nodded, hoping lunch would give her time to get her thoughts straight.

"Over there?" Caleb asked, indicating her round conference table, with four straight-back chairs encircling it.

She nodded. How could he seem so calm? Her insides were a fluttery mess.

He unpacked the bag, the scents of peppers, onions, and spicy spread mixed in the air. DeNucci's made the best Italian cheesesteaks.

She looked to the cup of pens in the center of the table, heat rushing her cheeks afresh.

She chewed on the ends of her pens whenever she paused while writing. It was a terrible habit she'd had since Mrs. Kendrick's first-grade math class. A nervous habit she couldn't seem to shake. She looked back at the cup full of chewed pen ends, and Caleb followed her gaze. The heat deepened in her cheeks. She must look like a beet. She always tucked the cup away before anyone entered her office, replacing it with one of the solid pens on the shelf to her right. But this visit had been unexpected. Just as the dizzying kiss had been.

She opened the foil around her sub, the peppery scent swirling in the air.

Caleb left his sub unopened. Instead, he picked up one of her pens and twirled it in his fingers.

*Great.* He knew she had a nervous habit.

This from a man who didn't have a single discernible one. In fact, the man never seemed nervous at all. She'd never met anyone steadier, but there had to be a reason he guarded his emotions so tightly.

Come to think of it, she'd rarely seen him laugh. Though he'd been smiling quite a bit more lately. Did that kiss mean she was the reason, or was that just wishful thinking?

Brooke woke after yet another restless nap that had lasted under twenty minutes. Noah wished he could calm her with his presence. At times it seemed he did, but the nightmares still plagued her. It was expected, given what had happened—one tragedy rapidly after another. He'd give anything for the haunting memories to stop. But it would take time.

"Sweet Home Alabama" played, and he retrieved his cell and walked to the door but didn't move into the hall. Mason again. Maybe he'd found the second man. "Hey, Mason, what ya got?"

Mason exhaled on the other end of the line.

Never a good start.

"I'm almost positive we found the place they held her."

Pain coiled his muscles. "Where?"

"In an old boathouse—large enough to store several boats, but none were in it. It's about a mile and a half from where she entered the road."

"What did you find there?"

"The only things in the building were a small table and a knocked-over chair." Mason was silent a moment. "There was blood on the chair."

Noah shut his eyes, trying not to envision what they'd done to the woman he loved.

"I'm sorry," Mason said.

Noah nodded, but words strangled in his throat.

Thankfully, Mason continued on. "Finn took samples. We'll need a sample of Brooke's to compare."

"Okay."

Brooke was studying him, but he'd hold off on telling her until he finished his call and could give her his undivided attention. "I'll have someone here take the sample. Send Em over to pick it up ASAP. She's running water samples from Caleb and Austin's chemical dumping case, but I want this to be priority one."

"Chemical dumping?" Mason said, surprise clinging to his voice.

"Long story. They'll explain at case board tonight."

"Roger that. I'll call Em now."

"Any other evidence?"

Mason exhaled. "Finn's working the rest of the building, but so far not a thing. Whoever these guys are, it seems they got in and out with barely a trace."

"Finn said he'll bring the crime-scene photos and an up-close pic of the man we assume to be Saul to case board. Hopefully, Brooke can ID him."

Noah prayed the same, prayed she'd be able to ID him from the photograph. Seeing the man who'd nearly killed her in the flesh at the morgue would surely be far more disturbing.

"Thanks, Mason," he said. "We'll see you at case board."

The call disconnected, and Noah turned to find Brooke still studying him.

"Evidence of what?" she asked. "What did Mason find?" She clutched the blanket between her fingers.

Noah reached out, and she placed her hand in his.

"He thinks he found where they held you."

She looked at the window, but he didn't miss the tear running down her cheek. She swiped at her face with her free hand.

"Hey." He caressed her palm with the pad of his thumb. "We'll get through this. I'll be here every step of the way." And then? The thought of not . . . of Brooke not being permanently in his life. Of her not being his and he not being hers . . . it was too painful to think on. He loved her, and she needed him, so he'd be there as long as she wanted him, and if after learning the truth about his past and his future . . . if she walked away then, he'd understand. It would kill him, but he'd understand.

Tears tumbled down Brooke's cheeks.

He ever-so-gently cupped her unbruised cheek. "I've got you."

She nodded.

He took a stiff inhale, hating to pull her back to the painful conversation, but she needed to be aware. "Em's going to need to come get a blood sample to compare to what they found."

"Sample?" She furrowed her brow. "I heard you mention needing to take a sample, but what did they . . . oh . . ." Her lips tightened. "Blood?"

He nodded, fighting back the hot tears pricking his eyes. He couldn't let her know how much what she'd endured—what they'd put her through—ate him alive.

# THIRTY-FOUR

A knock rapped on Brooke's hospital room door, and she jolted.

Noah stood, placing himself between her and the door.

*Great.* Her stupid reaction caused one of alert in him.

"Yes?" Noah said, grabbing his sidearm from its case on the windowsill.

"It's Mason."

"Come in," Brooke called.

Noah's taut stance settled, and he laid his gun back in its case. He was half tempted to wear a side holster with his pjs.

Mason entered with a manila folder in hand.

Her heart thumped erratically. Was that the folder. Was *he* in it?

"Noah, could I borrow you a moment?" Mason asked.

Noah looked to her.

"Of course," she said, giving Mason the closest thing to a smile she could muster.

"I'll be right back," Noah said.

The thumping in her chest spread to her eardrums, the sound erratic.

She hated that fear bounced in her gut whenever Noah stepped from the room, hated that what had happened during the last few days made her uncomfortable being alone. She was a soldier, a medic, and normally a strong woman, but now she felt innately vulnerable, and she hated it.

"Hey there," Noah said, returning with the folder in his hand.

She swallowed.

"Mason thought you'd probably prefer to look at these images in here."

"That's very thoughtful of you both, but I'd rather come to case board."

Noah's brow furrowed. "Are you sure?"

"Positive." Because she was far more likely to keep from bursting into tears in front of the whole team. "It'll be nice to get out of this room and to see everyone and feel useful."

She'd called Oscar to let him know she'd be discharged tomorrow and was ready to return to duty—Blotny's objection aside. But he'd informed her she was on a two-week leave to recuperate.

She'd respectfully insisted she was fine, but he didn't budge. Compared to Noah's injury, her wounds were nothing—and he was returning to full duty tomorrow. Oscar was no doubt concerned about the mental and emotional effects of the trauma she'd experienced, and it flat-out frustrated her. But she had no say in the matter. The decision had been made, and she'd been sidelined.

But she could try to be helpful to Noah and his team. Anything to be useful and anything to catch the men involved.

Noah's phone buzzed with an incoming text from Mason, letting him know the team—plus Austin, but minus Finn, who was waiting on some last-minute results at the lab—was ready for case board in his hospital room whenever he was ready.

He worried about Brooke, about the pain and nightmares

the case-board pictures might trigger, but he respected her decision to be present.

"You ready?" he asked.

"Yes." She climbed from bed and slipped into her robe. "I'm probably the first person to attend a case board in pjs."

He smiled. How did she do that? Carry such light inside after such darkness had attacked her? "Well, I'm guessing I'm the only boss to attend case board in flannel lounge pants and a long-sleeve T." He winked.

She chuckled and the sound did his heart good.

"We make quite a pair," she said with the soft hint of a smile.

Yes, they did.

"All right, folks," he said, entering the room with Brooke at his side. "Let's get started."

"Come sit by me, Brooke," Emmy said, patting the chair beside her.

"Thanks," Brooke said, lowering into the chair as Rissi took the one on the other side of her. That's why he loved his team—everyone was going out of their way to let Brooke know she was one of them. Not an official part of the investigative team, but an adopted member of their team family.

"Caleb and Austin, why don't you start us off?" He'd decided to begin with their case to give Brooke some time to settle in.

Austin and Caleb walked to the whiteboard. Caleb held the packet of case photos but gestured for her to begin.

"This started with my dog, Dirk, getting sick."

"I'm sorry," Emmy said, her face scrunching.

"Thank you," Austin said. "Turns out Dirk isn't the only pet in our neighborhood getting sick. Five other dogs along my side of the street have as well. Our houses all back to the sound. My vet ran some tests and saw something in his blood but had no idea what it was."

Caleb picked up the explanation. "I went out to take a sample

---

from the sound, and two neighbor kids were struggling in the water."

"In December?" Rissi said. "That water is freezing without the right wet suit."

"Apparently they were throwing a ball in the yard before school, and it went into the sound. The beastly wind we've been fighting was pushing it farther from land, and they decided to take a canoe out to retrieve it. Megan fell in the water trying to grab hold of it. Unable to climb over the side to get back in, she spotted the barrel. She thought standing on it would help her get in the tipsy canoe, but her foot busted through, and everything unleashed from there."

"Yikes!" Logan said.

"We quickly realized the barrel was leaking some sort of chemical," Caleb said, then explained everything through the USS *Diligence*'s retrieval of the barrels. "We only found half a dozen barrels, but we fear there are more out there, considering the vastness of the sound and its access to the ocean." It was hard to think of how devastating the full picture might be, especially not knowing the mystery chemical's toxicity.

Caleb glanced at Austin, and she stepped forward. "Emmy is analyzing the sample taken from the barrels, along with samples of the surface water and Dirk's blood." She looked back at Caleb, and he nodded. "We anticipate the three being a match."

"I hope to still have the results before the day is completely over, but I will for sure have them for you tomorrow morning." Emmy picked up a folder.

"Anything else on the chemical case?" he asked Caleb.

"No, boss."

"Good job, both of you." Noah inclined his head toward Austin.

"Thanks," she smiled as she and Caleb retook their seats.

Noah looked to Emmy. "You mentioned you'd found something on our last call?"

"Yes, sir." She stood, indicating the whiteboard.

"Please." Noah gestured to it.

"I think I've got something on the branding symbol."

"Wonderful," he said, thankful they were finally making traction on the shooting.

Em clipped several images to the whiteboard, and Noah studied them. One was of the branding mark picture he'd sent to Em of John Doe One's upper left arm. The other was a hand-drawn image of the same mark with three interlocking triangles.

"It took some digging, but I found the mark." Em smiled. "It's a Viking symbol called a valknut. It translates as 'the knot of the slain.' The Vikings believed that people who lived regular day-to-day lives ended up in a shadowy existence after death. However, those who died valiantly in battle would live on in Valhalla."

"Died valiantly in battle?" Noah said, tucking his chin in. "So we're looking at men who consider themselves warriors? Men who view what they did to be some valiant battle?"

"I'm afraid so." She nodded. "I've started researching, and it turns out some tattoo parlors offer branding. I'm scouring the area to see if any local ones do."

"Great work, Em," Noah said, disturbed at the notion of burning an image into oneself. "Keep on it."

# THIRTY-FIVE

"Okay." Noah cleared his throat. "Mason, you're up." A suffocating weight pressed down on him. Knowing what Brooke was about to face, he wished he could take all the pain and sorrow about to engulf her away. He'd happily carry it for her if he could.

Mason nodded and stood. With an exhale, he pulled the photographs from the packet and stuck them to the board—all except one.

Brooke blinked rapidly. Noah moved to her side as Mason strode over with Saul's photo and offered it to Brooke. She took it with a shaky hand.

"Is this one of the men on the boat with you?" Mason asked.

"Yes." Her voice quivered, and Noah fought the overwhelming urge to pull her into his arms, but he had to maintain propriety as team leader.

"Is this the man you saw chasing you once you escaped?" Mason asked.

"Yes . . . he was the closest." Her shoulders stiffened, and a few tears slipped down her cheeks.

Noah stood, grabbed the box of Kleenex, and stepped over to hand her several.

"Thanks." She swiped her face, then held the Kleenex in

her free hand, Saul's crime-scene photo clutched in the other. "I'm okay," she said to Mason, indicating for him to continue.

"You sure?" Mason asked.

"Yes." She nodded.

"Just to confirm," Mason said, doing his job thoroughly, "this is the man you heard called Saul?"

"Yes." Brooke nodded.

"Thank you," Mason said, gently taking the picture back and moving for the whiteboard.

Emmy reached over and clasped Brooke's hand, now free of the picture.

"Unfortunately, his prints didn't bring anything back." Mason sighed. "Neither did running his picture through the national databases, but we're hoping that when Hadley is able to get to his autopsy, dentals will bring back a hit."

"Thank you," Noah said before turning to Brooke. "I can take you back to your room now."

"I'm good with staying," she said. "If that's okay."

He lowered his head and his voice. "That's fine, but are you sure?"

She nodded. "Positive."

"Okay." Clearing his throat, he shifted gears to the next facet of their case, thankful that the most difficult part for Brooke was over.

"Rissi," he said, "please update us on your portion of the investigation."

"Certainly." She stood and moved to the whiteboard. "I'm continuing to interview everyone in the building at the time of the shooting." She lifted the top two sheets on her clipboard. "I've got four guardsmen left to question."

*Impressive.* "You're making swift progress," he said. "Is there anything that stands out to you so far? Anything odd or out of place?"

"Actually, yes." She placed three photos on the last square of real estate on the board. The first was a picture of three bodies with yellow crime-scene markers, their black numerals noting the various areas of the scene. The second was of a hallway, and the third, intriguingly, was a sketch diagram of Stiller Hall—no doubt Logan's meticulous handiwork.

Rissi turned to face the team. "If you'll recall, I previously met with a Mrs. Talbot about her husband and fellow instructors who were shot in the meeting room adjacent to the main hall. At the time, we considered the anomaly but didn't focus on what it might mean."

She took a deep breath and looked at her notes. "Mrs. Talbot contacted me this morning. She remembered a couple details she hadn't mentioned in our initial interview. She said when the shooters rushed by her, one of them pulled open the meeting-room door and said, 'This is it.' She hid behind a couch when the shooting started, and when they left the room, one said, 'That should take care of it.'"

Rissi looked to Noah. "I'm not sure if this will lead to anything yet, but I'll do some checking to see if I can find any links." Rissi's face softened. "I feel bad for Mrs. Talbot. She's really struggling to come to grips with the fact that she's still alive when her husband and his fellow instructors were killed so close by. She said it's like the shooters passed over her and chose them."

"She makes a solid point," Emmy said, her nose scrunched in thought. "Why *would* they pass by her but murder the three men in the room right next to her?" Em exhaled. "I guess we never know how close to death we really are. God knows, but we don't."

Everyone turned toward Logan, as this was the part where he typically made a snide comment or huffed at the concept of a loving God in control when atrocities happened. But nothing. Logan just sat there with his notes, surprising them all.

Brooke leaned forward, studying the case board with a frown. "Wait a minute—did you say Lieutenant Talbot?"

175

Rissi rechecked her notes. "Yep."

"Ken Talbot?" Brooke asked.

Rissi returned to her notes. "Yes, and his wife's name is—"

"Mari," Brooke said. "Well, her given name is Marigold, but everyone called her Mari during the investigation."

Noah frowned. "Investigation?"

"Yeah . . ." She looked around the room. "None of you are familiar with the case?"

Everyone shook their head or answered in the negative.

"I suppose it was before you all were stationed here," she said.

"Can you tell us about it?" Noah asked. It probably had nothing to do with their case, but she had him intrigued.

"Sure," she said, smoothing the thighs of her flannel jammies. "It was around eight years ago, not long after I started medic school," she said, standing and moving to inspect the photograph closer. "Yes," she said, pointing at each body in turn. "Ken Talbot, Alex . . . Ford, I think."

"That's right," Rissi said, skimming her notes.

"And Rich Sydell," Brooke said, pointing at the final instructor in the grouping.

"You knew them all," Noah said rather than asked.

"Yeah. They left quite an impression. They were the three IT instructors Scott Mirch implicated in his trial for the theft of cryptocurrency from the military."

"Someone stole cryptocurrency from the *military*?" Logan asked. "Which branch?"

She paused a moment. "Air Force."

"Can we back up for those of us with only a vague idea of cryptocurrency, and no idea of who Scott Mirch is?" Caleb asked.

"Sorry. I didn't mean to interrupt your flow of conversation. What happened with Scott was long ago. I'm sure it has no bearing on any of this." She shifted her stance. "Though it is odd. . . . Nope. Sorry." She looked to Rissi. "Go ahead, continue on. I'll head back to my seat."

"No," the entire group said in unison.

"We need to hear what you started," Rissi said. "You never know when something that might seem unrelated is actually very related."

"Okay." Brooke shrugged.

"Here." Rissi rolled the empty stool over and raised it for Brooke to sit by the whiteboard. "Take a seat and catch us up to speed on Scott Mirch."

"I met Scott soon after I arrived for Flight Medic A-School. He was here for IT C-School. He was a computer genius."

"And a hacker," Logan said, looking at his laptop. "It's all here online. I can't believe I haven't heard of this before."

# THIRTY-SIX

"Initially, it was all hush-hush," Brooke explained, "but whispers started circulating that someone had hacked into the Air Force's cryptocurrency . . . I don't know . . . account, I guess is the right term. They stole . . . a lot, though I'm not sure of the exact amount."

Logan tapped on his laptop, then looked up. "Close to five million dollars," he said.

Noah gaped. "Five million?"

"Worth five million then. In today's market . . . depending on the company they were traded through . . ." Logan said. "Okay, here it is, Alatheum."

"That's it," Brooke said.

"In today's market"—Logan's fingers danced over his laptop keys—"that would be the equivalent of fifty-five million dollars."

"Fifty-five million?" Mason said, his jaw slack.

Noah shifted in his seat. The amount *was* incredible, but it was more prudent to stick with Brooke's personal knowledge of the investigation. "Brooke," he said, "what do you remember about Scott and these three instructors?"

"Early on in the investigation all the evidence pointed to Scott, but the reason the prosecutor claimed Scott committed the crime was sad."

"What was the reason?" Noah asked.

"Something about Scott believing the military betrayed his dad."

Noah frowned. "Any idea why he'd think that?"

"Sorry," she said with a shrug. "It's been some time. And if I remember right, that was just a news blip I caught from the trial's news coverage."

"You didn't attend the trial?"

"No." She shook her head. "Scott and I weren't close. We shared lunch in the mess hall between classes now and again as we had a mutual friend. He seemed like a nice kid, though."

"Kid?" Noah arched a brow.

"Very early twenties, at most. I think he entered the Guard right out of high school."

Logan walked up to the whiteboard and tapped on the picture of the three bodies in the meeting room. "You said these three guys were implicated?"

"Yeah. When they arrested Scott, he plea-bargained, naming his coconspirators—Talbot, Ford, and Sydell."

"So they went to trial?" Rissi asked.

"No, but I believed Scott was telling the truth about their involvement."

Before Noah could ask why, Logan began. "It says here that Scott insisted these guys helped him hack into the military's black box and steal the cryptocurrency." Logan's gaze raced back and forth across his laptop screen.

"Did Scott ever claim he was innocent of the crime?" Mason asked.

"No. Just that he didn't do it alone," Brooke said. "Which is a big part of why I believed him. He wasn't trying to play innocent for something he did, and the three instructors had an interesting alibi."

"Which was?" Noah asked.

"Something about a group hangout with their wives."

Logan frowned. "So they claimed to be each other's alibi?"

"And their wives," Brooke added. "The kicker for me was when our mutual friend, Jack, talked about it as we continued having lunch together most days. He was an IT C-School student as well. He was convinced it had to be more than a one-man job."

"Is Jack still on base?" Noah asked. "I'd like to have a chat with him."

Brooke shook her head. "He mustered out when his reenlistment was up. I haven't seen him for years."

"Em," he said. "See if you can track Jack . . . ?"

"Milhorn," Brooke supplied his last name. "I heard he settled in one of North Carolina's beach towns but no clue which."

"Thanks," Em said. "The parameters help."

Em was their resident tracker. Well, she and Logan combined.

"I'll give Leavenworth a call, speak with Scott Mirch. See what he has to say," Noah said, jotting down some quick notes. "I'll also reach out to the original CGIS agent on Scott Mirch's case."

"I can pull the papers and news footage from the time," Emmy offered.

"That would be helpful," Noah said.

"And I can dig a little deeper into the three instructors and the crime. See how it was pulled off. See if I concur with Jack's assessment that it was more than a one-man job," Logan said. "And I can pay a visit to Marigold Talbot, get her take on the investigation of her husband's possible role."

"It's a great idea," Noah said. "Just be sensitive to the situation. She just lost her husband."

"You really think there could be some tie between Scott's theft and the mass shooting?" Brooke asked Noah as they walked back to her room.

Case board had wrapped up nearly an hour ago, but everyone had stayed to eat, chat, and then clean up the room. Tomorrow he and Brooke would be discharged, and things could move on in a more normal fashion. Though after all that had happened, he doubted normalcy would return to their lives anytime soon.

"My gut says there's something there," he said as she hopped back on the bed and pulled off her slippers.

"You follow that a lot, don't you?"

"My gut? I guess what I'm really talking about is a gift I believe God gave me, an instinct for solving crimes."

"This one is certainly branching out in a lot of different paths," she said as she settled back in her bed. Noah fluffed her pillows and straightened out her blanket before taking the recliner beside her.

"That's for sure," he said. "It's anything but straightforward. We've got a theft from the lab apparently synchronized with the shootings, and three men implicated in a long-ago crime they either didn't commit or didn't serve time for, who very well may have been targeted in the shooting."

Every event was a new thread in a spider's vastly expanding web, and he couldn't help but believe someone sat at the center of it.

"All right, Agent Rowley." Brooke's nurse, Amanda, entered the room. "Time for our end-of-shift rounds. I need to take a look at Miss Brooke, and Nurse Pamela is impatiently awaiting you next door."

"Yikes. I best hurry," he said, shuffling for the door. "See you in a bit." He smiled at Brooke and gave her a quick wink.

"You're trouble, you know that, right?" Amanda called as Noah rounded the corner and within a matter of steps entered his room to find Nurse Pamela as described—impatiently waiting.

"All right, mister. Sit up in the bed and slide up those flannel pants. I need to check your wound and freshen your bandages."

He'd argue but knew full well Nurse Pamela would win out.

Brooke was still chuckling about Amanda's comment a handful of minutes after Noah had hightailed it to his room. Case board had been hard but good. It was good being around everyone. Good being part of something.

The connection to Scott Mirch had been a surprise. She hadn't thought about him in years. It was odd, she supposed, about the three instructors being killed as they were—in a room off the back hall. It was like the shooters were after them specifically, and the comments Mrs. Talbot heard only served to back up that theory.

"Did you know they moved that boy to the ward this evening?" Amanda asked, removing the stethoscope from Brooke's back and easing her into a comfortable position.

"Connor Andrews?" Brooke looked over her shoulder at Amanda putting everything she'd used to check Brooke's vitals back in the rolling cart.

Amanda nodded. "He started coming to in the ICU and his vitals stabilized, so they moved him down here. Nurse Pamela got him settled in before seeing to that man of yours."

Brooke's cheeks flushed. "No, Noah and I aren't—"

Amanda cut her off with a knowing hand to the hip and arched brows. "Don't bother arguing, honey. We all know better. Now you rest up."

"So he's awake?" she asked before Amanda could roll her cart fully out of the room.

"Noah?" Amanda frowned.

"No, Connor Andrews."

"Last I heard, but I suspect he's back to resting now. It was touch and go with that one."

Brooke waited until Amanda left, and then another couple of minutes for her nurse to get invested in another patient, before hopping from her bed, sliding her slippers on, and peeking her head out the door.

# THIRTY-SEVEN

Brooke entered the hall. Noah's door was shut. Nurse Pamela must still be in with him. Looking the opposite way up the hall, she spotted a guardsman sitting outside a room about six doors down. She smiled. Connor Andrews's room.

She needed to know what *gator* meant, to know what was so valuable about such an innocuous word that she was abducted and—she swallowed—that she was harmed for it.

She wouldn't talk to Andrews without Noah present, though she was dying to. But it wouldn't hurt anything to talk to the guardsman in front of the room.

She made her way down the hall, her slippers padding softly. The guardsman rose at her approach.

"Hi," she said, "I'm Petty Officer Brooke Kesler."

He pulled off his hat and held it in his hands. "I know who you are, ma'am. Petty Officer First Class Macken. Pleased to meet you."

*Great.* The entire base probably knew about her abduction. She didn't know why that embarrassed her. It hadn't been her fault, and she hadn't done anything wrong. . . .

No, she knew full well why she felt that way. She'd broke, told them the word Connor Andrews whispered to her. They hadn't reacted to it verbally, but there had been a good pause before they started pressing her, torturing her, to find out if she knew anything else, or if she'd told anyone what Connor had said.

If she'd just mentioned it to Noah or one of the team, maybe it all could have been avoided.

"I'm sorry," she said, looking up at the guardsman. "Where are my manners." She reached out her hand. "Nice to meet you too."

Clutching his hat in one hand, he shook her extended one with his other.

"I'm just curious if he's spoken yet," she said, hoping Macken would be willing to share even if Noah wasn't at her side. She glanced back down the hall, but Noah's door was still shut.

"Nurse Pamela was the first one in after Andrews woke up," Macken said.

"Do you have any idea what he said?"

"She left the door open, so I heard most, if not all of it. It was just basic stuff."

She looked back down the hall. How much longer was Noah going to be? "So that was it?"

"Yes, but he might be saying more to the nurse who's in there now. He went in seconds before you arrived but closed the door, so I haven't heard anything."

Brooke's gut clenched. A second nurse. That wasn't right. Not if Pamela was assigned to Andrews's room.

Her body tensed. "Something's wrong."

Macken turned to open the door, but before he could, it opened from the other side.

The nurse—a male in blue scrubs—stood in the doorway.

"Sir, I need you to step over here," Macken said, his hand on his service weapon.

The nurse's gaze landed on Brooke, and a weird expression crossed his face. "I'm needed down the hall," he said.

A chill rippled through her body. She knew that voice.

"That's him," she hollered. The gravelly-voiced man who'd tortured her.

The man bolted for the emergency exit, busting through the door and setting the shrill alarm blaring.

Macken ran after him, and without thought Brooke followed.

"Brooke! Stop," Noah hollered from down the hall. "Stop!" His voice grew closer.

*I can't let him get away!* She burst through the emergency exit and caught sight of Macken racing down the stairs and only a flash of the man's blue scrubs as he rounded another level.

Noah hobbled as fast as his wounded leg would carry him, but Brooke was rounding the next level down when he finally made it into the stairwell, red lights flashing from the triggered emergency-exit alarm.

"Brooke!" he bellowed, his voice nearly drowned out by the shrieking alarm. He started to rush down the steps, only to nearly topple headlong down the concrete stairs. He had to move faster. He sat on his bum and slid down step-by-step at as rapid a pace as he could manage. Searing pain throbbed in his thigh, but he had to keep moving.

The pounding of footsteps stopped.

Shots fired—one, two, three bursts.

His chest constricted, the air knocked from his lungs.

*Brooke.*

# THIRTY-EIGHT

Her legs and arms trembling, Brooke hurried up the stairs, knowing Noah had followed. She rounded the stairwell onto the second-floor landing and froze.

Noah.

Crimson blood trailed down the steps behind him.

She rushed to his side and knelt down. His thigh was covered with blood. No doubt he'd busted open his stitches. "Are you crazy?"

He cupped the side of her face, his hand sliding along her hair. "You're safe." He closed his eyes for a moment, then opened them—a look of peace settling in his deep, brown eyes.

At the sound of footfalls, she looked back and saw Macken round the corner. "Noah, this is Petty Officer First Class Macken."

"The shots?" Noah asked.

"Hit the emergency door," Macken said, wiping the perspiration from his furrowed brow. "I had a split second to slam it shut before the rounds embedded in the door."

Noah clasped Brooke's hand. "I'll get my CSI man out here pronto. Finn can pull the slugs, and we might learn something."

"It was him," Brooke said, helplessness settling in the pit of her stomach. She'd been at that evil man's mercy, and he'd had none.

Noah's expression hardened. "Who?"

Brooke took a steeling breath. "The man who . . ." She looked at the marks on her arms. "Did this."

"You're sure?" he asked, his jaw tightening.

She nodded, her stomach lurching. "I never saw his face, but I recognized his gravelly voice."

Noah clearly tried to mask his deep concern, but it edged in the creases by his eyes. "Did you see his face now?"

She nodded.

Alarm fixed on Noah's brow.

She could identify her abductor, and the man knew it. She swallowed, needing to cut off those thoughts and focus on the present. "We need to get you back to your room," she said, hoping Noah would let that vein of discussion drop—at least for now.

Working in unison, Brooke and Macken slipped Noah's arms across their shoulders and lifted him up between them.

Halfway up the last flight of stairs, Noah wriggled in their hold. "I can hop the rest of the way."

"Not. Happening." Keeping her focus on Noah and off *him* was critical to her not losing it right now.

"I'm fine," Noah said, his voice tight.

She cocked her head. "Don't make me call Nana Jo." She wasn't playing fair, but she didn't care. His health and safety were what mattered.

His brows arched, but the hint of a smirk tugged at his lips. "That's a little beneath you, don't you think?"

"Whatever it takes for you to listen to reason and let us help you."

He released an exasperated sigh and let them continue, but one step up, he stiffened. "That was Andrews's room he came out of, wasn't it?" he asked Macken.

"Yes, sir."

He wrestled out of her and Macken's grasp and started hopping up the stairs. "We need to check on Andrews!"

As Noah topped the stairs, an earsplitting alarm sounded down the hall.

His jaw clenched. *No!* His gaze fixed on the red light blinking rapidly over a door twenty feet down the hall.

Pamela raced inside, followed by two hospital security guards. Noah hobbled to the door in time to see Connor Andrews convulsing, his wrist cuffed to the bed rail.

"Seizure," Pamela called out as Dr. Greene raced in, his open lab coat flapping about his scrubs.

He barked out orders.

Noah, Brooke, and Macken stepped back from the room and out of the medical team's way.

*Father, I can't believe I'm praying this for a man who took lives, but please let him pull through. We need answers, and he's the only shooter left.*

# THIRTY-NINE

They stood five feet from Connor Andrews's door. The young man lay dead. His head rolled to the side, his lifeless eyes staring in Noah's direction. One by one, the nurses and Dr. Greene filed out.

Noah balled his hands into fists. Determining why the shooters did it and who else was involved just got a million times harder. No fingerprint hits, no physical evidence they could pull DNA off of—but even if they could, Noah doubted it would bring back a hit.

This case was growing more frightening, complex, and frustrating by the minute.

He looked over at Brooke. She could have died chasing after Connor Andrews's killer—her abductor, torturer. Anger seethed, his limbs burning, his thigh blistering in pain.

"You okay?" Brooke asked.

He rubbed his hand over his close crop. "Just frustrated." Incensed that Connor Andrews was dead.

Dr. Greene, now in a fresh set of scrubs, approached them with a clipboard. "Would you like to stay until his body is taken to the morgue, given he was your prisoner?"

"Since foul play was involved, my CSI needs to process the body before the ME takes him," Noah said.

"I understand, but Hadley is quite particular. . . ."

True. "Hadley and our team work together often. I'm sure it won't be a problem."

"All right." Greene handed him the clipboard. "I need you to sign this chain of custody for Mr. Andrews's body until your CSI arrives, then have him sign on until Mr. Andrews's body is released into Hadley's custody."

"We need to get your leg cleaned up," Brooke said.

"I can take care of that for you," Dr. Greene said.

"Thank you," Brooke answered before Noah could argue.

"All right, but we'll need someone to remain with Andrews's body until Finn arrives," Noah said.

"Agreed," Greene said.

Noah stepped into the hall. "Macken, can you stay with Andrews's body until my CSI or Hadley arrives, whoever comes first?"

"Of course," Macken said.

Greene had Macken sign the chain of custody form instead and directed Noah back to his room.

Noah grimaced as Greene examined his wound. They also needed to review the security footage. He prayed there was something there that could lead them to the killer.

When Dr. Greene was finished, Noah returned to the hall to wait by Andrews's door.

"Noah." Hadley nodded as he rounded the corner. "I should have known you'd be here rather than resting."

"This takes precedence." And he'd taken the time—however reluctantly—to have his wound restitched and rebandaged. Greene had ordered antibiotics that would soon be arriving from the hospital pharmacy.

"Why am I not surprised." Hadley shook his head as he entered Andrews's room. Noah followed while Brooke remained just outside the door.

"Word is," Hadley continued, "your prisoner's death wasn't natural."

"Word travels fast around here," Noah said.

"I approach every autopsy the same—without judgment, regardless of what the grapevine says. One clean step at a time."

Noah didn't doubt that. Hadley's work was impeccable.

Hadley rocked back on his heels and turned to Brooke, who was definitely within earshot. "I hope you're able to get this one to settle down long enough to let his leg heal."

Brooke smirked and outed him. "He's on his third set of stitches."

"*Third*?" Hadley's brows rose, and he pinned his all-knowing gaze, or so it felt like, on Noah.

Noah shrugged. What could he say?

Brooke's eyes narrowed, and her mouth opened.

"Caleb!" Noah said, catching sight of his team member, thankful for the distraction.

"Hey, all." Caleb slipped his hands into his jogger pockets. "Finn and I were on the phone when you called in. Since Em had some big plans tonight, he asked if I'd mind helping him process the room. I was right down the street at Ringo's Records, so I'm happy to help."

"Find any?" Noah asked.

"Yeah. Got Kansas's *Leftoverture*."

"'Carry on Wayward Son,'" Brooke said.

"Yeah." Caleb smiled, clearly caught off guard that she knew that.

"What's our wayward son up to now?" Finn appeared in the doorway, rolling his equipment case behind him.

Caleb crossed his arms. "I'd hardly call *me* the wayward one of the team."

"True," Finn said. "But Logan isn't here, and you're next in line."

Caleb followed Finn to Connor's bed, sliding on his examination gloves. "And how do you figure that?"

Finn tipped his head in Noah's direction.

Noah held up his hands. "I'd love to stay and finish this conversation, but I still need to question Macken and Brooke."

He balanced on the bothersome crutch Greene insisted he use, hating the idea of being dependent on it. Brooke had pushed for a wheelchair, but that wasn't happening.

"Let's head to the nurses' station," he said to Brooke and Macken. Hearing their recollections before viewing the security footage would help him better understand the full situation and direct his viewing of the footage.

"Can you run through what happened, starting with the man coming out of Connor Andrews's room?"

Macken explained the order of events, and Brooke fully agreed with his statement.

"Did he turn and fire on you when you reached the bottom of the stairs?" Noah asked.

"No," Brooke said. "There were two men in the back of the van Connor's killer jumped in."

"A van?"

"Yes, sir," Macken concurred.

"The men in the van raised weapons. I pushed her back," he said, looking at Brooke, "and slammed the steel door shut."

"Quick thinking," Noah said, grateful he'd protected Brooke. "Could you see the color of the van?" he continued.

"White," Macken said.

That was not at all surprising. White van sightings had popped up along every curve of their investigation. Noah shifted and regretted the motion as fresh pain shot through his thigh.

"What about any identifying markers?"

"It all happened so fast," Macken said, "but after the shooting stopped, I heard them peel away."

Noah looked to Brooke.

"I only saw the white van and the men in the back for the briefest of seconds before the shooting started."

"Do you think you could identity the two men in the van?"

he asked them both. "Their faces, build, anything to help identify them?"

She shook her head.

"No," Macken said. "Only that they were dressed in black."

So it looked like the best lead was their close-up glimpse
of the man who killed Connor. He hated to put Brooke back
through this, but he had no choice. "Do you think you could
give enough detail of the man posing as a nurse for Logan to
do a sketch?"

"I'll do my best," she said. Beside her, Macken nodded his
agreement.

"I'll give him a call," Noah said, praying the sketch would
lead them to the man. Or even better, that the men or van had
been caught on camera.

# FORTY

Felix Cruz approached the security-station door at the same time as Noah.

"I hope I didn't keep you waiting," Felix said. "Leonard returned from his dinner break, and we made our rounds ensuring the hospital is secure."

"Far more important. I just appreciate you meeting me," Noah said. He supposed two security guards plus one in the booth were plenty for what was normally a quiet local hospital. But not tonight. Tonight, they could have used a whole force.

"I radioed Tom, our man in the booth, to let him know we were coming, but he didn't respond, which isn't like him," Felix said, pulling out his keys. "But he sometimes forgets his radio when he goes to hit the head or grab a soda from the vending machine."

Noah hoped Felix was right, because the body count was continuing to rise. He prayed Tom wasn't part of it.

"I'm assuming you're going to want a copy of all the video footage?" Felix said, unlocking the door.

"That'd be great." His skin pricked, eager to confirm Tom was okay.

Felix opened the door. "Dang fool is asleep." He shook his head and strode toward the chair as if he was about to ream Tom out. Instead, he froze in his tracks, his jaw slackening.

Just as Noah feared. The poor guy had been shot—once to the head, twice to center mass. Likely with a silencer. He highly doubted the booth was soundproof.

Felix stepped back. "I better call the ME to come get Tom . . . his . . . body." He covered his shock with a cough.

"Actually, I'll call up to our crime-scene investigator and have him process the scene before we hand him over to Hadley." Noah shifted his gaze to the monitors—black fuzz with intermittent flakes of white snow. "Looks like we got nothing."

"We have a backup storage device," Felix said. "If they didn't take it, you should still be able to access the footage."

When Logan finished the sketch of the man posing as a nurse, he turned it to face Brooke.

"How's this?" he asked.

Anxiety sucked the air from her lungs, realizing she was staring into the eyes of her torturer.

Noah entered her room wearing a fresh pair of gray Mickey Mouse lounge pants.

She smiled. "The kids?" she asked.

"Owen chose them."

His nephew was everything mouse, Mickey in particular.

"They suit you." Logan smothered a chuckle.

"How'd it go?" Noah asked, moving to her side.

"Hopefully, it's helpful." She shrugged.

"She did great," Logan said, holding up the sketch. "I'll start running his description and face through the database."

"I pray you find a hit," she said. But the way things were going, she wasn't betting on it.

"Brooke?" Emmy said in a rush as she rounded the corner, dressed in a gorgeous, flowing deep purple dress and matching pumps.

"Em," Brooke said. "You look . . ."

"Ravishing," Logan said, then quickly clamped his mouth. All eyes fixed on him.

"I just meant . . . that . . . that she looks . . . nice."

Brooke narrowed her gaze. Logan fumbling for words? That was a first. And was that a flush on his typically fair cheeks?

"Thanks," Em said, not paying the compliment much mind.

Brooke didn't blame her. Logan was a flirt, often playfully with Emmy, but never in a disrespectful way. Though . . . he hadn't been bragging on the number of dates he had of late, at least not when Brooke was around. Come to think of it, she didn't remember him mentioning a date at all for months.

"I heard what happened and wanted to make sure you're all right," Em said, moving toward Brooke's side where Logan sat.

He stood and gestured to the seat.

"Thanks," she said, taking a seat and crossing her legs, her silk dress shifting to reveal a modest slit up her calf.

Logan's gaze filled with something akin to tender affection. She knew he cared about Emmy, but had it become more? She shook off the thought and focused on sweet Emmy coming to make sure she was okay.

"I so appreciate you coming, but I hate that I interrupted whatever you're dressed so beautifully for."

"A date," she said, "but he fully understood. And we'll just reschedule."

"A date with who?" Logan asked.

Again, all three of them shifted their gaze to Logan.

"What?" He shrugged. "I'm just curious."

Emmy looked over at him with a smile. "I don't ask about your dating life."

"I share about my dating life."

"We know," Em said, "but not lately. Someone serious, perhaps?"

"Maybe I haven't been on a date lately," he said, slipping his hands into his well-tailored trousers.

Emmy laughed.

Logan didn't blink.

Emmy stopped and gave him that quizzical stare of hers. "*You* not date for more than a couple days?"

"Okay, folks, let's focus," Noah said.

Brooke wanted to swat him. She wanted to see Emmy's and Logan's verbal jousting play out. But he was the boss.

"Sorry," Emmy said.

"My fault," Logan said. "I'll head to the station and get started running the sketch."

"I appreciate that. I'd say wait until morning, but finding this man is critical."

Brooke studied Noah, not missing the worry in his eyes. He feared for her. She feared for herself now that she could identify the man in command.

"And I'll get started on the video footage," Emmy said, uncrossing her legs and standing.

"How did you—" Noah began.

"Ris told me."

"Again, I'd say wait until morning, but . . ."

"I'm on it," Emmy said.

Noah handed her the black video storage box.

"I guess I'll work at the station too," Em said, shifting her gaze to Logan, who hadn't been able to take his eyes off her, "if you don't mind giving me a ride in. My date dropped me off here."

"No problem," he said. "And when you're ready to head home, I'll take you."

"Thanks." She turned back to Brooke. "I'm so glad you're okay." She leaned down and gave her a hug.

Brooke hugged her friend back.

"I hope you're able to find something," Noah said.

"Hopefully we'll get a plate number or at least a better look at the van," Emmy said. "We're getting closer, Noah. I can feel it."

"I hope you're right," Noah said. "I'm praying."

Brooke shifted, praying too. Too many people were dying in the men's evil wake.

Entering his office, Dwayne chucked the nurse's scrubs on the table and swore.

"My sentiments precisely," a man said in the dark.

Dwayne's muscles constricted. He knew that voice well. "Sorry, sir."

"For?" the boss asked.

"Being seen." He'd met the primary objective. Connor was dead, but that woman recognized his voice, and now she knew his face.

The boss stood, his footsteps deliberate on the creaking boards. Everything he did was deliberate.

Dwayne pursed his lips, hoping he wasn't dead.

His breath hit Dwayne's in the face—mint and cigar, as always.

"You were seen, all right. By the guardsman and that woman. You've now failed twice with her."

He wanted to argue. The first time was Saul and Ted's fault, but the boss didn't tolerate fools. "Yes, sir."

"You aren't irreplaceable."

Adrenaline surged through him, his limbs burning to move, to flee, but that was the coward's way out, and he was no coward. "Yes, sir."

"We go way back, but don't think I won't pull this trigger." The muzzle of his gun rested against the center of Dwayne's forehead. "Take. Them. Out."

# FORTY-ONE

The following morning, Noah reviewed case notes while Brooke sat in the recliner in his room for a change, the soles of her black boots tapping a rhythm on his floor. They were both dressed and anxiously awaiting discharge, but it was taking far longer than anticipated.

Noah's phone vibrated in his pants pocket. He checked the number and answered. "Hi, Hadley. Anything new?" He hoped the ME had found something concrete. So far, it felt like they were chasing ghosts.

"Are you still at the hospital? If so, I've found something you might like to take a look at," he said.

"I'll be right down."

After he hung up, Brooke asked, "Did Hadley find something?"

"Yep. I'm going to head down to the morgue. Do you want to come along, or would you be more comfortable waiting here? I don't anticipate being long."

"Thanks for asking. I'd like to go with you."

After working their way to the bottom level of the hospital, Noah rapped on the morgue door, and it buzzed open.

Hadley looked up, his head lamp shining in Brooke's face. "Oh, sorry." He clicked it off as she blinked.

Lifting his face shield, he said, "Oh, Brooke dear, good to see you. I didn't know you were joining us."

"I hope that's okay," Noah said, placing a steadying hand on the small of her back.

"Of course. Miss Kesler is always welcome." Hadley looked between them and smiled but left whatever he was thinking unsaid.

"You said you had something you'd like me to look at?" Noah asked.

"Yes." Hadley positioned the swing light over Andrews's right shoulder.

"The same branding," Brooke said.

Noah bent, examining it closer. "But it's . . ."

"Still healing," Hadley said.

"So it seems our conjecture that Andrews was a new recruit holds true, or at least this is another clue supporting that theory."

Hadley adjusted his glasses. "I also got his toxicology report back."

"Great," Noah said, anxious to know what'd killed Andrews so quickly.

"Coniine," Hadley said.

"Excuse me?" Noah had never heard of it.

"It's an oily liquid made from hemlock. If injected into the bloodstream, it paralyzes the body until the heart and lungs fail. There are no postmortem signs except asphyxia." He lifted Andrews's right eyelid.

"Purple splotches," Noah said, noting the typical sign of suffocation.

"If you hadn't seen the man fleeing the scene of the crime, and Finn hadn't taken a sample of the IV fluid for me to test, I could have easily attributed Andrews's death to suffocation. But he was poisoned."

"With something very unique," Brooke said.

"Correct." Hadley smiled.

"Which makes tracking down the killer via the poison a strong possibility," Noah said.

"One other thing," Hadley said, reaching for an evidence bag laid out on the tray with a pair of gloves for Noah.

Noah slid them on, and Hadley opened the sealed bag, dropping the bullet that had been removed from Andrews during surgery into his open palm.

Noah frowned. "This is a .40 caliber. It would fit the standard issue Coast Guard Sig Sauer." Not the shooters' AK-47s, which used a 7.62 caliber. None of his team had shot Andrews, and based on the shooters in the building, the only other one left alive at the time of Andrews's shooting had been the one across the lobby, but Andrews had been shot from behind. SRT wasn't on-site yet, so the mystery of who shot Connor Andrews remained.

"Thanks, Hadley," he said, returning it to the ME. "That's helpful. If you don't mind, I'm going to take a picture of Connor's brand and send it on to Emmy for comparison."

"Of course." Hadley positioned Connor's body so Noah could get a proper shot. Noah's phone made a swoosh as he texted the pic to Emmy.

A minute later, she texted back.

"Well, that was good timing," he said. "She located three semi-local tattoo parlors, and she and Logan were just about to head out for them."

"Hopefully, they'll be able to find the right one," Hadley said.

"We need all the answers we can get," Noah agreed.

Back in his hospital room and still awaiting discharge, Noah decided to use the time to call Leavenworth. He'd called earlier to set up the appointment with Scott Mirch but had been told to call back in the early afternoon, and they would connect him to the commandant. It took a bit of time for them to patch him through, but eventually she answered.

"Colonel Brenda Horton."

"Colonel Horton, thank you so much for taking time to speak with me," Noah said.

"No problem. You said this was regarding Scott Mirch?"

"Yes, ma'am. We think there might be a link between Mirch and the mass shooting on our base."

"I was so very sorry to hear about the tragedy," Colonel Horton said. "Our hearts and prayers go out to all involved."

"Thank you."

"Though I have to say I'm very curious how the two might be related."

Noah explained the connections they'd uncovered. "It's a long shot, considering he is in prison, but I learned long ago, if there's any chance of a connection—"

"You follow it," she said.

"Yes, ma'am." He liked the colonel.

"So how can I be of help?"

"What can you tell me about Mirch? Is he a model prisoner or always pushing boundaries?"

"Oh, he's definitely a model prisoner."

"Does he interact with many people? Is he close with anyone in particular?"

"He mostly keeps to himself but occasionally interacts with a couple of the prisoners."

"Does he have many visitors?"

"None," Colonel Horton said.

"None?" His brows furrowed. "As in never?"

"That's correct," she said.

"What about mail, phone calls?" The guy had to have someone who cared.

"Those he gets."

"Do you know from who?"

"I read through his file before our call to reacquaint myself with his specifics. He gets a weekly call and a letter from the same PO box about once a month—sometimes more."

"He only gets mail from one person?" Noah rubbed his chin.

"That's correct."

"Is there a name on the return address?"

"Unfortunately, no. Just the PO box address."

"Could I get that from you?"

"Sure. I'll text it when we hang up."

"Thank you. And the phone calls?"

"We do random monitoring of the prisoners' calls. Every time we've monitored one of Scott's, it's been with a woman."

"The same woman?"

"Based on her voice, the guards who monitor calls believe so."

"Any chance you have a number?"

"I'm afraid not. Every time she calls in, the ID says 'private caller.'"

"Interesting. Thank you so much for your time today. You've been very helpful."

"Happy to be of help. If you think of anything else, don't hesitate to call."

"I appreciate that," he said.

"Would you like me to have Scott Mirch brought on the line now?" Colonel Burton asked.

"Yes."

After a brief pause, a man cleared his throat. "Hello?"

"Hi, Scott. This is CGIS Special Agent Noah Rowley from Wilmington, North Carolina."

"Yes?" Scott's voice cracked.

"I have a few questions."

"Can I ask what this is in reference to?"

"A mass shooting on our base here in Wilmington three days ago."

Scott cleared his throat again. "I heard about that on the news. Awful."

"Yes, it was." Noah shifted in his seat. A shock of pain shot through his thigh, and he resituated himself.

"I don't understand why you want to talk with me though." Wariness clung to Scott's scratchy voice.

"The three Coast Guard instructors you named as coconspirators in the crime you committed, Talbot, Ford, and Sydell—"

"Trust me, I know who they are. They're the ones who put me in here."

"Are you saying you didn't commit the crime?"

"I'm not going through this again. If that's why you're calling . . ."

"It's not. I'm calling because Instructors Talbot, Sydell, and Ford were killed during the mass shooting."

"Oh." Genuine surprise rang in his voice but not a hint of sorrow. "Okay, and what does that have to do with me?"

"There are unusual circumstances surrounding their deaths," Noah began.

"At a mass shooting? I don't see how any death would be normal."

"True, but it appears the three were singled out."

"What do you mean?"

"I can't go into more detail, but we suspect they might have been targeted."

No response.

"Scott?"

"Yeah, I'm here. I still don't understand what any of this has to do with me." The edge in his voice deepened. "You aren't suggesting I had anything to do with their deaths, are you?" He chuckled but no humor clung to it. "I'm in prison, remember?"

"It wouldn't be the first time a hit was ordered from prison," Noah said, certain that would end their call, but he had to put it out there, had to try to judge Scott's reaction.

"My communication with the outside world is monitored. In fact, I'm sure they are listening in on this call right now. If I'd planned something like that, the guards would know about it long before it could happen. And I wouldn't kill innocents just to get back at . . ." He swore under his breath. "Look, I'm done now." The line dropped.

Noah lowered his phone and looked over at Brooke.

"Well?" she asked.

"He still holds a lot of rage for those three."

Brooke pulled her knees to her chest in the recliner. "I'm not surprised. During the trial, he insisted they'd left him holding the bag."

"Hopefully I can glean more insight from the CGIS agent on Scott's case." Noah ran a hand through his hair. "It's hard to imagine how Scott would have worked it out, but something about their deaths . . . It just feels . . ."

"Like they were targeted?" she asked, using his earlier words.

"Yeah."

# FORTY-TWO

An hour later, finally discharged, Noah walked beside Brooke as they made their way to the hospital lobby and out to the parking lot.

The brisk December wind fluttered her long brown hair about her shoulders, and he smiled at her attire—an emerald green sweater, open black jacket, and a simple pair of jeans, but she wore them like no other.

"Noah?"

"Yes?" He swallowed. *Focus on her words and not her curves.*

"You okay?"

"Yes, I'm fine." He nodded. It was good to see her smile, to see her rested for the first time in days.

Reaching her two-seater '63 Shelby Cobra, he held the driver's side door open for her.

"Thanks," she said, climbing in.

He dropped into the passenger seat and buckled up as Brooke started the car. Cold air blasted out of the vents.

"Yikes!" She turned it down to the lowest setting. "It usually takes a little time before it heats up."

He looked over with a smile and held out his hand.

A blush crept over her still-swollen cheek. She placed her hand in his and interlaced their fingers.

She calmed his soul in a way no one other than God could.

He needed to tell her the truth before things progressed, though in unspoken ways, they'd progressed further in the last few days than they had during the previous months they'd spent together.

He surveyed their surroundings as she pulled out of the lot and onto the road—looking for a follow, for a white Sprinter van, for any hint of danger. He saw nothing, but that didn't ease the tautness in his gut.

His cell rang, and he slipped it from his pant pocket. "Hey, Logan. How's it going?" he asked as Brooke pulled onto the main road leading toward the station.

"Not good, I'm afraid," Logan said.

Noah stiffened. "What's wrong?"

"The police got a call from Petty Officer Macken's neighbor, a Mrs. Nelson. Yesterday, Macken told Mrs. Nelson he'd stop over before his shift today to fix her leaky faucet. When he didn't show and didn't answer his phone, she went over to check on him. She knocked, but the door wasn't fully shut. It swung open to reveal Macken dead ten feet from the door."

"I'm on my way."

Brooke arched her brows.

"Rissi and Mason are en route," Logan said.

Noah disconnected the call and slipped his phone back in his pocket.

Brooke glanced over at him again. "Do I want to ask?"

Noah exhaled. "Macken's dead."

After leaving Brooke at the station with Em and Logan, Noah headed for the crime scene. He wished he could keep her at his side. He hated having her out of his sight, given the horror of the last few days, but it made more sense for her to stay with them. Emmy and Logan would do everything in their power to keep her safe.

He tightened his grip on the steering wheel as he drew closer to the address Logan had provided.

Macken's death hit hard. Not just because he had liked the officer, but it was yet another confirmation that the men behind all that had happened wouldn't stop. They were relentless. The only way this ended was if Noah and his team caught them. And that's what they had to do.

The investigation webbed out in a cascade of threads—one more added with Macken's death. The key remained finding the center point—the heart of the case, where all the threads converged and, more importantly, led to the person pulling the strings.

Noah turned into the three-story brick apartment building's lot on the east side of town. A Wilmington police car, with lights spinning red circles, was parked at an angle in front of the building's main glass door. Mason stood talking to Officers Hardy and Jent, but he turned to Noah as he stepped out of the car.

With a nod of thanks to Hardy and Jent, Noah met Mason at the apartment building door, and they stepped inside.

"I know it's not the safest way," Mason began, "but with your leg and the crutch, we'd better take the elevator," he said.

Noah nodded. It wasn't safe being boxed in when the stairs provided multiple escape options, but he wasn't up to taking stairs.

Stepping into the empty elevator, Mason pressed 3. The elevator pinged its way up. Noah kept a grip on his gun as the elevator doors slid open. Rissi and a lady somewhere in her seventies, he'd guess, awaited them.

He hopped out, finally hitting the rhythm of moving with the crutch. It hadn't been his first time using a crutch, and he doubted it'd be his last.

He glanced at the crime-scene tape across the blue door to his left.

"Let's make sure we express our thanks to Hardy and Jent for sealing up Macken's apartment. Finn will be here soon." If there was anything to lead them to the killer, he'd find it. They were pulling him from the RAD lab yet again, though Emmy told Noah earlier in the day that Finn was nearly finished there, and that yet again the trace evidence found brought back no hits. Who were these guys?

Noah turned his attention to the elderly woman. "Special Agent Noah Rowley," he said.

"This is Mrs. Nelson," Rissi introduced the woman.

"Edith to you." She smiled at Noah and shook his hand, her skin soft, her fingers delicate.

"Edith." He nodded.

"Edith has been so helpful," Rissi said.

The woman's slender fingers fidgeted with the large purple gem on her necklace. She wore green-and-lavender floral pants and a purple blouse.

"Would you like to tell Agent Rowley what happened, or do you prefer I explain what you've so graciously shared with me?" Rissi asked.

"Please, go ahead, dear," Edith said. "I'd rather not go through it again."

Rissi nodded. "I completely understand."

Edith turned toward her door. "I think I'll make a cup of tea and try to settle my racing heart. If you need anything, just knock."

"Are you okay?" Noah asked, before she closed her door. "Should we call a paramedic to come and check your vitals . . . your heart?"

"Oh no, dear. Thank you for asking, but I'm as healthy as a horse, as they say. Just ruffled."

"Okay, if you need anything, please let us know," Noah said.

"Thank you." Edith shut the blue door behind her.

Once Edith was out of earshot, he turned to Rissi. "Run it for me."

"First . . ." Rissi checked the pink pearl face of her silver watch. "Finn's approximately two minutes out."

Noah nodded. They'd take an initial look but refrain from touching or contaminating anything until Finn could run the crime scene. Once done with the body, they'd call Hadley to escort Macken to the morgue.

"Edith said she heard someone knocking on Macken's door rather late last night, which she found odd as he rarely had visitors. She looked through the peephole and saw a man enter but shrugged it off and headed to bed. When Macken didn't come to fix her faucet—"

"She found him dead."

"Yep." Rissi nodded. "He's lying not far from the entryway, blood covering him."

Footsteps hurried up the concrete stairs.

"Hey, guys," Finn said, his CSI case in hand.

Entering Macken's apartment, they found him less than ten feet from his front door—three shots to center mass. No doubt the gunman had used a silencer as Edith didn't hear gunfire. Macken's TV was on. The killer had been swift. Noah wondered if it was the "nurse" striking again, or if it'd been one of the men Brooke and Macken had seen in the rear of the van.

Whoever it was, the number of men behind all this continued to grow. Noah couldn't help but wonder how vast a network had them in their sights, and when they'd strike next.

# FORTY-THREE

Three hours later, Noah picked up Brooke, and they stopped for supper at Sonic, where he filled Brooke in on all he'd learned. She insisted on driving him home—rather, driving *them* home. For her safety, he felt it best she stay in his guest room until the men behind the nightmare of the last four days were no longer a threat.

Rissi had invited Brooke to stay with her before he'd left the crime scene, but something burrowed deep inside compelled him to keep Brooke at his side. Could it be it was the Holy Spirit whispering to his soul that she was the one? Rissi had understood he wasn't doubting her abilities. And Brooke said she was comfortable staying with him. That knowledge alone propelled warmth through him.

But he was playing with fire. The deeper he fell in love with her, the graver the pain if she rejected him once he'd confessed his feelings and the truth of his situation. Maybe she'd surprise him and say it didn't matter. He wished he could hold on to that hope, but given the last time he told someone . . .

*Who am I trying to fool?* His heart would get pummeled. When Sherrie, his former fiancée, ended things, the rejection hurt, but it didn't grip his heart the way the mere thought of Brooke walking away did.

But for now, he needed to set that all aside and keep his head clear. His focus needed to remain on protecting Brooke. Once the threat was over, he'd tell her everything and beg God she didn't walk away.

The headlights of her car flashed across the stone and dark-stained wood of his one-story rancher as she pulled in the drive at 1940.

He reached into his pocket, pulled out his key ring, and clicked the garage-door opener. He'd paid a little extra to have the garage-door company make one small enough for him to keep on his person, but the cost was well worth it. In his line of work, he never knew when he might be away from his vehicle, yet still want the garage door to open remotely.

"That's a cool opener," she said as she pulled in next to his Jeep.

"Yeah. You can't imagine how many times this has come in handy."

"I'll need to see if I can get one of those." She jangled her keys as she opened her door and shifted to climb out. The keys slipped from her hands, dropping to the concrete floor with a clink. She bent, and something whizzed over her head, cracking into her open car door.

"Under the car!" Noah roared, clicking the garage-door opener. The door slowly lowered. *Faster.*

The driver-side tire popped by Brooke's head, air hissing out as he pulled his gun, shooting out the overhead light. Darkness covered them as shattered pieces of plastic casing clattered to the floor.

Finally, the door lowered all the way down, and Noah scrambled around her car, lying down next to her. "Are you okay?"

"Yes." She nodded, her limbs trembling.

He couldn't see her, but he sensed her fear.

"You can roll out now," he instructed. "We're going to get inside."

She did so and followed him in a low crawl to the interior

door. Once inside, he pressed her against the laundry room wall while hitting the emergency button on his security alarm.

A high-pitched warbling rang out.

"My team will be here ASAP," he said.

"Your team?" she whispered, her breath warm against his neck.

"Yes. The alarm company sends an emergency signal to the team rather than local police. I appreciate and trust local law enforcement, but if there's an emergency here, I want my team."

Noah didn't move, just stood solidly against her.

She inhaled, no doubt preparing to unleash a barrage of questions.

He held his finger to his lips.

They stood with maybe an inch between them—him shielding her with his body. He would have been content to stay there with her all night—just the two of them so close together, her heart beating against his chest, but the squealing of tires on asphalt, followed by an engine's hum, said the team had arrived, and their moment was gone.

# FORTY-FOUR

Noah waited until his team swept the area before moving with Brooke to his sister Kenzie's house. Wanting to keep Emmy and Logan fixed on the hospital video surveillance and criminal sketch search, he decided Rissi would drive the follow car, and Mason would drive Noah's Jeep, while he rode shotgun—frustrated as all get-out. He'd play along tonight, but tomorrow would be a different story. He wasn't kowtowing to his injury.

He looked back at Brooke curled up on his back seat, a pillow under her head and a fleece blanket pulled up to her chin. She looked adorable, beautiful, and fierce.

Once they safely entered Camp Lejeune, Noah relaxed . . . a bit.

Mason pulled the Jeep into Kenzie's drive, and Rissi pulled in behind in her red Fiat. She got out, waved to Kenzie standing at the storm door in cat pajamas, and gave Brooke a hug before popping back into the driver's seat. Mason joined her, and with a quick reverse, the two pulled out of the driveway and into the night.

"Come here," Kenzie said, wrapping an arm around Brooke.

"Thank you for letting us stay," Brooke said.

"Of course." Kenzie rubbed her arm. "You're family."

215

Noah started. So even his family knew she was the one.

"I've got the first room on the right all made up for you, Brooke, and there's a set of pjs on the bed."

"Thank you," she said.

"Noah"—his sister turned toward him—"you're in the back bedroom." She kept her voice barely above a whisper.

He didn't blame her. Once the minions were in bed, it was dangerous to wake them. *Dangerous . . .* A smile tugged at the corner of his lips. *But oh so fun.*

Last time he babysat, Kenzie came home to find the munchkins up at midnight, and he was thankful for his brother-in-law's intervention before his sister ran him through.

"Noah?" Kenzie said.

"Sorry. Was just thinking of my last time with the kiddos."

"Awww." Kenzie folded her arms over her chest. "That's sweet." She looked over at Brooke. "They adore him."

Brooke smiled at him. "I can see why."

He warmed. The woman got to his heart and soul in a way he never imagined possible.

"I better get some shut-eye," Kenzie said, her gaze shifting between the two. "Make yourselves at home."

"Thanks, sis." He hugged her in a choke hold, then kissed the top of her head. "For everything."

"Yes, thank you," Brooke said.

"Anytime," she said. "It's time for me to crash. Those rascals are always up far before I'm ready."

"'Night," Noah whispered, knowing if the adorable rug rats heard Uncle Noah, they'd be bounding down the stairs, and his sweet-natured sister would throttle him.

Kenzie smiled and wiggled her fingers to Brooke as she headed up the stairs. She had to miss Mark so much, especially with two little kiddos who loved their dad. Having a parent or spouse, or any loved one, deployed overseas had to be grueling.

At least he could rest easy knowing Brooke was safe for the

night. Given that Kenzie lived on a highly secure Marine base, it was the safest option for Brooke.

The room he'd be in was at the end of the first-floor hall, just past the kids' playroom—but in all honesty, the kids' "playroom" encompassed the entire house. Despite Kenzie's best efforts to wrangle everything together at the end of each day, by the time she rustled the kids into the tub, brushed their teeth, read Bible stories, and said prayers . . . It all took more strength than his morning exercise routine.

"I'm sure you're exhausted," Noah said after Brooke returned from the restroom.

She'd taken time to splash cold water and a bit of reality on her face. They'd been shot at. *She'd* been shot at. No doubt by the men who were behind everything that had happened in the last few days. If she hadn't dropped her keys . . . If Noah hadn't been there . . .

"I'll show you the guest room," he said, stepping toward the hall.

"Actually . . ." She rubbed her arm. "If the noise won't keep anyone up, would you mind if I watched a movie before I go to bed?" She was scared that as soon as she drifted off, the nightmares and flashbacks would return.

"I was just thinking a movie sounded like a great idea. I could use some decompression time myself. Why don't you pick the movie, and I'll make some popcorn?"

"Okay."

"The Blu-rays are along the far wall in the bookcase, in case you don't remember. And there's Amazon or Netflix. Oh, and unless you want to watch *Peppa Pig* or *Shaun the Sheep*—both of which are excellent—the adult movies are on the top three shelves."

"I don't know." She chuckled. "With some of the adult movies out there, I might prefer Peppa or Shaun."

Noah smiled, holding her gaze. He was such a great guy, so kind and strong and capable. The list of his solid character went on and on. But in moments like this, when his eyes held hers and her breath stalled in her throat . . . it was impossible not to notice what an incredibly handsome man he was.

She wasn't sure who broke the stare first, but the next thing she knew, she was standing in front of the movie bookcase, and he was rustling through Kenzie's cupboards on the other side of the cedar island that ran half the length of the family room.

"Can I get you a drink?" he asked, yanking her from her thoughts. "Sweet tea, maybe? Kenzie makes the best."

"Tea sounds good." So did knowing she wouldn't be alone the remainder of the night, though she doubted she'd sleep a wink. She glanced back over the counter as Noah hobbled about. "Are you sure you don't need help in there?" The man was working on a crutch, for goodness' sake.

"Nah, I got this."

He always did, it seemed. Forcing her eyes back to the Blu-rays, she trailed her fingers along each title, finally choosing two—*Fever Pitch* and the *Jumanji* remake with Dwayne Johnson.

Noah came hopping out on one crutch, balancing a silver bowl overflowing with popcorn and two movie-theater-sized candies in his free hand. "Milk Duds or Twizzlers?" he asked.

"Twizzlers."

He smiled. "I figured you for a Twizzlers girl. So what movie did you pick?"

She held up her two choices.

"Great taste and tough choice, but I'm thinking *Fever Pitch* tonight," he said. "Gotta love a good baseball story. And Jimmy Fallon is hilarious."

"I know, right?"

Noah pointed behind him, gesturing to the kitchen. "I'm just going to grab the drinks and—"

"Why don't you let me grab them? Not that I wouldn't enjoy seeing you attempt to carry two glasses while on a crutch, but I think we've had just about as much turmoil as we can take today."

"Fair enough." He took the case from her and moved toward the entertainment center as she moved for the kitchen.

Movie previews sounded as she poured the two tall glasses of iced tea.

Noah sat on the couch. Leaning forward, he pulled an over-sized navy fleece out of the blanket basket next to the couch.

Brooke handed Noah his drink and set hers on the end table before taking a seat.

He lifted the throw, offering to share.

"Thanks," she said, taking hold of the soft blanket.

He propped his socked feet on the coffee table, and she did the same, resting her feet beside his and cuddling up to him under the throw.

A half hour into the movie, Noah realized he'd fully relaxed for the first time since the mass shooting. His mind drifted to the intensifying depth of his feelings for Brooke.

He loved her.

*If you love her, then let her have all she deserves. And that's not you.*

He drummed his fingers against the side table, wrestling with the right thing to do, but heaven help him, he treasured the woman.

He paused the movie.

"Getting more popcorn?" she asked.

"Uh-uh." He reached over, cupping her face, his thumb caressing her uninjured cheek. "You are *breathtaking*. And I'm an imbecile for not telling you sooner."

She rested her cheek against his palm.

He pressed a soft kiss to her forehead but didn't pull back, his skin warm against hers, their foreheads pressed together.

"Brooke." Her name came out more a breath than a whisper.

She blinked, and he brushed his lips ever so softly across hers. *Please, Lord, let me be enough.*

Her lips parted and he deepened the kiss.

"Uncky Noah. Up." Owen, his two-year-old nephew, plopped on the center of his chest wearing a pair of PJ Masks pajamas.

"We're making unicorn waffles," Fiona, his four-year-old niece, said while pirouetting in her pink tutu over Peppa footie pajamas.

Noah rubbed the sleep from his eyes and looked to the window. "It's still dark out."

"Very good," Kenzie said, swirling a spatula in a blue mixing bowl. "You're the smart one of the family, right?" She winked as Fiona skipped back toward her, the girl's sparkly tiara tilting with the movement.

He checked his watch. 0535. He looked across the room, but the couch was empty. *Brooke?*

"Morning," Brooke said, as she stepped back from the refrigerator, a silver-and-pink rhinestone tiara fixed on her freshly brushed brown hair. "So Mr. Sleepyhead is finally up." She set a turquoise bowl on the counter beside the sink and lifted a colander of what he was guessing was fruit of some sort. The buttery scent of Kenzie's homemade waffles hung in the air.

Fiona raced over to Brooke, lifting up her arms.

"Fi, you're getting too big to be picked up," Kenzie said.

Noah stood and stretched. How did Brooke look so refreshed and awake? He recognized Kenzie's clothes on her. He was thankful to have such a kind and giving family.

"I'm going to take a shower." He jabbed his thumb over his shoulder toward the hall, hoping that would help him wake up.

"Okay," Kenzie said, "but don't take one of your typical half-an-hour ones. Breakfast will be ready in twenty."

Fifteen minutes later, he returned. "I'm sorry to bypass such a good-looking breakfast, but I need to head to the office." He looked to Brooke. "Wanna come along?"

"Or you're more than welcome to hang here," Kenzie said.

"Stay Auntie Brooke," Owen said.

Noah's eyes widened. *Auntie?*

"Isn't that cute?" Kenzie asked as Owen wobbled over to his little recliner by the TV. "Peppa's aunt paid a visit on the previous episode, and Owen decided Brooke was his aunt."

Pink flushed Brooke's cheeks.

He had to admit he liked the sound of it.

"We'd love for you to stay," Kenzie said. "I can always drop you off at the station later."

"That's a really kind offer, sis," Noah said. "But I want whoever Brooke rides with to be . . ." He glanced at the kids, and instead of saying *armed*, he patted his side where his holster hit.

"I'll head in with you," Brooke said, then turned to Kenzie. "But thank you so much for the offer."

Kenzie smiled. "It stands anytime."

# FORTY-FIVE

Noah held the door to the station open for Brooke.

The overhead lights were bright compared to the dismal gray sky. The click of typing on keyboards mingled with Em's and Logan's voices.

He caught sight of Caleb at his desk and Austin seated beside him. The two were quite the investigative pair.

Given the circumstances since the graduation shooting, the team had forgone their typical morning case-board meetings, but with everyone present, they could resume them—at least for today.

"Morning, everyone," Noah said.

Everyone turned and greeted him and Brooke.

"Since we're all here, let's go for our morning case board. We still have a ton to discuss, and I'd like to hear the latest updates."

Within minutes, everyone had settled on the U-shaped sofa facing the oversized whiteboard.

"Who'd like to start?" Noah asked.

"I'll go," Rissi said. "I've got some good news."

"Great," Noah said as Rissi stepped to the board. It was about time they had some good news.

"I've been following up with all the eyewitnesses from the shooting and one lady—a Mrs. Lois Hunter—recalled the catering van outside the graduation."

Noah rocked forward, ignoring the deep ache in his thigh. "Please tell me she remembered the logo."

"Jason's Delicacies," Rissi said with a smile.

"My neighbor's grandson, Grant Miller, said it began with a *J*," Austin said.

"He even offered Jacob or Jason as options," Caleb added.

*Finally! Thank you, Jesus.* Noah looked to Emmy.

"On it," she said, without him having to utter a word.

"Logan," Noah said, "see if Mrs. Hunter is able to provide the details for you to do a sketch."

"Will do," Logan said.

Noah shifted his attention back to Rissi. "Where are you on questioning the lab crew?" He'd added that to Rissi and Mason's docket with Caleb catching—or literally falling into—the environmental case.

"One of the female soldiers on the lab team, Army Lieutenant Amy Caldwell, stood out to me," Rissi said. "But I can't put my finger on why exactly."

"I trust your gut. Call her back in," Noah said.

"If it works schedule-wise, I'd like to have you sit in with me. I'd like your input," Rissi said.

"No problem." He was always happy to sit in and watch a master profiler work.

He turned to Mason next. "Where are you at with things?"

"I interviewed the guardsmen who responded to the shooting. Starting with first on-site. There was one who stood out to me as cagey—a Lieutenant Chris Malone. I could be wrong, but I'd like to bring him back in and have Ris take a crack at him."

"Makes sense. Go for it, Ris," Noah said. "And, Mason, since Connor Andrews is the only shooter we've identified, let's focus on that. I need you to catch a flight out to Georgia tonight to visit his hometown. See what else we can learn about him. Em's background check only pulled up a sister—parents deceased—but I'd like you to start with the sister and see if we can discover how he ties to the rest of our ghosts."

"You got it, boss." Mason nodded.

"Speaking of ghosts . . ." Noah shifted his gaze to Logan. "Where are you at?"

Logan lowered his glasses on his nose and looked out over them. It always threw Noah off on the rare days Logan wore glasses rather than contacts to work.

Logan exhaled, fully slipping his glasses off. He held the narrow brown frames in his hand. "I'm going through every little thing we know about the shooters—the brand of clothes they were wearing, their choice of weapon—though, as expected, the serial numbers were filed off so well Finn couldn't retrieve them. I'm continuing layer by layer, but I still have a ton of digging to do. Someone worked *very* hard to keep their identities hidden. Someone with a level of access that's frightening."

"Okay, keep at it."

"You got it," Logan said.

"How's it going on the chemical spill case?" Noah asked, wanting an update on that investigation.

Emmy stood and set her laptop on the stool beside the whiteboard. "I ran tests on the chemical leaking from the barrels and water samples Caleb gathered, then compared them to the sample Austin's vet provided. While the one from the surface of the water and Austin's dog were highly diluted, all were a match. It's a chemical I've never seen before and had to track down."

The entire team leaned forward.

"It's TCEP, and it's highly toxic, not just to pets but humans too. Had it leaked into, say, a well system, it could have fatal ramifications."

"What is TCEP?" Austin asked, her knuckles turning white as she balled her hands into fists. She was a fighter, that one. Noah glanced at everyone in the room. They were all fighters. It's what made his team so strong and effective.

He prayed her dog, and all the animals affected by the illegal dumping, would heal and that no humans would be affected.

"It's a flame retardant used in polyurethane foam manufacturing," Emmy said.

Mason's brow furrowed. "As in foam fingers?"

Emmy nodded. "That's one usage. Most foam manufacturers focus on car, airplane, or rocket cushioning, military foam casing for weapon cases, etc."

"So we're looking for a foam manufacturer?" Caleb said.

"Yes." Emmy nodded, then proceeded to write the chemical acronym on the board, the blue marker squeaking with the deliberate motion. "But TCEP was banned two years ago. Apparently, it was a major shock to the industry. If the manufacturers had been stocked up on TCEP, it would have cost them a fortune to properly dispose of it. Depending on the companies' focus, and how much they had in stock, it was enough to tank a few of them."

"Wow," Noah said, steepling his fingers. "So it seems someone took an alternate course of action."

"Dumping it in the inlet," Rissi said.

"Exactly," Emmy agreed.

"Do we know which local companies used TCEP?" Austin asked.

"Yes." Emmy started writing company names on the whiteboard under the TCEP heading. "There are three foam manufacturers within a two-hour drive. Huntington Foam is in the industrial park just outside of town." She added the location beside it. "Taylor & Greene Manufacturing is in Jacksonville," she continued. "And FoamTech is up in Goldsboro."

"That's a lot of foam in one area," Noah said, reclining back and battling the urge to wrap his arm around Brooke's shoulders.

"I looked into it, and apparently the state's economic policies make North Carolina very appealing to industries, which in turn brings business to the state." She handed a sheet to Caleb. "I printed out a list of the three companies with directions."

Caleb scanned it. His shoulders stiffened as Austin leaned up against him to look.

Noah bit back a smile. There was definitely something going on there, and if *he* noticed it, no doubt everyone else in the room did too. Those two worked—if they didn't kill each other.

He turned to fully focus on the team. "I have one more thing to report. Given how the three C-School instructors were killed and after my call with Scott Mirch, my gut says that thread is a critical piece of our puzzle."

He paused as the team nodded their agreement, then continued. "I called the original CGIS agent on the case, Brett Anderson. His voicemail says he's up north fishing, so I left him a message and hope to hear back soon."

"Now," he said, turning toward Em and Logan. "Any luck at the tattoo parlors?"

"Yes," Emmy said at the same time Logan said, "No."

They looked at each other.

Logan frowned. "What do you mean yes? We weren't told anything."

Em tilted her head. "Please, it was totally apparent that Leroy made the brand."

Noah watched the two of them spar back and forth, trying to smother a grin. When those two went at it . . . He shook his head.

Logan shifted to face her better. "Are you sure Leroy wasn't merely concentrating?"

"He could have been, but his expression when I showed him the picture of the brand seemed to indicate recognition."

"His gaze did harden, and his lips shifted sideways," Logan said, thoughtfully. "So perhaps you're right."

Emmy gave a triumphant smile.

Logan tilted his head, his gaze intent on Em. "You don't have to be smug about it," he teased.

"I'm sorry," Em said, smoothing her skirt across her lap. "I think I do."

Logan chuckled.

Em looked to Noah. "To get back to my point, I believe a man named Leroy at Custom Ink designed it. Roger, the guy at the front counter, recognized it, but he also got stiff when Leroy emerged."

"So how do we get Roger or Leroy to talk?" Noah asked.

"Leroy won't," Em said, "but Roger . . ." She tapped her booted foot. "I'll follow up with him. See if I can break through."

Logan tapped his pen against his notepad, his gaze fixed down on the page.

"Very good," Noah said. "Keep me posted."

# FORTY-SIX

A full day of casework and tracking down leads later, Noah was happy to be back at Kenzie's with Brooke.

Rissi and Mason were on their way to the airport for Mason to catch his flight to Georgia. Noah prayed there were answers waiting in Andrews's hometown—something, *anything*, that could help reveal the other shooters' identities. Finn arrived at Kenzie's not long after them, but Logan, Emmy, Caleb, and Austin remained at the station—all still fully entrenched in their work.

"Uncky Noah," Owen said, holding out his arms, "swing."

With a smile, Noah grabbed hold of Owen's hands and swung him back and forth. Around and around with his bum leg would have been a bit too much, but Owen's belly laugh said he didn't mind the modified version in the least.

A half hour later, Noah sat across his sister's family room from Brooke and Owen, who were on their third round of Don't Break the Ice. Owen's two-year-old face scrunched in concentration as his red plastic hammer hovered over the plastic pieces of ice.

Noah's second round of Don't Spill the Beans with Fiona was proceeding in a far more relaxed manner. Scents of red chili powder and freshly chopped onion swirled in the air as his mom stirred her famous chili con carne.

The smell of baking corn and honey emanated soon after, as Kenzie pulled her homemade cornbread from the oven. "Ten minutes," she called over the wide galley bar separating the kitchen from the family room.

Wood crackled in the fireplace, sparks flitting up the chimney as the flame's glow flickered along Brooke's fair skin. She was breathtaking.

A grunt escaped Owen's mouth, and his hammer flew along with the plastic ice. "Smash. Smash. Smash."

Noah leaned back, making eye contact with Kenzie over the kitchen island. "You haven't been letting him watch *The Avengers*, have you?" he teased.

Kenzie gave him a *plllleasse* look.

"He's just a boy. That's what they do." Nana Jo chuckled. "Take Noah, for instance," she said, and he followed her gaze across the room to Gabby. "He was such a boy—except for maybe that one time he got into my makeup."

"What?" Brooke burst out laughing.

Noah hung his head. *Here we go.* When his momma started on a story, there was no stopping her. And Brooke hadn't even heard the story yet, and she was already giggling. She looked at him, her eyes filled with mirth. "You? Makeup?"

He shifted his legs fully out in front of himself, taking pressure off his right thigh as brown plastic beans tumbled over the pot in the center of the game.

"Aw, man," Fiona said. "Oh well. I'll get you next time, Uncle Noah."

"See," Nana Jo said. "That's the difference between boys and girls."

"I'd love to hear the rest of the makeup story," Brooke said with a sweet tinge to her voice, but he knew she was only looking for information to razz him with.

"Me too." Finn chuckled as he entered from the back patio door.

Gabby set her mug of hot chocolate down, her fuzzy red-and-white snowflake-socked feet crossed on the ottoman behind Noah's head. "I wouldn't get too chuckley there, buddy," she said with a smirk in Finn's direction. "I heard a few whoppers from your mom when we visited."

"Yes, ma'am," Finn said with a sheepish grin as he handed Nana Jo the plate of sizzling strips of steak.

"Thank you, dear," she said, taking the plate from him.

Here came Noah's favorite part. When the steak met the carne asada sauce, he could hear it bubbling on the stove as his mom stirred it with the wooden spoon.

Finn took a seat beside Gabby on the sofa, wrapping his arms around her shoulders.

Everyone looked expectantly at Nana Jo.

Noah groaned. What was this? Family story hour?

Once his mom finished stirring the carne asada, she set it to a simmer, put the lid on, and moved to join them. "Okay," she said, swiping her hands on the *Cooking Queen* apron Gabby had gotten her last Christmas.

Was it nearly Christmas again? Noah shook his head. Time flew. It'd be his first Christmas with Brooke. He couldn't wait.

"So the kids used to play war games," his mom started.

Brooke's smile widened. "Why am I not surprised," she said, looking between him and Gabby.

"They'd climb into the tree fort their dad built in a big syca-more in our backyard up in Annapolis."

Gabby reached over and clutched their mom's hand. A catch always sounded in their mom's voice when she mentioned their dad. It'd been a couple of years, but after nearly a lifetime together, losing half your soul—as his mom put it—had to be devastating.

Nana Jo sniffed. "So they'd set up the small army guys, or whatever dolls Kenzie wanted to bring to the party, around the perimeter. It was Noah's job to secure the perimeter while

Gabby was on watch with a nerf gun, and Kenzie was on backup with a super soaker. They were quite the threesome."

"And the makeup part?" Finn asked, his grin as wide as Brooke's.

Noah grimaced before he smiled too. It was funny but oh-so-embarrassing.

"After securing the perimeter, they'd come in the house and do up their faces in war paint. Well, one day they ran out of the washable art paint they always used, so Kenzie convinced them to use my makeup for war paint."

"Oh, I like where this is going," Brooke said.

Nana Jo laughed. "You should have seen them—bright pink and deep red lipstick streaks across the bridge of their freckled noses and dark blue eye shadow under their eyes." She shook her head.

"Thankfully, we never left the backyard," Noah said, thinking how scarring that could have been if his friends had seen.

"True, but I did manage to get a snapshot of it. I'll find it and show it to you someday," Nana Jo said to Brooke.

"I'd love that," Brooke said between spurts of laughter.

Brooke looked so joyous and adorable with tears of laughter rolling down her face that Noah couldn't fake being stern. One tear rolled over her lip, another beading to it. He longed to kiss the drop away, but caught himself before he did, thank goodness. Oh, he'd be kissing her, because that holdout was long gone, but kissing her in front of his family and colleagues would be awkward. Despite his determination, though, he instinctively moved closer. "You find that funny, huh?"

Brooke tried to settle the laughter, pressing her lips together and holding her breath—like that would contain it. Rather, it only fueled the laughter like a pressurized rocket, and before she knew what was happening, she was doubled over in belly laughter, her eyes filling with tears of joy as she pictured Noah with hot pink lipstick across his cheeks as he patrolled the perimeter of his backyard. The laughter was a wonderful respite from the crushing anguish and fear that had been plaguing her.

Taking a deep inhale and exhale, she stemmed the tide of laughter as Nana Jo announced dinner was ready. Brooke got to her feet, fascinated that tears could be shed both in extreme sadness and extreme joy. She wondered, sometimes, why God created tears that way. To have two vastly opposite reasons behind the same physical reaction. She wondered what else He'd created like that.

A firm hand rested on her shoulder, giving it a playful squeeze. *Noah.* Warmth filled her. She glanced over her shoulder and smiled at him—his woodsy scent one of comfort and attraction. If this was any indicator of what a life with Noah would be like—time with his family, playing with the kids, laughing *a lot*—she yearned for nothing more.

Fiona and Owen raced for the kitchen. Kenzie met them at the edge of the island. "Nope. Go wash up first."

"Aw, Mom," Fiona whined.

Kenzie tilted her head, her brows arching.

"Yes, ma'am." Fiona turned and took Owen—who followed her every word and action—by the hand. The two siblings headed for the hall bath.

Noah started picking up the spilled beans from his and Fiona's game, as Brooke did the same with Don't Break the Ice, reaching all across the carpeted floor where Owen's smashes had landed them.

"Then pick up your games," Kenzie called after them.

"Yes, 'am," Owen said, attempting to sound like his sister.

Brooke chuckled and set the pieces she'd been gathering down in a pile by the box.

Noah did the same, knowing better than to argue with Kenzie's instructions to the kids. He'd tried doing that once or twice . . . or maybe a thousand times, but he'd finally learned. In their house, especially while their dad was deployed, what Mom said went.

Knowing they had a few minutes while the kids washed up and the rest of the adults were chatting in the kitchen, Noah reached out, snaked his arm around Brooke's curvy waist, and pulled her back against his bent left knee.

"Noah," she whispered.

"What?" He smiled, loving the feeling of her next to him. He ran his fingers up her neck, spreading into her silky hair. She giggled.

"Does that tickle?" He bit back a grin. He loved learning new things about her, loved learning everything about her that he could.

She squirmed but didn't move out of his hold. "Yes."

Fiona came skipping down the hall, followed by a half-waddling, half-running Owen.

"Games, please," Kenzie said.

Brooke straightened, and Noah glanced over his shoulder in his sister's direction to realize everyone—literally everyone—was lined up at the kitchen bar, their collective attention on him and Brooke.

He inhaled and leaned forward. "We should probably head in for dinner," he whispered against her ear.

"That tickles too," she murmured, turning to face him. Her gaze slipped over his shoulder and red rushed her cheeks as it landed on everyone staring in their direction.

Thankfully, they had the decency to at least pretend they were looking at something else, Finn choosing the ceiling of all things.

Noah shook his head, suppressing a laugh as Owen lunged into Brooke, tackling her in one of his baby bear hugs.

"Hey, big guy," she said, ruffling his blond curls.

"You're a natural with them," Kenzie said, smiling.

"You want a big family?" Finn asked, grinning. "Maybe six, or even eight kids?"

Noah grimaced. Finn was clearly razzing him. He had no clue about the situation. Unlike Gabby, who was clearly working to keep her expression unaffected. She was a good secret keeper when she needed to be.

Finn narrowed his eyes in Gabby's direction when she didn't join in the fun, but she simply shook her head, and he let it go.

Noah held his breath, waiting for Brooke's reply to Finn's question.

"I'd love a family," she said, tickling Owen, whose laughter was such a precious sound. "Probably not that big of one. I'm thinking more like maybe two or three."

Noah swallowed. There was his answer. He needed to tell her the truth so she could end things before either of them got in any deeper.

Who was he kidding? His heart was in all the way. He shouldn't have let this happen. He should have been stronger, but he'd failed. Now he'd break both their hearts.

# FORTY-SEVEN

Austin scooted back from Rissi's desk. She had generously let Austin use her space after she and Mason left for the night. Austin tilted her head from side to side, working out the kinks. Stretching her arms, she looked over her right shoulder. Emmy and Logan both sat at his desk, Em's chair rolled over beside him. Those two . . .

She shook her head. So much existed between them. At the very least, friendship, but she suspected there was much, much more, and her intuition had only failed her once. Though that failure had nearly cost her everything, the suffering that had resulted propelled her forward, leading her to this very moment—to her profession, her PI firm, and now to Caleb. She knew him well enough to know that he didn't kiss women just to kiss. He didn't date just to date. In fact, he basically didn't do anything without intense meaning behind it.

She inhaled, trying to keep her focus on work, and not on the kiss still lingering on her lips. Shifting to her left, she expected to see him hard at work, still researching disposal companies, while she acquainted herself with the foam companies they'd be visiting tomorrow. But he wasn't there. She swiveled the chair around, looking at the open kitchen door. Perhaps he'd gone to grab a bite or another cup of coffee. It had been a long day.

"He's outside," Logan said.

Heat flushed her cheeks. So it was obvious she was looking for Caleb. *Great.* They'd both worked so hard to act natural, like nothing had happened between them—no earth-shattering kiss—but perhaps they hadn't been as subtle as they'd hoped.

"Is he leaving?" she asked, a flutter of anxiety rising inside. He wouldn't do that without saying good-bye, so why had she even asked?

"Nah," Logan said. "He steps outside every night we're working. Hangs out there for a good twenty minutes for his break."

"Why?" she asked, unable to stem her curiosity.

"He says for fresh air," Emmy said, shrugging a shoulder. Clearly, she didn't buy that.

"But . . . ?" Austin nudged. She'd basically just given up any pretense of having no feelings beyond that of colleagues or friends. At least to someone as astute as Emmy.

"I think he goes outside to think," Emmy said.

That made sense. Austin swiveled back around. When she needed to clear her head and look at a case afresh, she went for a walk. Caleb going out for fresh air probably accomplished the same thing.

*Stay in your chair.* She tried to will herself not to move—well, sort of tried—but she couldn't help it. "I could use some fresh air myself."

She strode straight to the door, refusing to look at Emmy and Logan, knowing both were grinning. The wintry night air slapped her face, waking her afresh as she shut the station door behind her. She scanned the parking lot.

"You need me?" he asked, his voice coming from behind Logan's truck.

"I just wanted some fresh air," she said.

He leaned around the truck. "Hey," he said, pleasure and a twinge of surprise lacing his husky voice.

"Hey." She shoved her hands into her knee-length cardigan

sweater as she approached. "I hope it's okay if I join you," she said, suddenly feeling vulnerable and hating that feeling, but loving the sight of him waiting for her.

"Please," he said as she rounded the hood of the truck to find him leaning against the cab, his left knee bent, his boot anchored against the step-up rail. "Just getting some fresh air." He smiled, then gazed up. "The sky is pretty amazing tonight."

She looked up. He was right, but amazing didn't come close. Stars blanketed the crisp black sky. White glimmering dots on a beautiful canvas, like snowflakes on the ceiling. "Wow," she breathed. God's handiwork was gorgeous.

He looked over at her and frowned. "Where's your jacket?"

*Oops.* She'd completely forgotten to grab it. She pulled her sweater tighter about her, looping the belt. At least she'd had that on. "I spaced," she said, leaving it at that. She didn't need to say she'd forgotten everything but being with him.

"Here," he said, slipping out of his coat and draping it across her shoulders.

The black down coat was light but surprisingly warm—probably from his body heat. His spicy aftershave enveloped her senses, and she cuddled in tighter.

The moonlight cast a glow across his five o'clock shadow.

"Thanks." She inwardly cringed. Could she have taken any longer to respond? Sheesh, what was it about this man?

Slipping her arms in the sleeves, she realized she really ought to go back and grab her own jacket so he wouldn't be without one, but being in his presence had become so soothing—such a contrast to the way he used to irritate the dickens out of her. Though, if she was honest, he still did at least once a day. She smiled. Okay, probably more, but it seemed to be their unique way of flirting with each other.

He shifted to face her, his shoulder resting against the cab. "What has you smiling so sweetly?"

*You. No.* She couldn't jump the gun. Just because her emotions were pinging around, aching to kiss him again, didn't mean he felt the same. She shrugged. "Nothing."

He pushed off the cab, stepped fully in front of her, and closed in. He tipped her chin up with his finger. "Please tell me what you're thinking about."

"Did Caleb Eason just say *please*?" She smirked. Maybe he *was* feeling what she was.

"Yes," he said, his breath tickling her lips, fogging in the winter air.

The headiness in his eyes was irresistible, and before she realized it, the word slipped from her lips. "You."

"And I'm thinking of you, and how badly I want to do this again." He cupped her face with both hands and lowered his lips to hers.

Time melted away.

"Caleb," Logan's voice rang out.

They both stepped back, her head dizzy.

He steadied her by bracing his hands on her arms.

"Yeah?" he called.

Thankfully, Logan couldn't see them positioned behind the truck.

"Officer Jager's on the phone. It's your sister."

# FORTY-EIGHT

"I'm going to ask Logan to give you a ride home," Caleb said, rubbing Austin's arm and gesturing for her to go before him back to the station.

"Is everything okay?" she asked.

Logan remained in the doorway, holding the glass door open for them.

Humiliation and concern scorched Caleb's skin. "Hopefully," he said, never knowing to what extreme he'd find the situation.

"Line one," Logan said, lifting his chin as they stepped back inside.

"Thanks, man," Caleb said, moving for the closest desk and lifting the receiver to his ear. "Eason."

"Caleb," Officer Bill Jagers said, "sorry to bother you, but I thought you'd want to know there's been another call in."

He didn't need to say any more. "Thanks, Bill," Caleb said, raking a shaking hand through his hair as anger buzzed through him. "I'm on my way."

"I can give Austin a ride home," Logan offered.

Caleb looked at the open curiosity in Austin's eyes.

"Thanks, Logan." He ached to tell her, to let her know everything about him before he fell completely head over heels for her—as if he hadn't already.

"I don't mind going with you." She shrugged her shoulder, tilting her head so her ear brushed against the soft sweater she wore. "Maybe I could be of help."

No one could help this situation—that'd been a bitter lesson learned, but as Susie's brother, he still had to try. Try and pray—*hard*.

Logan and Emmy looked between them, awaiting his reply.

"Okay," he said to Austin. "But you may regret coming."

Austin quirked her brows but didn't ask. She simply grabbed her jacket off the back of Rissi's chair and handed his back to him. She'd looked adorable in it, and her lavender scent lingered.

"I'll see you guys in the morning," he said to Logan and Emmy as he grabbed his keys.

"Let us know if we can do anything," Em said.

"Thanks." He held the door open for Austin, and she stepped through.

Maybe he was crazy for taking her along, but if they were to have any type of real relationship, she might as well learn about his sister now.

"'Night, Mom," Noah said, giving her a hug as she headed out Kenzie's door.

"Good night, sweetheart," Nana Jo said.

"'Night, man," Finn said, clapping him on the shoulder.

Noah lifted his chin. "See you tomorrow."

Gabby came next, and the minute she told Finn she'd be right out, Noah knew she was going to pull him aside. Sure enough, she tugged him around the stairs. "You're going to tell her tonight, aren't you?" she asked in a hushed whisper.

"Yes, she needs to know."

"I agree, but please don't make the decision for her. She loves you."

He nodded, knowing if he argued, he and Gabby would be there in the stairwell debating all night. The end shot was Brooke deserved it all, and once the truth was known, despite how much she cared about him, she'd walk away. She had to.

Caleb tapped the steering wheel. "This isn't going to be pretty," he said, glancing over at Austin.

She waited, giving him the opportunity to continue.

He took a stiff inhale. "My sister . . ." he began, hearing his own voice crack. He cleared his throat and started again. "She and her boyfriend of the minute get into it pretty bad, and the neighbors call the cops."

Austin reached over and placed her hand on his shoulder. Her touch was warm and soft but steady. "I'm so sorry."

She didn't ask the obvious. Didn't need to. By indicating this had occurred before, she'd figured it out. His sister didn't leave, didn't even press charges. Worse still, she always bailed him out—them out. It'd been a string of losers and abusers as far back as Caleb could remember. She'd taken after their mom on the loser part. Thankfully, his mom had never gone for the abuser type. Just any other type. It'd cost her marriage to his dad. Cost him having a father. Cost him so much.

"It's good you try to help," Austin said, rubbing his shoulder.

He pursed his lips. "It doesn't seem to make any difference."

"But you try. You're there. That's what matters."

He nodded. That's what he kept telling himself. Praying one day Susie would walk away.

The usual red-and-blue lights swirled outside his sister's rental home.

An officer stood talking with Susie's neighbors to the left— the Hawkinses—who'd no doubt called it in, *again*. He was grateful they hadn't stopped calling.

He inhaled, then exhaled in a steadying whoosh before looking over at Austin. "Do you want to wait in the car?" he asked,
partly hoping she would and partly that she wouldn't. It'd be
nice to have someone at his side, to have *her* at his side. He was
getting used to her there. Loving her there, if he was honest.

Austin shook her head. "No. I want to be there with you,"
she said, her voice holding a steadfastness he admired.

"Okay." He stepped from the car and moved around to open
her door. She climbed out, and Officer Jager met them as they
approached the open front door. Screams flooded out.

"Thanks for calling," Caleb said.

"Anytime, man," Jager said.

"This is Miss Kelly," Caleb said introducing her.

Officer Jager dipped his chin. "Ma'am." He looked to Caleb.
"You want to follow me in?"

He nodded, thankful Bill Jager always called him, even
though Caleb had no jurisdiction here.

"You—" Susie screamed obscenities, and Bart gave them
right back.

Caleb shook his head, extending his hand to Austin. "You
sure?" he asked, giving her one last out.

"Positive."

He nodded as hot shame and indignation boiled beneath
his skin. He rounded the corner to the kitchen, Austin close
at his side.

Officer Samuels held Bart back, while the six-two burly man
wrestled in his hold.

"Duck!" Caleb said, pulling Austin down with him as a series
of plates flew over their heads, busting on the wall behind them.

"What are you doing here?" Susie screeched as he and Austin
righted themselves. "And who is she?"

Red marks in the size and shape of fingers marred Susie's
arms. Blood dripped from her lip, and her right eye was already
swelling.

His heart cracked. "Suz . . ." he said, pleading for this to stop.

"Don't 'Suz' me. I didn't ask for your help, and I don't want it." Another plate zinged.

"Enough!" roared Jager, stepping in front of her as Samuels wrangled Bart into cuffs. He looked back at his partner. "Get him in the car."

As Samuels walked him out, Bart glared at Caleb. "Like she said, you're not wanted."

Caleb's jaw clenched. "And you're arrested again."

"She'll bail me out in an hour. No 'arm. No foul."

Caleb got up in his face. "Look at her. She's bleeding. That sure as heck is harm." He bit back the rest of what he wanted to say, obeying what God called him to do instead.

"Who's the broad?" Bart asked, looking Austin up and down. Before Caleb could respond, Austin did. "I'm not a broad."

Bart chuckled. "You sure look like one, darlin'." He tugged against his restraints, trying to get in her space.

She didn't bat an eye. "I suggest you back up, or we're going to have a problem."

Caleb loved her tenacity.

"Yeah." Bart snorted. "And what kind of trouble could you possibly cause?" he asked as the officer pulled him away from her.

"This kind." She lifted her concealed Colt in her right hand, and her PI license in her left, showing it to Officer Samuels.

Samuels nodded with a sideways smile, then shoved Bart around the corner and out the door, their heavy footfalls hammering down the front steps.

Susie grabbed her purse and rushed forward. She stopped at Austin's side. "Don't you talk to him like that again, you little—"

"Mind. Your. Words," Caleb gritted out before she could finish.

"Whatever." Susie fished her keys out of her gray handbag, the jangling mess attached to a Panthers lanyard. "You're in my way."

"Don't do this, Suz," he said, trying yet again to break through to her.

"I don't need you," she said, storming around the corner and out the door.

Austin clutched his hand tighter as his stomach flipped. Why couldn't Susie see the truth? Why wouldn't she change? This time had only been a busted lip and eye, but next time . . . One of these drunken nights, Bart was going to move past the point of no return.

# FORTY-NINE

Brooke snuggled up to Noah on the couch, lifting the remote to put on *Miracle*. She'd seen the movie so many times, but it never got old, and it never stopped inspiring her to give her all in every area of her life.

Noah's hand rested over hers on the remote. "Hang on a second."

She stilled. Had his voice just cracked? "Sure."

He cleared his throat. "I need to tell you something."

She prayed he wasn't rethinking their relationship. "What's up?"

She set the remote on the oak coffee table, and he took her hand in his as he shifted to face her better.

"So . . ." He exhaled. "I was engaged once before, when I was young."

Her muscles tensed as she waited, her breath stuck in her throat. She hadn't known that. He'd never said . . . Gabby had never said . . .

"Obviously, we broke up." He clenched her hand tighter in his hold, the pad of his thumb caressing her palm. "But what no one knows, outside of my nosy sister . . ."

"Gabby?" She smiled.

He smiled back, but it was only a half smile. "Yeah."

"Goes with being a reporter, I'm sure."

"Unfortunately." He looked down at their joined hands, then back at her, pain etched on his face. "Not long before the wedding date, I was in a bad motorcycle accident. I sustained significant injuries and without going into explicit detail . . . the end result is . . ." He swallowed. "I can't have kids."

"Oh." She cupped his hand tighter. "Noah, I'm so sorry." Her heart ached at the raw sorrow clinging to his voice.

He continued, the words rushing out as his broad shoulders tensed. "I'm the sorry one. I should have told you sooner. I just fell hard and with everything going on. It's no excuse. I should have told you before." He released her hand and leaned back. "But now you know so you can walk away before we get in deeper."

"You're not in deep?" she asked.

His gaze fixed on her, creases forming at the corners of his eyes. "I'm drowning."

Her heart squeezed as a warmth she'd never felt before radiated through her. *Love. Immeasurable love.*

"And you?" he asked, his voice choked.

"Exactly the same." If not more so.

"I can't explain the joy hearing that fills me with, but . . ." His brow furrowed in thought.

She hated the word *but*.

"But it also fills me with agony."

She shook her head. "I don't understand."

"My fiancée, Sherrie, walked away because she wanted kids. She told me I wasn't enough. She needed it all—kids, dog, white-picket fence. And, while it was crushing, I understood." He clasped her hands in his again. "I want all of that for you. I love you too much to keep going, no matter how much I want to. You need a full life, and I can't give that to you."

She looked him deadpan in the eye. "I'm not walking away."

His eyes widened. "What? Why would you—"

"I want you."

He straightened. "But you want kids. I see you with Fiona and Owen. You need to be a mom. You'll be a fantastic one."

"Truth be told . . ." She hesitated, never having said this aloud. "For a long time, I didn't want kids. I'm a flight medic, and my job was my life. But that changed . . ."

His eyes narrowed, waiting for her to continue.

"That changed when I met you. When I started to envision a life with you. When I played with your niece and nephew." She looked down, feeling silly. "I started picturing our kids."

He tipped her chin up, forcing her to meet his gaze. "I love hearing that beyond measure, but I can't give you that. That's why you have to walk away."

"There's more than one way to have kids," she said, feeling God's Spirit leading her.

A hope she hadn't seen since the conversation started shone in Noah's eyes. "What are you saying?"

"Maybe we adopt." They'd still have a family. *Be a family.* And that's all she wanted—a life built with Noah.

"Not that adopting isn't wonderful, but are you sure you'd be happy adopting? Not having kids—" he cleared his throat— "the traditional way?"

"If we get married . . ." Despite the seriousness of the conversation and the near certainty of marriage, given the way he talked, she couldn't presume he was ready to get on one knee. "If we adopt, then they'd be *our* kids." She loved the sound of *our*.

"Are you sure?" he asked, deep longing pooling in his brown eyes.

She'd never been surer. She wanted a life with Noah, however that life looked. "Positive."

He leaned in, passion swelling in his gaze. He grazed his lips over hers. "I love you," he murmured against her mouth.

"I love you too," she whispered before his soft lips pressed fully to hers and he enveloped her in his embrace.

"Come on," Austin said as Caleb pulled to a stop in front of her house, unbuckling her seat belt and popping open the door. "There's something I want to show you."

His curiosity sparked at the tone of her voice. There was a sadness there but also something else. Was it joy?

Climbing out of his vehicle, Caleb stepped around the front of his car, his headlights still on until the automatic shutoff kicked in.

She stood there in the shaft of light, fog dancing around her, and he'd never seen her look more beautiful.

She held out her hand, and he took it, letting her lead him to her house. Pulling out her keys, she unlocked the door, and her alarm bleeped. She let go of his hand, her warmth slipping from his cold fingers. Dirk slid around the corner, his tail and tongue wagging.

"Hey, buddy," she said, pressing numbers on the security pad. The bleeping ceased, and she bent to pick up Dirk. He cuddled against her, licking her face.

"He looks like he's feeling much better."

"Yeah." She smiled at Caleb. "He is." She ruffled Dirk's wrinkled head, then set him down. He raced around the kitchen, his nails clinking along the tile floor.

"What's he in such a hurry for?" Caleb asked.

"He gets a bully stick when I get home."

"Ah."

A plate encircled with clear wrapping and topped with a white bow sat on her counter.

"Present?" he asked.

She looked over. "Carol is too stinking sweet." Rummaging

behind a cupboard door, she pulled out a chew stick for Dirk. He sat on his heels, his head at attention.

Caleb smiled. Dirk adored her, and he loved that. Animals loved unconditionally.

She handed Dirk the treat, and he scampered into the living room. "Carol is Megan and Billy's mom. She checks in on Dirk when I work late."

"That's nice of her," he said, shifting his focus to Austin. To them together.

"She makes the best chocolate chip cookies." She peeled back the wrapping and offered him one.

"Thanks," he said, biting into it. Chocolate, sugar, and a hint of vanilla swirled in his mouth. "You weren't joking. These are great."

"Mmm-hmm." She nodded, having bit into one. She took his hand in hers. "I want to show you something."

"Okay." Her soft skin caressed his as they walked into her bedroom.

She released his hand and knelt down in front of a cedar trunk. Stenciled artwork was painted across the top—a big sun in the center and wisps of rays reaching out with two cardinals flying.

"Nice trunk," he said.

"Thanks." It creaked as she lifted the lid.

"Did you paint the design?"

"Yeah." She smiled. "I wanted to brighten it up."

"Nice work."

"Thanks." She pulled out a wooden box the size of a shoebox with another sun and cardinal.

"You like cardinals."

"When I was a kid, there was a stretch of time when a cardinal used to come and sit on my ledge every morning and sing." She smiled, getting back to her feet and closing the lid. "He must have had a nest nearby. Every now and then, I saw the female, but she never came up on the ledge like he did."

"That's really cool."

"I viewed it as a gift from God." She headed for the door.

"He takes care of the sparrows," Caleb said, referencing the verse from Matthew.

Her cell rang. "Could you hold this?" she asked of the box.

"Sure." He took it and tucked it under his arm.

"Hello? Uh-huh. . . . Sure. No problem," Austin said, wrapping up the call.

"Everything okay?" he asked.

"It was Lucy. She's got a family emergency. She needs to drive up to Lynchburg as soon as possible and asked if I could watch Jaxon for a few days. She's been keeping him at the office until she finds a permanent home for him because of her cats, but since she's going out of town, I said no problem." Austin looked up at the clock. "She should be here in twenty."

"I hope everything will be all right," he said.

"Me too."

She reached for the box, and he handed it back to her.

"Thanks," she said. She opened the lid, and sifting through the contents, she pulled out a photograph. She angled it to face him.

He studied the picture clutched in her hand. It was a girl about Megan's age, but instead of the mop of curly red hair that Austin's neighbor had, this girl had blond hair—much like the shade of Austin's . . . and her eyes.

He looked up at her.

She offered a soft smile. "She's my daughter."

# FIFTY

Caleb took the photograph, his gaze shifting between Austin and her . . . *daughter*? He pushed down the detective side of him that wanted to drill her with questions. "She looks like you."

Austin smiled, but tears pooled in her eyes. "You think?"

"Definitely. She has your eyes and your beautiful hair."

Austin leaned against his arm and looked at the picture— almost afresh, it seemed. "Yeah, she does." She glanced up at him. "You're mustering some great self-control."

Of course, only Austin would call him out on it. "I don't want to press."

"But it goes against your nature?" She smirked.

"As it does yours." He smirked back. He was surrounded by gifted investigators, but Austin was the first one who seemed to share his need to understand things from all angles—to question and piece together an intricate puzzle that made up the whole, even if that curiosity went beyond the needed evidence and facts.

"I was seventeen and thought I was head over heels in love," she began. "He was nineteen and said all the right things. Did all the right things . . . until that night."

Austin shifted and ran a hand through her hair before walking over to put the picture up on the fridge with a magnet. Finally, she faced him again. "I told Heath it was okay, but then I changed my mind." She swallowed. "But he didn't."

Caleb pulled her in his arms, rubbing her back, resting his chin gently on top her head. "I'm so sorry," he said, his gut aching like a sucker punch had nailed it, and he fought the urge to track Heath down and throttle him or arrest him. Continuing when Austin said to stop constituted rape.

"Anyway," she said, sniffing and swiping at the tears beading down her face, "I got pregnant, and my parents said it was an embarrassment."

He leaned back an inch to look at her, his brow furrowing. "Seriously?"

"I grew up in Johns Creek, Georgia. My parents cared more about pretense and appearance than . . ." Pink colored her cheeks, and she looked away.

He'd heard of the area a bit north of Atlanta during a trip to the city last year. *Serious* money. While Austin was certainly refined, she was so down-to-earth and casual, he'd never guessed she grew up in such an affluent environment. "I've heard of it," he finally said.

"Then you know what it's like. Country clubs. Manicured lawns." She released a shaky exhale. "My mom sent me to stay with her sister, Tracey, who lived on a ranch out in Arizona. She said wild things belonged with wild things."

Tension racked his body, his breathing growing shallow. How could a parent be so cruel to their child? Though he knew that cruelty all too well. But treating someone as special as Austin like that? Realization of just how deeply he'd fallen for her—nosedive fallen—struck through him as he held her in his arms, never wanting to let go.

"Well," she said, slipping from his embrace and moving to lean against the kitchen counter, "my mom's idea of *wild* was a bit off. Aunt Tracey and her husband own a sprawling ranch in Scottsdale. Definitely not what most people picture when they hear the word *ranch*."

He stepped closer, leaning back against the kitchen counter

opposite her, the toes of their shoes touching—his large work boots, her petite navy flats. "Was she kind to you?"

Austin inhaled. "She was better than my mom and her snooty friends, who would have treated me terribly. Not to mention Heath, who I broke up with immediately and who basically pretended he barely knew me when I told him I was pregnant."

Caleb took a quick intake of air, cutting back his heat-fueled anger and desire to track this Heath down ASAP. But he remained silent, letting her talk as she was ready to.

"I gave birth in Scottsdale, and my parents insisted I 'get rid of the baby,' but giving her up for adoption after holding her in my arms was beyond painful." Tears streamed down Austin's face, and he pulled her back in his arms, enveloping her.

"After the adoption went through, there was no way I was going to go back home, so I moved into Tucson and tried to forget. But I couldn't, and that's what my tattoo is for." She swept her hair up into her hands, revealing the neck tattoo again. "Two hearts, one for me and one for my baby girl."

His heart broke for her and the loss that must have been. "It's nice you still get pictures of her." He didn't think that happened often with adoptions, but that definitely wasn't his area of expertise.

"Yeah. It took a while, but I found her." The lines around her eyes tightened. "With her new family."

"It's impressive you found them."

"I started working with a private investigation firm outside of Tucson, and the skills I garnered helped me track her down."

"You worked *with* the investigators rather than hiring them?"

She nodded. "After I left Tracey's, I was totally on my own. Thankfully, I still had some money in my bank account, and I sold my car, as it was in my name. It bought me enough time to find the right investigators."

"They hired you on?"

"In the first meeting, I broke down and explained why I

wanted to learn to be an investigator and how they were the first to even give me an audience. The owner of the firm must have seen the desperation in my eyes, but whatever the reason, he hired me on to help in the office.

"It didn't take him long to realize I wasn't going to stop trying to learn the PI ropes, so he paired me with his mentee, Deckard MacLeod, for basically an apprenticeship."

He brushed the hair from her face. "You learned quick?"

A soft smile curled at the corner of her lips, and he treasured the sight. Treasured her.

"Once I found Ella, I contacted her adoptive parents. The Spencers were super kind, and while they didn't let me formally see her, they let me watch her play in a park from a distance. She was beautiful."

He cupped her red-smudged cheek in his hand. "Like her momma."

"The Spencers send me a picture every December. They also let me send them a letter every year on Ella's birthday that they put in a manila envelope. And when she turns eighteen, they'll give it to her."

"How old is Ella now?"

"She'll be nine on Christmas Eve."

A rap on Austin's kitchen door shook both of them from the moment. Caleb automatically shifted his hand to the grip of his gun, as Austin moved for the door. "It's just Lucy with Jaxon."

"Habit," he said.

She pulled back the curtain on the door window and smiled as she turned the bolt.

Lucy hurried in, Jaxon bundled in her arms, a shopping bag in one hand, a dog bed in the other.

"Here," Caleb rushed forward before something dropped. "Let me help."

"Oh, thank you," Lucy said as he relieved her of the bed and bag.

Jaxon squirmed in her arms, whimpering to get down.

The minute she set him down, his nails tapped over to Caleb, where he'd set the bag and bed on the table. Jaxon jumped up on his right leg, pawing and whimpering to be picked up.

Caleb shook his head. This dog was too much. A smile crossed his lips as he bent and lifted him into his arms.

Jaxon's tail wagged, hitting Caleb's arm each time it went right, as he slathered Caleb's face with kisses.

"I'd say Jaxon's found his new home," Lucy said, smiling.

"Oh, I don't know." It had been so long ago, but after Skipper . . . after losing so much to his mom or her loser string of men, he never held tight to anything. Not until his team became his family . . . and now Austin, whom he ached to always hold tight.

"She's right," Austin said, inviting Lucy into the dining area where Caleb stood. "Look at how he is loving on you."

He looked down at the big eyes staring back at him. The mutt was pretty cute. Maybe he should adopt him. It'd be nice to hear padded paws around the house again.

Lucy pulled a bag of treats out of the shopping bag, setting it on the table. "I brought his water bowl and a bag of the food he likes. I feed him twice a day. Breakfast and dinner. Okay," Lucy said in a fluster. "I best run."

Austin took hold of her hands. "I'll be praying."

Lucy's rigid shoulders softened. "Thank you."

"Please keep me posted," Austin said, letting go of her hands.

"Will do." Lucy hurried for the door but paused before opening it. "Oh, I almost forgot. There was a black four-door car parked across the street from my house when I left. I didn't think much of it, but there's one outside your next-door neighbor's house too."

# FIFTY-ONE

Caleb grabbed his gun. "Where?" He'd scanned the perimeter when they arrived at Austin's, so the car either followed them extremely well for him not to notice or waited until Austin was sure to be home before parking down the street.

Lucy stood beside him in the living room, dark so as not to draw attention. "Right there," she whispered, pointing at the neighbor's house.

"Did you happen to notice how many people were sitting in it?"

"The car was running, and I think there were two people up front."

"That's helpful. You should wait here until I check it out."

"Okay." Lucy nodded, her dark bob bouncing with the movement.

Austin set Dirk—who'd clamored to be in her arms when Jaxon arrived—down and reached for her gun.

"You should stay here," he said.

"You aren't seriously playing a man card?" she asked, her brows hiked as high as possible.

Yes and no, if he was being honest. He couldn't help that he worried about the woman he'd fallen for, but he knew she was more than capable.

"If something goes awry, it would be best if one of us is with Lucy."

Lucy's eyes widened. "Am I in danger?"

He looked at Austin, and she gave one nod. "I'll stay with Lucy." She turned toward her vet. "It'll be fine," she said.

Surprised Austin didn't argue more to be the one going while he stayed with Lucy, Caleb headed for her rear door. Though he supposed it wasn't too surprising. Lucy knew Austin better than him, so her presence would be far more comforting.

"Be careful," Austin whispered.

"You too."

He stepped into the night—the temperature cold enough for him to see his breath. He hurried in a low crouch behind the row of bushes, then knelt at the edge of cover. He watched the car and finally spotted movement on the driver's side as the person stretched back, then someone shifting position on the passenger side. Two men. That's all he had to contend with.

Waiting until the driver's head turned toward his passenger, Caleb made the run behind the neighbor's house, moving around the far side, and then, once again, he knelt, assessing the situation.

The driver remained in a reclined position, hopefully giving Caleb an unseen approach. He moved along the neighbor's car parked behind the black sedan, coming up to its rear passenger door. His Glock gripped and ready to aim, he took a steadying breath and opened the rear door. "Hands in the air," he shouted.

The driver remained eerily still.

"Hands up," he yelled.

Slowly the passenger lifted his left hand. A shot burst through the seat back, followed by another and another. Caleb dove behind the car's trunk as the tires squealed, and the car pulled away.

Getting to his feet, Caleb returned fire, managing to bust the rear window before the car raced around the corner.

Caleb sprinted for his car.

Austin bolted out of the house. "Are you okay?"

"Just ticked off." He put his cherry on the dash.

"I'm coming with you," she said, moving to climb into the passenger seat.

"You should make sure Lucy gets off safely."

Austin looked torn but nodded and stepped back.

He peeled out of the driveway, taking the neighborhood roads that led fastest to Highway 40. Reaching 40, he depressed the pedal, the cherry radiating red circles on the pavement around him. He needed to close the distance between him and the sedan. Speeding forward, he searched the highway, but the sedan was nowhere to be found. He slammed the steering wheel and called Austin.

"Hey," she said. "You okay?"

"I can't find them. Are you and Lucy okay?"

"Yes. Doing fine."

He gripped the wheel, his knuckles turning white as he got off at the next exit. "Okay. I'm circling back."

Noah's cell buzzed as he was dozing off to the ending credits of *Miracle*. He grabbed it as fast as he could, praying it didn't wake Brooke.

"Rowley," he said, in a low register, raking a hand through his hair.

"Sorry to bother you," Caleb said. "But I thought you'd want to know that a black sedan was parked outside of Austin's."

Noah stood, moving away from the couch so he wouldn't disturb Brooke. "What happened?"

"When I approached the car, shots were fired, and the car peeled off. I managed to blow out the rear window, but it kept going. I got in my car and raced to follow but couldn't find them. I did get a visual on the license plate, though."

"Is everyone safe?"

"Yes."

"You did good. Send the plate number to Logan. I'm sure he'll get right on it."

The man stayed up to all hours. How he was never dragging, Noah would never know.

"I'll send out an APB on the car too. Maybe a patrol car will pick it up," Caleb said, and Noah could hear the frustration in his voice.

"It's a solid plan, and everyone is safe," he said, knowing the frustration of losing a mark. "Though it sounds like you're finding and retrieving the barrels pricked some serious nerves."

"Agreed."

"Get a good night's sleep. I have a feeling you and Austin are going to have your work cut out for you tomorrow."

"Thanks, boss. 'Night."

"'Night. And, Caleb . . ."

"Yes?"

"You two watch your backs tomorrow. And keep me posted."

"Will do."

"What's wrong?" Brooke asked in a sleepy voice as Noah hung up.

"Sorry." He turned to face her. "I didn't mean to wake you."

"What's going on?" She rubbed the sleep from her eyes.

"Caleb and Austin had some trouble."

She sat up. "Are they okay?"

"Yes." For now. But his gut said there was more to come.

Brooke stretched her arms on a yawn.

"You should really go sleep in the guest room. You need your rest."

"And you?" she murmured, still caught in the throes of slumber.

"I'll head to the third bedroom Kenz made up for me."

"Okay," she said, getting up.

He smiled. She was so beautiful. He couldn't wait until the day he could wake up beside her in bed. To see her first thing in the morning as his wife. After tonight, his mind was fixed. He loved her, and there was no way he was letting her go.

"What?" She smiled nervously as she ran her fingers through her hair.

"Just thinking how captivating you are."

"Oh, I'm sure I look just lovely right now." She chuckled.

"You do." He moved beside her. "I'd show you how much, but you need your sleep. So . . ." He took a steadying inhale. "I'll walk you to your room and say goodnight like a gentleman."

"It's only a few feet, but I won't argue."

They paused outside the first guest room door.

"Good night, love."

She smiled. "I like the sound of that on your lips."

He cupped her face. "Good, because I'm going to be calling you *love* a lot."

She smiled as he lowered his mouth to hers.

He never wanted it to end, but he forced himself to step back. "Sleep well," he managed to say, his mind flooded with the passionate kiss. He cleared his throat, hoping it'd clear his muddled brain. "I'll see you in the morning."

She nodded, clearly as reluctant as he was to part. But reaching for the doorknob, she entered the bedroom.

Noah exhaled and rested his forehead against the door. Man, he loved that woman. He pressed off the doorframe, heading for the back bedroom, doubting he'd sleep a wink. It'd been a roller coaster of a day, ending with the purest happiness he'd ever known with Brooke, but also including fury that someone had tried to take Caleb out. Whoever it was had no idea what was coming. When someone came after one teammate, he came after them all.

Caleb knocked on Austin's locked front door.

It quickly opened. "Hey," she said, stepping back to usher him in.

"How's Lucy?" he asked.

"I'm good," she said, rounding the corner. "Is it safe for me to leave?"

"Yes. The car is gone, but I'll escort you out."

"Thank you," Lucy said. "And thanks for keeping Jaxon for a few days," she said to Austin.

"No problem. Take as much time as you need."

Lucy gave Austin a hug, grabbed her purse, and followed Caleb out to the driveway. She climbed inside her SUV and took off.

Caleb watched her taillights until she made a right onto Beacon. Then he scanned every inch of the neighborhood within sight. The fact that they hadn't even interviewed anyone yet, hadn't done anything but retrieve the barrels and set up appointments at the three foam manufacturers, gave him pause.

If someone was watching them already, what would happen once they really started poking around?

His breath fogged in puffs, the temps dropping steeper than anticipated, and yet he remained, surveying her street and the leafless tree line across from it.

"Thanks for seeing her off," Austin said.

He turned to find her leaning against the doorframe, the kitchen light spilling out around her. She held Jaxon in her arms. He wiggled and squirmed as Caleb approached.

"I'd say someone definitely likes you." She smiled.

Jaxon nearly burst from her arms as Caleb entered the house and shut the door behind them, locking it.

"All right," she said, laughing as she set the wiggly dog down.

He raced straight for Caleb, jumping up and pawing at his legs.

Caleb leaned down and picked him up.

"Looks like I've got some competition for those arms." She winked.

"I'll dump the dog right now," he offered.

"Don't you dare," she said as Jaxon nuzzled into his chest. "I'm just kidding." She turned and headed for the living room. "Sort of . . ." She smiled over her shoulder.

The air left his lungs. He was falling hard and fast.

"I'll grab you some bedding," she said.

He frowned. While he did plan to bunk on her couch, given the men watching her place, he hadn't said anything yet. "Am I that readable?" he asked. For a special agent, readable was never a good thing.

"More like predictable," she said, opening the small closet on the back wall of her living room.

His frown didn't lessen.

"That's a compliment," she said, moving to set the folded pile of bedding onto the far end of the sofa.

He arched his brows. "*Predictable* is a compliment? Maybe for a tax accountant." Certainly not the adjective he hoped to hear from the woman his heart was racing for.

She stepped back toward him. "*Reliable* might be a more apt description. You're . . . dependable."

"Not exactly the words that describe a man trying to whisk you off your feet."

She pattered across the kitchen floor separating them, her feet bare. She halted a matter of inches in front of him and raised up on her tiptoes. "On the contrary," she whispered. "Consider me whisked." She pressed her lips to his.

# FIFTY-TWO

Austin exited her bedroom at 0505, dressed in her wet suit, half hoping not to wake Caleb when he needed sleep, and half hoping to wake him as she longed to share this with him.

A laugh slipped passed her lips at the sight of Jaxon curled around Caleb's neck, but she stifled it.

"Why are you going diving at five a.m.?" he asked, his eyes still closed.

"How'd . . . ?" She shook her head. "Never mind. I'm not diving. I'm going for my sunrise swim."

"In fifty-degree water?"

"Hence the 3/2mm wet suit."

"Ah, so you wake up snarky," he said with a grin. "I've always wondered."

"If it wasn't true, I'd take offense," she said. "You want to go with me?"

"I'd love to. I just have to unfasten this heavyweight from my neck and grab my wet suit from the trunk."

After the short drive over to Wrightsville Beach, Austin stepped into the ocean, water rushing over her toes. Broken seashells, left in the outgoing tide's wake, tickled the soles of her bare feet. She looked at Caleb, standing at the water's edge beside her, his physique highlighted by the remaining moonlight mixed with the breaking dawn. How had she gotten so lucky? And did he feel the same?

Before her mind went all the way down a rabbit hole, they had best hurry to reach the cove in time. "Shall we?"

"Definitely." He grinned, a mischievous glint to his eyes.

Walking out, her feet sunk in the wet sand, squishing between her toes. Waves lapped higher and higher up her legs. Another dozen yards, and she dove under a breaking wave.

Reveling in the rush of adrenaline coursing through her, she swam for the surface. Now past the line of breaking waves, she leaned back into a float, letting the movement of the ocean carry her. The outgoing tide took her up and over the next line of burgeoning waves. The taste of salt water danced through her mouth, tickling her tongue.

Caleb swam to her side, bobbing seemingly without effort, only his head and shoulders breached the water. She straightened, treading water with only a breath's span between them. Her heart throbbed, echoing through her ears, mingling with the melody of the waves.

He reached out, cradled her head in his right hand, and nudged her nose with his, dipping in closer. The moment she lifted her lips toward his, he engulfed them. He tasted of the salt of the sea as the lulling waves lifted them up and lowered them down—their kiss never breaking except for a breath of sea air. He encircled her waist with his left arm, pulling her closer still, and she melded into his embrace.

Time evaporated until Caleb eased back. A deep sigh escaped his lips as water rushed around her where his arm had just been. Still dizzied, she looked up at him.

He slowly trailed his fingers along the side of her face and across her jaw before skimming the pad of his thumb across her lips.

She took a deep breath, conflict vacillating inside. She wanted to stay right here in this perfect moment, but if they lingered much longer, he'd miss the surprise. "We better get swimming, or we're going to miss it."

His brow furrowed. "Miss what?"

She started swimming in the cove's direction, warmth spiraling through her despite the brisk water lapping her face. She'd known Caleb's soul was a deep well of goodness and loyalty not long after they'd met—despite their sparring early on. But after *that* kiss, he also possessed an intensely passionate side she definitely loved.

Swimming freestyle between the lines of forming waves, Caleb rippled through the water beside her.

She struggled to shake off the well of emotion they'd shared in that kiss. *Clear your head. Focus on reaching the cove.* Rolling her nose and mouth just above the water line, she inhaled the chilly air, praying it'd shake her out of the stupor.

Within another hundred yards, she saw they'd reached the cove just in time. She shifted to treading water, smiling as Caleb treaded beside her.

"Look," she said, pointing at the horizon. The sun rose slowly, casting streaks of orange and pink across the sky. As if God were painting His canvas right in front of them.

Caleb spun to face the horizon. "Wow. Killer sunrise spot."

She smiled. She'd never shared this with anyone before. But watching the sunrise was even more special now that she had someone she wanted to share it with.

He swam behind her, wrapping his arms around her waist, resting his chin gently on her head. "It's beautiful. Just like you."

She smiled, wondering if they'd talk about what was happening between them—were they dating, courting, in a relationship? That talk had to happen sooner rather than later, but not in this perfect moment. Instead, she leaned back into him, his strong torso flush with her back as they watched the sun rise higher in the sky.

The opening riff of "Sweet Home Alabama" jolted Noah awake. Grabbing his phone off the end table, he fumbled it.

"Rowley." He pinched the bridge of his nose, trying to shake himself awake as he looked at his watch—*0640*. Definitely time to get up. The coffee pot gurgled, brewing the pot Kenzie had preset last night before heading up to bed.

"Hey, boss," Logan said. "Sorry to disturb you, but thought you'd want to know the license number came back as a stolen plate."

"Why am I not surprised."

"Stolen from a Floridian tourist visiting Wilmington."

Noah sighed. "Another dead end."

"But on a good note, Mrs. Hunter, the woman who remembered the catering van outside of the graduation, was able to provide enough detail for me to do a sketch of the logo on its side."

*Finally! A strong lead.* "That's excellent news."

"And Em has more good news," Logan said. "Hang on."

Noah checked his watch again. How long had the pair been at the station?

"Hi, boss. I told Logan I can just go over this at our next case board—"

"No problem. What do you have?"

"Unfortunately, the catering company on the logo doesn't exist—not anywhere I could find."

Noah sighed. Another dead end. If Emmy couldn't find it, it didn't exist. "I expected you were going to say that." But Logan had said good news . . .

"Yeah, but I did find other vehicle logos with a similar style. Apparently, it's a special technique, or medium used, if you will."

"Interesting." He stifled a yawn and took a sip of coffee while he waited for her to continue.

"There are only two shops that carry the supplies for that method of logo within a two-hour vicinity of Wilmington."

"Great. Text the names over, and Brooke and I will visit them right away this morning. We'll take the sketch Mrs. Hunter provided."

"Sounds good. So a late case board?"

"I think we'll just go with our p.m. case board since we all have our assignments for today. Brooke and I will hit the logo stores, Caleb and Austin are on foam companies. Finn's got plenty to keep him busy in the lab, and Rissi is still knee-deep in the mass shooting and lab theft investigation. But I'll text everyone to make sure we're all on board. I'll be back to the station this afternoon for the interviews of Lieutenants Caldwell and Malone."

He prayed that at least one of their other leads provided answers.

# FIFTY-THREE

Caleb tapped the steering wheel on the way to FoamTech—the first company they'd be visiting. His tapping increased. He and Austin needed to talk. "I've been thinking . . ." he began, his words sounding awkward to his ears.

"So have I," she said.

He arched a brow and glanced over at her. "Oh?" he asked, before darting his gaze back to the road.

"I don't know how you view things . . ." she began.

"View what?" Was she about to bring up the very same thing he'd been pondering?

"Us." She swallowed. "I mean . . . the kissing."

She *was* thinking the same thing. "Yes?" he asked, letting her take the lead.

"I don't know how you feel about it . . . about me, but I . . ." She sighed. "I'm hoping . . ."

He'd never seen Austin nervous.

"I'm hoping that . . . you're . . . that we're . . ."

"Dating?" he said.

She nodded.

"We probably should have talked first . . ." he began.

She shifted. "Oh?"

He cleared his throat. Why was this so difficult? "I don't kiss just to fool around, and I don't date just for the heck of it."

Her brow furrowed. "What are you saying?"

He loosened his collar. How was it hot in the midst of one of their coldest winters yet? "That, I—" Here went nothing. "That I like you."

Her beautiful eyes narrowed. "But?"

"No but." He shook his head, and her shoulders relaxed. "I care for you deeply. I just want . . . just think . . ."

"We should be a couple?" Austin supplied.

Why did the words come so easily for her when he'd sounded like a bumbling fool? "Yes." Not wanting to drive distracted and already fully there, he looked for a place to pull over and found one the next block up. He shifted the car in park, unbuckled his seat belt, and shifted to face her.

"What are we doing?" she asked, a soft smile on those lips he loved to kiss.

Words first. He needed to know, though from the way she kissed him back he thought he already did, or at least he hoped. "How do you feel about us being a couple?"

She bit her bottom lip, then smiled. "I'd love to be your girlfriend if you're asking."

He smiled. "Oh, I'm most definitely asking." He reached over and slipped his fingers through hers. "And dating . . ." He looked up at her. "I don't date if I don't see it going anywhere."

Her gaze held his. "Are you asking me to marry you?"

He choked. He cared deeply, but they'd just started—

She laughed, hard. "I'm sorry." She struggled to contain her laughter but did a terrible job of it. Tears even sprang from her eyes. "I couldn't help myself."

"You little . . ." He wanted to say *vixen* but had zero clue where that word had come from.

She continued to crack up. "You should have seen your face."

"That wasn't funny." She'd nearly given him a heart attack, partially from the joy the mere thought had brought to his mind.

"Oh, I disagree. It was hilarious."

He snaked his arms around her waist, pulling her tight. "I can see now this is going to be one heck of an adventure."

She caressed his jawline, lowering her lips to his. "But never a dull moment."

He chuckled as she kissed him, then swallowed his laughter as her kiss grew deeper.

Austin's heart was still abuzz when they pulled into Foam-Tech's lot. *They*—her and her boyfriend. She smiled, basking in the thought he was hers.

"Who are we seeing here?" Caleb asked as he hopped out and walked around to open her door.

"Len Heisman, the director of manufacturing," she said, stepping out of the Forester.

Len was out on the inventory floor when they arrived, so they waited in the dismal gray lobby.

A half hour later, a tall man in his upper forties strode toward them with an iPad tucked under his arm. "Len Heisman," he said. "Sorry to have kept you waiting. It's inventory day."

"We understand," Caleb said.

"How can I help you folks?" Len asked.

"We'd like to ask you a few questions about TCEP," Austin said.

"TCEP." Len shook his head on a whistle. "That was a real money sucker once they banned it."

"We heard it was extremely expensive to properly dispose of," Austin said.

"You're telling me. Fortunately, we only had a dozen barrels left when the ruling came down, but it still cost us a pretty penny."

"And how did you dispose of it?" Caleb asked.

"We used an EPA-approved company to dispose of it at the hazardous waste site up in Leland."

Austin made a note in her phone. Yet another place to check on.

"Mind giving us a quick tour of the plant?" Caleb asked.

"Sure," Len said. "Let's grab you some hard hats."

"Hard hats?" Austin arched her brows.

"Safety protocol," Len said. "We've got a new safety-assurance gal, and she's implemented a number of precautionary procedures."

*Gal?* Austin let that one go. Maybe he hadn't meant anything by it, but his tone certainly hadn't sounded flattering.

Len led them into the plant, where a pungent smell filled the air. Part strong chemical, part . . . Whatever it was, it was definitely unique.

"What kind of products do you specialize in?" Caleb asked.

"Car seats, shoe linings, mattress and pillow filling, along with a number of items for the medical market."

"Medical?" Austin asked as they followed Len deeper into the plant and past blue scaffolding with gigantic rolls of foam nearly touching the thirty-foot-high warehouse ceiling. They entered another set of gray double doors, and the odor intensified, saws whirred, and black ooze slithered down a large chute.

"Put these on." Len handed them both protective eye gear.

The last time Austin had worn a pair was in high school chemistry.

"Running," a man called from the machine's control panel.

A high-pitched whirring sounded as a yellow light circled on the scaffolding overhead. Len scooted them along. What looked like a combination of lava mixed with bright blue liquid poured down the chute in front of them, the liquid thickening into foam by the time it reached the end of the shaft.

Austin had never seen foam made. It was interesting. But far more so were the off-limits sections Len claimed were too dangerous to enter without the proper training and gear.

A half hour later, they thanked Len for the tour and for answering their questions, then exited the plant.

"I didn't see anything that stuck out as a concern," Caleb said, opening his car door for Austin. "But I think we better follow up on the disposal of TCEP—see if what they have to say matches up with what Len said."

"Agreed."

# FIFTY-FOUR

"Hopefully we'll have better luck here," Noah said, opening the glass door of Lance's Logo Supplies for Brooke. The first logo shop had been a bust.

"Thanks," she said, stepping inside as a bell jangled overhead.

A man approached the other side of the roughhewn wooden counter in a plaid shirt and faded blue jeans. "How you folks doing today?"

"Fine, thanks," Noah said, lifting his badge on the chain around his neck. "Special Agent Noah Rowley."

"Jim Larson," the man said, shaking Noah's extended hand.

"This is Miss Kesler," Noah said.

"Miss." Jim gave a nod.

"We're hoping you might be able to help us out," Noah said.

"Oh?" Jim leaned forward, planting his palms on the counter. "What kind of help?"

Noah slid him the drawing of the logo Logan had rendered. "Any idea whose work this might be?"

Jim studied it for a moment. "It's Dwayne's."

Noah arched a brow. That was quicker than anticipated. "Dwayne?"

"Dwayne . . ." Jim's eyes squinted. "I'm trying to think of his last name, but not sure he ever gave it."

"Does he come in often?" Noah asked.

"He did, pretty regularly."

"Did?"

Jim straightened and rubbed his chin. "Is Dwayne in some sort of trouble?"

"We need to ask him some questions," Noah said, being as vague as possible.

"Good luck finding him." Jim leaned against the rear counter, linking his arms across his chest. "He hasn't been in for months."

"Any idea why?" Brooke asked.

Jim shrugged. "No clue. Guy was in here probably once a week. Everyone in town who wanted a good logo called Dwayne. Then one day he just up and disappeared."

"Do you have his number?" Noah asked.

"I have his old number," Jim said. "It says it's out of service. All his customers are calling here looking for him."

"Why here?" Noah asked.

"His customers know Dwayne worked with the best supplies, which he got here. They haven't been able to get a hold of him at his old number, so they've tried here." Jim shuffled through some papers beneath his register. Noah hadn't seen an actual register in years. Everyone used Square or some card reader nowadays.

"Here," Jim said, sliding the list over to Noah.

Clasping the steno sheet in his hand, Noah trailed his gaze down the mint green page. Names with numbers next to them. "Dwayne's customers?"

Jim nodded. "I have no clue where he is. I don't think any of them do either, but maybe . . ."

"Thanks, I appreciate it," Noah said. "One more thing, could you describe Dwayne?"

Jim rubbed his chin. "I'd say about your height, brawnier build—sort of thick, ya know?"

Noah nodded. "Hair color? Eyes?"

"Dark hair."

"Brown? Black?"

Jim studied him. "A few shades darker than yours, I'd say. His eyes . . . don't know that I ever noticed, to be honest."

Noah always waited to get the person's description without leading with any details and then, if it sounded like a match, he'd show the sketch or photograph—if only they were so lucky to have found that.

He slid the sketch of the "nurse" across the counter to Jim. "Any chance this is Dwayne?"

Jim lifted the sketch and studied it a moment. "Yeah. That's him. Good drawing."

"Thanks. We've got a talented artist on the team," Noah said, though Logan would never think of himself as such. "Appreciate your help." Now they had a name—at least a first name—along with a positive ID on Logan's sketch. It was a great start to the day.

"So," Brooke said as they stepped outside, the temps feeling even colder than when they'd entered. "We have a first name to go with the sketch." Brooke shrugged. "I suppose it's better than nothing."

"Definitely better than nothing," Noah said. "And a list of customers as well."

"True," she said, slipping her braided hair behind her shoulder and slipping on her white wool cap.

"It is kind of odd that Jim worked with Dwayne on a weekly basis and yet didn't know his last name."

"I'd bet Dwayne worked solely in cash."

"You think?" Noah asked.

"Sounds like a man who kept things close to the vest."

Usually the most dangerous kind.

Noah hung up from his call, crossing the sixth number off the list Jim Larson had given him of Dwayne's customers. Only two customers left to call and one to hear back from. Thus far, every customer had always paid cash, as apparently that's all Dwayne took, as Brooke had correctly guessed. Several customers had a last name for him, but none were the same—Thomas, Smith, Jones—easy, simple names that drew no attention.

Noah's cell rang. Brooke looked over from the driver's seat as he glanced at the number. "Hey, Caleb," he said, switching the call to Bluetooth. "How's it going?"

"We just left Taylor & Greene Manufacturing, the second foam plant we've visited."

"Any luck?" Noah asked, the wind flapping the thick plastic windows of the soft-top Jeep.

"The managers at both plants were helpful and gave us tours," Caleb said, but he was holding an opinion back. Noah could always tell by the hitch in his voice.

"But?" Noah prodded.

"But I feel like we're getting the same party line. Austin, you want to chime in?" he asked.

"Hi, guys," Austin said. "Like Caleb said, we basically got the same story at both places, and the same tour. It was like both had been rehearsed, and maybe that's the case. Sort of like any group tour you go on where things are basically verbatim."

"Right," Caleb said. "But we don't imagine they give enough tours to sound so . . ."

"Similar," Caleb and Austin said in unison.

Noah looked over at Brooke, and she smiled.

When this case was over, he was very curious where Caleb and Austin would be. Deep in the midst of a relationship if

Rissi's and Brooke's musings were right, and he wouldn't bet against those two.

"What party line did they give you about the chemical in question?" Noah asked, regathering his thoughts.

"Len Heisman of FoamTech said they'd lost, and I quote, 'a pretty penny,' properly disposing of the TCEP," Caleb said, "and he provided us with the hazmat waste disposal company they utilized."

"Tony Shapiro from Taylor & Greene said they saw the writing on the wall and began phasing out of TCEP before it was banned, so they only had a small quantity to dispose of."

"Did he say who they used to dispose of it?" Noah asked as Brooke entered the traffic circle at the bottom of Main Street. Time for a much-needed coffee break at Port City Java.

"He couldn't recall offhand," Caleb said.

Brooke's brows arched as she darted a glance over at him, echoing his own questioning response.

"He claimed he could locate the name of the company if required," Caleb said with that investigative edge to his voice.

"As in, if a warrant was produced?" Noah asked.

"Not in so many words," Austin said, "but that was clearly the point he was making."

"So you'll be keeping an eye on Taylor & Greene." It wasn't a question, as he already heard the conviction of it in both of their voices.

"I'm already digging up what I can on them while Caleb drives," Austin said.

"Good. Keep me posted." His other line rang. "Sorry, guys, I have to take this."

"Take care," Austin said before the call dropped.

Noah answered the incoming one. "Rowley."

"Hi. This is Don Lang. You left a message on my voicemail about my logo guy, Dwayne."

"Yes, Mr. Lang. Thanks for returning my call."

"No problem. Have you found him?" Lang asked.

Noah furrowed his brow. Interesting choice of words. "Found him?"

"I've been trying to get a hold of him for months but can't reach him. Seems Jim Larson can't either."

"Do you have a last name for Dwayne?"

"Jackson, I believe," Lang said.

Yet another one. "And do you have any idea where Dwayne lives?"

"I think he rents a room at the Strasburg Hotel over on West Avenue."

Surprise rattled through Noah. He was at the point where he'd stopped anticipating a lead.

"I tried calling over there once," Lang continued, "but the lady at the desk said she hadn't seen him in ages. I gave up and went with someone else for the job."

"Is there anything you can tell us about Dwayne? Any physical features, markings, anything about his life that stood out to you?" He'd asked everyone on the list and gotten the same response Jim Larson had provided—tall, broad, dark brown hair. Though the customers had filled in a few more details—brown eyes, and that he wore jeans and patriotic T-shirts.

"Any tattoos?" Noah asked. "Anything specific or unique about the man?"

"Well, he did have this weird tattoo on his upper left arm, just below the shoulder."

"Could you describe it?" he asked

"I mean, I only got a quick glance, but it was odd for a tattoo."

"Odd how?"

"It looked like it was seared into his skin."

# FIFTY-FIVE

Caleb followed Austin into Huntington Foam to find himself in a completely different environment from the previous two foam manufacturing companies. The walls were a cheery yellow, and a blond secretary with red nails, red lipstick, and a perky smile greeted them. "Good morning, y'all. Welcome to Huntington Foam. I'm Cheri. How can I be of help?"

"Thanks for the welcome." Caleb smiled.

"Do y'all have an appointment?" Cheri asked, picking up the phone.

"We do, with Mr. Gower." Caleb lifted his badge. "I'm Special Agent Caleb Eason with the Coast Guard Investigative Service, and this is private investigator Austin Kelly."

Cheri pressed an extension. After a moment's pause, she said, "Mr. Gower, your next appointment is here. A CGIS agent and a private investigator. Uh-huh . . ."

She covered the receiver. "He'd like to know what this is in reference to?"

Caleb held his badge up again. "We've got some questions about chemicals used to make foam."

After half an hour of waiting in the bright yellow lobby with upbeat elevator music that was trying Caleb's last nerve, a man in a tailored three-piece suit stepped through the double set of gleaming white doors. The man was younger than Caleb had anticipated for being the CEO of such a lucrative company—based on Austin's initial findings.

Caleb got to his feet, and Austin did the same.

"Mr. Gower?" Caleb asked.

"Yes," the man strode forward, his shoulders taut. "Braxton, please," he said, extending a hand. "Sorry to keep you both waiting. One meeting after another today."

"Everything okay?" Austin asked.

Gower smiled at her. *Really* smiled at her. Caleb silently dared Gower to play the "you're too beautiful to be a private eye" card with Austin. She would level him flat.

But the man just cleared his throat and said, "The foam business is a massive juggling act, and there's a delicate balance between maintaining enough supply of the necessary chemicals to make the foam and fulfilling orders, but not being too heavy on inventory or overhead."

"That's actually what we're here to ask you about," Caleb said. "We would like to speak with you about TCEP, specifically."

Gower blanched, then smoothed his tie down to the V in his coat. "Let's speak in my office, shall we?" He gestured to the white doors. "Right this way."

"Thanks," Caleb said as Braxton held the door open for him, then in turn for Austin.

"We'd also love a tour of your facility," Austin said, coming up beside Braxton in the white hall with gray doors every ten feet or so.

Gower smiled. "You would?"

"Yes." Austin smiled back. "We've been to two other foam companies today and received tours, but I have a feeling yours will be far different."

"We like to think so." Braxton shifted directions, heading down a small hall with an emergency exit door at the end. "Might as well start the tour now."

Austin looked around as they moved through an immaculate section of the plant, the metal scaffolding and ramps a similar bright yellow as that of the lobby. "Your plant is highly impressive."

"That's quite a compliment." Gower nodded. "Thank you. I'm guessing you visited FoamTech?"

"Mmm-hmm," Austin said, "And Taylor & Greene."

"They produce decent foam, but we've worked hard to upgrade our standards and innovation. Here," he said, reaching for yellow hard hats, handing one to Austin and then Caleb.

Austin slipped hers on, and Caleb tried not to smile at how adorable she looked.

*Mind on case. Mind on case.* "How long have you been CEO?" Caleb asked.

"About three years," Braxton said.

So only a year before TCEP was banned. If he'd been fully stocked up, the legal disposal of it according to EPA guidelines could have bankrupted the company—one he'd only recently taken over.

"How'd you come to Huntington Foam, Mr. Gower?" Caleb asked.

"Braxton, please. It's a family business, over sixty years old. I took it over when my father retired."

"That's a lot of pressure," Austin said.

Braxton nodded. "It can be, but I thrive under pressure. I bet this guy does too." He angled his head back at Caleb.

"Miss Kelly does as well," Caleb said. As passionate as she was about her work and various aspects of life, when it came to pressure, instead of getting overwhelmed, it sparked her to life.

"Is that so?" Braxton said, appraising her as they worked their way into the next section of the plant—passing a mail station mounted along the far wall between office doors.

People walked by them, excusing themselves as they shuffled by in the narrow space. Phones rang up and down the halls, and that unique scent from the other two plants filled the air here as well.

After winding through section after section of the plant, Braxton invited them back to his office to talk in less noisy surroundings.

"Here we are," he said, gesturing them inside. Windows ran the length of the back wall, displaying trees and the parking lot.

Once they were all seated, Braxton asked, "What do you want to know about TCEP?" He reclined in his chair, steepling his fingers. "I have to admit, I'm very curious why the Coast Guard Investigative Service and a private eye are interested in a foam manufacturing chemical."

"Understandable," Caleb said, pulling his notepad out of his pocket, followed by his pen, which he clicked to begin writing. "Let's start with the basics. Is TCEP a chemical you use in production?"

Braxton reclined farther, his chair creaking with the motion. "We did use TCEP until it was banned, which basically affected our entire line of products, so we switched to an innovative technology resulting in eco-friendly foams."

"Eco-friendly?" Austin asked.

"Six months back, we overhauled our plant. We use enclosed chambers to control the foam-pouring conditions, which no longer require the use of hazardous air-pollutant auxiliary blowing agents to manufacture our products. In fact, our process is now virtually emissions free. We've developed patented technology and are quickly becoming leaders in the green foam field."

"So leaders in environmentally friendly foaming?" Austin asked. "Just to clarify."

Braxton smiled. "That's correct." He reached into the cabinet behind him and grabbed two brochures, handing one to each of them.

Caleb unfolded the trifold brochure, scanning the contents.

"That's quite a change from manufacturing flame-retardant foam," he said.

"Yes." Braxton took a stiff inhale and nodded on the exhale. "It was a multimillion-dollar overhaul, but it was worth it for our environment and our customers."

A big foam plant suddenly worrying about the environment when they'd worked with chemicals like TCEP for years seemed a rapid turnaround. "What did you do with the TCEP you had on hand?" Caleb asked. "They had to be expensive to dispose of."

Braxton tapped his fingertips together. "It would have been, but thankfully we weren't left holding any. We got wind of the ban coming and pumped out product as fast as we could."

"You had *none* left to dispose of?" Austin asked, clearly not convinced Braxton Gower was telling the truth.

"Correct." Braxton said, straightening, his chair creaking on the way up. "Unlike some of the other poor saps in our industry. Cost a few in the biz their entire plants."

He looked at his watch. "I apologize, but I have a meeting in five."

"Of course," Caleb said. "Thanks for your time and for showing us around."

"My pleasure," Braxton said.

Austin pulled a card from her bag as Caleb pulled one from his pocket. Both handed them to Braxton.

"If you think of anything that might be helpful in the search for who might be dumping TCEP illegally, please give either of us a call," Caleb said.

"Is that what this is about?" Braxton asked, slipping their cards in his vest pocket.

"I'm afraid so," Austin said.

"That's terrible. I will absolutely reach out if I think of anything," he said over his shoulder as he hurried off.

"What do you think?" Austin asked as Caleb held the Forester's passenger door open for her.

He inhaled. Three plants. The first two nearly carbon copies. The last held a very different vibe with its environmentally friendly process and claim they'd been left holding no TCEP. "I'm thinking we discuss it over burgers at Dockside." Lunch would give them time to discuss everything.

"Sounds great." Austin smiled.

Reaching the one-lane bridge leading into Wrightsville Beach, they waited for their turn to cross. Caleb looked in his rearview mirror and frowned.

"What's up?" Austin asked.

"That blue sedan," he said, tilting his chin. "I saw one like it as we pulled out of Huntington Foam and now here."

"Is it the same one?" she asked.

He glanced in the rearview mirror again. "Well, both had an air freshener hanging from the rearview mirror."

She glanced in the side mirror.

The sedan was far enough back that he couldn't make out much of the man behind the wheel other than he was average size, wearing a dark baseball cap tucked low on his forehead and a pair of sunglasses. Given the cold temp and gray cover blanketing the sky, his attire definitely piqued Caleb's attention. "It could be a coincidence."

"Could be, but your gut is saying it's not?"

Caleb exhaled. "I don't know, but the odds we're headed to the same place all the way from Huntington Foam doesn't sit right with me."

"What do you suggest?" she asked.

"We lose him, then track back around and see if we can't get behind him and—"

"Grab his plate number," she finished.

Once clear of the bridge, Caleb pulled up to the left lane and signaled to the car beside them, asking with hand motions if they could cut in front to make a left at the light. The driver in the yellow VW nodded, and Caleb nosed his Forester toward her. The light changed, and the lady in the VW waved him forward, allowing him to pull fully in front of her and make the quick left. The sedan fell behind, having a harder time finding someone to let them in the turn lane before the light turned red.

Caleb smiled. *Perfect*. He U-turned and pulled back on the road, going the opposite way. "Grab the number," he said.

"Got it." Austin scribbled it down. "I'll send it to Emmy. See what comes back."

"Hopefully something other than another stolen plate."

# FIFTY-SIX

Brooke slowed as they drove by the Strasburg Hotel on West Avenue. Hotel was a very generous word. Motel would have been too. What they were looking at was more of a halfway house with rooms rented by the month or hour.

The ick factor, or *isky* factor as her grandma always said, slid over her like tar on a briar patch.

Noah surveyed the area, then pointed to their left. "Let's park over there."

She followed his outstretched finger to a small paid parking lot, scanned the area as she flipped on her blinker, and turned in. It was the best, and basically only, option if they wanted his Jeep to remain intact.

A guard sat in the metal box, for lack of a better word.

He handed her a ticket, not bothering to glance over. "Put it on your dash. We close at ten."

"Thank you," she said, sliding the yellow ticket onto the dash. It slipped down to nestle between the defrost vents and the windshield.

The white bar with red reflectors raised, allowing them passage into the square lot enclosed by a low brick wall.

After she parked and locked the Jeep, Noah held her hand as they crossed West Avenue.

Two men sat on metal folding chairs outside the Strasburg's

office, both drinking from Styrofoam cups. Maybe midfifties, round in the belly with receding hairlines. The only difference between them was the style of their attire. One was in a thick winter coat, the other in a striped shirt and brown argyle sweater vest, but he carried on as if it were a nice fall day.

"Don't get the likes of you around here much," the man in the sweater vest said as Noah held the door open for Brooke.

Offering the man a pleasant smile, she stepped through the doorway as Noah placed his hand on the center of her lower back.

Tomato sauce and garlic assaulted her nostrils. Both were normally pleasant, soothing scents, but not now. The stench hung thick in the smoke-filled lobby, a rancid odor imbibing the air.

She leaned back. "I didn't think you could smoke indoors anymore," she whispered over her shoulder at Noah, whose body she could feel at a tight three o'clock.

"I don't think rules apply here."

She hesitantly stepped forward as she took in the scene. Bicycles lined the right wall, mostly kid-sized, which twinged her heart. Two women in less than modest clothing stood in the alcove by the front door. She smiled at them, but they ignored her, one flicking the ashes off her cigarette, which fluttered to the thin black carpet.

Noah indicated the bank-teller-style front desk down the narrow brown-paneled hall about fifty feet in.

"Hi, ma'am," Noah greeted the elderly lady behind the Plexiglas.

"Room?" she asked, without looking up.

Why were people so unwilling to make eye contact? Eye contact was crucial in Brooke's job. If the patient couldn't see her intent and her reassuring gaze, they often slipped through her fingers rather than hanging on. She swallowed back stinging pain. Molly slipping through her fingers rattled Brooke's brain and heart in painful conjunction.

"You okay?" Noah whispered.

She nodded.

"Room?" the lady asked again, still not bothering to look up.

"No, ma'am." Noah held his badge up to the glass. "We have some questions."

The woman's gray brows bunched as her dim brown eyes flickered up at the shield. "Cop?" she said, squinting.

"Special Agent Noah Rowley."

"Josh," she called over her shoulder. "Josh!" she hollered after no one appeared.

A man about Noah's height but probably a decade older, with mussed brown hair, stepped through a door behind the desk. Wearing a blue silk shirt and black trousers, he looked oddly out of place. "Can I help you?" he asked.

"I hope so," Noah said, holding up his badge again. "I'm Special Agent Noah Rowley."

"Josh," the guy said, lifting his chin.

"Josh . . . ?"

"Gilbert."

"Thanks, Josh. We're hoping you can be of help. We're looking for Dwayne."

"Last name?" Josh asked.

"We have at least four possible last names but don't believe any of them are accurate," Noah said.

"Look . . ." Josh skimmed his hand slowly along the top of his hair. "We get a lot of folks in and out of here."

"He's tall—about my height, maybe an inch or two over. Has brown hair a few shades darker than mine, brown eyes, and a beard. Oh, and he wears a lot of patriotic T-shirts."

"Oh yeah." Josh nodded. "I know who you mean. He was in 3B."

Noah released a stiff exhale. "Was?"

"Yeah. He disappeared a few months back."

"Any idea where he went?"

"Nah." Josh shook his head with an amused smile, as if Noah had just asked the most absurd thing. "Guys take off, don't leave a forwarding address. You get my drift?"

"Yeah." Noah's jaw tightened, then he cleared his throat. "Could we look around 3B?"

"Someone else is living there now," Josh said.

"Did he leave anything behind?"

"Rooms come furnished, so everything like that stayed."

Brooke winced, trying not to imagine what Josh's idea of *furnished* was.

"But . . ." Josh began. "I let the more long-term renters store stuff up in the attic." He shrugged. "I suppose it's possible he left something up there. The rule was mark your junk with your apartment number."

"Can we take a look?" Noah asked.

"Sure," Josh said. "No sweat off my back, but you and"— his eyes shifted to Brooke—"your lady friend should be careful. There's no floor beyond the entry platform, just structure beams."

Noah held Brooke's hand as she climbed up beside him on the platform.

"Careful on the beams," he said as they split up to look for anything labeled *3B*. He hoped but wasn't holding his breath.

He watched Brooke head for the right front side of the attic, balancing with precision across the beams.

"Impressive," he said.

She shrugged. "Years of ballet."

"I didn't know you danced." There was still so much to know. He couldn't wait for the time spent learning everything about her.

"Hey," she said ten minutes in.

He turned, and she waved him over to the far corner of the

attic. He worked his way over beam by beam until he was at her side.

"3B." She smiled.

"Fantastic." He honestly hadn't expected to find anything, not at the rate this case was going.

He slipped his gloves on and then, positioning a foot on two parallel planks, knelt to examine the box. It looked intact enough to transport as is. "Let's take it back to the lab for Finn to go through."

"Sounds good." She stood as he lifted the box in his arm, and they gingerly made their way back to the platform and out to his Jeep.

Though a *3B* label didn't necessarily mean the box had belonged to Dwayne, Noah prayed they'd finally found tactile evidence on the man who had eluded them thus far.

# FIFTY-SEVEN

Brooke pulled into the station parking lot with only minutes to spare before Noah's interviews with the Army lieutenant and guardsman who'd both brought up red flags when initially questioned.

Em stepped past them as they entered the station. "Hey, boss." She balanced a tower of files and a mishmash of notepads before off-loading them onto her desk. She certainly had her work cut out for her.

"Ris," Noah called, heading toward the lab with the box they'd found, "I'll be right back."

"Neither Caldwell nor Malone have arrived yet, so take your time," Rissi said, lifting her coffee tumbler as Noah went by.

Noah turned to Brooke as he set down the box. "You're welcome to join Em while she processes the box's contents. I know you're as anxious as I am to see what's inside."

Her eyes lit. "You sure that's okay?"

"You're as big a part of this case as any of us."

She shifted her weight, unable to smother her smile. "Okay. Thanks."

"Ready?" Emmy said with a bounce in her step as she entered the lab.

"Most definitely. My curiosity is sky-high," Brooke said.

"On that note," Noah said, "I'm going to get ready for the interviews. You two try not to get into too much trouble."

Emmy batted her eyes. "Us? Trouble?"

"Mind if I join you ladies?" Austin asked, entering.

Noah exhaled. All three of them in a room. Trouble was sure to abound.

He longed to press a kiss to Brooke's lips before leaving her, but they were in the station and within sight of his team, so he restrained himself, but very begrudgingly.

"Hey, Caleb," he said, heading back for his desk. "How'd it go?"

"All along the party line, though each foam company differed in feel and size."

"Any gut feelings?"

Caleb shook his head. "Not yet. Well, I wasn't the biggest fan of the head honcho at FoamTech. Something about him rubbed me the wrong way."

"Your instincts always serve you well," Noah said. "Pay heed to them."

Caleb nodded. "Will do."

"They're still not here," Rissi said, taking a sip of her coffee. How she could inhale so much caffeine and not talk a mile a minute like Gabby did befuddled him.

"Is it just me," Noah said, "or are you finding it odd that both of them are late?"

"Yeah, it's quite the coincidence."

Noah glanced at his watch. "I say we give them five minutes, then we call."

"And if they don't answer?" Rissi asked.

"I'll send you and Caleb to find Malone, and Finn can meet Logan to check on Caldwell."

Em looked up at Austin and smiled. "I'm glad you're here."

Austin smiled. She was glad to be there too and prayed with all her heart that both cases—with their myriad layers—would be solved. Prayed that God would open Finn's and Emmy's eyes to process the evidence and to see it for what it was. To see the links in the chain that would wrap around the necks of the guilty.

"I got a hit on that plate number you and Caleb called in," Em said.

"Really?" Excitement sparked inside her.

Emmy nodded. "The plate is registered to a Hector Valdez on Water Street. He reported it stolen a couple days ago."

Austin narrowed her eyes. "Stolen?"

"Yep." Em nodded.

She frowned. "So he came out that day and his license plate was missing?"

Em chuckled. "Nope. Whoever stole it replaced it with a similar-looking plate."

"So he checks his plates regularly enough that he immediately noticed the switch?" Austin asked. She knew her plate number by heart, but she didn't check it regularly.

"You sound about as skeptical as I was," Emmy said. "Mr. Valdez said he called in right away to file a report, but apparently he didn't feel like sitting around waiting for the police to come check things out, so he drove the car anyway, going about his day. But he got pulled over for speeding. The cop ran the plate and . . ."

"And?" Austin said.

"He'd already reported his plates stolen and replaced."

"And the cop seriously bought that?" Austin said. It was a scam if she'd ever heard one. Report something you planned to use in a crime as missing, and then it couldn't be pinned on you.

"I contacted the officer who took the report and let him know the stolen plate had been spotted and gave him the make and model of the car. They put out an APB."

"Any sightings yet?" Austin asked, twirling a pencil she'd pulled from her purse between her index finger and thumb. She had so much restless energy coursing through her, she needed some place to direct it.

"Not yet," Em said.

"Did you get an address for Mr. Valdez?" she asked.

"Yep. It's written on the orange Post-it note on my desk," Em said.

"Thanks. I'll grab it on the way out." But first she was curious about the box.

"Okay, ladies." Em rubbed her gloved hands together. "Let's get started."

Austin stepped back with Brooke while Em did her customary round of photographs, capturing each side of the box.

"Where'd it come from?" she asked Brooke as Em's flash bounced off the examination table's silver legs.

"We found it at the hotel where Dwayne stayed—the man I saw at the hospital in the nurse's costume," Brooke said. "The man who killed Andrews . . . the man who had me . . ." Her voice shook a bit as she trailed off, but she seemed determined to stay in the middle of the investigation.

Austin placed her hand on Brooke's shoulder. "You okay?"

Brooke looked up with a tight-lipped smile, but also a fire in her eyes. "Yes."

"All right," Austin said, highly impressed at Brooke's fortitude. "Did you find out his last name?"

"Not yet."

"Maybe something in this box will hold the answer," she said.

Brooke's taut shoulders eased. "That would be awesome."

"Let's open her up," Em said, handing the box of gloves to Brooke, who handed it on to Austin.

Grabbing a utility knife, Emmy sliced the packaging tape. Setting the knife aside, she pulled back the flaps. Musty dust poofed out, and Em quickly collected a sample from what had fluttered back into the box.

"Lovely," Austin said, half-afraid of what might be inside. Over the years of private investigation, she'd found plenty of funky and outright scary things in abandoned boxes.

Reaching in, Emmy pulled out a T-shirt with the American flag emblazoned across the front, its ends tattered. She turned it over. *Restore Our Country* was written in white block letters across the top.

"So he's patriotic but disillusioned, perhaps," Austin said, as Emmy laid the T-shirt on the paper-covered table, where all items would go until she labeled each, inspecting everything for trace evidence.

Next out was a stack of three hardcover books. "First up . . ." Em said, turning the book on its side, "*The Constitution of the United States.*"

"So Dwayne wasn't a light reader," Brooke said.

"Yeah, and he is growing more interesting with each item," Austin said.

"Next we have . . ." Emmy turned to its spine. "*The Federalist Papers.*"

"He's definitely patriotic," Austin said.

Brooke shook her head. "I just don't understand a guy who lives in a literal fleabag rent-by-the-hour motel, goes by more last names than fingers on my hand, but reads serious books on our nation's founding."

All of that mixed together was painting a very complex portrait. *Who is this guy?*

"And the mystery continues," Emmy said, holding up the third and final book. "*Scapegoats: Thirteen Victims of Military Injustice* by Michael Newton."

"Oh boy." Brooke shifted to face Austin. "I'd say you nailed it with 'patriotic but disillusioned.'"

Emmy reached into the box and lifted out something bundled

in a tattered, mustard-yellow towel. She held it away from her body. "Not going to lie, I'm a tad fearful of what we might find in this."

"That makes two of us," Brooke said.

"Three." Austin held up her hand.

Emmy took a deep inhale and released it. "Here we go." She laid the bundle onto the table and slowly unraveled the towel to reveal a Colt pistol.

"May I?" Austin asked, indicating the gun.

Emmy stepped back. "Be my guest."

"It's a Colt 1911," Austin said. "These things were made as a tribute to the revered Commercial Government Model pistols of the past."

"But why did Dwayne—if that is his actual name—leave this behind?" Brooke asked.

"Maybe he left in a hurry," Em said.

"Yes, that's highly likely. But why?" Austin asked.

"Just one more in a long line of questions about this guy." Brooke said, her shoulders growing taut again, her brow furrowing. "That's all we have with this guy—questions."

"We should pray for answers," Emmy said.

"Definitely," Austin said. "The combination of this guy's lifestyle and the contents of that box . . . I'm afraid we haven't seen the worst of it."

# FIFTY-EIGHT

Noah paced impatiently as Rissi placed calls to Lieutenants Malone and Caldwell.

"No answer for either," she said, slipping her cell back into her black trouser pocket.

"Caleb," Noah said, "you and Rissi head over to Malone's place."

"Roger that." He leaned his head toward the back hall and the lab. "I'll just let Austin know. I'll be quick."

"No problem." Noah smothered a smirk. Caleb was hooked.

"Logan, I'll call Finn and have him meet you at Caldwell's apartment."

"You got it, sir."

They both turned to Em's cell phone as it rang on her desk for the third time since she'd entered the lab.

"I'm going to answer it," Logan said. "It's not like her to leave her phone lying around and maybe it's important." He picked up the cell. "Emmy's phone, can I help you?" His jaw tightened. "Uh-huh. Okay, hang on." He covered the phone. "I need to run this to Em. I'll be right back."

Logan returned, and within a minute Caleb, Em, Austin, and Brooke exited the lab.

Noah smiled at Brooke, then turned his attention to the call Logan had taken. "Everything okay?" he asked.

"Yes," Emmy said, grabbing her purse. "I got a lead on the

branding from Roger, the guy I followed up with from Custom Ink."

"Great," Noah said. "What'd you learn?"

"Nothing yet. He invited me for happy hour at Dockside. Said we could talk then." She tucked her phone in her purse.

"Do you think it's wise to go alone?" Logan asked.

"It's Dockside," she said. "The place will be packed."

"Be safe and keep us posted," Noah said as she hurried for the door.

"Hey, Em," Logan said.

"Yeah?" She turned, her fingers wrapped around the door handle.

"Like Noah said, be safe."

She nodded, and a brisk wind blew in as she exited.

Caleb climbed from his Forester after parking outside of Lieutenant Chris Malone's apartment complex. Three stories. Brick with black iron balconies. Rissi pulled up beside him and cut her engine. He climbed out and moved around the parked cars to meet her at the sidewalk's edge. When he'd told Austin that he could ask Noah about her riding with him and Rissi on the call, she'd told him that wasn't necessary, which sounded absolutely unlike Austin. Add in that glint in her eye . . . she was most definitely up to something, but what? And more importantly, was she being safe?

"Malone lives in 2A," he said. His full attention fixed to their detail, he held the metal door open for Rissi, then followed her inside.

"How do you want to play this?" he asked as they rounded the second floor.

"I'll knock. You cover," Rissi said as they approached Malone's door.

Caleb positioned himself at Rissi's nine—out of the line of sight of the door—his gun aimed at where it would open.

Rissi knocked. "Lieutenant Malone," she called.

Only a soft creaking sound whispered from inside.

Rissi knocked again, holding her badge up to the peephole. "Malone. It's Special Agent Rissi Dawson. We had an appointment."

Nothing but the creaking.

"I don't have a good feeling about this," Rissi whispered.

Caleb exhaled. "That makes two of us."

"On three," she said, then kicked in the door.

He followed, covering her.

Lieutenant Malone hung from a rope around his neck, a chair flat on the floor behind him.

Noah's cell rang. "Hey, Caleb."

"It appears Malone hung himself. We found him with a noose around his neck, a chair kicked out from under him."

"I'll call Finn, see if they located Caldwell, and have him head your way. Is there a suicide note?"

"No, sir. Hadley's on his way here now."

"Okay, ask him to give me a call when he's headed back to the morgue with Malone, so I can meet him there. My gut says there's more to this than a suicide."

"Mine as well."

Disconnecting the call, Noah rang Finn. He answered on the second ring. "Hey, Finn. Any luck finding Lieutenant Caldwell?"

"No. I think she took off in a hurry. She took some clothing, toiletries, etc., but pretty much everything else is still here, like she just left for a quick vacation. But considering the circumstances, I'm guessing it's more than that. Logan found an interesting photograph stuck between the pages of a magazine."

"Oh yeah?"

"Yeah. I'm looking at Caldwell with her arm around Scott Mirch."

Noah's brows hiked. Scott Mirch was personally connected to Lieutenant Caldwell, a member of the team developing a laser. "Why does this guy's name keep popping up?"

"Was just thinking that myself," Finn said. "The next guy in the photograph looks a lot like the man we know as Dwayne, and his name is confirmed by a notation on the back."

*Thank you, Lord.* They were finally getting somewhere.

"There are two more men. One looks like he could be Scott Mirch's brother or some relation. The picture's back indicates his name is John. And the last guy looks twenty-some years older than Mirch, but here comes the good part . . ."

Noah waited impatiently.

"He's listed as Gator, with a capital *G* on the backside."

"The word Connor Andrews whispered to Brooke was a name?"

"Yep. Do you think he's the one behind all this?" Finn asked.

"Very possibly, but the key question is, Who is he really?"

# FIFTY-NINE

While Caleb was busy tracking down Malone, Austin had a person of her own to question. No sense tagging along for something unrelated to their chemical case, not when she could get one more interview under her belt.

She'd called to schedule the appointment with Mr. Valdez as soon as Emmy provided the information, assuming Caleb would be free to go with her, but when Noah sent him to check out the no-show interviewee, she decided she could handle Valdez.

She noted a gold-tinted Nissan sedan in the driveway—probably the car the plate had supposedly been stolen from. She wished she could get a quick glimpse inside the two-car garage, but she was pressing her appointment time, so she announced her presence with the gold-lion door knocker.

The door opened, and a burly man with dark wavy hair stepped forward. "Yes."

"I'm Austin Kelly. We spoke on the phone. Thanks for seeing me," she said.

"Let's just make it quick. I have an errand to run." He stepped back, allowing her into his ranch-style home.

"You said this was about my car?" He gestured for her to take a seat in the front room facing Water Street. Sunlight streamed through the sheer curtains pulled across the bay window.

"Yes. About your stolen license plate."

"Oh." Hector Valdez visibly relaxed, which set Austin's investigative antenna pulsing. He sank down into the floral-upholstered chair opposite her. "That makes sense."

She studied Hector—stout with dark freckles covering his caramel skin. "Could you tell me what happened?"

His chocolate brown eyes narrowed. "I already told the cops." He sat forward on the chair. "Who'd you say you are again?"

"Austin Kelly with Kelly Investigations."

"Like a private eye?" he asked with a chuckle.

"Exactly," she said.

"What kind of business does a PI have with my stolen plate?"

"I'm looking into the people who stole it."

His eyes narrowed again, his shoulders widening as his chest puffed out. "You know who stole it?"

"Not their identity, but they followed my colleague and me."

He shifted again, his dress shoes sliding through the high-pile cream carpet. "They *followed* you?"

"Yes, sir." Hoping to ease his tension by making a personal observation, she glanced around for pictures of a family, or at least of a wife, based on the female decorating touches, but found none. "Your wife has wonderful decorating tastes."

"Yes, she did," he said through thinned lips.

"Oh, I'm sorry. I didn't realize you're widowed."

"Not widowed. Divorced." He stood, smoothing out the thighs of his trousers. "Look, lady, I get that you want to investigate whoever stole my plate, but people following you has nothing to do with me."

"If I could just ask you a few more questions."

He headed for his front door. "I'm asking you politely to leave."

She stood, slipped on her coat, and headed for the door.

"Thank you for your time." She handed him a card. "If anything comes to mind that might be helpful, please give me a call."

"Uh-huh."

She stepped outside and had barely cleared the door before he swung it shut.

Hector Valdez thought he'd gotten rid of her, but all he'd done was convince her she needed to come back tonight. It was stakeout time.

---

"Agent Anderson," Noah said, striding to the booth at their favorite burger joint. "Thanks for agreeing to meet me."

The man stood to shake his hand. "You must be Agent Rowley. And . . ." He looked over Noah's shoulder.

"This is Petty Officer Brooke Kesler."

"Ma'am." Agent Anderson removed his CGIS navy-and-white ball cap and tipped it at her.

"Brooke, please," she said.

"And Brett to you both," he said, waiting until Brooke was settled in the booth before retaking his seat. Noah guessed the retired agent was in his early sixties.

"We appreciate you meeting with us."

The waitress sidled her way over to the bench, her white apron askew over her pink dress uniform. "I'm Darlene. I'll be your server today. Can I get you folks started with anything?"

Noah eyed Brett's slice of pie and coffee. "Brooke, what would you like?"

"I think I'll have the same as Mr. Anderson," she said. "That pie looks scrumptious."

"Chocolate cream," he said. "My favorite."

"Make mine the same, please," Noah said.

Darlene put the pie order in and returned with a pot of coffee.

They flipped over the mugs on their table, and she filled them up. "Any cream?" She rustled some cream packets out of her apron pocket.

"None for me," Brooke said. "But thanks."

"I take mine black as well," Noah said.

"Something that never leaves you when you leave the military," Brett Anderson said.

"How many years did you serve?" Brooke asked.

"Ten in the Guard after college. Another twenty-three in the investigative service."

"That's impressive."

"All in a day's work."

"Are you enjoying retirement?" Brooke asked.

He nodded. "A lot more time with my wife, Kim, more time with the grandkids."

"That's great."

"Yeah, it is." He smiled. "But enough about me, I know you wanted to chat about Scott Mirch's case." He tapped the rim of his coffee cup. "That's a name I haven't heard in years."

"Same for me," Brooke said.

He lifted his chin at her. "Did you know Scott?"

She shrugged. "Knew him a little."

"He was a friendly guy," Brett said.

"Yes, he was," Brooke responded.

"That is, until you asked him about something he didn't want to talk about," Brett added.

Brooke nodded. "That's true. I asked about his family once. You'd have thought I'd asked for State secrets."

"I got the same response when I asked him something he didn't want to talk about. He'd flat-out refuse." Brett took a sip of his coffee, then set the cup back on the saucer. "The whole case was strange, if you ask me."

Noah cocked his head. "How so?"

"Well, I'm sure you've done your research," he said to Noah.

"My buddies still on the base tell me you run one stellar CGIS unit."

Quite the compliment. "Thank you, sir."

"No *sir*." He swished his age-spotted hand. "Brett."

"Brett," Noah said with a nod.

"So I'm sure you've read that Scott implicated three partners in the crime?" he began.

"Yes, s—" Noah cut himself off before saying *sir* again.

Brett leaned his head toward his right shoulder, shifting his posture on the bench, to look at Brooke. "And what did you think at the time?"

"I knew Scott was brilliant with computers. I shared lunch with him and another C-School student often. I had no clue what half the things they talked about were, but they were fun and pleasant to be around. I knew who the instructors he implicated were, too, but didn't know them personally."

"Do you think Scott was telling the truth about their involvement?" Brett asked.

Brooke took a deep inhale, giving herself time to ponder. "I know the basics of what happened, but only from the news. It seems like it would be an awful tricky job to pull off by oneself. I assumed he was telling the truth until . . ."

"Until the men he implicated had alibis," Brett said.

"Right."

Noah studied the man before him, the glint in his eye. "You believed Scott?"

"I did. I think those men were guilty too, but we couldn't find anything to tie them to the crime. No fingerprints on the wires that someone used to disrupt and loop the video feed, making Scott the invisible man, no evidence on their home computers of schematics of the office Scott needed to break into, or fingerprints on the computer he used to steal the currency."

"Not even Scott's?"

"No."

"Then how did you know Scott did it?"

"The technical details were above my level of expertise. We had our computer expert . . . I'm sure you've got one."

"Logan Perry and Emmy Thorton—both are fabulous."

"Our computer genius was Eddie Gardner. I'm not exaggerating about his skills, but it took even him two straight days to finally track down Scott's trail on the laptop he used. Apparently, every person leaves a digital footprint, and Eddie found Scott's. I don't fully understand it all myself, but Eddie is still around, and he'd be happy to chat with you, if you'd like."

"That would be great," Noah said.

"I'll text him your number."

"Okay, thanks," Noah said, then returned to the thread of their conversation. "So we knew investigators followed the money trail to Scott, that he stole five million in cryptocurrency that's worth a lot more today, but we didn't delve much deeper into the investigation. What more can you tell us?" Noah asked.

"Well, again, Eddie would be the technical resource on all the digital currency details, but there are these things called wallets where you keep your currency and private keys for access. Somehow Scott accessed a wallet's private key for a military-and-intelligence-agency joint fund and transferred the cryptocurrency into a wallet he owned. The instructors he implicated had no money trail leading back to them."

"Is it possible they planned to initially put it in one fund and split it later, but Scott got busted before he could transfer it to separate accounts?"

"It's possible, but the money is gone, moved again *after* he was arrested, and Scott claimed he had no clue where it went."

"Yes, we learned that in our research. Any idea how Scott might have moved the cryptocurrency?" Noah asked.

"Eddie believes he used something called Lazarus to launder the funds, but how that occurred *after* his arrest—when computer access is monitored—doesn't make much sense unless one of the instructors was lying and he did it, or there was someone else working with Scott."

"Any idea who that might be?" Brooke asked.

"That's a question for Scott's defense attorney, Jack Weaver. He had this whole fifth-man theory."

"One you didn't buy into?" Noah said.

"It was his theory, so I'll let him tell you about it."

"Fair enough." Noah tapped the table, everything racing through his mind. "The joint account—I'm assuming we're talking CIA."

"Above my pay grade," Brett said, "but it was definitely tied to the military, and Eddie believed an intelligence community too. It's not unheard of for the two to band together to undertake joint missions in war zones. A fund is kept for anything that occurs off the books. With cryptocurrency, according to Eddie, especially through an open-ended decentralized software program like Alatheum, you're naturally talking far less, if any, oversight."

Brett rolled his hands out, palms up. "We had solid proof Scott was guilty—that part progressed easily. Unfortunately, though we believed the instructors were involved, there was no proof, but at least they didn't get any money."

"Any idea who did?"

Brett shook his head. "Unless it's been spent or otherwise disbursed, someone is sitting on a great deal of money in cryptocurrency, and we haven't a clue who."

# SIXTY

Two hours later, after dropping Brooke off at the station, Noah entered the morgue.

"Noah," Hadley greeted him.

"Nice to see you, sir, but as always, it would be nicer under different circumstances."

"My sentiments exactly." Hadley smiled, the creases at the corner of his eyes and mouth deepening.

"Thank you for expediting this one," Noah said, knowing how much weight Hadley's report would hold in the case. Had Malone committed suicide or not? The answer to that question would take the investigation in one of two vastly different directions.

Malone was already undressed, washed, and laid out on the autopsy table, a baby-blue paper sheet covering him from the clavicle down.

"Any impressions yet?" Noah asked.

"Two," Hadley said. "First . . ." He lowered the sheet to expose Malone's upper right arm.

Noah's eyes widened. It was the same brand they'd found on all the mass shooters. He shook his head at the implications that held. "And second?" he asked.

"Lieutenant Malone did not commit suicide. He was murdered."

Noah returned to the station five minutes before evening case board was set to begin. The meeting was going to run late tonight. They had *a lot* to cover.

He spotted Brooke across the way and walked over to her.

"Hey." She smiled.

"You have a good time with Gabby?" He glanced at his sister, who'd dropped by the station to bring Finn dinner and spend time with Brooke.

"Always." Brooke's smile widened, and Gabby smiled in turn.

He furrowed his brow. "Why do I feel like I'm staring at trouble?"

"Nonsense." Gabby got to her feet. "Us? Trouble?" She gave Brooke a mischievous look if he'd ever seen one. "I'm going to chat with Finn until you start the meeting."

"Sounds good." Brooke chuckled.

Noah arched his brows.

"Oh, stop worrying." She got to her feet and lifted her empty mug. "We were just plotting and planning."

"That's what worries me." He hated to imagine the misadventures they'd get into over the years.

*Over the years.* He loved the thought of being with Brooke for years.

"What?" Brooke asked, studying him, her empty mug in hand.

"What?" he repeated.

"Your expression . . ." She frowned. "Something good or something bad?"

"Oh. Something very good," he said, glancing around the room. The team was still gathering materials for case-board time. They had a couple of minutes. He tugged her in the kitchen and closed the door behind him.

"Noah . . ." she said, a playful expression dancing on her beautiful face. "Why do I think you're the one who's up to trouble?"

He closed the space between them, his fingers sliding through her hair, his mouth on hers.

A moment later, begrudgingly pulling away, he pressed his forehead to hers. "I love you," he whispered.

"I love you too," she whispered back.

"Oops," Logan said, opening the door, only to do a one-eighty and head back out.

Noah sighed. "I guess we best get to it."

She nodded, smothering a smile.

"But first, coffee," he said, hitching before he hit the door. He refilled Brooke's mug and then his.

They headed for the sofa and chairs lined up in front of the whiteboard. Brooke took a seat between Austin and Emmy while he stepped to the front.

"All right, guys," Noah began. "I know it's late, and we all want to get home to grab some rest."

Gabby approached. "Before you dig in, I caught a story I think you'll all be very interested in."

"Oh?" Noah arched a brow. His sister lived to break stories. "Why don't you come on up and share." He wouldn't mind taking a load off in the meantime. It had been a long day—make that a long week.

His sister swapped places with him, hopping up on the silver swivel stool. "My boss called with a story for me to investigate while Brooke and I were chatting." She smiled.

He knew that smile well. This was going to be good. *And helpful, Lord. Let it be helpful. This case is wearing me out. I need your strength, your guidance . . . I need you, period.*

"It involves four missing Holly Ridge caterers and their van," she said as casually as if they were discussing the weather.

Noah nearly dropped his coffee. "Seriously?"

310

"Yep." She crossed one leg over the other.

"I'm assuming you feel it's related?" Logan said but continued before Gabby could respond. "But why is it just coming up now? You'd think four missing persons would be news right away."

"Apparently it was a four-person operation—a bunch of kids fresh out of culinary school who decided to start their own business," she said. "They lived together in a loft above their kitchen and had no family in the area, so there was no one to immediately report them missing. But eventually the aunt of one of the ladies, and the mother of another, called their respective niece and daughter and didn't hear back. At first, they didn't think that much of it because the catering business was booming and the kids worked nonstop, but eventually they both contacted the local police."

"And?" Austin asked, inching forward.

"Police checked out their shop," Gabby continued. "They found a bunch of notes on the door, complaining that the caterers stopped returning their calls, and they then found the same sort of messages on their answering service. It looks like the caterers missed two of their events—one the day of the graduation, the other the following day, but the police found nothing suggesting foul play in the shop or their loft. And their last job said they finished the event and left without incident."

"Has their van been found?" Rissi asked.

Gabby shook her head.

"So we probably just found our white van," Noah said. "What's the name of their business?"

"Annie's Edibles." Gabby wrote it and the missing caterers' names on the board.

"Any idea of their logo?" Mason, just back from Georgia, asked.

"Green and yellow," Gabby said, attempting to draw it on the board, but she drew about as well as Noah did—not their gift.

"According to Jim Larson, who we talked to at the supply shop, Dwayne was a master at logos," Noah said. "He probably replaced the logo as soon as they had the van."

"Stealing the van was smart," Logan said. "No eyes to identify them—at least none still alive."

Noah's stomach twisted at the senseless tragedy of their "smart" choices.

"And no paper trail," Rissi added.

Noah nodded.

Emmy slipped her pen over her ear and rested her notepad on her lap. "Why not just use the existing logo?" She shook her head on a sigh. "Never mind, I just got it." She looked in her empty mug. "Clearly, I need more of this."

"You're good," Noah said. "It's late, and we've been working hard. I think we're all wiped. Hopefully, we'll rest well tonight." A solid night's rest. They all could use it.

"Any idea what happened to the bodies?" Mason asked.

"Unfortunately, yes," Gabby said. "This morning, an elderly woman went to visit her husband in the family mausoleum at Fairpark Cemetery and nearly had a heart attack—quite literally—at finding four bodies in the tomb."

"Is she okay now?" Brooke asked.

"Her daughter said she's resting but is still in shock," Gabby said. "The bodies are at the morgue, and relatives have been called in to ID them. None live locally, so it could be another day or so before we know for sure."

Noah's muscles constricted. "The body count keeps rising."

# SIXTY-ONE

Noah shifted his weight. His wound itched tonight—no doubt it was starting to heal, but the itching was more irritating than the pain at times. He looked at the clock, wishing he could just call case board for the night, but they had important information still to cover. "After our conversation with Brett Anderson, I'm growing more convinced that the three instructors Scott accused of being his partners in crime were in fact involved. I'm also coming to believe our theory that they were specifically targeted in the shooting is correct."

"From what you've shared, I wholeheartedly agree," Rissi said. "We also know they used the shooting as a distraction to steal the laser plans."

"Whoever planned all of this—Dwayne and who knows who else—doesn't give a second thought to taking innocent lives," Noah said with an exhale. How could one care so little for human life?

He shook off the thought and moved on. "So far the investigation keeps circling back to Scott Mirch. Was he, in spite of his denial, calling the shots from prison? Or was someone else in the photograph Finn and Logan found in Lieutenant Caldwell's apartment the ringleader? The questions just keep coming."

He looked up to find Brooke staring at him, concern marring her brow. She was worried about him but wouldn't ask in front of everybody.

He was fine. Just worn out a bit, but he'd crash hard tonight and feel ready to go in the morning.

"How about you, Em?" he asked. "Did you learn anything from the guy who works at Custom Ink?"

Logan bristled, and by the curious expression on Emmy's face, she hadn't missed his reaction.

"I had appetizers with Roger, and he was very helpful. He said he'd heard rumors about the group that had Leroy—the owner of the tat shop—design the brand."

Gabby scooched forward on the couch, resting her elbows on her knees. "What kind of rumors?"

Noah gave her a look.

"I know. Nothing leaves this room," she reassured him. She'd been extremely helpful, and he honestly didn't mind having her stay. She often offered a fresh perspective.

"Roger said the man who ordered the brand had Leroy design it," Emmy said. "But instead of the group members coming in to have Leroy do the branding, the man just picked it up and said they'd be branding themselves."

Austin's mouth slackened. "Ouch!"

Emmy nodded. "Yeah, and it gets worse. The guy who bought it is rumored to be part of an extreme patriotic group that functions much as a paramilitary operation."

"Former military?" Rissi asked.

"That's the feel Roger got from the guy who bought the brand. Oh, and that guy just happens to match Dwayne's sketch."

Noah shook his head. Who was Dwayne to Scott Mirch—friend, fellow soldier, relative? And how did it all fit together?

"Roger said he's heard speculation that the group is living and training out on some farm outside of town."

The hairs on the nape of Noah's neck stood on end. "Training for *what?*"

Em pressed her lips together and shrugged. "He didn't know, but he reiterated that he thinks the group of them are former military. To use his words, they are 'not the sort to mess with.'"

"Well, that's frightening," Rissi said. "Especially considering the theft of plans for the final laser component." She crossed her legs. "Do you suppose Lieutenant Caldwell is helping build one for the group? She has the expertise and was in the photograph with Scott Mirch, Dwayne, and whoever Gator is. And now she's in the wind."

Adrenaline coursed through Noah's limbs. "Do we even want to consider what they plan to do with the weapon if they get a functioning one finished?"

Everyone sat silently, the intent expressions on their faces said they were all pondering the magnitude of that question.

He checked the clock. They had to get moving. His team needed rest, though he had a feeling at least a few wouldn't take it. "Em, you and Logan start digging to see if you can find anything on this group and isolated farms. I'd guess they'd have a large parcel of land and no neighbors for miles."

"On it," Em said, "and the contents of the box you found at the Strasburg Hotel fit perfectly with the type of group you're describing. I'd say that's even more evidence that it belonged to Dwayne."

"Okay." Noah nodded, wondering just how big this group was and how far out there they were. "You and Logan keep on Dwayne and the farm."

"Yes, sir," Em said, and Logan nodded his agreement.

"Finn, can you update us about anything you found at Malone's?" Noah asked, shifting to yet another branch of their investigation.

"Absolutely." Finn stepped to the whiteboard and hung up a series of photos. "Malone's suicide looked clean at first," he said. "But I found something on his wrists. I ran tests, and it's duct tape residue."

"So someone restrained his hands?"

"Yes," Finn confirmed.

"Good work," Noah said. "Hadley's autopsy findings agree—Lieutenant Malone did not commit suicide. He was murdered." Noah kicked one foot over the other, grimacing at the twinge in his thigh. He cleared his throat and continued, "For those of you who haven't heard, Malone had the same branding mark as our mass shooters."

"So we can assume he was part of the shooting plot?" Caleb asked.

"The branding mark associates him with the shooters, so my inclination is to say affirmative," Noah said. "Not to mention the .40 caliber bullet pulled out of Connor Andrews is the standard Coast Guard–issued service weapon—the Sig Sauer P229."

"During my interview with him," Mason said, "Malone told me he was the first guardsman on scene, but no one remembers seeing him there until after the paramedics arrived, so he very well could have been out of sight, monitoring the shooters to make sure none surrendered."

"And when Connor Andrews did, Malone took him out," Noah said.

"But how does Malone tie to the group? To Mirch?" Rissi asked.

"I think this will help," Finn said. He slid another blown-up picture on the board. "Chris Malone and Scott Mirch as Eagle Scouts."

Yet again, everything circled back to Scott Mirch. It was time to pay him an in-person visit. Noah had a ton of questions for the man. Maybe he really was organizing all this from prison. Scott had plenty of time on his hands, and it certainly wouldn't be the first time an inmate planned and directed criminal activity on the outside.

Noah stretched his coiled neck muscles. When he interviewed Scott Mirch in person, he'd show him Malone's picture and the one Logan found. See his reaction when he mentioned Dwayne's name. But first he'd talk with Scott's defense attorney tomorrow morning as planned. He wanted all the information he could get before flying to meet with Scott. And the fact Brooke knew Scott from before the arrest meant he was far more likely to talk to him if she was along.

He shifted to face Logan. "Could you share the photograph you found at Lieutenant Caldwell's place with the group? We've discussed various aspects about it, but it would be good to see and review."

"Of course." Logan stood and moved to the front. "Finn and I found this at her efficiency." He clipped a blown-up image to the whiteboard.

"He looks younger than when I knew him," Brooke said, "but that's definitely Scott Mirch."

"The notation on the back of the photograph indicates this third man from the left is Dwayne."

She hesitated and then nodded. "Yes, that's him."

Logan continued, "We know the woman with her arm around Scott Mirch is Lieutenant Amy Caldwell. Do you know if they were dating at the time of his arrest?"

"No, I never heard anything about him having a girlfriend," Brooke said, "But Scott wasn't a sharer. Never talked about his family, dating, anything personal."

"Do you recognize the other two men?" Logan asked.

"No." She shook her head. "But the guy on the far right looks so much like Scott, he's got to be related."

"Based on your previous comment, I'm assuming Scott never mentioned a brother?"

"No." Brooke shook her head.

"Lots to look into," Logan said. "But we finally figured out what *gator* means, or rather, *who* it refers to."

Brooke stiffened. Noah gave up all pretense and went to her side. Both Austin and Emmy started to move.

"You stay," Emmy said to Austin as she sweetly moved into the seat Logan had just vacated.

Noah sat, needing Brooke to feel his support—his love. He reached out and took hold of her hand. She gripped it tightly.

Logan hung up a second blown-up image of the back of the photograph. Names were scrolled across the back: *Me, Scotty, Dwayne, John, Gator.*

"So based on the picture, we can surmise," Finn said, "Amy Caldwell and Scott Mirch had some level of a personal relationship. And Caldwell worked in the lab where the plans for the laser had been stolen, which means she could have given them access to the lab."

"This picture also tells us Scott knew Dwayne close to a decade ago," Noah said, picking up the thread Finn had begun weaving, "and now Dwayne is involved at a high level—most likely coordinating the mass shooting, where the three men Scott claimed set him up to take the fall were killed."

He shifted, still holding Brooke's hand tightly. "Additionally, I am starting to think this group has someone else above Dwayne orchestrating it all."

"Maybe that's what Connor Andrews was trying to tell Brooke," Emmy said. "Maybe this guy Gator is the center of it."

"I agree. Let's focus our energy on him and on discovering if the man noted as John is a relative of Scott's, and if so, where he is."

Em nodded. "On it."

Rissi stood and moved to examine the picture Logan found closer. "Gator's stance is military," she said, clearly beginning a profile. "His shirt is patriotic but crass," she continued. "The logo on his baseball cap has an insignia that I'd bet has military origins. For a man who I'm guessing is at least double Scott's age, he looks just as fit." She turned to face the group. "They all look military to me."

"Good eye, Rissi," Em said. "I did a search on the insignia on his cap just before the meeting, and it's that of the Marine Raiders."

"Seriously?" Logan said. "The guy is special ops?"

"Or was," Finn responded.

"Em, fax his picture to the Marines, provide them with the information we have, and see if they can be of some help," Noah said.

"Will do."

"Okay, last but not least, Mason, did you learn anything in Georgia?"

"Mostly general family things, but one thing, after listening to all this, has become extremely pertinent," Mason said. "Connor Andrews's dad was a Marine Raider who was killed in Afghanistan."

"So far, they all are military or former military," Noah said. "I bet if we can figure out Dwayne's full name, we'll find out that he was in the Marine Raiders too. He's only a decade or so younger than Gator. For all we know, they served in the same unit."

# SIXTY-TWO

Soon after case board wrapped up, Caleb followed Austin out of the station into the brisk December air. The only ones still in the office were Emmy and Logan, but that was par for the course. They often worked all hours hunting down leads.

"I need to go get supplies," Austin said with a bounce in her step.

He stopped, his hands deep in his jacket pockets as the temperature continued to drop. "Supplies for what?"

"A stakeout." Shafts of streetlight danced off her face.

So beautiful . . . "Wait." He collected his thoughts. "Did you just say you're going on a stakeout?"

"Yes, and I'd love for you to come with me."

The thought of the two of them cozied up in a car, fixated on whatever lead she was focused on, filled him with excitement and pleasure.

"Who are we staking out?"

"Hector Valdez."

"The guy who reported his license plate stolen? Why?"

"While you were checking on Malone, I went and spoke with Valdez."

"Did you learn anything?"

"Not straight out about the case, but he was cocky and most

320

definitely hiding something. I have a hunch I should be watching tonight."

Austin's hunches almost always paid off. "All right." He rubbed his gloved hands together. "Let's get supplies. You get the food, and I'll take care of keeping us warm."

She glanced around the parking lot, then lifted on her tiptoes and pressed a kiss to his lips. "I like the sound of that."

Caleb swallowed. Maybe the brisk slap of the wind in his face wasn't a bad thing after all.

Half an hour later, outfitted for a stakeout, Caleb parked and slid his seat back as far as it would go. Might as well get comfortable. They could be here all night, but if he had to spend all night on a stakeout, there was no one else he'd rather spend it with.

A little less than two hours after they parked, Austin tapped his leg. "The garage door's opening and . . . he's leaving . . ."—she lifted her binoculars to her eyes and slapped her knee—"in the blue sedan that followed us with his supposedly stolen plates." She smirked, knowing she'd nailed it again.

Caleb shifted his seat back in place and buckled his seat belt for the follow. "Don't let it go to your head." He chuckled, pulling out, headlights off.

"Uh-huh." Her smirk deepened.

"You are ridiculous." But adorable. He shook his head, now turning on his headlights and keeping a fair distance between them and Valdez.

As a former homicide detective, he'd been on his fair share of stakeouts. He'd found, for some crazy reason, killers almost always returned to the scene of the crime. It was practically textbook. So where was Valdez leading them?

Turning his headlights off again, Caleb followed Valdez into an industrial park just on the outskirts of Wilmington. Unsurprised, he coasted to a stop behind a warehouse diagonal from Huntington Foam—parking between a yellow forklift and an older Mercedes so they were out of sight.

Austin leaned forward, focused on the sedan. "I knew that story Gower tried to feed us about having no TCEP left when the ban came in was too good to be true."

"The more perfect the story, the more likely it's all a lie," Caleb said.

"I never thought of it like that, but I suppose that is true."

"People telling the truth make mistakes, can't recall everything. The truth usually has a more disconnected ring to it," he said as he quietly opened his door and climbed into the night. Austin did the same, wearing only her fuzzy fleece. He'd suggested she dress warmer, but she'd insisted the fleece was enough. He hoped she was right because he had a feeling they'd be fighting the wind awhile.

Sneaking around the front of the next warehouse over, they scrambled behind the line of forklifts and trailers lining the front.

"Can you see him?" he asked as she positioned at the edge of a forklift.

"I think so." She sat into a low crouch and, taking a steadying breath, poked her head around the lift. "Got him—down by the loading docks."

One of the steel warehouse doors rolled up—creaking metal plate by creaking metal plate. So much for being clandestine.

More light spilled out across the pavement the higher it raised, until it locked into place with a clanging echo.

"And would you look at that," she said, "Braxton Gower."

Chalk another one up for Austin.

He crouched behind her, her back pressed against his chest as he rested his chin on her head. "Don't get me wrong. I love having you so close, but we're going to have to move in to hear what they're saying."

"I think we'll be within earshot but out of their direct line of sight over there." She indicated a medium-sized shed next to Huntington Foam.

"Next to it?" he said. "Isn't that pushing it?"

"Come on, scaredy-cat," she said, tugging on his knee.

He had no fear for himself—ever—but he had an innate desire to protect Austin, even though she did a bang-up job of protecting herself.

"Okay," he said, pulling his gun from his waist holster.

"You go first," she said. "I'll follow."

He nodded and raced in a low crouch across the pavement. Headlights banked over the hill.

Moving behind the shed, Caleb looked back. Austin was still a couple dozen feet from cover.

He gestured for her to hurry, and she sped her pace, but it wasn't going to be fast enough. The field of light was almost upon her. Rushing back out, he grabbed her and dove with her under the closest trailer.

The headlights swiped over the pavement where they'd just been but continued on.

Caleb let go of the breath he'd been holding and looked down at Austin wrapped up in his arms. "Sorry for slamming you. Are you okay?"

She smiled. "Better than okay."

He shook his head as a breath of laughter escaped his lips. He reluctantly rolled off her, and they both moved onto their stomachs, staring out from under the parked trailer. She handed him the binoculars as she lifted the camera.

Only the loading dock's auxiliary lights were on, but a black Lexus SUV they'd noted on their earlier visit was parked nearby in Braxton Gower's parking spot, along with three security cars.

Caleb adjusted the binoculars and scanned what he could see of the grounds from their position. He'd only seen one security car patrolling when they'd visited, but it made sense they'd have more at night.

So why was Gower meeting Valdez at—Caleb glanced at his watch—*0105?*

Gower said something Austin couldn't make out, then shook Valdez's hand.

"Where's Sid?" Gower asked, his voice louder.

"How am I supposed to know," Valdez said.

Gower bent forward at the waist, getting closer to Valdez's face. "Don't take that tone with me. I pay your salary. Don't forget that." Gower straightened. "If this whole thing goes south, you're the one whose car was seen following that agent and girl."

"And you're the one who ordered me to follow them, among other things," Valdez barked back.

Gower inhaled so deeply his entire torso lengthened. He raised his index finger, pointing it at Valdez. "Don't make me . . ."

"Don't make you *what* exactly?" Valdez cracked his knuckles.

Another set of headlights swept across the drive, and Austin and Caleb flattened against the gravelly pavement, the loose pellets of asphalt biting into her cheek. Caleb's breath mingled with hers. She wasn't sure if it was her heart pounding or his. If this were any other moment in time . . .

"Finally," Gower said as the hum of the engine's motor stopped.

"About time," Valdez said as a car door opened and shut.

She eased back up onto her elbows, and Caleb did the same beside her.

A short man who wobbled as he walked joined Valdez and Gower. He reminded Austin of Paulie, Adrian's brother in the *Rocky* franchise. The man wore a dark flat hat, dark sweater with his white undershirt sticking an inch out of the bottom, and a pair of loose-fitting jeans.

"About time, Sid," Braxton said, tapping his watch. "We have a problem. Do you not get that?"

Sid frowned in the light fanning out across the warehouse's loading dock. "What kind of problem?" He hitched up his jeans.

Gower looked at Valdez like *Is this guy serious?*

"He was your hire."

Gower grunted as he scanned the area. "Let's go inside. We never know if they're watching."

"They?" Sid asked.

"The two investigators who paid me a visit," Gower said.

"Whoa!" Sid exclaimed. "You didn't say anything about investigators."

"Inside!" Gower growled, then turned and walked back into the warehouse, followed by Valdez. Sid shifted from side to side for a moment but finally followed suit.

Austin released a sigh of relief, then looked at Caleb. "We gotta get closer."

"I hate to say this, but you're right," he agreed.

She winked before rolling out from under the trailer.

Caleb rolled out and met her on her side of the trailer. When they reached the warehouse door, the men's voices were clear. She prayed they hadn't missed anything vital.

". . . agent and PI are getting too close," Gower said. "Sooner or later, they'll show up with a subpoena. I know it. And if it's while we're moving the cargo, we'll end up in jail."

Austin leaned forward just far enough to get a glimpse inside.

Gower paced in a square of his own making. "Do you realize—" he yelled, then paused, clutching his hand into a fist, and taking in torso-raising inhales. "Do you realize," he began again, his voice far more level and controlled, "the amount of

TCEP we still have? We need to get rid of those barrels ASAP. We have close to a hundred left."

Gower snapped his fingers, and three security guards Austin doubted were legit entered the area, forming a triangle around the men—each armed, each in military at-ease stance. "I've taken the liberty of hiring some extra help to aid us in this endeavor."

Sid's eyes widened. "I'll resume dumping, but it's going to take a ton of time with that quantity."

"Which is why we're going to move the barrels by railcar," Gower said.

"Railcar?" Sid frowned. "I don't get it."

"Isn't that far too visible?" Hector asked.

"That's the point," Braxton said. "No one would think we'd put illegal chemicals on our railroad cars. We'll transfer the chemicals to different containers, and anyone who happens to see them will assume it's one of our orders."

"Then what?" Sid asked.

"Then we'll ship them down to south Florida, where my brother will meet you, Sid. He'll get you outfitted to do your thing in the Everglades. Covering over seven-thousand miles, a hundred barrels in the Everglades will be like drops of rain in the ocean. Besides, who's going to care if a few gators die?"

"And the two snooping around?" Hector asked.

Gower's jaw tightened. "They are a thistle in my loafers." He grunted. "The soonest I can get the pieces in place is five a.m. We do this predawn, and the railroad containers will be happily chugging down the line before they show back up."

"Why do you think they'll be back?" Sid asked.

"Because they're the type."

Austin looked at Caleb and leaned forward. He shook his head. Now was not the time to move in. They didn't have a warrant.

She shifted to step back and kicked a rock that skittered

across the pavement. Caleb reached out, tugging her into the shadows.

"Did you hear that?" Gower asked.

"Hear what?" Sid said.

"I heard something outside. Turn on the floodlights."

Austin's muscles tensed, adrenaline burning through her limbs. They'd never make it back to the car unseen.

"Quick," Caleb whispered, pulling her into an alley between the buildings as bright lights flashed on.

They bolted out of the light's reach, racing across the cracked and crumbled asphalt.

Once far from the flooding light, Caleb pulled up short, and her Keds skidded out from under her on the damp pavement. His hand grasped her tightly, swinging her back upright.

Cold sweat beaded her brow. That was too close.

"Go check it out," Braxton roared in the warehouse.

"Don't you think—"

"What I *think* is that both of you need to keep your mouth shut and make sure no one is watching us. Because if they are, they're dead," he yelled, making sure anyone present heard him, and hear him they did.

Caleb took a quick assessment. "Down the outcropping."

*Is he crazy?* The outcropping sat at the edge of the manufacturing warehouse—a sheer wall of rocks and boulders thirty-feet high with a shallow retaining pool at the bottom. One wrong foothold and . . . She didn't want to think about *and*.

Caleb intertwined his long fingers with hers and took the first step.

Shifting his boots for the steadiest placement, he reached out his other hand, placing its wide grasp on her waist. He guided her down to the first boulder with decent footing for her already-slick sneakers.

They held in place, listening, the cold of the boulder seeping through her fleece.

"You go that way, Sid," Hector directed. "I'll take the rocks."

"Nobody'd be crazy enough to go down there. It's a thirty-foot drop."

"Just do what I said," Hector roared. "Boss said if they're out there, we know what to do."

"We've got to move," Caleb whispered against her ear. "We need to get below that boulder."

Austin looked down. The boulder he was talking about balanced precariously on the edge of the other rocks, jutting out a good three feet. If they got under it, they'd be out of view, but if it shifted, they'd be toast.

Using a combination of footholds, handholds, and even her fingernails in the edgier spots, she made the transition in Caleb's firm grasp, down to the boulder jutting out. Now to just finagle beneath it.

Why did she always get herself in these predicaments?

She froze as a flashlight panned out, reflecting off the still water below.

Caleb reached out and swung her under the boulder, moving to press against her.

"Over here," Hector yelled. "I think I saw movement."

Footfalls and flashlight beams grew closer, and so did Caleb, his smooth cheek pressed to hers, his breath echoing in her ear. His heart thumped against her chest, his muscular torso and arms enveloping her.

"I guess it was nothing," Hector said after a very tense minute.

"Fine," Braxton said, apparently having joined the search. "Get back inside. We have to get these barrels ready to go by five a.m."

A few moments later, the loading dock door rolled shut, and darkness swooped back in, leaving only a slit of moonlight breaking through the cloud cover.

Caleb pulled back. "Sorry if I smashed you."

"I'm not," she said, tugging his jacket, pulling him back against her. She pressed her lips to his. His body was chilled from the air temp, but his lips were warm and soft. He leaned into the kiss, his one hand splayed out on the rock for purchase, the other spreading through her hair.

Finally pulling away, he groaned. "As much as I hate to break up this fantastic moment, we better get out of here. We need a warrant. I'll call Noah, the local EPA office, and Wilmington police." He looked at his watch. "We've got less than four hours."

# SIXTY-THREE

Dawn not yet breaking, Caleb studied Huntington Foam through his binoculars. Everyone was waiting on his call.

He watched Gower pace the railroad loading dock in shafts of light emanating from an open factory door——his shadow growing tall as he neared the railroad tracks, then shrinking as he headed back for the factory.

All exterior lights remained off, but more than a dozen cars littered the lot.

Gower checked his watch, then disappeared inside, only to reappear moments later and repeat the process.

Caleb heard Austin's barely audible footsteps approach. "Ready for this?" he asked without looking over his shoulder.

"How do you do that?" Frustration laced her tone. "Everyone else I can sneak up on."

"Maybe I'm just drawn to your presence," he said, this time looking over at her standing beside him.

She smirked, then nibbled at her lip. "Well played, Mr. Eason."

Metal clinked as the railroad loading door raised, and Gower ceased pacing. He waved to someone on the other side of the loading door.

Caleb waited, his breath smooth and even.

A man wheeled a blue plastic drum out on a dolly.

"That's a go," Caleb said on his radio. He looked forward to the joy of presenting Gower with a warrant.

Austin pulled her Colt from its holster, and they moved stride-in-stride across the parking lot as the first Wilmington police cars crested the hill. Blue-and-red lights swirled off the dew-covered pavement, sirens blaring. More followed.

Gower's eyes widened. He shoved his way past the line of men with dollies, tripping over one on his way back into the plant.

"Armed security guards are somewhere on the grounds or in the building, but no eyes on them," Caleb said on the radio before the wave of police officers climbed from their cars.

"Roger that," Celia Tracy, head of investigative operations, said.

Three EPA vehicles were the last to pull in.

On Celia's command, the officers streamed into the factory, two escorting the EPA officials straight for the plastic drums on the dock.

Caleb and Austin moved through the building toward the offices, thankful for the thorough tour Gower had provided yesterday. The long wing was still bathed in darkness, only the emergency exit signs lit red, and a few auxiliary lights.

"One security guard in custody," one of the officers reported over Caleb's earpiece.

Which left two by last night's count. He'd bet money Gower had them protecting him. *Fool.* With the parking lot exits blocked, he had nowhere to go but the ravine out in front of the docks or the thick woods on the eastern side of the factory—accessed best through the office wing.

Caleb expected Gower to go for the woods.

The sound of footsteps scuffling on the carpet came from the other side of a partition dividing a large open space where employees took breaks and ate meals. Caleb held his finger to his lips, and Austin nodded, covering his six while he moved forward. If he remembered correctly, a set of doors on the far side of the room led to the outside patio area, and just beyond that sat the woods.

Austin indicated she'd slip around the other end of the dividing wall. Caleb nodded, giving her time to get in position before he rounded the corner. His gun aimed at the first guard's chest. The second guard stood behind him—both of their revolvers aimed at Caleb.

The first guard cocked his head, a slight smile crossing his lips. "Looks like you're outnumbered."

Austin crept up behind the second guard, pressing her gun to his temple. "I'd say we're more than even now."

The outer door opened and clanked shut. *Gower.*

They didn't have time for this.

"Lay down your weapons," Caleb said, his gaze pinned on the guard in front of him. "There are police swarming the building. You really want to take a murder rap for a loser like Gower?"

"We don't want no trouble," the guard said, laying down his weapon.

"Kick it over here," Caleb said.

"Do the same," Austin said to the second guard. He complied.

"We've got the two security guards, unarmed in the office wing. Gower ran—we're taking chase," Caleb called over the radio.

"On my way," an officer said.

Caleb looked back at the guards. "Is Gower armed?"

The first guard nodded. "He grabbed a gun from his desk, though I doubt he has a clue how to use it."

An officer rounded the corner.

"Thanks," Caleb said as he and Austin rushed for the outer door.

Racing across the patio sitting area, they dropped down the four-foot retaining wall and crossed to the tree line.

Fog rose nearly a foot high, thickening the deeper they moved through the woods. Dampness clung in the air, their breath highlighted by first cracks of light.

Austin stilled, surveying the landscape. "Anchor Road is about a thousand yards due east."

"Good thinking."

The peach hue of streetlights glowed like globes in the distance as streaks of orange crested the horizon.

"Gower," Caleb called, catching sight of the man's retreating form. "There's nowhere to go."

Gower stumbled as he spun around, firing his gun.

Caleb pressed his back against the knotty trunk of the closest tree as Austin did the same.

"This is a dead end," Austin called.

He fired again. This time up in the air.

*What an idiot.*

Austin gestured for Caleb to take the go-around route this time, and she'd continue moving forward.

Caleb nodded and made a wide arc around the trees to the north.

Gower hit the road, his form outlined by the streetlights. He lifted his hand to shade his eyes as he looked up and down the road.

"Nowhere," Caleb said, his gun aimed, his stance firm.

Gower whined. Literally whined. "I can't go to jail."

Austin crept up behind him, gun aimed, and relieved him of his gun. "You should have thought of that before you started dumping toxic chemicals in our waters."

Caleb stepped across the short space and handcuffed Gower.

Forty-five minutes later, Austin leaned back against Caleb as they stood by his car, his chin resting on her head.

A patrol car drove past with Gower secured in the back.

Austin's shoulders dipped as she turned with a smile. "That was fun."

He chuckled. "You have a very interesting idea of fun."

"You know what else is fun . . ." A sparkle lit her eyes as she opened the passenger door and slipped inside.

Climbing in, he shifted to face her.

She leaned across the seat, pressing a long, slow kiss against his lips.

He could get used to this.

Spreading his fingers through her silky hair, he kissed her back, unable to keep a smile from curling on his lips.

"What's the smile for?" she murmured against his mouth.

"You."

# SIXTY-FOUR

Noah held the station door open for Brooke, and she passed through. The day had started on a high note with Caleb and Austin busting Huntington Foam and its CEO, Braxton Gower. Noah hoped for more good news.

"Hey, guys," Em said. She strode over to Noah and handed him a printed-out article. "A present for you."

His eyes scanned the page. The image was of the man labeled *John* on the back of the photograph they found at Caldwell's. His gaze tracked down.

"Senior chief corpsman in the Navy," he said.

"Yep." Emmy leaned against her desk, crossing one leg over the other.

"You are good."

He caught Logan's smile at his compliment for Emmy.

"How did you find this?" Noah asked.

"I followed a hunch. Because of his resemblance to Scott, I started searching for John Mirch. Of course, nothing came up, which is freakishly weird, given he's active duty in the Navy. Anyway, I ended up finding this small news article about John's latest commendation. Guess whoever was busy wiping out identities dropped the ball on this one."

"Any idea of his relation to Scott?"

"No. But my spidey-sense says brother."

"You're probably right. And he's active duty?"

Noah scanned the fine print at the bottom just as Emmy said it aloud. "Stationed at Pensacola, Florida."

"We're meeting with Jack Weaver, Scott Mirch's defense attorney in . . ." Noah glanced at his watch, "in a half hour. See how soon after you can get Brooke and me on a flight to Pensacola."

"On it," Emmy said, pushing off her desk and moving to sit at it.

"Me too?" Brooke said.

"First, I don't like you out of my sight." He grinned. "For more reasons than one."

She shook her head on a smile. "And second?"

"You knew Scott. However this man is related to him, you might be able to strike up a conversation about Scott that can lead to some helpful information." Any information on Scott Mirch or his elusive family would be a huge leap forward in the investigation.

The man at the front desk of Weaver & Sons, Attorneys at Law stood. "Mr. Weaver is ready to see you now," he said, holding his tie against his chest as he directed them to an imposing dark wood door.

He opened the door, announced them, and politely excused himself.

Jack Weaver, a robust man with wavy blond hair and a dark tan—quite unusual for this time of year—stood and reached across his large cherry desk to shake their hands. "Agent Rowley and Petty Officer Kesler. Please sit." He gestured to the two chairs facing his desk. "How can I be of assistance?"

As she sat, Brooke took in the pictures lining the long wall of bookcases. Weaver and who she assumed was his family on a sailboat in clear blue waters and on a white, sandy beach and smiling for a selfie under a palm tree. Now the tan was making sense. They were the tropical-traveler types.

"We met with Brett Anderson yesterday," Noah began.

"Brett Anderson," Weaver said, rocking back in his desk chair as he folded his hands across his belly. "How is he doing? I've missed seeing him since I went into private practice."

"You're former JAG?" Noah prompted.

"Yeah." Jack rocked forward and moved to retrieve a picture off his credenza. He smiled at it, then handed it to Brooke.

It was Jack in his JAG uniform probably twenty years ago. She passed the picture to Noah.

"As you can see, that was a long time ago." Jack retook his seat. "Brett and I used to go at it back in the day. Good man, that guy." He rested his forearms on his desktop. "You said you wanted to discuss Scott Mirch?"

"Yes, sir," Noah said.

"Jack, please. But I'm curious why now? Scott went to prison seven years ago." He tapped the shiny surface of his desk, piles of folders on either side. "I can't help but notice the timing of events. There's a mass shooting on base, and within days, you're in my office asking about a seven-year-old case. Are you thinking there's a link between the two?"

"That's what we're trying to determine," Noah said. "Brett said you had a theory about a fifth man on the job."

"Oh . . ." Weaver chuckled. "He thought I was crazy, and Scott adamantly denied it, but in addition to believing Scott that the instructors were in cahoots, yes, I believe there was a fifth man he wasn't willing to reveal."

"Why's that?"

"Someone had to move that money after Scott was arrested. And someone had to tell Scott about the off-the-books cryptocurrency fund in the first place." He poured himself a glass of water from a crystal pitcher on the gold trivet at the far corner of his desk. "Would you care for any?" he asked.

"I'll take a glass," Brooke said while Noah passed.

"You mentioned you're a flight medic on the phone. I'm curious, how does a medic fit into all this?" Jack asked.

"I knew Scott, and unfortunately, I was involved in the mass shooting."

"I'm sorry to hear that but glad to see you're doing okay," Jack said, handing her an etched-glass tumbler with ice-cold water. "How did you know Scott?"

"He was in IT C-School while I was in Flight Medic A-School, and our mess hall slots hit at the same time."

"Would you say you knew him well?" Jack asked.

"I think as well as anyone could know Scott," she said.

"So you *did* know him well." Jack exhaled. "His was the hardest defense I ever had to pull together."

"Because he kept things close to the vest?" Brooke said.

"Exactly." He reached for the pile of files to his left and fingered through them. "Ah. Here we go. I pulled this when you called. I'm not sure how much use it'll be. You won't find much in there on Scott. Only what he was willing to say."

"What do you mean?" Noah asked.

"When building a defense, it's important to have as many character witnesses as you can get. I tried to talk Scott into letting me call his brother, John, to speak on his behalf, but Scott refused to talk about his family or anyone else who might have spoken for him."

Brooke smiled. So John *was* his brother. Knowing that should make their conversation in Florida go easier.

"Scott acted as if John didn't exist, though the background check I did proved otherwise. Try as I might to convince him, Scott refused to let John testify."

"Did he say why?" Noah asked.

"No. Just denied his existence."

"And his parents?" Brooke asked, trying to remember if Scott had ever mentioned parents or even where he was from.

"Again, only from the background check, but his mom—Margie, I believe—is deceased. She died when Scott was seventeen. John, I think, is close to a decade older than Scott."

"And their dad?"

"In the wind since he left the service."

"Their dad was military too?" Noah looked at Brooke. They were both thinking it. The older man with the Marine Raiders hat in the photograph.

"Yes. He was in the Marines, but that's as far as I got. His records were sealed. Labeled classified. I went a little higher up the chain, and suddenly Frank Mirch's records vanished."

# SIXTY-FIVE

The announcement to prepare for their final descent into Pensacola came over the plane speakers. Noah and Brooke spent the entire flight combing through Scott Mirch's file. It was clear that Jack Weaver believed the three men Scott implicated as guilty were just that. And based on the evidence Jack collected—as circumstantial and theoretical as it was—there seemed a strong and intriguing possibility that a silent fifth man existed.

The biggest takeaway, though, was learning the father's name, along with confirmation that Frank was a former Marine Raider with his service disappearing.

Noah looked out the window as the plane touched down, bouncing along the runway until it screeched to a stop.

"It's sunny," Brooke said, looking past him.

"And warm." He showed her his phone with the local weather page. "Sixty-five degrees. Not too shabby."

"Is John expecting us?" she asked as they made their way up the ramp to the airport.

"Yep. I gave him a call while you grabbed some snacks in the sundry shop. He seemed intrigued about our visit but didn't seem surprised when I mentioned it was about his brother, saying he figured someone would visit again."

Brooke dipped her chin. "Again?"

"Apparently, we aren't the first authorities who've visited John Mirch."

Having no checked luggage, they breezed through the airport, picked up their car, and were on the freeway in no time.

"You know, I keep thinking . . ." Brooke said.

"Oh boy, that could be dangerous." Noah grinned.

"Don't you know it." She winked. "But seriously, Weaver's fifth-man theory . . . What if Frank or John was the fifth man? They are in the photograph with Scott, Amy Caldwell, and Dwayne. But considering John is still active military and Frank went dark after Scott was arrested, my money's on Frank."

Caleb and Austin celebrated the arrests of Braxton Gower, Sid Sawicki, and Hector Valdez with burgers followed by milkshakes from Gracie & Johnny's, which sat just around the corner from UNC-Wilmington. The ma-and-pa diner catered to the college crowd but had a booming business with the whole town.

"How's the raspberry shake?" he asked as they stepped outside, the day finally warming into the fifties.

"Delicious," she said. "And yours, Mr. Vanilla?"

"Vanilla is a perfectly good flavor." Once he found one he liked, why switch?

"I know what we're doing for your birthday next month . . ."

"Oh?" He was half-afraid to hear. And how did she even know when it was? No doubt she did a full background check when they first worked a case together. He couldn't say anything. He'd done the same.

"An ice cream party"—she walked toward his car with a spring in her step—"with twenty different flavors."

He laughed. "Only you."

His cell rang, and he fished it out of his jeans pocket. "Eason," he answered.

"Hey, Caleb," Emmy said. "Glad to hear the raid went well."

"Thanks."

She cleared her throat. "I have some bad news."

Caleb sighed. That hadn't lasted long.

"A group of petty officers just found a body washed up on the shore of the base," Em said.

"Any identification?" he asked, though he feared he already knew who it was.

"No, but it's a woman, and she's blond. The petty officers didn't touch her, just cordoned off the area and called it in."

"Okay, ETA fifteen."

Finn was waiting for him when they arrived.

Caleb climbed through the yellow crime-scene tape. Austin waited at the edge, looking on.

"What do we got?" he asked.

"I've photographed the body as she was found and started marking the scene," Finn said.

Caleb knelt by the body.

The woman was dressed in a long white nightgown, her blond hair halfway down her back, matted to her body.

"I think we both have a feeling about who this is," he said. "Let me know when it's okay to move the body."

"I'm ready," Finn said, crouching down, his camera ready to start shooting.

His muscles coiling, Caleb carefully rolled the body over and sank back on his heels. Just as he suspected. Lieutenant Amy Caldwell. He shook his head as Finn's flash bounced off her pale face and blue lips.

"Is Hadley on the way?"

"Yes." Finn nodded.

"I'll be curious to see if she died from drowning, or if she was killed and dumped. Though the bruising around her neck suggests either she was strangled—"

"Or held underwater until she drowned," Finn said.

"Right." Caleb scanned the area. "The chance of her randomly washing up on our base is slim to none."

"Agreed." Finn lowered his camera. "So why here?"

"To send us a message. To signal that his reach is long and close." Whoever *he* was. Caleb agreed with Noah. Dwayne was the on-the-field player, but he wasn't the one calling the plays.

# SIXTY-SIX

NAS Pensacola was located on a peninsula a few miles south-west of the town.

Noah pulled up to the gate under the blue sign with yellow lettering and powered down his window. After dispensing with formalities, he and Brooke were both handed visitor badges and given clearance to enter.

"We're here to see Senior Chief Mirch. Could you direct us to him?"

"He's expecting you. Said he'll be waiting at the Naval Education and Training Command building. You want to head to the fork, then head left, follow it all the way around, and the NETC is on your far left. Four-story brick building. You can't miss it."

When they arrived, Noah opened Brooke's door for her.

"Thank you." She climbed out with a smile, sliding her sunglasses up on her head.

They stepped into the building and asked the first soldier they passed where to find John.

"In the main room, back table," the baby-faced soldier said, pointing down the hall. Man, he'd forgotten how young he'd been when he joined.

They entered the main room filled with silver tables and

chairs. Knowing what John looked like—a near-exact replica of his brother—made him easy to spot.

"Senior Chief," Noah said, holding out his hand. "Special Agent Noah Rowley."

He shook Noah's hand.

"And this is my colleague, Petty Officer Brooke Kesler."

"Ma'am." John nodded once. "I thought we'd head to the mess hall, grab a bad cup of coffee, and talk. That work?"

"Lead the way," Noah said.

John strode for the door. Once outside, he said, "Or we can go to McDonald's. Coffee is a mite better there."

"Whichever you prefer," Noah said. "We just appreciate you taking the time to speak with us."

"Mess hall is only a hundred yards. McDonald's is quite a bit farther." He looked over at them.

"The mess hall works," Noah said, knowing he had to take it easy on his leg as he was able, but after being cooped up on a plane and then in a car, stretching his legs sounded good.

"Sorry about the shooting on your base," Mirch said.

"Thank you. I know you had your own mass shooting here a couple years ago," Noah said.

"Far fewer people killed and injured, but even one is too many."

"Agreed." Noah nodded.

They walked in silence for a while until Brooke said, "So you served three combat duties?"

"Yes, ma'am. Three tours in Afghanistan."

"I can't imagine."

"It ain't pretty. Whoever said 'war is hell' wasn't lying, but I know you're here to talk about my derelict brother." His jaw tightened on the word *brother*. "Might as well get to it on our walk."

Noah went straight to the point. "We believe your brother ties in some way to the mass shooting."

The lines on John's face tightened. "I knew that boy was going to cause serious trouble one day."

Noah climbed in the black rented Escalade, his head spinning with all the information John Mirch shared.

"Well, he certainly was helpful," Brooke said, buckling her seat belt.

"Yes, he was." He glanced at his phone and saw a text from Emmy asking him to call.

"Call Emmy," he said to Siri as he pulled out of the lot and headed back to the base gate.

The phone rang twice, and she picked up. "Thorton."

"Hey, Em. It's me."

"Hey, Noah. How'd it go?"

"Really well. Now I need you to work your magic and get me and Brooke on the first flight out to Leavenworth. We need to interview Scott Mirch face-to-face."

"On it, but before I let you go, Logan and I found two farms where the group might be staying. One is an abandoned forty acres of land in Murrayville. The second is a thirty-acre farm bought by a corporation a year ago out by Skipper's Corner."

"Is the corporation legit?" he asked.

"It's an offshore company. Trent & Foster."

"Companies don't buy farms unless they are going to raze them to the ground."

"And"—he could practically hear Emmy smiling—"I have to do a bit more digging for specifics, but it looks like Trent & Foster deals in cryptocurrency."

Noah smiled with relief. "I'd say you probably just found our farm."

"I hope so," she said.

"But just to be thorough, let's check the other farm as well. Go ahead and send Logan and Rissi to the Murrayville farm, and Mason and Caleb to Skipper's Corner."

"Caleb . . . might be tied up. If so, I can go. He asked that you give him a call when you get the chance. When you're finished, let me know what you'd like me to do."

"Okay. Calling him now."

He'd barely disconnected the call with Emmy when he had Siri dialing Caleb.

"Eason," Caleb said, picking up on the first ring.

"Em said you wanted me to call?"

"Yeah. I'm afraid I have some bad news." Caleb cleared his throat. "Lieutenant Caldwell's body washed up on the base's shore today."

"Oh no," Brooke whispered.

"It looks like she was strangled or forcibly held underwater until she drowned. Finn's working the crime scene, Hadley is on-site, and since she was Army, we've called Army CID in to take over the investigation."

Noah shook his head. How many people were going to die before this ended? "Thanks for letting me know."

"Of course. How'd your talk with John Mirch go?"

"Good. Brooke and I are heading to Leavenworth to interview Scott. Em found two likely farm locations, and I need you and Mason out at one of them as soon as you can make it. She can give you the details."

"Roger that."

Noah disconnected his call and less than a minute later picked up Em's. "Whatcha got for us?"

"Okay, it was a little tricky. Nothing worked for tonight, but I've got you on an 0700 flight tomorrow morning. It'll get you on the ground by 1030, and then I've arranged a rental car for the half-hour drive to the disciplinary barracks at Leavenworth."

"Thanks, Em. I spoke with Caleb, and he's good for the farm. He'll be calling you to get the details."

"Sounds good."

"Since Brooke and I aren't leaving until morning, let's have a Zoom case board this evening after they return from checking out the farms. I need to update you all on what Brooke and I learned from John Mirch, and I want to hear the follow-up on both the farms and Caldwell's death."

"I'll set it for 1800," she said.

"Great. I'll log in then." He started to disconnect the call, then paused. "And Em?"

"Yes?"

"Good work."

Disconnecting the call, he looked at Brooke. "Guess we're going to need to find a hotel for the night." Truth be told, he was happy to have Brooke out of Wilmington as this powder keg felt ready to blow.

# SIXTY-SEVEN

Taking a steadying breath from his position on the wooded hill, Caleb looked through his binoculars at the farm near Skipper's Corner. He spotted a man patrolling the northeast perimeter line of the fenced property—an AR-15 in his grip.

A ten-foot chain-link fence surrounded what he could see of the property, though at thirty-two acres, it was a vast piece of land. Surely the entire property wasn't fenced—at least not with a high chain-link fence all the way around. Or . . . He spotted a second man patrolling with the same AR. Maybe it was.

He traded his binoculars for his camera with a scope lens, clicking images of the fence and guards.

Mason had taken the southwest side of the property, and Caleb was anxious to learn if he was seeing much of the same.

His muscles grew taut as he continued taking pictures of the farm that had been transformed into a compound.

There was a vast shooting range in the distance with close to a dozen men firing on it. Three red barns stood between the fence and the range. A large metal barn stood out—far newer than the wooden ones.

He slowed his breath, easing his focus. His rifle was strapped over his shoulder, the weapon resting along his back. The temp was dropping with the sun, and soon darkness would overtake the farm.

Caleb spotted what appeared to be two large bunkhouses, and on the edge of a rolling hill sat an old farmhouse with faded green siding, a white porch with peeling paint, and an old wooden rocking chair.

If he had to guess, there had to be at least twenty people on the compound, and that was just based on the acreage he could see from his vantage point.

He hiked back more than a mile through the woods to his Forester, which he'd left hidden down an old dirt drive.

Placing the rifle in its case in the rear, he moved around to the door and climbed in, his Glock still in his waist holster. He started the ignition and paused for a minute, scanning the area. Finding it empty, he eased down the dirt driveway and onto the winding country road—headed to retrieve his teammate.

Caleb knocked on Logan's door as Austin wrapped her coat tighter around herself. The blistering wind was swirling, kicking up her skirt, and she was ready for the warmth of Logan's home—and anxious to see the inside, as it was her first time visiting. Deciding they all needed a break, Logan had invited her, Caleb, and Emmy to dinner to celebrate closing the chemical dumping case.

"Hey, guys," Logan said as he propped the storm door open for them to pass through.

Emmy stood up from the velvet sofa. It was a cloudy gray with slate undertones that matched the wall, which held a large stone fireplace with flames dancing inside and the homey sound of crackling wood.

"Make yourself comfortable," Logan said. "Can I get you anything?"

"I'll take a root beer," Caleb said. He turned to her. "Logan ships in the best handcrafted root beer—Dominion."

"Would you like one too, Austin?" Logan asked.

"It really is delicious," Emmy said, scooting over on the couch so Austin could take a seat.

"That would be great."

"Three frosty root beers coming up." Logan disappeared down the white hall on the left.

She waited until he was out of earshot. "I didn't picture Logan's home looking so . . . refined." She studied the canvas travel pictures donning the right wall. "Does he travel a lot?" Had he really been to all those places?

"Yes," Emmy said.

"I didn't realize CGIS paid so well," Austin said.

Caleb chuckled. "It doesn't." He lowered his mouth to her ear and whispered, "Trust-fund kid," as Logan rounded the corner, three literal frosty mugs in hand.

"Three root beers." Logan handed a vintage glass mug with a red Frostie logo to Austin. She wrapped her fingers around the handle, the cold penetrating her otherwise warm fingers. "Careful, the mugs have been in the freezer," Logan said.

"Got it." She wiggled her fingers. "Thanks."

"Dinner's almost ready," he said.

"Can I help set the table?" Emmy offered.

"That would be great."

Emmy stood and followed him into the kitchen.

Austin hadn't seen Logan as a trust-fund kid, but it fit now that she thought about it. But why work as a CGIS agent when he could live off his inheritance? Apparently, he wasn't a sit-on-your-bahookie type of guy. Her esteem for him grew even more.

"Give it a taste," Caleb said, a line of froth donning his upper lip.

She fought the urge to reach out and wipe it away. Anything to touch his strong yet gentle lips, but she held herself at bay. Besides, after her first sip, she'd probably have the same. Lifting the mug to her lips, she took a swallow. "Wow!"

"Good, right?" Caleb said, swiping the foam from his lips—lips he had pressed to hers not long ago.

"It's delicious."

"If you'll excuse me, I'm going to wash up before dinner," Caleb said, standing.

"Of course." Sitting by herself, she reached over for the *Coastal Living* magazine on the end table. To her surprise, she discovered a Bible under it. It had notes sticking out of it. She wanted to pick it up and flip through it, but respecting Logan's privacy, she restrained herself and re-covered it with the magazine.

Caleb returned and sat next to her.

She leaned over and whispered in his ear. "Logan has a Bible on that end table."

Caleb's brows arched. "Seriously?"

"I took the magazine off the table to flip through, and it was sitting under it." She tapped the magazine. "I wonder if Emmy knows."

"That would make a big difference for them," Caleb said.

Austin wrestled with the desire to tell Emmy, but it wasn't really her place. If Emmy didn't already know whether Logan had committed his life to Christ or was just searching, he would tell her when he was ready.

"Hey, guys," Noah greeted his team via Zoom from his hotel room. He and Brooke found a hotel near the airport, but he doubted he'd be able to sleep. Too much was happening for them and his team.

"So how did your meeting with John Mirch go?" Rissi asked.

"Well, he was really helpful," Noah said. "As a twice-decorated senior chief corpsman who did three tours in Afghanistan, you can imagine how he felt when Scott's crimes brought disgrace on his family's reputation, but it gets worse."

"Seriously?" Logan gave a sarcastic chuckle. "How does it get worse than that?"

"John's dad was dishonorably discharged too," Noah said.

"What?" Emmy spewed her root beer across Logan's pressed white shirt. "Sorry," she murmured.

"No problem." He chuckled, handing her a handkerchief.

She used it to dab the fizz from her mouth. "Sorry, boss," Emmy said.

"All good," Noah replied.

"Are you sure about Frank Mirch?" Emmy said. "It took calling in some serious favors, but I got a copy of Frank Mirch's military records."

"I'm highly impressed," Noah said.

"Well, don't get too excited. Ninety-five percent was redacted, and I'm not exaggerating. The longest phrase I got was 'trained at Camp Lejeune.'"

"Frank trained on my brother-in-law's base?" Noah's chest constricted. "If he wasn't dishonorably discharged, it would give me great pause to know a killer lived on the same base as my sister, brother-in-law, and, most especially, the kiddos."

"We know what Scott did to warrant discharge," Emmy said. "Did John say what his dad did? It wasn't in his file, or it was part of what was redacted."

"He and his Raiders team were resting in between ops at an enemy internment camp in Afghanistan when a riot broke out among the detainees," Noah said. "They were overtaking the few Marine guards, so Frank stepped in—put a maul to the head of the detainee stirring up all the trouble. Killed him flat. The body was disposed of. No one said a thing. Nothing came of it until his team returned to the States, and one of the men outed him. It almost went to trial, but that wasn't something the US military or government wanted to come to light, so they quietly dishonorably discharged him and sealed his records."

"I can only imagine how quiet they wanted to keep that," Logan said.

"Needless to say, Frank didn't take what he deemed a betrayal by his brother-in-arms and the military leaders he'd served for nearly thirty-five years well."

"He fell off the map, so to speak," Brooke said. "When Scott committed the heist, John believed it was payback for what the military had done to their father."

"And the dad?" Logan asked.

"He was nowhere to be found while Scott was on trial. Nor has he visited him in prison, according to the man in charge. However," Noah said, "Brooke has a theory."

"It's our theory, really."

She'd come up with it. She was just being gracious.

"Please," Noah said, indicating for her to go ahead.

"Jack Weaver, Scott's defense attorney, said two pivotal things," Brooke began. "One, Scott refused to ask his family to speak on his behalf. And two, Weaver believed there was a fifth man involved. Someone who knew the off-the-books cryptocurrency account existed in the first place."

"Someone who'd participated in off-the-book missions and worked with the intelligence community on several key missions," Noah said.

"Frank Mirch," Mason said.

"We can't be sure with his redacted record, but Marine Raiders are serious special ops. According to John Mirch, we know his father did tours in the Persian Gulf War, Operation Desert Storm, and Afghanistan. He was right in there."

"So you think Frank was incensed at being 'betrayed,'" Logan said, using air quotes, "knew about this cryptocurrency account, reached out to his son with brilliant computer skills, and got him to steal the money? They most likely worked with the three instructors, intending to use their skills for what they needed, then set them up to take the blame, but the three double-crossed Scott, leaving him holding the bag."

"You've got it," Noah said.

"So now all of this is payback for his son going to prison?" Rissi asked.

"Well, the money Scott stole disappeared after he was in custody, and it's untraceable," Brooke said. "We think Frank bided his time and used some of the money to plan and coordinate this entire offensive, if you will. He gets back at the military and takes out the three instructors who set up his son to take the fall in one fell swoop."

"Unbelievable," Em said, shaking her head.

Noah leaned forward, resting his hands on his knees. "What did you guys find at the farms?" He prayed they found Dwayne, who—if he was right—was Frank's second-in-command.

Caleb filled him in on the compound they found on the farm in Skipper's Corner.

Noah pinched the bridge of his nose. These guys were completely unhinged, though that had been clear since the mass shooting.

"I'll give ATF and the local FBI field office a call," Caleb said.

"Ask for Bill Todd over at ATF. He's a good man—a great agent."

"Will do."

"I worry with Lieutenant Caldwell's death and her expertise on the laser weapon that . . ."

Caleb sat back, his face paling on the screen. "That she finished it."

"So are we looking at an impending act of domestic terrorism, or is he selling it to one of our nation's enemies on the black market?" Noah asked, thinking out loud. "Either way, we need to pray you guys find it first."

# SIXTY-EIGHT

Caleb knelt, his knee sinking into the cold earth, the predawn moisture seeping through his pants.

ATF agents, FBI special agents, and his teammates, save Noah and Emmy, were present. Em was on logistics, and Noah and Brooke would soon be flying to see Scott Mirch.

Caleb scanned the compound through his night-vision binoculars. If Frank Mirch was running this, he certainly had a well-trained team. Most former military, if Caleb was reading the men right. And he wouldn't be surprised if there was an extensive weapons cache on-site.

He made a visual check with ATF's Bill Todd and beyond him with Federal Agent Axel Murphy, the three of them running their coordinated teams.

Adrenaline coursed through his limbs, and Caleb forced himself to remain still. He was itching to move in, to get this guy behind bars and end this, but they were in a hold pattern until the FBI snipers were in place and they received the go order.

He turned his attention back to the gated compound, watching the two men armed with modified AK-47s along the northeast perimeter. As he'd suspected, recon revealed two men patrolling each fenced property line. Just before dawn was usually the perfect time for a raid. Just enough light not to go in blind, but with most of the men asleep or easily caught off guard.

But Mirch's team clearly maintained around-the-clock watch, which meant this could turn ugly fast.

*Father, please protect everyone here. We have an idea, but definitely don't know the extent of what we're walking into or the skill of those we're raiding.*

He took a steeling breath and prepared for whatever lay ahead, knowing God went before them.

"Snipers are in place," Agent Murphy said. Caleb was point on the raid. However, given the situation and Noah's direction, they were passing the remainder of the investigation of the compound to Axel and the FBI.

CGIS was here for Dwayne and, hopefully, Frank Mirch.

"Holding on snipers," Axel said over the comms. "We count ten guards, armed and moving."

Caleb lay on the ground beside Bill Todd, binoculars in hand, his weight propped up on his elbows. "My concern is how many we aren't seeing."

"Agreed," Bill Todd said. "And based on what I am seeing, I also agree with your assumption of a weapons cache. We'll need to move swiftly."

Caleb gave a nod.

"Thanks for the call," Bill said.

"Snipers are reporting back," Axel said over comms. "They're seeing movement in the bunkhouses and believe there could be hidden sectors."

Caleb's chest compressed. Just as they feared. He took a resolute inhale, knowing whatever they faced, God was watching over them and would go before them.

# SIXTY-NINE

Plumes of smoke rose in in the dawn air, mixing with clouds of white from their breath. His heart thwapping in his ears, Caleb ran low, gun in hand. The underground charges spaced around the perimeter had been unexpected, but the gunfire once they'd rammed their way into the compound had not.

Bullets ripped over his head as he dove behind a military-green Jeep.

The metal pinged as the bullets encased in the vehicle's siding mere inches from his head. Rolling onto his stomach, he aimed at the shooter's feet, visible from under the Jeep's wheel well. He held his breath, then slowly exhaled as he squeezed the trigger.

The man cursed and hobbled away, blood trailing behind him. Impressive he hadn't dropped, but futile—Caleb had him.

Standing, Caleb tracked the man, his aim focused on the center of his back. "Halt," he said.

The man turned, raising his gun to fire, leaving Caleb no recourse.

He fired—one, two, three—until the man dropped to the ground, his AR-15 slipping from his open palm.

Caleb moved toward him, confirmed his death, and picked

up his weapon. Having an extra weapon in this melee wasn't a bad idea.

He moved with Mason, making their way deeper into the compound.

A half hour later, Axel Murphy announced over their headsets that they had control of the compound.

Caleb's breath released on a prayer. *Thank you, Jesus.*

Now they just needed to find Dwayne and Frank Mirch among the men. Along with the laser plans or, heaven forbid, the weapon itself.

He shook his head as he took in the dead scattered across the hard-packed dirt. So many who could have lived if they just would have laid down their guns. "How many of ours are gone?" he asked, unable to see all his team members over the vast acreage and through the still-dissipating smoke.

"Two ATF. Two FBI," came Bill Todd's reply.

Caleb's gut clinched. "I'm sorry to hear that." But he hadn't gotten a number on his team. "CGIS," he said over the headset. "Report."

Gratitude and thankfulness filled him as one by one his entire team present responded.

*Thank you, Father, that none of my team died today, but good law enforcement members did. Please be with their families and those left behind.*

"Eason," Rissi said over the headset.

"Eason here. Go ahead, Rissi."

"You need to see something in the basement of the farmhouse."

Caleb's gaze flashed five hundred yards northeast of his position to the old farmhouse he'd scoped out yesterday. "On my way."

"Roger that," Rissi said.

Two ATF agents stood guard on the porch, along with a sniper combing the perimeter to assess if any had escaped through a hidden exit.

Caleb nodded as he stepped passed them. "Good work."

"You too," one of the agents said as they both nodded.

Entering, Caleb found Finn guarding four prisoners secured on chairs.

"I'll run prints as soon as things settle," Finn said.

Caleb nodded his thanks, but they both knew the men's identities had been scrubbed.

"Rissi and Logan are in the basement," Finn said.

Caleb climbed down the narrow cellar steps into a full logistics room. Was it possible they'd finally made it to the end of the horror unleashed little more than a week ago? Two men were restrained in chairs, their hands zip-tied behind their backs— definitely not Frank or Dwayne.

Disappointment surging, Caleb turned his attention to the computer screens mounted on the wall running video surveillance of the entire compound.

"It appears," Rissi said, "these two were left in command."

"Yeah. They left us in charge, top-tier," the prisoner with cropped red hair boasted. "The rest are just foot soldiers."

The man next to him cussed. "What do you mean *foot soldiers*, Ted? My brother is out there."

Ted glared at the man next to him. "Thanks, *Max*."

Caleb's jaw shifted. "So Ted, is it?" He stepped closer, hovering in Ted's space. If these jokers had been left in charge, was it possible the operation had moved to the next phase? A chill raced up his spine. "Where are Dwayne and Frank?"

Ted laughed. "Nowhere you'll find them."

"It's interesting that, considering you're top-tier, they had no trouble leaving you behind."

Ted's jaw clamped, his teeth grinding. Finally, he opened his mouth. "A good soldier takes orders." His eyes narrowed. "Or don't you get that?"

"Caleb," Logan said, "you're going to want to see this."

Taking a sharp inhale, he walked away from the trash that

was Ted and followed Logan through the door on the far side of the room.

He stepped into the room to find all of the laser plans pinned to a corkboard in connecting squares. His breath froze. He looked at the table, at the small parts and tools strewn across it, but no laser weapon.

His heart sank. They were too late.

Ted's laughter filled the space, and it took all Caleb's restraint not to strangle the man as he moved back to him. "Where are they headed?"

Ted's laughter only increased.

Taking a sharp breath, Caleb surveyed the room. There had to be a clue. Something.

He surveyed the laser plans and the notations in what appeared to be a woman's script strewn across them—Lieutenant Caldwell.

He shook his head and kept scanning until his gaze hit the metal trash bin. Mainly scorched papers lay nestled inside. "Logan," he called.

"Yes?" Logan leaned through the doorway. "Go swap with Finn. I need him."

Logan nodded, and in less than a minute, Finn entered the room.

"We need to dump the trash. You've got gloves?"

"Yes." Finn pulled out a handful of pairs he always kept on hand, and a plastic evidence bag that always sat in his back pocket during situations like this. He'd bring his full CSI kit in once they were ready.

"Thanks," Caleb said, slipping on a pair.

Finn did the same.

"Here we go," Caleb said, praying there would be even the slightest lead to where Dwayne and Frank might have gone.

The papers spilled across the far end of the worktable, and they began going through them piece by piece.

"Oh no," Caleb said, the words coming out in a rush.

Finn stilled. "What is it?"

He clutched what remained of a blueprint and lifted his hand. "The disciplinary barracks at Leavenworth. They might already be there. I've got to call Noah."

# SEVENTY

Noah sat back as their plane soared up in the sky nearly twenty minutes early. Everyone had been aboard, so they lucked out with an early takeoff. He looked over at Brooke and smiled, thankful she was able to grab a few hours of rest last night. Sleep had eluded him.

He hadn't heard from his team before boarding, and as much as he wanted an update, he wouldn't risk calling during a raid. Caleb would reach out to him as soon as he was able. He took a sip of his Dunkin' red-eye and glanced out the window at the sun breaking through the darkness.

A flight attendant headed their way, and he smiled, but the smile faded as she stopped at their seats. Leaning over, she whispered, "There's an emergency patch-through for you. If you follow me . . ."

He gave Brooke's hand a squeeze and followed the attendant to the cockpit. She knocked and stood with her face in line with the large peephole.

The copilot opened the door. "Agent Rowley, I take it."

"Yes, sir."

"Please, come in. There's someone on the line for you."

The pilot greeted him and handed him a set of headphones. "Agent Rowley. Go ahead, please."

"It's Caleb."

His chest constricted, making breathing laborious. "What's wrong?"

*Please don't let it be that anyone died in the raid. Please, Lord.*

"It's bad," Caleb said, getting straight to it. "The weapon was finished, and it's gone. No Dwayne or Frank either." Caleb sighed. "They're heading to Leavenworth."

The lunatic was going to try to use a laser weapon to break his son out of prison? Was he crazy? Didn't he realize he was more likely to kill his son in the explosion?

"Warn them immediately," he said, careful with his choice of words with others present.

"Already done," Caleb said.

"Any idea how much of a head start they have?" he asked.

"No, but we found a hangar disguised as a barn and a dirt runway in the midst of the back fields."

"They have their own plane?" *That meant . . .*

A Marine helicopter waited for Noah and Brooke when they touched down. It would be faster than a rental car.

"Thanks for the lift," Noah said. "I'm Noah Rowley, and this is Brooke Kesler."

"George, and no problem. I hear your team warned Leavenworth."

Noah clamped his hand on the dash, leaning forward as if he could will himself there faster. "I just pray we're not too late."

Fifteen minutes later, Noah looked down in horror.

The Castle, the barracks' unofficial name, was on fire. Smoke rose in gray billows as red lights swirled in a mass of chaos below.

"Hang on tight," George said. "We've got snow mixed with ice—black ice from the looks of the landing helipad. Make sure you're both all buckled up."

Noah reached back and clasped Brooke's hand.

Thankfully, George was a stellar pilot. He wasn't exaggerating about the wintry mix, but he touched down without issue.

"Thanks, George," Noah said as he and Brooke rushed out of the copter.

"Godspeed," George called after them.

Noah pulled his phone from his pocket as they raced toward the roaring fire. How many had the madman killed? He glanced at his phone. "The disciplinary barracks are located one klick north and two klicks east from the top edge of the helipad."

Brooke nodded as the snow crunched beneath their shoes and fat snowflakes tumbled from the sky.

About a hundred yards out from the barracks, the stench of smoke filled the air. They crested the slope, and the enormity of the devastation greeted them. The center of the state-of-the-art prison was gone, and a bright orange glow, like the tip of an inhaled cigar, rose and sparked in its place.

Fire teams were battling against the heat to douse the flames with water. Ash rained down with the intensifying snowflakes, making long-range sight nigh impossible.

Red lights swirled about them as the piercing base alarm pealed.

Groaning soldiers and inmates littered the ground as medics surveyed the field, assessing greatest need.

Brooke grabbed hold of his arm, stopping him. "I need to stay and help."

The idea of her away from his side troubled him.

She scanned the grounds before them. "There are too many wounded and not enough medics to help."

He looked at the blood soaking into the white snow around

wounded Marines, the sparse number of medics, and EMTs rushing between the wounded as fast as they could while a triage tent was being set up.

"Noah, I need to do this."

"I understand. You go do your thing. They can definitely use your help. Just be safe, okay?" He squeezed her hand, then slipped off his coat. "Take this."

"No." She wrapped her light jacket tighter about her. "I'm fine."

"I don't mind the cold," he said. "Take it. Please."

She grabbed hold and slipped into it. "Thanks. Now you go do your thing."

He nodded and rushed toward the inferno. Glancing back, he saw her moving to the soldier closest to her.

"Fire is fifty-percent contained," a fireman said over his radio as Noah approached.

"The men are just making it into Pod One, pulling back and squeezing through the rubble," the firefighter on the other end replied. "Pod Two is shot all to heck, and the fire is still ablaze in there."

"And Pod Three?" the fireman asked.

"It's just about breachable. We don't yet have a count of how many inmates are injured, or how many have escaped. US Marshals are en route."

The fireman signed off and turned to Noah. "Yeah?"

"CGIS Agent Noah Rowley, Wilmington, North Carolina. Do you know who is in charge of the barracks?"

"You want that guy." The firefighter pointed to the back of a man towering over six-four.

"Thanks." Noah hurried over and made the same introduction.

"Lieutenant Colonel Miller. What are you doing here all the way from North Carolina?" He moved about, radioing out instructions, calling in more troops. "Call in the National Guard if you need to, local police—I don't care. And where are the Marshals?"

"ETA ten minutes."

He turned his attention to Noah. "Is it your team that sent the warning about this?" he asked.

"Yes, sir," Noah said.

"Thanks for what warning we did get. Unfortunately, it wasn't enough." He shook his head as he stared out over the destruction. "Not nearly enough."

"I'm so sorry. We're here about—"

"Prisoner Mirch—I know. He's in Pod Three. We're just about to breach it. Peterson!" he hollered.

"Yes, sir," MP Peterson said.

"This is the CGIS agent who sent the warning. Take him with you into Pod Three. He needs to confirm Mirch's presence."

"Yes, sir." Peterson saluted.

Noah followed Peterson, a small contingent of Marines, and several of the fort MPs.

"We have five hundred and two prisoners," Peterson said. He turned to the men escorting him. "Marshals are less than ten out. I want a list ready for them of who they need to be searching for from Pod Three, so take note as we go through it. Understood?"

"Yes, sir," they all said.

"Into teams of two."

MP Peterson and MP Lancer accompanied Noah toward the rear of the pod as the rest of the team peeled off two-by-two. "Death row prisoners are housed in Pod One, which was basically destroyed upon impact. Pod Two houses war crimes, and there's a chance the majority are still alive."

"And Pod Three?" Noah asked.

"Every other violation of the Uniform Code of Military Justice. It was the least damaged."

They moved down the remainder of the corridor, looking

into the shoebox-sized windows of each cell with a flashlight while the auxiliary lights flickered on and off.

"And if we find any injured prisoners?" Lancer asked.

"Right now, our primary objective is to determine if there are any escapees. Second is to assess that the pod is secure, and third, medical can move in."

"We've got one missing from 103," one of the MPs said over the radio.

"Roger that."

"Which cell is Scott Mirch in?" Noah asked.

"He's the one you think this is all about?"

"Yes, sir."

"Cell 107," Peterson said. "Next cell up."

*Please, Lord, let him still be in it.*

Noah coughed through the smoke, approaching 107. His gut clenched at finding the door ajar. He pushed it open, gun at the ready, and his stomach plummeted. *Empty.*

# SEVENTY-ONE

Brooke knelt by a wounded soldier, assessing his injuries. "It's okay," she said. "I just need to stop the bleeding." She pulled off Noah's coat, the deep chill seeping through her light jacket into her bones. She wrapped the coat as a temporary tourniquet around his upper arm and hollered for gauze from the medic tent. Seconds later a medic stood over her, his face obscured by the smoke.

He knelt beside her. "Remember me?"

Fear skittered along every nerve ending. *Dwayne.*

The muzzle of a gun poked into her side as his arm snaked around her.

"Stand up nice and slow. We're going to take a walk to the woods."

Her mind raced between yelling for help, trying to fight her way out, trying—

He shoved the muzzle deeper into her side. "Don't even think about it. Now walk."

She stood and walked in the direction he steered her. She tried to glance over her shoulder.

"Don't turn around. Just keep walking."

*Noah will come. Please, Lord, let Noah find me.*

They passed into the woods and down to a creek, her tennis

shoes slipping along the snow. Water with chunks of ice flowed along it. Dwayne whistled, and Scott and Frank Mirch came into sight.

Scott had changed out of his prison garb into what looked like a federal agent's attire. Frank wore the same. Both held guns at their sides.

Scott's eyes widened. "Brooke? Brooke Kesler? What are you . . . ?"

"Hi, Scott." She turned her glare on his dad. "And Frank. Or should I say Gator?"

"You're right," Frank said to Dwayne. "She is nothing but trouble, but we'll take care of that."

Dwayne laughed.

"And one more thing to take care of." Without a blink of an eye, Frank raised his gun and shot Dwayne, the bullet embedding in the center of his forehead.

"Dad, what are you doing?" Scott gaped at Dwayne's lifeless body.

"Extra weight. He'll just slow us down," Frank said.

"But . . . you've known him for twenty years."

"And he was a good soldier. Took orders. Now I need you to do the same and move."

"But why is Brooke . . . ?"

"Insurance."

"For what?" Scott frowned, zipping up his down jacket.

"In case her boyfriend catches up."

As he exited what remained of the barracks, Noah surveyed the grounds. A group of people approached from the east. He caught sight of the back of one of their blue jackets with yellow lettering. US Marshals. He needed to find out who was in charge but wanted to check on Brooke first. His gut had been uneasy ever since they'd parted, and knowing Scott Mirch was on the loose only compounded it.

He headed to the medic tent but didn't see her. He scanned the grounds, nothing.

His heart hitched. *No. Please, Lord. No.*

One of the medics in the tent was busy directing the rest of them.

Noah rushed to his side. "I'm looking for Brooke Kesler. She's a medic from North Carolina. She was helping."

"I'm going to need more," he said.

"She isn't in uniform—tall, long brown hair, jeans, and a thick brown jacket."

"I know who you're talking about, but she was wearing a thin gray jacket."

"That's her." She must have taken his jacket off for some reason. "Do you know where she is?" He looked back at the opening of the tent and saw a US Marshal striding toward them.

"She was helping a soldier over by the tree line," the medic said. "I was about to bring a kit to her, but another medic went to help. I looked over again, and they were gone."

"The other medic," Noah said, trying to keep the panic from setting in, "did you know him?"

"No. I'd never seen him before, but there are so many flooding in."

Knives sliced down Noah's throat. "Can you show me where you last saw her?"

"Over there," the medic said, pointing at the tree line.

The marshal stepped to Noah's side. "US Marshal Gus Harris. I was told you're the one who alerted Leavenworth. Can I—"

"Marshal Harris, a medic has been taken hostage," Noah said. "I need to find her now."

"How can I be of assistance?" he asked.

"This medic was just telling me where he last saw her."

Turning his attention back to the medic, he said, "Can you show me exactly where you last saw her?"

"Of course." The medic turned to another. "Carl, you're in charge."

Noah studied the footprints in the snow as they walked to the tree line.

"They were right here," the medic said as he kneeled to examine the patient Brooke had been assisting.

Noah noted two sets of footprints about a stance apart. Side by side. He'd no doubt held her at gunpoint. Whichever *he* it was who took her.

Noah thanked the medic and turned to Marshal Harris. "They've definitely taken her."

# SEVENTY-TWO

Yanking her by a rope secured around her wrists, Frank Mirch kept Brooke's pace at a run. Snow crunching beneath her soaked tennis shoes, she struggled not to trip over tree roots or slip on patches of ice.

"Dad," Scott said, his breath white puffs in the thickening snowfall. "What did you do?"

*He did it all*, thought Brooke. Frank Mirch had deployed the laser, killed and injured countless people, and broken his son out of prison.

Frank didn't slow his pace, her rope in one hand, an AK-47 in the other.

"What do you mean, what have I done?" Frank said. "I've given you your freedom."

He frowned.. "You were behind the mass shooting, weren't you?"

"I took care of the men who set you up. I got the weapon that set you free."

"But you've killed so many people. Innocents . . ."

"Collateral damage," Frank said.

"Is that what Amy Caldwell was?" Brooke said, hoping to jar Scott, to make him question his dad further. It was probably a long shot, but she prayed he'd even turn on him.

Scott stopped. "What happened to Amy?"

"Your dad killed her."

Frank's fist collided with her cheekbone. Pain ricocheted through her face. "Enough!" he hollered.

Warm liquid slipped down her face. She wiped the blood trailing from her nose. Scott looked horrified, but he did nothing, just stood silent.

"One more word, and you're dead," Frank said.

"You won't kill me until you make it safely away," Brooke said.

"Don't try me," he clipped out, and she believed him.

Dogs barked and howled in the distance, the woods crawling with search teams. Having found Dwayne shot in the head, Noah and Harris now followed three sets of shoe prints—two larger, one smaller. The Mirches and Brooke.

*Thank you, Lord, for the snow.*

Noah's breath caught in his chest. Brooke had become his heart, and until he had her safe and back in his arms, nothing would feel right.

*Please, Jesus, don't let them harm her, I beg you.*

Harris's arm came out and nearly clotheslined him.

Noah teetered on the top edge of a ravine. He looked over to thank Harris, but the marshal held a finger to his lips and pointed. "Half a klick downstream," he whispered.

Noah's gaze landed on Frank Mirch tugging on a thick rope secured around Brooke's wrists. Noah gritted his teeth as adrenaline and anger seethed inside.

"If we hurry around, we might be able to cut them off where the stream narrows," Harris said.

Moving as swiftly and silently as possible, they made it to a narrow hollow before Brooke and the Mirches reached it. With one of them positioned on either side of the stream, Noah held his breath until the precise moment the group passed in front of him. It took everything in him not to move early and lunge for Brooke, but timing was everything.

Harris stepped out in front of them, gun aimed at Scott Mirch's head. "Guns down and release the girl," he said.

Frank Mirch laughed. "She'll be dead before you pull the trigger."

Noah pressed the muzzle of his gun into the base of Frank Mirch's skull. "And so will you."

"Dad," Scott gritted out.

"Let her go," Noah said.

Frank tugged her closer. "Nuh-uh. Either we're getting out of here, or no one does."

Scott gaped at his dad. "Are you crazy?"

"Don't you dare back talk, boy. Not after all I've done."

"You mean guilt-tripping me into stealing the cryptocurrency because of what the military did to you? Or leaving me to rot in prison for seven years without a word from you?"

"You were only too happy to steal that currency. You wanted your half, and I saved it for you. I've put a ton of my share of the money into this very moment. But a mission like this isn't accomplished overnight. It takes years to plan and even more to execute. I disappeared because I wanted you to be innocent of what was happening. I did it to protect you."

"Protect me!" Scott roared. "Are you out of your mind?"

"I did what I did to right injustice. Those men set you up. They left you in prison to rot."

Scott stared at Frank as if he didn't recognize him.

"The military betrayed me," Frank said. "Your brother betrayed me. Don't you dare betray me, boy." Frank jabbed the gun against Brooke's head.

"I'm sorry, Dad, but I can't do this." He dropped his gun on the ground and raised his hands.

Frank shifted as he gaped at his son, moving just enough for Harris to take the shot.

Noah met Harris's gaze, giving him the silent go-ahead, and the shot rang out, echoing through the woods.

"Dad!" Scott screamed as Frank's lifeless body fell back—a single gunshot wound to the head.

Noah rushed for Brooke, wrapping his arms around her as Scott sobbed over his dad's body.

Harris radioed in their position, and half an hour later, Noah sat beside Brooke in the back of the ambulance as the paramedic treated the rope burn and open flesh on her wrists.

They watched as a US Marshal by the name of Theisen escorted Scott Mirch into the back of a transport van.

It would take time to rebuild the disciplinary barracks back into a long-term facility. In the meantime, the remaining prisoners were being transferred to an unknown location, and according to Marshal Theisen, it was going to stay that way.

"So we were right. Scott was guilty of the theft, his dad was the fifth man, and the instructors left Scott holding the bag," Brooke said.

"Yep." Noah brushed the hair from her face.

"Unbelievable." Brooke rested her head on his shoulder after the paramedic finished tending to her wounds.

Noah waited until the paramedic stepped away before saying, "Let's go home."

"Home." Brooke smiled softly up at him. "I like the sound of that."

He placed a kiss on her forehead. *Soon it'll be our home.* He just needed the ring.

# SEVENTY-THREE

The sun was a welcome sight at Molly's memorial service after the dismal previous two days of rain they'd endured in Wilmington. Brooke and Noah had flown into Molly's hometown the night before and would be flying out that evening. Standing over a loved one's grave had been hard enough. Doing it in the pouring rain would have been harder still—the heaviness of rain only adding to the weight of sorrow. But because Molly was a believer and home with Jesus, in no pain and rejoicing at her Savior's side, it was also inspiring and joyful.

Brooke had bawled as they played Brad Paisley's "When I Get Where I'm Going." It was such a beautiful song, reminding Brooke every time she heard it of the joy and reunion to come. One day she'd see Molly again, and they'd laugh and talk as if they'd never been apart. But until then, she'd remember her friend with fond heartfelt memories.

As they headed for the rental car, she clutched Noah's arm tighter, the events of the past couple of weeks racing through her mind.

"You okay?" he asked.

She nodded as tears smarted.

He pulled off one of his black leather gloves and clasped her hand. "I'm right here, *always*."

"I know." And she was so grateful.

*Thank You, Jesus, for blessing me with this strong, steady man. Having him by my side today and your Holy Spirit inside of me helped me celebrate Molly's life the way she would have wanted, rather than falling to pieces in sorrow. You have upheld me by your righteous right hand. Thank you, Jesus.*

Austin had insisted on hanging the Christmas lights across the top of her porch herself. She wouldn't let Caleb help, other than to hold the ladder, but part of him—a big part—loved that about her. Loved her. He'd never thought, when she'd burst into his life, inserting herself into their case, that he'd fall for the headstrong woman. Forget fall—try plummet, in the best possible way. As he held the ladder for her, she held his heart.

*Okay, Eason, that was way too sappy. Focus on holding the ladder so she stays steady.*

He looked up at her stringing the old-fashioned, multicolored bulbs along the lipped edge of her front porch. She wore white leggings, a navy sweater, and brown UGG boots.

"Later, you can hold the ladder while I put the angel on top of the tree," she teased.

"And you can do the same when we decorate my tree," he teased back.

"We'll discuss that after I get down."

"Take your time." He offered a charming smile as she glanced back over her shoulder at him. "I'm quite enjoying the view."

Her eyes opened wide, but in a playful, surprised way. "Agent Eason!"

He smirked. "I can't help it if the view is stunning."

"I'm not sure if I should be offended or flattered."

"I think kissed is a better option."

"Oh, you do, do you?"

"Most definitely."

Grinning the entire way, she climbed down the ladder and into his arms.

He kissed her with all the passion sparking inside, then pulled back slightly. "I love you," he said, hoping she didn't think it too soon.

She bit her bottom lip, then smiled. "I love you too."

Relief swelled inside. He'd said he wasn't ready to get married yet, and that still held true, but finding the woman he'd one day marry—well, that search seemed over as he held Austin in his arms.

Dirk and Jaxon pawed at her front window, barking to come out and join them. Who would have ever thought he'd adopt another dog? But Jaxon had taken to him, and truth be told, the goofball mop of a pup had already stolen a piece of his heart.

"It's okay, boys," he said through the glass. "We won't be long."

Her brows arched. "Won't be long? Where are we going?"

He pulled her tighter into his embrace. "On our first date."

"We've had plenty of dates," she said.

He chuckled. "Stakeouts don't count."

"Are you sure?"

"Positive." He pressed his lips back to hers. He'd been right. This love was going to be quite the adventure.

# Epilogue

## CHRISTMAS EVE

"Stop it!" Kenzie said.

Noah looked across the table at her. "Stop what?"

"Bouncing your knee. You're shaking the whole table."

"Sorry." He hadn't even realized he was doing it—never did.

"I think it's sweet," Gabby said, pulling her cinnamon roll into pieces before taking a bite.

"Since when?" Kenzie asked, popping the last of her roll into her mouth.

Their mom made the best cinnamon rolls ever.

"He's anxious for Mom to come back," Gabby said.

It was annoying she knew him so well. She'd figured out why he'd come to breakfast sans Brooke for the first time in at least a month.

"Why?" Kenzie asked, narrowing her eyes, then her mouth slackened. "Is she . . . ? Are you . . . ?"

Noah exhaled. He might as well just tell her. Otherwise, she wouldn't stop bugging him.

"Here you go," his mom said, handing him the velvet bag.

"Is that what I think it is?" Kenzie asked, her eyes wide with delight.

"Grandma's ring," Noah said.

Kenzie's face lit.

"But not a word," he said.

She made the zip-my-lips sign with her fingers across her mouth.

"Okay. I better go." He stood. "Thanks, Mom," he said, pressing a kiss to her cheek.

"You're welcome." She patted his cheek, tears glistening in her eyes.

He opened the front door to find Finn on the other side, his arm up, poised to knock.

"Hey," Finn said.

"Hey." Noah slipped the velvet pouch into his pocket.

"Heading out?" Finn said, swapping places with Noah.

"Yep."

"See you tonight, and don't forget your white elephant gifts," Finn said.

"You got it. We'll be there at eight."

"What's in the pouch?" Finn asked, lifting his chin.

That was the danger of working with investigators. You couldn't keep a secret to save your life.

Noah patted his pocket, the ring nestled inside, and smiled. "Let's just say it's a happy ending."

Noah pulled to a stop in front of Finn's house, which was fully decked out for Christmas. Bright strings of pink and white lights donned the roof, porch, and fan palms clustered about the house. He chuckled at the neon flamingos situated by the palms, but his absolute fave was the flock of plastic sea gulls wearing necklaces of blinking Christmas lights and Santa hats.

Brooke laughed.

Man, he loved that sound. Loved hearing happiness in her voice. He prayed that's what he heard after their walk.

He climbed out of the car to open Brooke's door, but she'd already hopped out and was gathering the presents from the back seat into a big bundle.

He rested a hand on her arm. "These can wait for a minute. There's something I want to show you first."

Taking the presents from her hold, he placed them on the back seat and closed the door. She scanned the drive, noting the cars present. "It looks like everyone's here. Shouldn't we head inside?"

"It'll take Gabby and Finn forever to get all the food out. You know how my sister likes to turn each plate into an artistic treasure."

Brooke laughed. "That's definitely true." She slipped her hand in his, and he reveled in the warmth, in the caress of her soft skin. "Where are we going?" she asked as he led her around the side of the house.

"For a quick walk."

She frowned. "Now?"

"Yep. Come on," he said with a smile.

She smiled back but curiosity lingered there. "I thought you said you wanted to show me something?"

"I do."

"On the beach?"

"Yep."

"Okay." She stilled, and for a second his heart froze. Was she going to grill him or suggest they turn back?

"Let me take my heels off." She glanced down at her feet. "They aren't exactly made for beach walks. You should have told me so I could've brought a pair of flops."

"I'll keep you out of the cold water. The sand should still be warm from the sun."

She arched a brow.

"Warm-ish." He shrugged.

She shook her head. "You're a mess."

"But I'm your mess." He winked.

"And I wouldn't have you any other way." She chuckled.

He knelt down to one knee.

Her brows shot up. "What are you doing?"

"Helping you with your heels," he said, lifting her right foot. She braced her hand on his shoulder, balancing her weight as he slid one shoe off and then the other.

"Ready?' he asked, getting back to his feet and holding out his hand.

She smiled. "Always."

They walked a quarter mile along the shore, weaving between the ocean's rippling edge and the sand dunes to their right.

The sun was just a sliver of orange peeking out from the horizon as it lowered in the sky, taking its warmth with it.

Brooke cuddled against his arm.

"Here," he said, slipping his V-neck sweater over her emerald green dress.

"I must look quite hilarious," she said as she fussed with the sweater's hem.

"You look anything but," he said, unable to keep his gaze off her.

"Noah?" she said after a moment.

"Yes?"

"Did you want to show me something?"

"Right," he said, snapping himself out of his stare. "Just around the next dune."

They followed the natural sloping curve of the beach, and as they rounded the six-foot sand dune, she stopped in her tracks. "Noah." His name came out a breathless whisper.

The two sand "snowmen" he'd built stood there with scarfs

around their necks, coal for buttons, reeds for arms, carrots for noses, Santa hats, and his second-favorite touch—sunglasses.

Brooke's hands cupped her nose and mouth as she laughed into them.

"Merry Christmas," he said, standing beside her.

"I love them." Her laughter grew. "It's my favorite Christmas gift of all time."

"You might be jumping the gun."

She frowned, confusion rippling across her furrowed brow.

"The snowmen aren't the gift," he said.

"I don't understand. . . ."

"Take a closer look."

Curiosity flickered in her eyes, before she moved to inspect the sand snowmen.

He watched, wanting to catch the exact moment she found the gift.

She stilled. "Noah . . . is that . . . ?"

That was his cue. He dropped to one knee.

She reached out her hand, slipping it off the snowlady's reed finger. "Is this?" She turned, his grandma's ring in hand, and her vivid brown eyes widened at the sight of him a whisper behind her kneeling in the sand.

"Noah . . . " Her hand started to shake as his knee sunk deeper in the sand.

"I think you're supposed to give that to me." He winked, reaching for the ring.

She placed it in his hand, her eyes still wide, though beading with tears.

"You know I love you."

She nodded, more tears forming.

"You know I always will."

She nodded, tears slipping down her rosy cheeks.

"So will you allow me a lifetime to show you just how much?"

A soft gasp escaped her lips as the reeds rustled on the dunes beside them.

He held up the ring. "Will you marry me?"

She nodded, tears of joy streaming down her face as he slipped the ring on her finger.

She dropped to her knees in front of him.

"Your dress," he said.

"Who cares about a dress in a moment like this." She didn't lose a second's time in pressing her lips to his.

"Oomph!" a voice sounded from behind the dune.

Hating to break the kiss, Noah glanced over in time to see his sister Gabby tumbling down the dune with a squeal.

"Gabs?" Seriously? She was the rustling? Of course, she'd be the one to watch.

"Sorry, babe," Finn said, standing up, his head poking over the reeds atop the sloping dune.

"You too?" Noah shook his head, too happy to care about the invasion of privacy.

Finn cleared his throat. "Your sister . . . " He cleared his throat again.

Gabby stood, brushing the sand off her outfit. "Don't you dare blame me. You all wanted to come."

Noah got to his feet and helped Brooke up. "All?" He dipped his head.

One by one, his entire team and their significant others stood, their heads cresting the reeds.

"Sorry." Gabby bit her bottom lip. "We really didn't mean to interrupt. I just lost my footing. We'll leave you two alone." She turned to head back up the dune, then paused and, turning around, streaked to Brooke and wrapped her arms around her. "You're going to be my sister!"

Noah chuckled. "You all might as well come down."

Finn started, and the rest followed, Austin losing her footing and tumbling forward into Mason's back.

"Sorry!" she hollered as Mason bumbled forward into Rissi, and before Noah could stop laughing long enough to take a solid breath, the entire group—save Caleb, who was bringing up the rear—landed in a pile at the base of the dune.

"Serves you all right for eavesdropping," Noah said, trying to hold a stern expression, but he just couldn't do it. He was too happy. He pulled Brooke away from Gabby and back into his arms. Lifting her hand to his mouth, he pressed a kiss to her ring finger as the goofball group flailing in the sand had the decency to stare at the sky. He pressed a second kiss.

She shivered.

"Are you cold?"

She leaned close, her breath tickling his ear. "Far from it."

# Acknowledgments

Thank you, Lord, for placing the call to write on my heart and for meeting me every time I pick up a pen or sit at the computer. I love the special time of creating with you.

To my family for all their love and support. And for dealing with "Deadline Mom," as my daughters call me. Writing is quite an adventurous journey. Thank you for being by my side every step of the way and for filling my life with joy.

To Dave, Karen, and Kate. You are an amazing editorial team. I'm blessed by you all. Every story is stronger because of your hard work.

To Crissy, Amy, and Joy for your love of story and constant support.

To Dee for your generous heart to always read my stories, for your loving-kindness, and for the treasures you place on my heart. Thank you, friend.

To Kelly for staying up to Zoom-write with me at all hours while I was on deadline for this book. For all the writing sprints, prayers, and encouragement. I got through those long rough weeks because of you. Thank you, friend!

To Stephanne for always being willing to lend a hand, for helping me keep my story organized (a monumental task in and of itself), and for your hilarious T-shirts that always make me smile. Most of all, thank you for the wonderful idea that brought it all home for me.

To the Darlings for being such an awesome group. God surely brought us together!

To Christen for keeping me on track, for your grace and patience, and for your awesome work. I appreciate you!

Last, but certainly not least. Thank you, Janet, for your years of support, guidance, sage wisdom, and friendship. I'm so thankful for you.

Praised by *New York Times* bestselling author Dee Henderson as "a name to look for in romantic suspense," **Dani Pettrey** has sold nearly eight hundred thousand copies of her novels to readers eagerly awaiting the next release. Dani combines the page-turning adrenaline of a thriller with the chemistry and happy-ever-after of a romance. Her novels stand out for their "wicked pace, snappy dialogue, and likable characters" (*Publishers Weekly*), "gripping storyline[s]" (*RT Book Reviews*), and "sizzling undercurrent[s] of romance" (*USA Today*). Her Alaskan Courage, Chesapeake Valor, and Coastal Guardian series have received praise from readers and critics alike and have appeared on *Publishers Weekly*, ECPA, and CBA bestseller lists.

From her early years eagerly reading Nancy Drew mysteries, Dani has always enjoyed mystery and suspense. She considers herself blessed to be able to write the kind of stories she loves—full of plot twists and peril, love, and longing for hope and redemption. Her greatest joy as an author is sharing the stories God lays on her heart. She researches murder and mayhem from her home in Maryland, where she lives with her husband. For more information about her novels, visit www .danipettrey.com.

# Sign Up for Dani's Newsletter

Keep up to date with Dani's news on book releases and events by signing up for her email list at danipettrey.com.

---

# More from Dani Pettrey

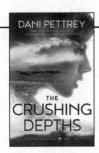

When an accident claims the life of an oil-rig worker off the North Carolina coast, Coast Guard investigators Rissi Dawson and Mason Rogers are sent to take the case. But mounting evidence shows the death may not have been an accident at all, and they find themselves racing to discover the killer's identity before he eliminates the threat they pose.

*The Crushing Depths*
Coastal Guardians #2

# You May Also Like . . .

When a Coast Guard officer is found dead and another goes missing, Special Agent Finn Walker faces his most dangerous assignment yet. Complicating matters is the arrival of investigative reporter Gabby Rowley, who's on a mission to discover the truth. Can they ignore the sparks between them and track down this elusive killer?

*The Killing Tide* by Dani Pettrey
COASTAL GUARDIANS #1
danipettrey.com

Private Investigator Kate Maxwell never stopped loving Luke Gallagher after he disappeared. Now he's back, and together they must unravel a twisting thread of secrets, lies, and betrayal while on the brink of a biological disaster that will shake America to its core. Will they and their love survive, or will Luke and Kate become the terrorist's next target?

*Dead Drift* by Dani Pettrey
CHESAPEAKE VALOR #4
danipettrey.com

When a terrorist investigation leads FBI agent Declan Grey to a closed immigrant community, he turns to crisis counselor Tanner Shaw for help. Despite the tension between them, he needs the best of the best on this case. Under imminent threat, they'll have to race against the clock to stop a plot that could cost thousands of lives—including theirs.

*The Blind Spot* by Dani Pettrey
CHESAPEAKE VALOR #3
danipettrey.com

BETHANYHOUSE

# More from Bethany House

When dark-haired women across Virginia begin to suddenly disappear, FBI behavioral analyst Alex Donovan is tasked with hunting the kidnapper down. But when Alex herself is baited and abducted at an abandoned amusement park, her partner Logan Hart and the BAU team fear Alex might not make it out alive this time.

*Free Fall* by Nancy Mehl
THE QUANTICO FILES #3
nancymehl.com

When Luke Dempsey's fellow inmate lay dying, Luke promised to protect the man's daughter, Finley, and help her find the treasure he had hidden. Upon Luke's release, he and Finley uncover the clues, and their reasons for resisting each other begin to crumble. Luke will shield her from unseen threats, but who's going to shield him from losing his heart?

*Turn to Me* by Becky Wade
A MISTY RIVER ROMANCE #3
beckywade.com

Allie Massey's dream to use her grandparents' estate for equine therapy is crushed when she discovers the property has been sold to a contractor. With weeks until demolition, Allie unearths some of Nana Dale's best-kept secrets—including her champion filly, a handsome man, and one fateful night during WWII—and perhaps a clue to keep her own dream alive.

*By Way of the Moonlight* by Elizabeth Musser
elizabethmusser.com

◆ BETHANYHOUSE